Praise for Fa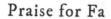

"As a storyteller in the oldest tradition, Halter effortlessly weaves a tale of friendship, secrets, and magic."
—Kathleen Kerr, Acquisitions Editor at Harvest House Publishers

"Even for a non-fantasy reader like me, *Fairyeater* was an enchanting, can't-put-it-down journey, full of as much heart as magic."
—Nancy Rue, Christy Award-winning author of *The Reluctant Prophet*

"An enthralling, heartfelt adventure that will draw you in at the first page and never let go—even after the end."
—Kyle Robert Shultz, author of the Beaumont and Beasley series

"Fantasy lovers will be enthralled with Akeela's quest for love, family, and duty to the fairies as dark forces rise to stop her. Pam Halter's debut novel is a winner!"
—Rona Shirdan, Assistant Regional Advisor, SCBWI Eastern PA

"Pam Halter transports her readers to a new, vibrant realm filled with rich world-building and characters as complex as they are engaging. I had no idea what would happen from one moment to the next, but I knew I needed to see Akeela's journey through to its end. Although it broke my heart a few times, at its core *Fairyeater* radiates light, hope, and joy. A beautiful book."
—Laurie Lucking, award-winning author of *Common*

FAIRYEATER

The Fairy Guardian Chronicles

ONE

$\mathcal{F}$AIRYEATER

The Fairy Guardian Chronicles
ONE

PAM HALTER

McKenzi —

everyone is
created with a
purpose!

Pam Halter
11-2019

Love2ReadLove2Write Publishing, LLC
Indianapolis, Indiana

Copyright © 2018 by Pam Halter

Published by Love2ReadLove2Write Publishing, LLC

Indianapolis, Indiana

www.love2readlove2writepublishing.com

ISBN-13: 978-1-943788-36-1 (Ebook edition)

ISBN-13: 978-1-943788-35-4 (Paperback edition)

LCCN: 2018961150 (Paperback edition)

Library of Congress Cataloging-in-Publication Data is on file at the Library of Congress, Washington, DC.

This is a work of fiction. Names, characters, incidents, and dialogues are products of the author's imagination and are not to be construed as real. Any resemblance to actual events or persons, living or dead, is entirely coincidental.

Cover Design by Sara Helwe (www.sara-helwe.com)

Illustrations © Kim Sponaugle (www.picturekitchenstudio.com)

For my husband, Daryl,
my rock and my love

Northern Province

Undaeus Mountains

Olde Janmar's Cave

Cave Opening

Se'Vrawd Settlement

Acadian Kin Tribe

Earth Fountain

The Prophecy

Ashes deep in slumber
Will rip the ground asunder.

Foul, yet fair, he will ascend,
Consuming earth, enslaving men.

Fairy and folk will hide and cower,
But only one can wield the power.

When triple moon hides sun so fair,
Then Fairystone in runes must wear.

Back to ashes, evil mourns,
The guardian will be reborn.

Part One

RISING

Chapter One

"I do not want this task."

Kraylor sat silent on the throne.

"I do *not* want this task!" Krezma repeated. "Why should I have to raise another woman's child?"

For a moment, she thought Kraylor would give in, but then Kray frowned.

"Sister, I know what you've been through. I know what you desire, and I wish I could allow it. But you know how our people feel about what you did."

"Aye, I know, but that was so long ago. Surely I have redeemed myself by now."

Kray leaned forward. The morning sunlight glinted off the crystals in her crown, making tiny rainbows shimmer at Krezma's feet. "How many years could it take? Eighteen at the most? You've been working to get to your daughter for almost one hundred now."

Krezma blinked back burning tears. "Why me? Just because I was at the birth of the child shouldn't mean I have to take on the responsibility of raising it."

Kray started to speak, but Krezma went on.

"Let someone else take it. A baby! I am three hundred years old. I don't want to raise a baby at my age." She threw her hands up. "And a girl? Will Celtar ever stop punishing me for the mistake I made as a younger? I want my *own* daughter, not someone else's! Surely the Fairy Council could find someone more suitable. More willing."

"But the damage you caused, even though it was two hundred years ago, had great consequences," Kray said. "And no one knows more about the prophecy than you."

Krezma wiped a tear from her cheek.

"You're not being punished," Kray continued. "If it weren't for you, the kingdom would have been destroyed. Can't you see? This isn't a punishment—it's an honor! The Fairy Council trusts you. *We* trust you. Think about it. If you hadn't been there, the baby would have died. All hope for our future would have died. Celtar placed you there for this!"

Krezma turned and stalked to the end of the room. Celtar had placed her there? No, she'd placed herself there. She'd known who was attacking that village. She'd *wanted* to go there. She'd *had* to.

She sighed. Of course, Celtar knew that. And so He'd placed her at just the right place at just the right time. Krezma turned and looked at her little sister. Stars, Kray might be queen, but she could still make Krezma feel like smacking her.

"Very well," she finally said. "I will take the child and raise it. But I will not do it here. I'll take it—"

"Her," Kray said.

"*Her.* I'll take *her* and raise *her* where I see fit." Krezma folded her arms.

Kray studied Krezma's face. Then she nodded. "I will inform the Vestry and the Fairy Council. You will need to let the fairies know where you and the girl are."

Krezma bowed her head. She turned to go, but Kray stopped her.

"What will you name her?"

Krezma frowned. She supposed the child must have a name. "Akeela."

Kray's eyebrows arched. "Akeela? *Burden*?"

"Yes!" Krezma snapped. "That is what she is, and that is what I will call her. I'll raise her properly. I'll keep in contact with the Fairy Council. She will be ready when the time comes. But I will not relent on the name."

"I'm sorry you are so unmoved," Kray said. "Dear sister, please soften your heart toward the child. She's done you no harm. Remember that."

Krezma hurried to her bedroom, packed what she could carry in a shoulder sack, and dismissed the nursemaid.

She looked down on the sleeping infant. "It seems you and I will be spending some time together, child."

The baby girl squirmed and sighed in her sleep. Krezma swallowed the lump forming in her throat. She would raise this child. No one would be able to say she hadn't done her duty.

But no one could make her love it.

Chapter Two

Fifteen Years Later

Akeela yanked the leather archery glove on her right hand. She sat on the stump of a tree, examined her bow, and waited for the forest to wake up. Hunting was the only escape she had from Krezma's sharp tongue, and she was sick of both. The latest lecture came because Akeela had missed that deer. Well, deer were fast sometimes. And she wasn't perfect.

The glimmer of a bird's aura appeared in an oak tree, followed by the call of a mourning dove. Within a few seconds, several glowing auras appeared between the leaves, and birds began to greet the morning.

Akeela walked along her usual path toward the lake. Another aura, yellow-orange, filtered through the reeds. A pheasant. This was an excellent find! She hadn't seen one for a couple of weeks.

She stomped, kicking up leaves as she moved toward the aura. It looked to be a good-sized bird, maybe ten pounds.

When she was within a few yards of the reeds, she stopped. The pheasant would try to escape now that she was silent. She reached back and drew an arrow from the newly made leather quiver.

Steady. Steady.

She aimed just above the glowing aura, relaxed her fingers, and released. The pheasant exploded out of the grass. The string snapped against the glove, but the arrow held true as it sped through the air. It struck just below the wing.

Akeela ground her teeth. Fairy feet! She'd been aiming for the neck. Time to brace for another lecture. Her jaw couldn't take much more stress.

She bent to remove the arrow, stuffed the bird into a canvas bag, and headed toward home.

As she walked under a patch of oak trees, several acorns dropped on her head.

"Ho there, you little pests!" Akeela called. "Do you want to see the inside of Krezma's cooking pot?" She chuckled, thinking of how much Krezma hated to clean squirrels.

The squirrels flung themselves into a neighboring tree. Their auras left an unusual dark red trail. Akeela frowned. An animal's aura darkened when they sensed danger.

She glanced around. The woods were calm. No other auras were present. In fact, she couldn't see any animal auras, only the gentle shimmer of life that came from the plants.

Strange.

As she approached home, seven robins shot out of the trees, their auras leaving deep orange lines behind them. Akeela's eyes narrowed. A tingly feeling played around her stomach. She glanced behind her. The highest tower of the witch's castle peeked above the trees. Perhaps she was up and moving early. Thank Celtar for Krezma's protection spell that made the cottage unseen by the witch. Akeela had long ago stopped asking why they lived so close to her. Krezma never gave an answer.

She pushed through the garden gate of the stone cottage and paused. Everything looked as it always did. The moss-covered roof, the vines of yellow bell flowers growing along the stony walls, the gardens, both vegetable and herb . . . all undisturbed. The earth fairies who usually visited the gardens hadn't made an appearance yet. However, that was nothing to worry about. They came and went at their leisure.

Krezma must be awake by now, yet she wasn't in the small labyrinth set to the far side of the cottage. It was Krezma's habit to walk the labyrinth and pray first thing in the morning.

Akeela clenched her jaw. Prayer. What was the point? Akeela tried praying now and then for Celtar to help her, but here she was, stuck with a crotchety old woman in the forest. Away from the village and all her friends. In the shadow of the witch's castle. Akeela huffed out a breath. Iari, and everyone else who was normal, lived in Broem. Krezma didn't go there often, even though it was only an hour's walk, and she didn't allow Akeela to go without her.

So did Celtar really hear her prayers for help? If He did, He didn't answer. Ever. Was she so horrible Celtar had to take away her mother and father and leave her with Krezma?

Her stomach growled as she stepped through the back door and hung the bow and quiver on a hook. "Good morn."

Krezma looked up from her task at the kitchen table. "It will be a good morn if you have something for the evening meal."

Akeela tossed the canvas bag on the table. "I have."

Krezma grunted. "Only one? I would think with the spirit-sight you'd be able to get three or four." She picked up the bird and threw it back on the table. "And you've damaged the meat! Careless girl. You know this means you'll be going back out."

Akeela's face flushed. Aye, she was gifted with spirit-sight. So what? Little good it did her. She forced down a retort and nodded at the basket of herbs. "That's more than usual. Getting ready to do something special?"

Krezma picked up a bunch of lavender. "It's bartering time for us. We're in need of a few items from the village."

Akeela's heart leaped. "When do we leave?"

"Tomorrow. We'll barter at the festival. I see no need to go to the village two days in a row."

Akeela's shoulders slumped, but she quickly recovered. The

Planting Festival was tomorrow. The promise of that eased the sting of Krezma's words.

Nooph jumped onto the table with more grace than a cat his size should have. He sniffed the pheasant and put out an inquiring paw. Akeela ran a hand down his back. He meowed, and Akeela rubbed his head. "Be patient, Nooph. Breakfast is coming soon enough. I got a pheasant. There will be some tasty morsels for you after I've cleaned it."

Krezma picked him up and dropped him on the floor. "Nooph, you witless cat. Always thinking about your stomach. Shoo now, shoo!"

"What did Nooph ever do to you?" Akeela asked under her breath.

Krezma tapped the stems of a bunch of yarrow on the table. The stalks separated, and Krezma lifted one to inspect it. "What are you mumbling about?"

Akeela clenched her jaw again. Fairy feet! She hadn't realized she'd spoken aloud. "Nothing. I just want to see my friends."

Krezma grunted. "You will see Iari and the others at the festival tomorrow, child."

Akeela's fists tightened. "I'm not a child!"

Krezma glanced at her. "Is that so?" She continued tying the herbs together. When Akeela didn't answer, she said, "Take the large basket and bring me all the strawberries you can."

"Right after I eat."

Krezma reached over to the counter, grabbed a piece of bread out of the basket, and tossed it on the table. "Get going. I have much to do today."

Akeela's heart twisted. Krezma never gave words of thanks or courtesy. At least not to her. Mean old hag. She picked up the basket and glanced out the window. Several bird auras filtered through the trees. It reminded her of the animals' strange reactions. "Something is wrong with the squirrels and birds."

"I've noticed nothing amiss. Your concern should be with getting my strawberries."

Akeela hesitated at the doorway.

Krezma placed five bunches of sage in a basket. "Go on, now!"

Akeela gripped the basket until it cracked. She turned to the doorway. If Celtar wasn't going to help her, she'd do something herself. As she clutched the basket and ran to the strawberry patch, she made a decision, one that had been playing in her thoughts. Tomorrow night, after Krezma slept, tired from the Planting Festival, she was going to leave. She would make a new home far, far away from here. Someplace where she could meet someone and start her own family. A family that would love her.

Finally.

Chapter Three

Tzmet paced her balcony. Rat's teeth! Why did it always take so long for fairies to wilt? She strode to the wooden rack in the court-yard atop the castle tower. Two wingless earth fairies hung upside down, barely moving in the bright sunlight, their life essence slowly draining away. One opened her eyes and peered up at the sky with a look that begged for mercy.

"Hah, beg. Yes, beg! It moves me not." Tzmet threw her hands in the air and stalked off. She stopped to look at herself in the mirror and ran a hand over her bald head. Why did she torture herself by keeping a mirror in the tower?

The Hinwari stared at her with deep, melancholy eyes. Miserable things. Before she'd begun wilting forest fairies, she'd had the notion to make servants out of them. She'd removed their wings and magically stretched them into a useful size, four or five hands tall. They resembled long, thin, leafless trees with two legs, two arms, and hair that stuck out like branches. They never spoke but wept silently from time to time. They also neither ate nor drank, and Tzmet could not figure out how they continued to live.

She'd fully expected them to retain their magic for her use, but they had not. She'd named them "Hinwari," meaning hollow, and they may have served her faithfully, but they were always filled with a deep, fathomless sadness. It was irritating.

Now when she caught fairies, instead of stretching them, she ripped off their wings and shaved their heads before she wilted and ate them. Killing them outright wasn't good enough. The wings she saved for a cape, a mighty cape of power, which she would wear when the time was right. The hair? Well, who wanted to eat hair? Besides, she thought it fitting, since their interference caused her father's great spell to backfire and her hair to fall out.

"Don't give me your sad look!" She swung a hand at the nearest Hinwar. *Crack!* Tzmet's hand met the thin face. "You frustrating, lazy things! Get to the kitchen and make me something to eat. I'm famished."

When the Hinwari emptied the room, Tzmet walked to the window and gazed at the plain that stretched to the east of the castle. Somewhere out there were the ashes of her lord and father, Riss'aird, waiting, growing, longing for the time of regeneration. She repeated the verses of the prophecy from the scrap of ancient scroll she'd snatched from an old man in the forest several years earlier.

"Ashes deep in slumber
Will rip the ground asunder.
Foul, yet fair, he will ascend,
Consuming earth, enslaving men.
Fairy and folk will hide and cower,
But only one can wield the power.

"I will see you restored, mighty Dark Lord. The one who can wield the power," Tzmet whispered. "Yea, you will be restored, if I have to eat every single fairy in Fedestia."

A single, slender cry came from one of the drying fairies. Tzmet whirled around and flew to the courtyard. One of the fairies had wilted. She lifted the lifeless creature and smiled. Why wait to cook it?

"For you, Father."

Krezma placed the last bunch of herbs in a basket. Even after her prayer time in the labyrinth, thoughts weighed heavily on her today, and the words of the prophecy rang unbidden in her head. She had to tell Akeela the truth. But when? Not that she would be unhappy to see Akeela go. She'd never asked for this responsibility, after all. She was too old to raise children. Besides, she had her own plans that had been laid aside, and she was anxious to get back to them.

Still, a grudging affection had grown in her heart for the child, and the importance of the child's true destiny could not be denied. Then there was the promise she'd made to the fairies. A promise she hadn't kept entirely.

The fire in the stove crackled and jolted Krezma from her thoughts. "Greetings, message-bearer."

"Greetings, Krezma," the fire fairy called. "Earth fairies continue to vanish. We have contacted the Guardian."

Krezma nodded, and the fairy sped up the stove chimney in a burst of sparks.

Nooph leaped up on the table and rubbed his head against Krezma's arm. He purred and mewed, asking for breakfast.

Krezma chuckled. "Patience, my fat feline friend. I have rabbit livers on the counter. I'll get them for you when I'm done here."

Nooph meowed and rolled over.

"Ah, Nooph, if you could give me words of wisdom, what would they be?" Krezma stood stiffly and moved to the water basin. "By all that's good, I must reveal Akeela's destiny to her, but she is still so young."

Krezma's thoughts flew back once again to the fateful day of Akeela's birth. Tzmet had arrived at the village midmorning. As noon approached, the people of Tindan were faring poorly. Most didn't know why the witch had systematically attacked all the villages in the area, but Krezma did. She'd seen the shooting star and knew a special child would be born. Tzmet must've also seen. The words of the prophecy rang in Krezma's head.

Word came that Akeela's father had fallen in battle, and upon hearing the news, her mother, Ardythe, immediately went into labor.

"When I saw the birthmark on the babe's hand, I knew the prophecy was being revealed before my very eyes." Krezma rinsed her hands and wiped them on a towel.

Nooph began to groom his claws. He gave a grunt as if to say, *I've heard this story before.*

Krezma put another log in the iron stove and poked the burning embers into flame. "It is almost time to explain everything to Akeela, and my heart is urging me to. But I've not heard from Oret in months. What to do? What to do."

Nooph curled up next to the fireplace and went to sleep. Krezma poured a mug of chamomile tea and sat, thinking, until Akeela returned with the basket of strawberries.

Akeela and Krezma walked to the village, surrounded by the song of the birds, the squeaky wheel of their cart, and the clopping of their mule's hooves. Akeela's anticipated the festival, but also her plans of running away that night. Her thoughts flew back and forth, and it must've shown on her face because after several minutes, Krezma pulled their mule, who had no name but "Mule," to a stop and spoke.

"Child, today is the Planting Festival, a day of blessing and joy. I would see you smile and put away dark thoughts."

Akeela forced a smile.

Krezma ran a hand down Akeela's hair, which was braided today to keep it out of the way for the games. "Dear Akeela . . ." she started to say.

Akeela could probably count on one hand the number of times Krezma had called her Akeela and not "child." What pixie had come in the night and replaced Krezma?

"There is a time for work and a time for rest," Krezma continued. "Work is ahead of you. Today is for rest and refreshment. You would be unwise to forgo it."

Akeela clenched her hands into fists. "What are you saying? Rest? All I ever do is work for you, and you never appreciate it!" She finished with a sob, but she kept her eyes on Krezma. "Why do you hate me?"

Krezma sighed. "I do not hate you. Aye, I know I've been hard on you, and you've borne it well. I'm proud."

Akeela's mouth dropped open.

Krezma chuckled. "I see I've surprised you."

Akeela crossed her arms.

"You worked for two weeks on your dress, child, and you chose the material well. It matches your eyes." Krezma smiled, and an unfamiliar, warm look came over her face. "The young men of the village would be blind not to notice."

"I am not interested in the young men of the village." Akeela lifted the violet skirt and dropped it. "They are all frivolous."

Krezma slowly shook her head. "Mayhap I have raised you to be too serious."

Akeela frowned. She was not going to be fooled by Krezma's uncharacteristic friendliness. "You have raised me just fine. Now, let's continue, or we'll miss the festival."

Krezma stared at her a moment, then clicked to Mule. They started their slow walk again.

With her thoughts racing, the walk to the village passed swiftly for Akeela, and soon they approached the main entrance.

"Keela! Keela!" Anon trotted up, giving Mule a wide berth.

Akeela hugged the little faun. "Hello, Anon. Today is the festival. Are you ready?"

Anon nodded his furry head. He held out a small linen bag tied closed with string. "Have stones, Keela." Anon loved his collection.

"I see." Akeela placed her hand on his shoulder. "You be careful with them. You don't want to lose any."

Anon shook the bag. "Yah."

Akeela smiled at her little half-boy, half-goat friend. He'd taken to her and she to him right away. He'd shown up three years earlier in Broem, dirty and weeping, and the minister, Queth, took him in. The fire fairies had brought the news that poor Anon had been rejected by his herd when it was known his mind had not developed as it should've.

The children in the village either avoided or teased him because he looked and acted so differently. His lower body was covered in curly, brown fur, and his feet were hooves. And while he had a boy's face, hands, and chest, his ears were long and droopy. And he had wild, spiky brown hair.

Krezma, Akeela, and Anon walked to the booth for the jam contest first and left a jar of spiced strawberry jam for judging. The rest would be sold later, right from the cart. Akeela smiled a greeting to everyone who passed and searched the many auras for Iari.

An only child, Iari was the daughter of Boryard the blacksmith and Issdra the village weaver. And she'd been Akeela's best friend since childhood.

She'd come many times to Krezma's hut with her mother, who sought help with her barrenness. None of the herbs Krezma mixed had worked. Finally, Issdra had given up and doted on her only daughter.

"Got you!"

Akeela jumped as fingers poked her sides. She whirled around to see her smiling friend standing there with Gilron, the tailor's son. Iari wore a new deep-green dress with cream sleeves and red ribbons. The shimmery material had obviously come from the peddler. Her mother spun wool into thread and wove it into the ordinary cloth the villagers used for everyday clothing. If they wanted something fancy, they had to wait until a peddler came.

Every woman and girl made a new outfit for the festival—which then became their Worship Day attire. Not that Akeela got to wear hers often. Krezma preferred to worship in the small labyrinth at home.

Akeela held out her arm to Iari, and they hugged close. "You only got me because you sneaked up on me." She laughed and tucked her right hand in her dress pocket. The archery glove she always carried felt soft and warm, and Akeela slipped her hand into it. "Besides, there are so many people, the colors all run together."

Iari laughed as well. "It matters not. I still got you." She clapped her hands.

Gilron held out his hand. Akeela touched her fingers to his and curtsied.

"I'm starved," Gilron said. "Let's see if the honey cakes are ready."

The three friends walked arm in arm toward the baker's hut, with Anon trotting behind, his tail swishing in excitement. A minute later, they emerged with cakes in hand. It was tradition to start the festival with the sweet, moist cakes covered in honey.

Iari leaned close to Akeela and lowered her voice to a whisper. She nodded toward Anon, who still followed. "Does he *have* to follow us?"

Akeela elbowed her friend. "Yes. He always comes with us."

Iari rolled her eyes. "How will we ever get to talk to Gilron and Ham with that little *tekla* hanging around?"

"He's not a *tekla*!" Akeela bristled at the derogatory name. "He can't help the way he was born, and besides, we always talk to Gilron and Ham with Anon hanging around."

Iari laughed. "You're right, Akeela. Don't be mad at me. I just wanted to share news with you."

"News?"

"Do I have to explain it to you?" Iari shoved Akeela. She nodded toward Gilron and smiled at Akeela.

Akeela started to answer when Ham, the baker's son, ran up to them. "Happy Festival!" he panted, catching his breath. He held out his hand, which still had remnants of flour on it. He blushed, wiped it on his trousers, and stuck it back out.

"Happy Festival," they replied. The girls took turns touching his fingers and dipping into a small curtsy.

"That's a nice dress, Akeela." Ham looked at his feet. His blush crept all the way into his short, blond hair.

Akeela fought to keep from frowning. Ham was acting as strangely as Iari and Gilron. "Thank you."

Gilron tugged on her fingers. "What's with the archery glove? This isn't a hunting party."

Akeela pulled her hand out of his. "I'm, um, breaking it in. It's new."

Iari glanced at her and then turned to face Gilron. "Gil, I'm starved. Let's get the next course."

"Sure." Gilron smiled down at Iari, and they walked hand in hand toward the food tables. Akeela breathed a sigh of relief. Iari knew about her birthmark, but Akeela hid it from everyone else.

"Akeela?" Ham's voice broke into her thoughts. "Are you ready?"

Akeela smiled and nodded. She allowed Ham to tuck her arm in his, and they followed Iari and Gilron.

The sun shone warm on the village, and Akeela pushed thoughts about running away and her friends' strange behavior to the back of her mind. She enjoyed squirrel- and bread-stuffed mushrooms, grilled onions and goat cheese, creamed apples, and flatbread with rich, herbed butter.

She and Iari won the three-legged race. Ham won the pie-eating contest. Gilron took first place in the javelin throw.

Minstrels wove their way through the crowd, playing and singing favorite songs. A group of young people started a circle dance, but Akeela grabbed Iari before Ham could ask her to join. Iari gave her a questioning look.

"Come on," Akeela said. "Let's get something to drink. Mayhap Krezma will give us some bell-dew this year."

The girls walked off arm in arm, Anon ever trotting behind.

Tzmet rode through the woods, carried in her sedan chair by four Hinwari. She lounged against the cushions as they followed two wild pigs which were snuffing out her favorite delicacy, truffles. How lovely that her castle sat in the most southern part of the

Northern Province. So much easier and quicker to get to the forest.

The heat of the day caused her wig-covered head to burn, and she tugged on the mink fur in frustration. As they neared the simple village on the edge of the woods, Tzmet heard sounds of laughter and revelry.

"Ah yes." She sat up in the chair. "The Planting Festival. Silly peasants. Turn around and follow that path." She pointed in the direction of Akeela and Krezma's home. "I have no desire for gaiety."

After stopping once for the fifth Hinwar to dig up a few truffles, they came upon a little stone cottage she'd never seen before. Strange. She thought she'd been through every part of the forest in the last fifteen years. Ever since she woke up from the great spell.

Tzmet held up her hand. "Hold!" She stepped on the back of a Hinwar to descend from the sedan and walked to the hut. She pushed open the door. "Are there any peasants here?" she called.

Silence.

"How delightful," she murmured. "I was getting bored. I think I'll explore a little. And why not? This will all be mine once my lord and father has risen from the ashes."

A fat gray cat with black stripes leaped off the table as she entered. It hissed and growled.

Tzmet kicked at it. "Vile animal! Get out of my way."

It jumped out the open window and ran off.

Tzmet strolled around the kitchen, opening drawers and smelling the many bowls of herbs. She picked up a plate of cakes and bit into one.

The cake tasted familiar, like something she'd eaten long ago, but she couldn't place it.

However, the flavor lingered. Curious. She took another bite. *Mm* . . . she lifted it to her lips again, then caught herself. Suddenly angry, she tossed it to the floor. "Bah! Peasant food. It disgusts me."

Then she glanced out the window. Movement in the garden

caught her eye, and she darted out the door and into the back clearing.

There, in front of her very eyes, dozens of fairies moved around and through the plants, diving into the ground as if it were water, laughing and playing. She put a hand to her throat and gasped.

At the sound of her voice, the fairies stopped their playful antics. As Tzmet blinked, they vanished. In their place, butterflies and honeybees fluttered around the garden. She watched for a moment before stepping closer. In a heartbeat, angry, buzzing bees surrounded her. She flailed her arms, trying to free herself of the storm of insects, but she only succeeded in knocking off her wig. She ran blindly to the house.

Gasping for breath, she leaned against the table until her breathing slowed. Then she raised her head and glared out the window. The butterflies continued their flighty dance around the plants, but the bees had vanished. Something was not quite right with the loathsome bugs.

Tzmet slapped the table. "I'm sure I saw fairies. But where did they go? And who lives here? I must find out."

With that, she swept out of the cottage and climbed into the sedan chair. Curse the wig. It could stay where it fell.

"Remain here among the trees and report to me when the peasants who live here return," she commanded the Hinwar holding the basket. "And give me my truffles!"

After snatching her treats, she ordered the remaining Hinwari to take her home. She may not have caught fairies on this outing, but she would enjoy truffles, sautéed with slugs and garlic, for her evening meal.

She glanced back at the cottage as the Hinwar blended into the forest. Then a quick movement caught her eye, and she watched the wretched cat drag her wig into the forest.

Chapter Four

"Good people of Broem," Queth began. "Gather your offering for the blessing!"

Several villagers brought forth baskets of seeds for the minister to ask Celtar's blessing on their crops.

Akeela looked around at the families standing together. She wondered what life would be like right now if her parents had lived. A twinge of sadness pierced her, and she blinked away tears. Deep in thought, she heard voices and looked up to see Iari, Gilron, and Ham walking toward her.

"Akeela, what are you thinking about? I said your name three times," Iari called.

"It's nothing," Akeela said. "Please forgive me. I was just thinking of everything that has to be done tomorrow when our planting starts."

Iari laughed. "But that's not today. Today, we have fun." She turned to the boys. "What do you want to do next?"

Akeela turned to Anon, who stood by her elbow, shifting from hoof to hoof. "Anon, have you had enough to eat?"

"I like pie," he said.

"Let's get some then." She turned to her friends. "Do you want to come with us?"

Iari shook her head. "We've already had pie. You go with Anon. We'll catch up later."

So Akeela took Anon's arm, and they walked to the baker's table.

After selecting a slice of apple for Anon and huckleberry for herself, Akeela sat with her friend at an empty table. Anon gobbled up his piece in a few seconds, and flashing Akeela a pie-crusty grin, he opened his linen bag.

"New stone, Keela." He handed a smooth, speckled stone to Akeela.

"It's very nice, Anon." Akeela smiled and made a big deal of admiring the stone before handing it back.

"Love you, Keela."

"I love you, too, Anon." Akeela took his hand and brought it to her cheek. Anon embodied such innocence and trust, it almost took her breath away. She thanked Celtar for bringing this poor little faun into her life. If only more people were like him, the world would be better for it.

Queth approached the table. "Pleasant day, dear Akeela. Hello, Anon. Are you having a good time?"

"Yah. Me and Keela eat pie."

Queth nodded. "That sounds good. Will you bring me a piece of apple pie, Anon?"

Anon hopped up, and Queth turned to Akeela. "My dear, are you all right? You don't seem your usual self."

Akeela shrugged. "I have things on my mind."

"Would you care to talk about it? Sometimes that helps."

Akeela considered that. If anyone would understand, it might be Queth. She took a breath. "I'm feeling a little lost, I guess." She shrugged again. "I wish I knew more about my parents. I want to live in the village. I want to be part of a family."

Queth patted her hands. "I can't help you with information about your parents, but I can assure you that you are, indeed, part of a family. The family of Celtar."

Akeela raised her eyebrows.

"Children who are not naturally born into a family are children of choice. Krezma has chosen to take you in as her daughter. She has raised you, taught you, loved you. It is the same with Celtar."

It took all her strength not to snort when Queth said Krezma loved her. "How?"

Queth smiled as Anon brought a slice of blueberry pie. Akeela knew he'd asked for apple, but he didn't correct Anon. He simply accepted what his adopted son brought.

"People are not naturally born into Celtar's family," Queth said. He took a bite of his pie. A blueberry dropped onto the table. "Those of us who believe in, love, and worship Celtar have been chosen as adopted sons and daughters. As the Holy Writings say, He loved us first. That's why we can love Him."

Akeela rested her chin on her hand. "I hadn't thought of it that way."

Queth finished his pie and wiped his hands on a cloth. "Akeela, you are loved with a rich and holy love. First by Celtar, second by Krezma, third by your family here in the village." He took her hands in his. "I will pray for peace in your soul, my dear."

"Thank you, Minister Queth. You have eased my mind considerably." Akeela squeezed his hands and smiled.

Queth nodded and stood. "Happy Festival."

"Happy Festival." Akeela rubbed her gloved hand. She hardly knew what to think. Queth said Krezma loved her. *Loved* her? With sharp words and constant nagging? True, she had a home, food, clothes. Krezma made sure she knew numbers and how to read. She taught Akeela about plants and herbs and how to sew. She allowed Akeela to have friends in the village and always warned her to keep her birthmark hidden. There were even times they laughed together. But love?

Gilron, Iari, and Ham walked up, laughing. Ham waved a white ribbon. "Look what I got for winning the pie-eating contest, Akeela!"

Akeela smiled stiffly. "Congratulations."

Anon shoved his bag of stones under the table.

"Whatcha got there, Anon?" Gilron leaned forward, reaching out his hand.

Anon shook his head.

"Oh, come on, Anon," Ham said. "It won't hurt to show us. We're your friends."

Anon shook his head harder.

Gilron pointed up. "Look, what's that?"

Everyone looked up, and Ham snatched Anon's bag and hid it behind his back.

"No!" Anon shrieked. He jumped up from the table and ran after Ham, who jogged a few feet away and tossed the bag to Gilron.

Anon charged toward Gilron. "Give stones!"

The bag went sailing back to Ham, who lifted it and shook it.

"Stop!" Tears poured down Anon's face. His body trembled as he leaped toward Ham.

Ham tossed the bag back to Gilron.

Akeela stood. "That's enough! What is wrong with you? You know Anon treasures his bag of stones. Leave him be!"

Gilron swung the bag around. "Aw, Akeela, we're just having fun."

Akeela grabbed the bag. "Does it look like Anon's having fun?" She gently laid the bag in Anon's shaking hands and smoothed the fur between his ears. "Here you go, Anon."

Anon drew in a deep, sobbing breath and ran off.

Akeela turned back to the boys and narrowed her eyes. She stared them down for a few seconds and then walked away.

Iari, who'd stood silently by the whole time, ran after her and grabbed her shoulder. "Wait, Akeela. Truly, Gilron and Ham didn't mean any harm."

Akeela resisted the urge to shrug Iari's hand off her shoulder. "One look at Anon's face would've told you differently."

"Please, Akeela, accept our apologies." Ham jogged up, his face flushed, Gilron right behind him. "We just got caught up in the spirit of the day."

A cool breeze stirred the grass. Akeela shivered and shaded

her eyes as she glanced at the soon-to-be-setting sun. "The spirit of the day is not teasing those weaker than you." She turned to her friends. "I forgive you, but please apologize to Anon. He doesn't understand, and he's especially attached to his little bag of stones."

Gilron nodded.

"We will!" Ham was quick to put in.

Iari rubbed her arms. "Come, Akeela, let's get our shawls." She stepped away from Gilron. "It will soon be time for the bonfire and singing."

"Hurry back," Gilron said, his eyes lingering on Iari.

A strange, fluttery feeling came back to Akeela's stomach. As they approached Krezma's cart, Akeela had to say something. "Your aura changes when you're with Gilron." She reached into a cloth bag and pulled out her cream-colored, woolen shawl.

Iari blushed. "I've been wanting to talk to you. My father is going to announce it tonight." She took a breath. "Gilron and I are promised. Our hand fasting will be after the planting."

Akeela's mouth dropped open. "Oh!" She threw her arms around her friend. "I should've guessed."

Iari laughed and tightened her arms around Akeela. "I'm so glad you're not upset. You haven't been yourself all day, and I so wanted you to be happy for me."

"I'm sorry. Truly, I'm happy for you." Akeela held Iari at arm's length. "Gilron is a fine young man, and I know he'll take good care of you."

The girls walked arm in arm toward the pond. "Our marriage will take place next spring," Iari said. "It's a year away, and I wish it could be now."

Akeela nudged her. "A year is not a lot of time to get everything ready for a home. I will personally pick some of Krezma's best herbs for your kitchen garden."

"What about you?" Iari asked.

"What do you mean?"

"You're fifteen."

Akeela chuckled. "So?"

"So there must be someone who's caught your eye." Iari nudged Akeela back. "What about Ham? He seems to like you."

Akeela shook her head. "Ham is my friend, and he's nice, but I don't believe he's for me."

"Akeela! Iari!" a voice called. Akeela looked up to see Ham waving furiously at them.

Iari sighed. "I hope you tell him gently. He's smitten with you."

Akeela gave Ham a small smile, hoping he wouldn't be encouraged. She had a feeling it didn't work.

Krezma sold the last jar of spiced jam to Mosset, Ham's mother, for a loaf of raisin bread.

"Kintcha will be disappointed to have only one jar," she said to Krezma.

"Your husband knows I can supply him with more," Krezma retorted.

She knew she sounded sharp, but a persistent feeling of alarm had worn on her, and she'd grown weary of carrying it all day. Kintcha, the village baker, often came to her for jams to fill his pastries, so she kept some at the hut for him every year. If this year was the same as previous years, he would be by tomorrow with a sack of flour to barter.

Mosset hesitated by the table and clutched the jar of jam to her chest.

"Is there something else?" Krezma's patience snapped, and her voice rose.

"I . . . well . . ." Mosset looked as though she were about to faint. "Kintcha wishes to speak to you regarding your . . ."

Krezma stared her down.

Mosset opened her mouth and closed it. She took a breath. "Akeela."

Krezma's eyebrows rose. "Akeela? What business does he have with Akeela?"

"She's fifteen, after all, and Ham favors her above others in the village, and we do a goodly business. She would be well taken care of." Mosset finished in a rush.

Krezma's heart pounded. Someone was actually asking for Akeela's hand. She knew the day might come, but knowing it did not keep her from feeling a strange sadness. And guilt. She was supposed to have prepared Akeela for her responsibility one day, and she'd not entirely done that.

"I will talk with your husband," she finally said. "But I promise nothing."

Mosset scurried off with her jam, and Krezma turned back to the cart. Akeela's shawl was gone. She must be heading for the bonfire. The feeling of alarm increased, and Krezma decided the time to go home was now.

It wasn't hard to spot Akeela with her creamy-white shawl in the fading sunlight. Krezma watched her with Iari, Gilron, and Ham for a few moments. She seemed happy enough, yet not quite herself. Krezma nodded. Yes, it was time to head home. She muttered a quick prayer and approached the group.

Akeela turned and looked at her before she could say a word. The fire illuminated her hair, and Krezma held her breath as the light outlined Akeela's body, giving her a glowing appearance. It was a sign, but Krezma didn't know what it meant.

Krezma reached out her hand. "Come, child."

Akeela turned to her friends. "I must go. A blessed planting for your families."

Iari and Gilron said their goodbyes and turned back to the fire, but Krezma glanced back and noticed Ham watching them until they turned behind the stables where Mule and the cart waited.

"Is all well with you?" Akeela asked.

Krezma shook her head. "Something is amiss. I feel the need to return home."

"I've been on edge, too."

Akeela untied Mule and held the harness. Krezma patted her hand and, with a grunt, heaved herself up on the seat. Akeela handed her the reins and climbed up next to her.

Sounds of singing and laughter faded as Mule trudged along the path, knowing the way home, even in the dark.

Krezma glanced at Akeela. "Child?"

Akeela sighed. "Iari and Gilron are promised."

"Does this bother you?"

Akeela shook her head. "No."

"What bothers you then?"

"Something Iari said." Akeela sat silent a moment. "She said Ham favors me. He's a nice boy, but I don't care for him in that way."

Krezma gave the reins a light snap. "Mule, get along."

"You know about this?"

Mule stepped up to a slow trot while Krezma thought. Should she reveal Ham's intentions to Akeela? The child would find out sooner or later. Better to be forewarned.

"Mosset spoke to me earlier. Ham's father will come by tomorrow to speak with me."

Akeela's body stiffened. "What will you say?"

"I have not the words tonight, but I will ask Celtar for wisdom in this matter." Krezma snapped the reins again.

They rode home in silence, if the singing of the crickets and frogs could be determined quiet. As Mule slowed to a stop in front of the cottage, Akeela gasped. "The witch has been here!"

"Are you sure?"

Akeela nodded and pulled her shawl tighter. "I can smell her aura."

"Wait here." Krezma handed Akeela the reins. She climbed down with a grunt and crept to the front door. If Tzmet were here, the last person Krezma wanted her to see was Akeela.

She peered into the window and nearly jumped off the ground when she felt a hand on her shoulder.

"It's just me," Akeela whispered.

"I told you to wait!" Krezma ground out. "Celtar forgive me, I forgot to set the protection spell."

"Why? The witch is gone," Akeela said. "We need to get inside where I can reach my bow in the event she returns."

They stepped through the doorway. Nothing looked out of place except the plate of *krenda* cakes on the counter. Krezma started to relax, until she heard a branch snap.

🐝

Akeela peered into the dark woods and noticed a strange golden-brown aura she'd never seen before. "Who's there?"

Silence met her.

The hair on her arms prickled.

Then the aura swam toward her. She gasped as a large spotted wildcat stepped out from behind a pine tree, his aura so bright, it crackled. Akeela's feet seemed to have rooted themselves to the ground, and she stood, stunned.

The ocelot moved gingerly as he drew near her. He stopped and bowed his head. Akeela held her breath as she realized she could hear the big cat's thoughts.

Chosen one, I have traveled far to see you.

Nooph shot through the door, hissing and spitting.

"Nooph, you witless cat, calm down." Krezma stepped forward and, to Akeela's surprise, bowed her head in respect toward the ocelot. "The blessing of Celtar be with you."

Krezma, it's been a long time.

Akeela's eyes opened wide. Krezma knew the wildcat? Why then did he say he'd been searching for her and not Krezma?

"Come in, come in," Krezma said. "The witch has been here. I do not wish to be caught lingering if she's still around."

They entered the cottage, and Krezma set the bar in place to lock the door. She lifted her hands and whispered. Then she turned around. "Oret, your appearance can mean only one thing."

Oret lowered his head. *Yes, the time is near. Is the child prepared?*

Krezma shook her head. "By all that's good, it cannot be time."

The urgent fear in her voice caused Akeela's defenses to rise.

It should not be time, but circumstances have arisen that force it.

"Ach, where are my manners?" Krezma threw her hands up.

"Please, sit and be welcome. I have rabbit livers I've been saving in the cupboard."

Nooph meowed as if to say, *Weren't they my livers?* Krezma shooed him into the bedroom and shut the door.

Akeela put her hands on her hips. "What's going on? How can we hear this cat's thoughts? Who is he?"

"Hush, child, and let Oret speak."

The girl knows nothing?

Krezma looked ashamed. "Nay. Well, she knows about fairies and a little about the witch."

Krezma.

"I was going to start teaching her this spring. She's only fifteen!"

"I'm right here, you know," Akeela said.

They both looked at her as though she'd suddenly appeared out of the air. Krezma stood and poured hot water into a mug. She sprinkled some herbs in and set it before Akeela.

Akeela, you must learn and learn quickly. Krezma, get the prophecy. We must start teaching Akeela now.

Krezma went into the bedroom and came out with a rolled animal skin. She placed it on the table and settled with a grunt into a chair. A faint silver glow came off the skin as if the light of the moons illuminated it. Akeela closed her eyes. What kind of animal skin had an aura? Only living things had glowing energy around them.

The rustling of the skin interrupted her thoughts, and she opened her eyes. Krezma spread the skin on the table. "This is the original prophecy."

Akeela nodded.

"A copy of the scroll was torn and a piece stolen by the witch when my sister's scribe was bringing it back to my people," Krezma went on. "Thanks be to Celtar she does not have the entire thing. She has only the part she managed to run off with."

Read the words, Krezma. Let me hear them once more.

Krezma closed her eyes. Then she looked directly at Akeela.

"Ashes deep in slumber
Will rip the ground asunder.
Foul, yet fair, he will ascend,
Consuming earth, enslaving men.
Fairy and folk hide and cower,
But only one can wield the power.

"That much the witch knows. But she knows nothing of the Chosen One." She closed her eyes again and recited:

"When triple moon hides sun so fair,
Then Fairystone in runes must wear.
Back to ashes, evil mourns,
The guardian will be reborn."

Krezma grew silent, smoothing her hand over the scroll. "I never asked for this. I did not want to raise another child."

Akeela blinked. Another child?

Is that why you named her "burden"?

Akeela held a hand over her mouth. Her name meant burden? Of course it did. Krezma often made her feel as though she were something to be tolerated.

"Aye, I did name her that," Krezma said slowly. She turned to Akeela. "I do regret that now, child."

A tear slipped down Akeela's cheek.

Where else could we have turned? You know better than anyone the power of the Dark Lord and the history of the Guardian.

"Yes, I know. I know. And I'm the only one the Fairy Council trusted." Krezma slid back from the table and stood. She rolled up the scroll. "But I have my own life! My own plans. I have given up much."

Oret bowed his head. *We know this and are grateful. Has it been so terrible, raising Akeela?*

Krezma sighed. "Nay, it has not been terrible. She has not been the burden I believed she would be. Akeela is like my own child, and yet, she is not. I'm torn. It's not time to reveal her destiny. She is so young, I'm not sure she can handle it."

Are you saying Akeela does not know who she is?

"Nay, I have not told her."

This is bad. Krezma, we depended on you to prepare her! There is little time. We must tell her and teach her.

"I have taught her about Celtar. The fairies," Krezma said. "And she knows about plants and herbs."

But she does not know her history. Her responsibility. Her destiny.

"Aye, I know," Krezma said.

Akeela felt overwhelmed. Her head whirled with questions. She cleared her throat. "I've always known Krezma had no great love for me, but what is the meaning of the prophecy? What am I supposed to learn?"

Since the Dark Lord Riss'aird's destruction, the earth fairies' magic has been keeping his ashes asleep in the ground. This is changing. I have learned Tzmet has been going through the forest for the last seven years and capturing earth fairies. What she does with them, I do not know.

"That's why the animals are so frightened," Akeela said.

Krezma leaned forward. "You do not understand, child. The animals are not important. If Tzmet eliminates enough earth fairies, their power will weaken."

Akeela's mouth went dry. "Weaken?"

Oret looked into Akeela's eyes and held her gaze. *The prophecy speaks of the rising of Riss'aird from the ashes. If this were to happen, terrible evil would fill the land. But it also speaks of hope with the rebirth of the Fairy Guardian.*

Akeela stared at the wildcat. "What does this have to do with me?"

"The birthmark on your hand, child." Krezma touched Akeela's right hand. "It's a circle of runes."

Akeela clasped her hands together.

Your gift of spirit-sight, the auras, and the fairies you can see and communicate with.

Akeela's eyes widened. "How do you know these things?"

I am the Fairy Guardian.

"But Krezma can communicate with fairies. What does any of this have to do with me?"

Krezma leaned forward. "Child, you have heard the words of the prophecy. Do you not know?"

Akeela shook her head. "It can't have anything to do with me. Yes, I have a strange birthmark, but it's nothing more."

"Take off your glove, child."

"I don't want to."

I too have a mark of runes, Akeela. And I also have the gift of spirit-sight.

"Yes, but you are the Fairy Guardian."

Oret seemed to have a smile on his face. *That is true.*

He and Krezma stared at Akeela.

"What? Me? No." She jumped from her seat. "I have only seen fifteen summers!"

Krezma leaned forward, frowning. "Can you not see the spirit beings flitting around our plants, skimming the water, sparkling in the fire, dancing in the fields?"

Akeela sank back into her chair. "Yes," she said, feebly.

"And are you not the only one who sees this?"

Akeela shook her head. "You see them . . ."

Does Krezma have a birthmark?

Akeela shook her head again.

Does Krezma see auras?

Akeela didn't respond. The weight of the truth rested on her chest, and she struggled to take a deep breath. Finally, she found her voice. "Why me?"

You are the one chosen by Celtar.

Akeela felt lightheaded. She shook her head. "Not possible."

Oret gave a rumbling sound, as though he chuckled. *Quite possible. And quite imperative for you to learn your role now.*

All the breath left Akeela, and she struggled to get out her next question. "Why is it imperative now?"

Oret's golden eyes met hers. *I am dying.*

Chapter Five

"Dying?" Krezma's voice rose to an unfamiliar pitch. "Why? What has happened?"

I had an encounter with the witch. It seems, somehow, I was expected. Her fingernails were laced with some kind of poison. Nothing I have tried has worked a cure.

Akeela's throat constricted. "I don't understand. You went to find the witch?"

Yes. When three earth fairies brought news that fairies were disappearing from the forest, I suspected the witch was involved. I didn't want to risk sending fire fairies to spy just yet, so I went to the castle. She was waiting just outside the gates.

Krezma brought out her mortar and pestle, her precious herb book, and her bag of herbs. "Tell me what you've tried, and I'll see what I can do."

"I'll help," Akeela said.

"Nay, child," Krezma said. "The hour is late. You'll need to be up with the sun to hunt, so you must sleep now."

Akeela gave a short laugh. "Sleep? You really expect me to sleep?"

39

Krezma waved her hands. "I care not if you sleep, but you need to leave us. I have work to do. When Oret is rested, we'll talk more."

Akeela was going to argue when she glanced at Oret. His eyes were fixed on her face, and he still seemed to smile. A surge of anticipation and a strange peace suffused her, and she smiled back.

"Fine. I'll try to sleep. But we *will* continue this in the morning."

But Krezma was deep into her herb book and didn't respond.

"Curses and firestone! Where is that wretched Hinwar?" Tzmet paced the length of the kitchen. She'd left the Hinwar at the cottage last night. Surely it should've been back by now.

What if it had been caught? Tzmet pondered this possibility and dismissed it. The Hinwar blended perfectly with the forest. No one would've been able to see it, not even herself.

The other Hinwari shuffled into the kitchen and began preparations for breakfast. Tzmet smacked her forehead. "*Tov tekla!*" she mumbled.

The Hinwari continued their work as they chopped, stirred, and cooked Tzmet's choice of black snake with mushrooms and *hicata* peppers.

Tzmet threw her head back and laughed. She laughed until her sides hurt and she had to sit on a bench. "Fool that I am," she gasped. "I left a creature to spy and report to me, and the creature cannot speak! It's probably still standing in the same place I left it."

She gave a short laugh and sighed.

"I've wasted enough time. I believe I may have to try out my experiment." She smiled and tapped her fingers on the table. "Yes, I'm tired of searching for these vile fairy creatures, only to capture one or two at a time. I need more. *More!*"

A Hinwar brought her a goblet. She wrapped her hands around the cup. "First, I'll enjoy my meal. I work better with a full stomach."

Breakfast was barely over and the dishes washed when Kintcha arrived to collect the extra jars of jam Krezma had promised.

Akeela helped him load several jars of Krezma's spiced jam into his cart. If she helped, maybe she'd be able to hear some of the conversation between Krezma and Kintcha. They were going to be talking about her, for goodness' sake.

"I thank you, Krezma, for your generous supply of jam," he said. "Here is the bag of flour and *caavea* beans I promised."

"If you would, set them on the kitchen table." Krezma rubbed her knuckles. "I fear my hands are not up to the task of carrying such heavy items."

"It is no problem." Kintcha lifted the bags, one on each shoulder. "And if I might have a word with you in private . . ." He smiled at Akeela as they walked into the cottage.

Akeela grabbed her sewing off the table. "I'll work on my sewing in the back room."

She leaned against the wall by the kitchen door, listening, as Kintcha offered his proposal. It was not complicated: Ham and Akeela would marry, and they would inherit the bakery.

Krezma told him she needed time to pray.

"I will come again in one month's time for your delicious honey —and also for your answer."

Akeela ducked away from the window and scurried into the back room where she slept. Oret was sleeping in Krezma's room. Krezma moved about in the kitchen. Panic gripped her, and she nearly flew to sit on the bed, picked up the deerskin boots she'd been sewing, and jabbed the bone needle into the leather. She tried not to think of how closely she'd come to becoming Ham's bride today. Krezma had secured her a month.

Her plans to run away came to her again.

What was wrong with her? Why couldn't she be happy like Iari? Why shouldn't she marry Ham and live in the village? At least she'd have her own family.

But a change had occurred in her heart since Oret's appearance. She didn't feel such an urge to run away, even though the thought lingered.

Krezma stood at the doorway. "He is gone." She came and sat next to Akeela. "I presume you heard everything."

Akeela put the needle down. Krezma always knew. She nodded. "Ham is my friend. He would make a good husband. Why am I not happy to have him ask for my hand?"

Krezma ran her hand over the deer leather. "Mayhap Celtar has another plan for your life, and that is why He hasn't put the desire to marry into your heart."

A warm feeling grew between them Akeela had never felt before. She grasped on to the hope that she might not have to run away. "Do you think it has something to do with the witch?"

"I know not," Krezma murmured. "Her coming to the cottage is surely a sign, yet I cannot discern what it may be."

The two sat silently for a few minutes. The sun cast its rays through the window and made dancing designs on the wooden floor. Akeela rested her chin on her hand, the needle pointed away from her face.

"I think I'm linked to the witch."

"What gives you this thought, child?"

"I can see and smell her aura. She found the cottage—*our* cottage—without any provocation. And I can feel the animals' fear. Even you cannot do that."

Krezma pinched her arm, the camaraderie gone. "Enough, child. All will be revealed in due time. I will prepare our midday meal. When Oret awakens, we'll talk." She went to the door and turned. "Patience is a virtue of Celtar."

Akeela nodded and continued her sewing while Krezma started the noon meal. She was going to need these boots when she left. If she left. As she sewed, she thought of what else she would need to take and how quickly she could get them together if the time came.

Soon she smelled the rich aroma of baking bread. If she married Ham, she'd never be without bread.

Oret joined them at the table. Akeela thought it odd Krezma

allowed the wildcat to sit at the table. Nooph always took his meals by the back door.

Akeela dipped a piece of bread into the gravy. "I'm ready to talk now."

"I have the last of the preserved gooseberries ready with cream," Krezma said, ignoring her.

Oret licked his chops. *Just cream for me.*

"Didn't you hear me?" Akeela asked.

Krezma brought a small bowl of cream to the table. "Take this to Nooph, or he'll think himself left out."

Akeela slammed her spoon on the table. "You promised when Oret woke, we would talk! It's my life, and I want to know what's going on."

Krezma waved her hand toward the door.

"I hate you." Akeela's heart pounded as the words she'd been wanting to say for years burst out.

Krezma raised her eyebrows.

Frustrated, Akeela stomped to the back doorway and set the bowl on the ground. Nooph was nowhere to be seen. No matter. He'd appear at some point. What she really wanted was to speak with Oret. In fact, she wasn't going to stop asking until she got answers.

She started to turn when a strange color caught her eye. Peering into the woods beside the hut, she could make out a grayish aura which would've been invisible if not for the brown bark of the sycamore tree where it stood.

She took a step toward the shape. The gray aura trembled, but before Akeela could say anything, a creature she'd never seen before sprang away from the tree and darted into the forest. It was very thin, like a young sapling, with hair that stuck out wildly around its head.

"Wait! Stop!" Akeela ran after it, keeping her eyes on the tree-like creature with the gray aura.

They hadn't gone but a few lengths into the forest when a man stepped out from behind a pine and caught the creature by the neck. It wriggled desperately but made no sound. Akeela stopped before them and stared. Now that she was closer, she could see the man was as foreign to her as the creature he held.

They stood studying each other. Akeela observed his aura first. It shimmered, giving off shades of orange and blue. How strange that it was two colors. She continued her assessment of him, taking in golden eyes, a hawk-like nose, close-cropped brown hair, and what seemed to be a tight weaving of white feathers around his neck. He carried a bow and a quiver of arrows on his shoulder.

The man studied her as well. He glanced at her right hand, and Akeela quickly put it behind her. Her eyes dropped to his hands, and she gasped as she realized the hand that held the creature was not a hand at all, but a talon. Big, like the foot of an eagle.

Finally she found her voice, giving the standard polite greeting of Broem. "Good noon day greetings to you."

He nodded.

"May—may I be of help?" Akeela stammered. The man's strange aura and lack of voice unnerved her. If only Krezma would come out of the cottage to see why she hadn't come back.

The creature continued to kick and wiggle silently. The man gave it a shake, and it ceased its movements.

"I have come in response to Oret's message." The man's voice was quick and clipped, yet gentle.

"He's staying with us," she said.

The man glanced at the cottage.

"What is this creature?" Akeela felt a great sadness when she gazed into its eyes. "I sense something familiar, yet I've never seen anything like it."

"I must speak with Oret." The man took a step toward her. "This creature is part of the reason I've come."

Akeela turned and strode back to the house, completely forgetting to invite the man in. She glanced over her shoulder as she pushed through the gate.

Oret came to the door. When he saw the man following Akeela, he gave a rumble of welcome. Then he did something which made Akeela almost faint. He transformed into a man.

"Tar, you are most welcome." Oret stepped forward and grasped the man's free hand. "I thank Celtar you got my message."

"I feared the worst for you, my friend," Tar said.

Akeela looked from man to man, aura to aura. Oret stood before her in the form of an older man, tall, handsome, with golden eyes and long, golden-brown hair streaked with gray. Three angry-looking scratches were on his right cheek. Yet his aura remained unchanged.

Oret put his hand on her shoulder. "Tar, I am pleased to introduce to you a most special young lady." He turned to Akeela. "This is Akeela."

Tar nodded.

"Akeela, this is my closest friend. His name is Tar."

Akeela could only manage a nod back. She stared at the scratches on Oret's cheek. He glanced at her and smiled, touching his fingers to the wounds.

"What are you two doing?" Krezma stuck her head out the window. She gasped. "In the name of Celtar! Tar! Is it really you?"

Oret gestured toward the house. "Come inside, friends. There is much to be said."

Tar raised his claw-hand, and the creature desperately attempted escape. Tar grabbed it with both hands and held it before him. "What shall I do with this?"

"What is it?" Akeela blurted.

Krezma snorted. "Child, you always have questions. Come inside! All will be revealed."

Tar followed Oret into the house. Akeela hesitated and glanced back at the woods. Were other creatures out there?

An earth fairy flew to her and hovered a hand's breadth before her face. "Akeela, please restore our sister."

Akeela started out of her thoughts. The fairy's lack of protocol, giving no greeting, shook her to the core. What was happening?

"Restore our sister!" the fairy cried out again.

"I—I don't know what you mean."

The fairy lifted her chin. Tears ran down her brown cheeks. "The creature in the birdman's hand is our sister!"

Akeela's eyes widened. The creature with the gray aura was a *fairy*? What evil had done this? And how could *she* heal it?

Chapter Six

"Here, Tar, I was about to serve gooseberries and cream." Krezma pulled another wooden bowl from the cupboard. "They are the last of what I put by last summer."

Akeela wanted to scream but couldn't find her voice. First, Oret showed up, now this strange man held a creature that was supposed to be a fairy, and Krezma was worried about gooseberries?

"I thank you." Tar sat stiffly at the table, still holding the fairy creature with his claw.

Oret reached for it. "Allow me."

Tar handed the creature over, and it kicked furiously as Oret held tight. He leaned toward its terrified face, looking deeply into its eyes. "Hmm, yes. I see your pain, dear one. Please trust me."

The creature calmed and hung limp in Oret's hand. All the life seemed to drain from it.

Akeela came to stand by Oret's shoulder. "You know this creature?"

"I knew what it was."

"What it was?"

Oret looked at Krezma and then at Akeela. "I believe you know, don't you?"

Akeela nodded.

Krezma lifted her spoon, dripping with cream, and slipped it in her mouth before pointing it at Akeela. "Child, be not afraid. Tell us what is in your heart."

"It's a fairy. But how can this be?"

Oret smiled. "Come, place your hands on it."

Akeela knelt and put her fingertips on the creature's shoulders. It shuddered at her touch. She gazed into its eyes. "I can't see the fairy light."

Oret sighed. "You wouldn't. This creature has had most of its life pulled out, including the fairy light."

"Pulled out?"

"By the witch," Tar said.

Krezma leaned forward. "There is much to tell you, child."

Akeela gave a weak smile. "There is much I want to know."

"First we must attend to this poor creature," Oret said. "Then we will answer your questions." He set the creature on the edge of the table. It looked pitifully at Akeela.

"Please don't be frightened," she whispered. "I spoke to your sister. They are waiting."

Oret bowed his head. A tense moment passed. Akeela held her breath and prayed the earth fairy had been right, and if so, Oret could help this poor creature.

A fluttering sound caused Akeela to look toward the window. Several fairies gathered on the sill. They held hands and bowed their heads as if praying with Oret.

Oret raised his head. "I have not the strength to do it. It will take too much of my life force."

Tar stepped forward. "This does not have to be done now. We will keep the creature safe until the changing can be done."

"Yes, we have need of you, Oret. Do not tax your energy," Krezma said.

The fairies left the window one by one.

A feeling of incredible sadness overwhelmed Akeela. "We have to help! The pain is so great. Please, Oret."

"Child, silence! The creature will be helped." Krezma rose from her seat and hobbled to the stove. "Sit. The time has come for you to learn the truth."

Akeela sat and lay her head on the table. Krezma placed a steaming mug before her.

"Here, child, drink. It will soothe you."

Akeela turned away from the pungent smell of cinnamon and yarrow. It eased the spirits and gave comfort to the body.

She didn't want to be comforted.

Dear Akeela, please trust me. I understand your confusion.

Akeela glanced at Oret, who sat in ocelot form once more. "I don't understand. How can we all hear your thoughts? Why do you appear as a wildcat?"

Even though I am the Fairy Guardian, I am human, but the fairy magic infused in my body keeps me in animal form as a protection against those who would harm me. I can use human form when necessary, but it is draining. And, unfortunately, the witch has discovered me. I know not how she did it. This places me in great danger.

"Why?"

Krezma, please take this poor creature out to the forest fairies. They will keep it safe until we can heal it.

Krezma carried it out the back door. She was back in a minute.

First, you can hear only the thoughts I wish you to hear. Tar and Krezma can only hear what I wish them to hear. As Fairy Guardian, I have this ability.

Akeela picked up the mug of herbal tea. "I see."

It is similar to when you talk. I can hear the words you say aloud, but I can't hear what you don't say.

Oret placed his paw on the table. *Now, we must pray to Celtar and ask for wisdom.*

Krezma nodded. "Of course."

Oret prayed, and a tingling sensation stirred within Akeela. His voice pierced her thoughts and questions as a peace she couldn't explain filled her mind. She looked up expectedly when Oret finished.

Krezma cleared her throat.

Oret began. *The location of the earth fountain must be protected at any cost.*

"Where is it?" Akeela leaned forward. She tried not to sound anxious, but she couldn't hold back the questions. "*What* is it?"

He took a deep breath. *There is a map. Four fountains. Earth, fire, air, and water. They give life to the fairies. The four fountains have separate locations. The head of the council keeps the location of each fountain on a map, and the map is guarded at all times by three fairies. The joining of the fountains is called the Fairysong. Without the Fairysong, all fairy life would cease to exist.*

"What's so important about the earth fountain?"

Oret took a trembling breath. *The earth fountain sustains the earth fairies, whose goodness keeps Riss'aird's ashes safe under the ground. If the earth fountain is attacked, the fairies' power will weaken.*

Akeela's heart beat quicker. "And how do we protect it?"

There are fairy protectors, trained in prayer and warfare. As Guardian, I travel between the fountains, energizing each one through the Fairystone in my birthmark.

"Fairystone in runes must wear," Akeela murmured.

"What, child?" Krezma asked.

Akeela turned to look at her. "Part of the prophecy. Remember?"

"Aye, of course I remember." Krezma chuckled. "I was just surprised you did. You've only heard the prophecy once."

Oret nodded. *Akeela, listen to me. My power is draining. You must follow the words of the prophecy. Just as there are four fountains, there are also four pieces to the Fairystone. Find these pieces, then join them by placing them in the runes on your hand when the triple moons come together and hide the light of the sun. If you do not, you will not have the power to destroy Riss'aird.*

"When will he regenerate?"

Oret stretched out his paw and touched Akeela's hand. *The prophecy tells of his rising. Although the time is not known, it will happen. If you cannot join yourself with the stone, you will not be able to stand against him, and he will destroy our world.*

Akeela frowned. "Why can't I simply take the Fairystone from you?"

Krezma snorted. "Child, the Fairystone and the Guardian are joined. Could you remove your heart and give it to anyone who asked?"

Akeela blanched at Krezma's rebuke. Even though she was now so important, Krezma still treated her as though she were nothing but foolish.

Tar stepped next to Oret. "I have seen the destruction Riss'aird can bring. When he rises, he will not rise alone. He will call his army of whiptails together. These simple village folk will not survive."

Akeela swallowed. "What are whiptails?"

"They are mutants, created by Riss'aird for his evil purposes," Krezma said. "Heinous creatures that are part man and part rat. Their tails are deadly whips. Their saliva is burning sulfur. It is sufficient to say that someone without a warrior's training would not stand against them."

"But I have no warrior's training," Akeela said. "How am I supposed to guard against such creatures?"

Krezma began to pace. "It is not the Guardian's job to fight Riss'aird's army. It's your job to find the four parts of the Fairystone and *become* the Guardian. This will enable you to strike down Riss'aird because you'll be connected to the power of the entire fairy realm. Tar will gather those strong enough to fight."

Faces of her friends flashed in Akeela's mind. She couldn't bear the thought of everyone she loved being destroyed by Riss'aird and his army. She straightened her back. "I'll do it. Tell me where the Fairystone pieces are, and I'll get them."

Oret was silent for a moment. *When Riss'aird's spell went wrong, even the fairy realm was affected, so we scattered the new stone. I have the first piece for you.*

He nodded to Krezma, who handed Akeela a small, white stone.

The second piece is below ground with the Kazmura cave people. The third is with the Salt Dwarves. The fourth with the Fidesians, Krezma's people, south of Broem. When all four pieces are in the runes in your hand, they will meld together and join with the runes.

Akeela examined the stone. "What then? Will I become a cat?"

"The Stone will choose," Krezma said. "Do not worry your head over it. You must be protected somehow, child."

Akeela pondered that. What if she didn't want to become something other than she was? What if she lost herself? No, she wouldn't allow it. She'd find a way to keep who she was.

"How do I find the Kazmura and the Salt Dwarves?"

"I have a map," Tar said. "I will accompany you on this quest."

Akeela didn't want to travel with a stranger. She sent Krezma a panicked glance, but Krezma was nodding her approval. What could Akeela say? She'd already promised to find the Fairystone pieces.

"The sun is late in the sky," Krezma said. "I will prepare the evening meal. We can talk more in the morning. Oret needs to rest and fight the witch's poison."

Akeela stood. "I'll help you."

She didn't know how she'd sleep tonight. Her plans for running away didn't include a quest or fighting the witch. She wanted a family! And there was more she wanted to talk to Oret about. She prayed Celtar would bring healing to the ocelot before it was too late.

The cool night air brushed Tzmet's cheeks as she gazed toward the starry sky. The Hinwari hitched her horse, Nightshade, to the carriage, and she set off, breathing in the mossy perfume of the ground.

Leaning forward, she looked at the three waning crescent moons hanging in the sky like sickles. If all went according to plan, her father would rise from the ground before the moons showed their full faces, a mere thirty days away.

The box next to her on the seat glimmered with a faint green glow. Tzmet patted it and let out a dry laugh. "Patience, my pets. Your time is coming."

Nightshade trotted along the dark path as the crickets sang and the tree frogs frolicked. Exhilaration bubbled up, and she laughed out loud as she contemplated her future as the daughter of the master of the universe.

A sudden flash of light streaked across the sky and over the village of Broem. Tzmet's peace shattered. A similar shooting star had appeared fifteen years ago, indicating the birth of a special child. She'd destroyed every village in the area, looking for it. "But I found no evidence of a birth. Only burning little hovels," she whispered.

Nightshade whinnied in response.

"But what if one of those huts held the remnants of childbirth? Where would that child be now?" Tzmet's fingers entwined, opening and closing.

Nightshade snorted.

"Enough, you fool horse. Pay attention to the path." Tzmet gazed at the faint trail of the star. "I must pull out my star charts when I return to determine the meaning of this appearance."

The box shifted on the seat, and Tzmet rested her hand atop it. She wished she hadn't eaten such a large meal now.

"My imagination is getting the best of me." She laughed. "Even if a child was born that night, it would only be fifteen, and what could a mere child of that age mean to me?"

Still, the presence of that star was a sign. She'd have to be more alert.

The carriage neared the stone cottage. She signaled the Hinwar to stop. "I will walk from here. Wait for me in the shadows."

Tzmet picked up the box and stepped down from the carriage. She looked around, satisfied the carriage was invisible to anyone passing by, and headed down the path. This cottage would be a sign to the villagers. If they were hiding Oret, they would pay.

Tzmet stood without moving. The cottage should be here! Where was it? Her heart raced, and blood pulsed in her head. She clutched the box to her chest and crept forward like a growing shadow. She'd only taken three steps when she felt the tingle of magic.

So the peasants who lived here had a protection spell. Interesting. It must have something to do with the fairies she'd seen in the garden.

A branch snapped, and she cursed under her breath and ducked behind a tree. The musty smell of fungus filled her nostrils. She rubbed her nose to keep from sneezing. Holding her breath, she peered around the trunk. Then she whispered a revealing spell, and the cottage came into view. A man stood at a window.

"Good, someone's home," she murmured.

She knelt and opened the box. Three glowing figures floated up and hovered before her face. Tzmet smiled as she gazed at the earth fairies. They were true fairies and not ones she'd conjured. No matter how hard she'd tried, she couldn't conjure a fairy that would fool real ones.

These, however, *were* real. After a hundred failures, she'd mixed the right potion that transformed fairies into her servants. True, she only had these three, but did she really need more? They proved themselves undetectable when she put them in the holding cell with other fairies. They learned Oret was coming to her castle, and that enabled her to catch him by surprise. She never would've gotten close enough to use her deadly fingernails otherwise.

She stifled a laugh. Once she had Oret's body, she'd be able to read the runes rumored to be on his chest and find the source of fairy life. Unless her fairies could bring the information themselves. But then, what fun would that be?

"Easy, my pets," she whispered. "You know what to do. Warn them of my coming. Gain their trust. Go, now!"

The fairies whizzed off into the night. Tzmet heard them shriek an alarm and smiled.

"Daaanger! Daaanger!"

Akeela sucked in her breath. Three earth fairies careened through the open doorway, screeching like bats.

"Daaanger! Daaanger!"

Oret lifted his chin. *Peace, my children. What is wrong?*

The fairies spoke in unison. "The witch is approaching!" Then they flew out through the front window, obviously frightened out of their wits.

Akeela jumped up. "The witch!"

Krezma's mug thumped on the table. She pulled Akeela's arm. "In the name of Celtar! Come, child. You must make haste." She nodded to Tar. "Take her to the village. Oret and I will stand against the witch."

Tar slipped his bow on his shoulder. His gold eyes glittered as he lifted Akeela's bow and quiver of arrows off the peg and handed them to her.

"But I—"

"Shush now, child! Take these with you." Krezma handed her the finished deerskin boots. "And your heavy cape."

Akeela, you must go with Tar. We cannot afford to reveal your existence to the witch.

Krezma took her hands and squeezed. "May Celtar protect you."

Akeela snatched them away from Krezma. "Come with me. Please, don't stay here."

"Foolish child! Don't you understand we can't?" Krezma pushed her toward Tar. "If the witch should follow, the village would be in danger."

Oret leaped onto the table. *Tar will get you through the woods. There is none better to guide you at night.*

More fairies appeared at the back door. They must've heard the alarm. Akeela paused at the door and tried to speak again. "Krezma, I'm afraid. Please don't—"

"Pffft, go now, child." She waved her hands at Akeela and Tar. "Go!"

Akeela gasped as Tar grabbed her arm and pushed her through

the door and into the dark garden. Before she could take a breath, they were through the garden and into the woods. Akeela clung to Tar's arm, unable to see a thing, but Tar didn't seem to have a problem guiding them through the woods without benefit of a path or torch. They moved quicker than Akeela thought possible, and she tried to brush away the branches slapping at her face. The light from Krezma's kitchen disappeared in a matter of seconds.

Krezma peered out the window. At first, she saw nothing, but then she noticed a slight movement in the shadows. "She's here," she whispered to Oret.

I will help as much as I'm able. However, I do not have my full strength.

"I know. We can't fight her now. I said that to get Akeela out. Let me see if she'll talk to me."

That will do no good. Tzmet has never been one for talking.

"Let me try."

At that moment, Tzmet's harsh laugh rang out. A chill ran down her spine, and she knew then they should've left with Akeela. She looked out the window in time to see Tzmet thrust her hand up. Blue lightening flashed, and in an instant, the thatched roof burst into flames.

"Oret, quickly!" Krezma cried. The fire crackled as it ate through the hay on the roof. Only the tightness of the woven stalks kept it from spreading at a greater speed.

Krezma rushed to her bedroom to fetch the prophecy.

"We must make haste," she gasped. "Can you transform again so soon?"

I will try.

Krezma nodded. "If you can, hitch Mule to the cart. I will carry what we'll need to the garden."

Oret bounded through the back door. Mule let out a surprised bray, but then he grew quiet.

She worked feverishly, stuffing herbs and food into sacks and tossing them through the window. As she shuffled out of the bedroom with extra clothing, the first bit of charred hay fell to the floor and burst apart with flying sparks.

Oret appeared at the door. "Here, give them to me. I don't have much time left in this form. I'll meet you at the cart."

Krezma shoved the clothing into his hands. She glanced around her beloved kitchen, the roof now fully engulfed in flames.

"Celtar, have mercy," she whispered and shuffled out the door as quickly as her old legs could carry her. As she approached the stall, she noticed Oret, once again in cat form, lying in the cart. Mule stamped his hooves and strained against the rope.

Krezma lifted the rope over the post, heaved herself into the seat, picked up the reins, and clicked her tongue. Mule complied, and they set off into the night.

Chapter Seven

Akeela sat with a steaming mug of hot cardamom and chocolate near the fireplace. In spite of the warmth of the fire and the quilt that covered her legs, she trembled. Her legs ached from the frantic trek through the forest. Tar paced the room, still holding his bow.

"My dear, can't you tell me anything?" Queth asked. He sat near Akeela, glancing at Tar now and then.

Akeela shook her head. "I'm not sure what's going on."

"Can you tell me if Krezma will be here soon?"

"I cannot."

Akeela turned back to the fire, wishing with all her might there would be a fire fairy in the flickering flames to bring news. Queth sighed. She started to speak when a soft knock sounded at the door.

Tar peered out the window. He nodded to Queth, who opened the door a crack. "Finally!" he cried. "Come in, come in. I've been worried. Akeela won't say a word. How can I help if I don't know what's going on?"

Krezma stepped into the house. She had Nooph in her arms. "Tar, see to Oret. Minister Queth, we are in need of a safe haven."

Queth took Krezma's arm. "Of course."

Akeela jumped up from her seat. "What happened to Oret?"

Queth walked Krezma to the chair opposite Akeela and helped her sit. Nooph jumped down and made himself at home on the hearth. Krezma stretched her gnarled hands toward the fire and sighed. Her aura looked thin, like part of it had been sliced away. It seemed she'd aged over the last few hours.

"Krezma?"

"Let me rest, child. All is well. Oret is simply weak, and Tar can tend to him." Krezma sat back in the chair. "I could use some hot tea."

Queth rushed to the kitchen. He hadn't awakened his housekeeper or Anon, and Akeela was relieved. She didn't think she could deal with anyone else tonight.

Tar came in carrying Oret at the same moment Queth walked into the room carrying a steaming mug. Queth gasped, spilling tea on the floor. "My goodness."

Tar nodded. "I need a room for him."

"Is he going to be all right?" Akeela asked.

Tar shifted Oret's weight in his arms. "He needs rest."

Queth's hand trembled as he gestured toward the stairs. "Follow me. I have guest rooms which are always prepared to take in the weary stranger . . . or friend." He handed Krezma the mug and scurried to the steps. The swish of his robes stirred the embers in the fireplace.

Akeela sat up. "Krezma, what took you so long?"

"We didn't want to lead the witch straight here." Krezma settled in her seat. "And we barely escaped the fire."

"Fire?"

Distress crossed Krezma's face, and she winced. "The witch has destroyed our home."

Akeela put her hand over her mouth.

"Do not dwell on it, child. What's done is done." Krezma blew across the mug. "It's time you learn of the past and your destiny."

Akeela's eyes burned with unshed tears. Her home! The only home she knew. She stared at Krezma, searching her face for any emotion beyond exhaustion. She saw none. "Are you sure everything is gone?"

"Yes, child. I saved the prophecy and a few precious things, but there was no time to linger."

Akeela rubbed her gloved hand. She couldn't believe Krezma's eyes held no sorrow. Not even Krezma, with all her gruff ways, could feel nothing over the loss of her home. "And you think this has something to do with my destiny? You've always known and never said anything to me."

"Hush now, child. What would this knowledge have done for you if I had told you earlier? Knowledge can be a heavy—burden —and you were not strong enough."

That word again. Akeela shook it off. "What if I'm not now?"

Krezma gazed at Akeela. "You must grow up quickly, for times have come that require you to carry it, whether you have the strength or not."

An icy hand gripped Akeela's stomach. She shivered in spite of the fire's heat. She barely registered Queth returning.

Krezma had closed her eyes. She didn't move for several moments. Had she fallen asleep? Akeela whispered, "Krezma?"

Krezma brought herself up. Her eyes, now open, were fierce and dark. "His name was Riss'aird. He was the son of the steward for the King of the Northern Province. When we met, his love of learning and joy in music and art captivated me."

Akeela leaned forward to hear Krezma's low voice.

"I fell in love. And even though it was forbidden by my people to marry one of the Mal'fiks, I did anyway. But his heart was black, and once I knew this, it was too late."

"Too late for what?" Akeela no longer felt sleepy. She bunched up the quilt and held it on her lap.

The corners of Krezma's mouth lifted into a half smile. "Yes, that's the question, isn't it? Too late, I suppose, for everything. After we married, things were peaceful. We were happy, I thought. But soon after the birth of our baby, his obsession for power filled his mind, and he turned to the dark arts."

Akeela's eyes widened.

"Yes, child." Krezma chuckled. "I was young. But that is not important. Love, as it has been said, can be blind, and I was indeed blind. Blind to the small, intricate changes happening within Riss'aird's heart."

Krezma grew silent as she tugged on her braid. Akeela could hardly stay in the chair, but she managed to clamp down on her impatience and wait. She tried to picture a younger Krezma—one who was in love. Impossible.

Tar entered the room and stood near the front window. Krezma nodded his way. She drew in a breath and let it out slowly. "I pleaded with Riss'aird to turn away from darkness, but he laughed. He had the king assassinated, I am sure of that, and set himself up as lord. When I sensed how black his heart had become, it took all my skill and prowess to escape. I managed, as you can see, but not without a price. An overwhelming, terrible price."

"I'm sorry," Akeela murmured.

"Thank you, child. I cannot honestly say I'm entirely over it, but most of my wounds have healed with the help of Celtar and my friends."

Queth came and stood next to Krezma's chair. "Celtar will often send difficult and even tragic circumstances to strengthen us. His ways are mysterious beyond all reasoning, but He has a purpose for everything."

Tar spoke from his place near the door. "As much as I agree with you, we do not have time to debate Celtar's ways. We must plan. The witch will surely come to the conclusion this village is of some significance, and when she does, she will strike quickly. People will die."

Krezma nodded. "Peace, Tar. I know what you say is true, but Akeela must learn of the past if she is to help the future."

"How?" Akeela clutched the quilt tighter, her eyes wide with fright.

Krezma leaned forward and touched Akeela's right hand. "You have been marked since birth, child. Set apart. Just as Oret and his grandfather before him."

"I don't—"

"Shh. Listen now. The story of Riss'aird does not end with my escape. No, it only begins." Krezma sat back and pressed her fingertips together. "For the next several years, since I couldn't go home, I hid and moved from place to place. I studied to make my own powers stronger. I have been a peddler, a teacher, a midwife. All the while, Riss'aird gathered an army with the intention of wiping all good from the world. He would, of course, set himself up as Supreme Lord, keeping the inhabitants he left alive under his mighty fist."

Akeela frowned. "I don't understand. What does any of this have to do with me?"

Krezma put one hand up. "One thing at a time, child." She sipped her tea. "Riss'aird. He comes from the race of people called the Mal'fiks. Their very nature it is to cause harm, especially by supernatural means. I, in my foolishness, thought him different. He was beautiful. Winsome. Engaging. Powerful. He made me laugh, which I dearly loved to do then. But he has no faith in the power of Celtar, which gives us the advantage."

Tar looked at Akeela, his eyes reflecting the dying light of the fire. Akeela could almost see his strength in the reflection. Her heart quaked, and she thought if anyone could stand up to Riss'aird, it would be Tar.

"The battles were bloody and short," Krezma continued. "Riss'aird's army, strengthened by his magic, was a force beyond the might of simple peasants. One by one, villages fell. Women and children were taken as slaves. Men were—changed—and forced into his dreadful army. The elderly he killed. Riss'aird had no use for the weak."

Akeela's cheeks flushed. She felt young and foolish. Up to this point, her life had been so sheltered . . . and safe. Why hadn't she realized there was more to the world than fairies, the forest, and Broem? Even Krezma's sharp, unkind tongue now seemed insignificant.

"Elves and fairies joined the battle by infusing the ground with magic. Good magic," Krezma continued. "They did this secretly when fire fairies, acting as spies, discovered Riss'aird's plan to wipe out all who opposed him. By then the witch was assisting him. They worked up a spell so powerful, if they were to successfully cast it, we would not be here today."

"What did you do?" Akeela asked.

"The Fairy Council determined something more was needed," Krezma went on, "so we combined the Fidesians' magic with fairy magic. And with Celtar's power, a stone was formed. A stone which would transform a person, linking them with the Ruling Fairy. We chose a human male, gave him a circle of runes on his hand, and the stone was placed in the middle. This man became the first Fairy Guardian."

Akeela buried her face in the quilt and pulled her knees to her chest. Her voice was muffled through the blanket. "Is that why the spell didn't work?"

"The good magic in the ground worked its way into plants and trees and all creatures that fed on them. With Celtar's intervention and the power coursing through nature, the spell turned back toward Riss'aird's castle. As best as I can tell, evil magic met good magic, and the spell rebounded. He and his army disintegrated, and his ashes settled into the ground. Ever since, the earth fairies have been sowing goodness into the earth, keeping the ashes dormant."

Akeela lifted her head. "Why didn't the witch die?"

Krezma shrugged. "I know not. But Riss'aird is not dead. No, he only sleeps." As she leaned forward, her eyes bore into Akeela's. "This is why Oret's job is so important and why you *must* accept your destiny. If fairies continue to disappear, the magic keeping his ashes in the ground will weaken."

Akeela's heart pounded. She choked out the question she knew the answer to but had to hear anyway. "What happens then?"

"Riss'aird will regenerate."

"And?"

Tar stepped forward, his face hard. "We will all die."

Queth gasped. "May Celtar forbid it!"

"But it's the witch, Tzmet," Akeela said. "She's the one who's causing fairies to disappear. We need to stop her."

"Indeed, child." Krezma drank the last of her tea. "However, the witch is a force to reckon with. She is strong and filled with hate. Even as a child, Tzmet would have nothing to do with anything she considered good. She is a formidable woman, especially since we know not how she escaped Riss'aird's spell."

"Krezma?" Akeela asked.

"Yes, child."

"How do you know so much about the witch?"

Krezma didn't answer. Akeela waited for a stinging retort. The silence was deafening. Then, in a voice almost unrecognizable as Krezma's, came the quiet and heart-stopping words.

"She is my daughter."

Tzmet shrieked and cursed as she threw candlesticks, goblets, books, and anything else not tied down. Not even the fairies that hung wilting could ease her anger. The peasants had escaped! How was this possible?

"Argh! Blood and firestone!"

The Hinwari stood in a huddled group across the great room. Tzmet ignored their presence, ranting and hurling threats on the peasants, whoever they were. And she was furious at herself for destroying the cottage. It must be important somehow. Fairies were there. That must mean something, and now she'd never know.

Tzmet's hand settled on her potion bowl. She lifted it, realized what she was about to destroy, and set it down with a *thump*. As she clutched her hands over her bare head, she grimaced until it hurt. Then she heaved a great sigh and lowered her hands.

"I must not let this cause me to forget who I am," she whispered. "I am Tzmet, daughter of the great Riss'aird, Lord of the entire universe! My plans will prevail."

She whirled around and marched to the courtyard. Four fairies hung on the rack, their skin hardening, bodies slowly drying—the agonizing, suffocating death they deserved.

Tzmet watched a moment, picked up the wings she'd yanked off their bodies, and held them up. They sparkled in the torchlight. "Why, I believe my cape is just about finished," she purred. "Would you like to see it? What a good idea. I'll go get it. Don't go away, now."

She laughed at her joke and rushed into the great room. The Hinwari still huddled in the corner.

"What are you miserable creatures doing? I'm hungry. Get me some cheese and bread." She waved her hand toward the group. "Go now, before I lose my temper. And don't forget the wine."

The Hinwari shuffled to the kitchen, and Tzmet smiled as she knelt before a wooden trunk. She ran her hands over the carvings and inlaid rubies and sighed with delight. Then she reached into her skirt pocket and pulled out a key.

"The key to my future."

A raven in a cage next to the fireplace flapped its wings and squawked.

"Silence, you foul thing. If not for your abundant source of eggs, I would feed you to the vultures." Tzmet tapped the key on her chin. "Hmm, eggs. Yes, that sounds good." She raised her voice and called, "Scramble some raven eggs with leeks and night crawlers to go with my bread and cheese!"

She turned to the trunk. "And now . . ." She stuck the key in the lock and turned it.

"I must not forget my spies. It takes patience to get information, and I can be very patient."

She lifted the cape of fairy wings she'd been working on for seven years. How frustrating that she'd wasted years before that, trying to figure out how to release her father. Until she'd realized the fairies held the key.

"If only I'd been able to capture more fairies at a time, this would've been done long ago." She gave the cape a shake. The wings fluttered and shimmered.

Tzmet spread the cape on the table. She took the wings from her most recent catch and laid them in a row. Then she skipped to the cabinet and brought out a needle and thread. Yes, oh yes, thoughts of the power she'd gain over the fairies filled her mind, and she felt almost giddy with delight.

A Hinwar brought her a goblet of wine, and she sipped as she sewed, humming to herself. The aroma of cooking eggs drifted past, and she breathed deeply. Then she heard the slender cry of a wilted fairy and giggled. Lifting the goblet, she toasted the mirror.

"To the downfall of Oret and his god, the weak and impotent Celtar. Fate has determined my place in history to be great, and I will be revered by all!"

Chapter Eight

Krezma lay awake, listening to Akeela's slow breathing. *It is good the child is resting. I fear the time is coming when rest will not be easily attained.*

Queth's house was eerily silent. Krezma had lived many years in the forest, surrounded by sounds of night creatures. It was comforting, the chirping and whirring of crickets and tree frogs. The absence of familiar sounds put Krezma's senses on full alert. Queth snored upstairs, and Tar prowled outside as he kept watch lest the witch come.

Her thoughts turned back to the recent happenings. When Oret awoke, Akeela would learn more about her destiny, and Krezma would have less responsibility for the child. What a relief! She'd never thought this day would come. Now she could continue with her interrupted plans. But even as she thought about this, her heart grew heavy. She felt torn. True, the child was an unwanted burden, yet she cared for her. And that brought shame when she remembered her harsh words and constant frustration. She should've been honored to be the caretaker of the line of Guardians. But she was tired. So very tired.

A sudden movement outside the window caught her eye. It was

gone in a flash, but Krezma's heart swelled with fear. "Dear Celtar!" she whispered. "A shooting star! The witch will know we're here, if she has seen it."

Krezma turned toward Akeela's bed, trying to discern her face in the dark. She shouldn't have spoken out loud, even in only a whisper. Akeela needed to sleep, and Krezma needed to pray.

Celtar, what shall we do? Where should we go?

Silence met her, and after several minutes of waiting for an answer, Krezma fell into a troubled sleep.

Akeela opened her eyes. Sunlight streamed through the slats of the wooden shutters. For a moment she couldn't remember where she was. Krezma's familiar snoring surrounded her, but this was not her room in the cottage.

The fireplace burned brightly, and someone had placed a teapot and two mugs on the nightstand between the beds. The simple room had no décor except for dark-red curtains with blue trim.

Akeela sat up and touched the kettle. It was still hot. Memories of last night flooded her. She was at Queth's. Stifling a sob, Akeela fell back onto the pillow. If only this were a bad dream. Could Celtar really have brought her to this place in her life?

A shuffling at the door caught Akeela's attention. The door creaked as it edged open. A small hand curled around the door, and Anon peeked in the room.

"Keela?" he whispered.

Akeela smiled and reached out to him. "Hello, Anon!"

Anon pushed the door all the way open and trotted to the bed. He fell into Akeela's arms. "You sleep, Keela?"

Akeela hugged him tightly. "Yes, Anon, I slept here last night."

"Come play?"

"First, let's get something to eat. I'm hungry." Akeela let go of Anon and smoothed his furry brow. "And let's be quiet. Krezma is still sleeping."

Akeela slipped on the archery glove, and they tiptoed out of the room. She closed the door and took Anon's hand. His little goat feet clicked on the wooden floor until they came to the braided rug in the sitting room. The kitchen was down the hall on the right, and sweet smells led the way.

"Oh, 'tis a fine morning," said Nirit, Queth's cook and house-keeper. "Come in, come in. I have fresh sweetcakes. They're almost ready. Just be needing a bit of dusting."

Akeela smiled at the short, round-faced woman. "Thank you, Nirit. They sound wonderful."

Anon climbed onto the bench. "Have chocolate, Nir?"

"Of course, darlin'. It's still hot, so just you be patient." Nirit poured a cup of white sugar in a bowl and added a sprinkle of cinnamon. She picked up the bowl and flipped it in deft, circular motions to mix the ingredients.

Akeela breathed in the sweet cinnamon-sugar dust, and her stomach rumbled.

"Have new stone, Keela." Anon reached in his bag and pulled out a gray pebble. He showed it to Akeela.

"It's beautiful, Anon."

He grinned and dropped the pebble back into the bag, then sighed and leaned his head on Akeela's shoulder. She kissed the top of his furry head.

Nirit brought Anon's mug of chocolate and a mug of plain tea for Akeela. Then she took the sweetcakes from the oven and dropped them two at a time into the bowl of cinnamon and sugar. She stirred them with a wooden spoon to coat them all over, then lifted them onto a plate.

"Hot, Anon. Hot," she said.

Akeela took one and cut it in half. Swirls of steam rose from the cake, and Akeela blew on it. "I'll help him." *One last time.*

Breakfast passed peacefully. When they were done, Akeela and Anon went into the garden. Akeela gazed at the plants and wondered if her beloved garden at the cottage had survived the fire. She put her face into her hands.

"Keela sad?"

"Yes, Anon."

"Pray?"

Akeela lifted her head and looked in wonder at the little faun. "Oh yes, Anon. Let's pray and ask Celtar to help us."

They held hands and Akeela prayed. She poured her heart out to Celtar, knowing Anon wouldn't understand, so her secret fears would be safe. The sun felt warm on her head, and bees buzzed around the flowers as her prayers ended. A tingling sensation came over her, and she looked up. Relief flooded her chest. The three forest fairies who'd called a warning last night hovered near a lilac bush.

"Good morning, dear fairies. Please tell me any news of our cottage."

"The cottage is destroyed," the fairies said in unison.

Akeela was surprised they didn't return her greeting, but she didn't dwell on it. "It's gone? All gone? The garden? The labyrinth?"

The fairies looked at each other. Their auras changed from light green to dark green. "We don't know."

Akeela's eyes narrowed. "Is something wrong?"

The tall fairy smiled. "We are upset, as you must be. It's a terrible thing."

"Yes, terrible," said the other fairies.

What was wrong with these fairies? "Is there any sign of the witch?"

"No! No witch," they said.

"But you must have seen —"

"No! No witch!" Their voices rose in alarm.

Akeela started to speak, but a footstep at the door scared the fairies away.

"Good morning, my dear." Queth said. "Did you sleep well?"

Akeela whirled around. She took a breath to steady herself. "I didn't think I would, but yes, I did. Is Krezma awake?"

Queth stepped into the garden. "Yes. She is breaking her fast now." He gave Anon a tender smile. "Hello, little one. You're up early."

Anon yawned and stretched. "Qeth. Keela here."

72

Queth chuckled. "Why, yes. Yes, she is."

Anon grinned at Akeela.

Akeela took his hand and tugged. "Come on, Anon. I want to talk to Krezma."

They entered the kitchen, and it took a moment for Akeela's eyes to adjust to the dim kitchen. Krezma sat at the table sipping tea. Nirit stood at the stove, cooking something with garlic, if Akeela's nose was working properly.

"Duck eggs and deer strips will be ready shortly," she announced, rubbing a dried leaf between her fingers and sprinkling it on the sautéing meat.

"Wonderful, Nirit," Queth said. He gave a small grunt as he settled in a chair at the end of the table. "Come, Akeela, have some food with us."

Akeela sat next to Krezma on the bench. Anon climbed up beside her.

"I saw three forest fairies in the garden. They said the cottage is completely destroyed."

Krezma nodded. "I thought as much."

"They acted strange," Akeela said. "Like they were afraid, or at least distracted."

"I'm a bit distracted myself," Krezma commented.

Nirit placed a platter on the table. She served Queth a full plate and gestured to Krezma and Akeela. Krezma nodded, and Akeela said, "Just a little for me."

Queth and Krezma ate without speaking. Akeela pushed the meat around the plate. It smelled delicious, and she didn't want to insult Nirit, so she dipped the meat into an egg yolk. The rich golden liquid ran over the white and mixed with the venison. As soon as she tasted it, the thought came to her that this was the very reason Queth was so large. Fairy feet! Why was she even thinking this right now?

She took another bite. "This is good, Nirit."

Nirit bobbed her head. "Thank you, miss. And there's plenty, so don't be shy."

Akeela surprised herself by eating everything on her plate. She pushed it away and sighed. Anon stirred next to her, and she looked down to see he'd fallen asleep, his head resting on his hand on the table. He smiled slightly. Probably dreaming of finding a new stone. Akeela stroked his head. Then she turned to Krezma. "Is Oret up?"

Krezma shook her head as she sipped from a mug. "No. He still sleeps."

"Can you tell me anything more? You said something about my destiny last night."

"Not beyond what I've already told you." Krezma looked at the sleeping Anon. "You should take some time with your friends. When Oret's strength returns, we'll have to leave."

Akeela's throat tightened. "Why must we leave? Can't we wait and see what happens?"

Krezma turned to her. "Wait for what? The witch to destroy the village? Is that what you want?"

Akeela shook her head.

"Child, the night you were born, your village was in the midst of defending itself from the witch. The people knew no reason she would attack since they were poor, barely able to support themselves."

"But why—"

Krezma put up her hand. "Listen to what I'm saying. A shooting star appeared that week, and within a day of sighting it, the witch attacked."

"I see shooting stars all the time."

"Yes, child, but there's a difference between those stars and ones that give a sign." Krezma pushed away her mug. "Those who are trained can see the signs a shooting star tells. The star which appeared over your village foretold the birth of a special child. A child with special abilities. A child who might even destroy the Dark Lord."

Queth interrupted. "Are you saying Akeela is this special child?"

"No," Akeela said at the same time Krezma said, "Yes."

"And the witch knows she's here?" Queth continued.

Krezma's shoulders slumped. "It's possible. If she doesn't, she'll soon figure out that something is going on in the village."

Akeela shook her head. "How could she possibly know about me and where I am?"

Krezma paused, and Akeela braced herself, because when Krezma paused, she was about to say something no one wanted to hear.

"A shooting star passed over this village last night."

Iari clutched Akeela's hand over the kitchen table. "I just can't believe your cottage is gone! It's a miracle you got out."

Ham nodded. "I gave thanks to Celtar when I heard."

Gilron laughed. "When you heard the cottage burned?"

"No!" Ham's horrified look almost made Akeela giggle. "When I heard Akeela was safe."

Akeela looked at her half-full plate of roast pheasant and mashed tubers. "Thank you, Ham. I can't believe it was just last night."

Ham blushed and took a drink from his mug.

What was she going to do about Ham? Of course, she'd be leaving soon, and he'd find someone else. He'd *have* to.

Her thoughts were interrupted by Iari. "What will you and Krezma do now? You can't stay at Queth's forever."

Akeela shook her head. She couldn't tell the truth, and she didn't want to lie. "I guess we'll find another place to live." A weak answer, but she didn't know what else to say. And if Krezma was right about the shooting star, they didn't have much time. Perhaps she could simply hide. No, that would only put her friends in danger. The weight of responsibility grew, and she sighed.

"I'll ask my parents if you can live with us," Iari said. "Then we could be together all the time. Wouldn't that be fun?"

If only she *could* stay with Iari and her parents. They were the closest thing she had for a real family. Krezma didn't count. Still, knowing she was the adopted daughter of Celtar gave her some comfort. Akeela smiled weakly. "What about when you and Gilron marry?"

Iari shrugged. "That's not for a year and"—she glanced at Ham—"who knows what'll happen in that amount of time?"

Akeela kicked her under the table.

Iari's mother came into the kitchen, unknowingly cutting the tension. "Has everyone had enough to eat?"

They all nodded, and Gilron patted his stomach. "Yes, thank you. It was very good."

Iari giggled. "You don't have to impress my mother, Gil. We're already promised."

The group laughed, and for a moment, everything felt normal.

Ham cleared his throat. "Well, I should be getting back to the bakery. My father expects me to finish the bread for the evening meal." He stood and wiped his mouth on the back of his hand. "Akeela, would you like to walk with me so I can give you Queth's order? He asked for our braided nut bread."

Akeela's throat went dry. "I thought Nirit did all the baking for them?"

Ham shrugged. "I know not, but my father said he was going to bake the nut bread for Queth."

"I'll come along in a little while."

Ham's face dropped, then he straightened and smiled. "I'll look for you later then. Pleasant day."

"Pleasant day," Akeela murmured.

Gilron stood as well. "I too must be getting home. Father needs my help with repairs on Rissat's door hinges."

After wishing everyone well, Gilron strode out the door. Iari's eyes lingered on him until he turned the corner. She sat back and sighed. "I can't wait to start my own home. I've known since I was a little girl that I wanted to marry Gilron."

Akeela's stomach twisted. A husband and home were most likely out of the question for her. Krezma hadn't said so, but there was no obvious way it could work.

Iari picked up the plates and carried them to the washbasin. She started to wipe them with a wet cloth and soap. "Bring me the mugs please, Akeela. I'll wash up so you can pick up Queth's bread. And you can tell me why you don't want to be alone with Ham."

Akeela thumped the mugs down on the counter. "Stop!"

Iari stopped midwash. "What's wrong?"

"You don't understand. I *can't* marry Ham." Akeela leaned against the counter and put a hand on her forehead. "Even if I could, I wouldn't. I just don't like him that way."

Iari reached for a mug. "Hmph. What are you waiting for? Akeela, there is no other boy in the village I would match you with, and you can't say there is."

Akeela looked around the small kitchen where she'd spent many hours eating, laughing, and playing games. The hearth with its ever-present fire and kettle. Issdra's soup pot. Flowers growing in a box at the window. Linen curtains, tablecloth, and napkins, which were a luxury for most families, but Issdra's skill in weaving cloth and sewing added a homey touch to the kitchen.

"I wish I could tell you." The words were out before Akeela could catch them.

"Tell me what? What are you keeping from your best friend?"

Iari knew her so well. What could she say that would satisfy her curiosity?

"Come on, out with it." Iari set a plate on the counter. "If it's not Ham or any other boy, what can it be?"

"I can't tell you."

Iari put her soapy hands on her hips. "What do you mean you can't tell me? Since when do we have any secrets between us?"

"Since Gilron," Akeela flung back.

The girls glared at each other. Akeela looked away first.

She rubbed her gloved hand. "I'm sorry, Iari. I can't tell you. It's too dangerous."

"Oh, now you *really* have to tell me!"

Akeela started to protest when a movement in the fire caught her eye. A fire fairy danced in the flames. The fairy smiled and nodded. News. Akeela put her hands on Iari's shoulders. "You're my best friend. That will never change. Maybe someday I'll be able to tell you, but please trust me for now."

Iari's eyes reflected her hurt. "I will trust you—for now. But you must promise to be careful and tell me the very minute you can."

Akeela wanted to slap herself. How could she hurt Iari this way? But she didn't have a choice. "I will. I should pick up Minister Queth's bread."

Iari gave her a small smile. "Have a pleasant evening."

"I'm only picking up bread."

Iari nodded. She picked up another mug and wiped around the edge. "Uh-hmm."

Akeela paused in the doorway. "I love you."

Iari's eyebrows lifted in silent question. Akeela turned and slipped out the door.

Akeela walked at a fast pace to the bakery. She needed to get back to Queth's. Hopefully, the fire in the small bedroom downstairs would still be burning. Then she'd be able to get whatever news the fire fairy had. Taking a deep breath, she stepped through the open doorway.

"Akeela, so nice to see you." Kintcha, Ham's father, grinned from behind a counter piled with breads of every sort. Soon it would be time for the villagers to trade for loaves for the evening meal. "What can I do for you?"

"I, well, Ham said Queth ordered braided nut bread," she said in a rush. "I'm here to pick it up."

Kintcha looked confused for a moment, then he smiled and nodded. "Of course, how could I forget? I'll call Ham. It must be ready by now."

Akeela groaned inwardly. Ham's father was obviously in on the so-called bread order. She glanced around the bakery as she waited. It was simple with a large counter where several baskets held freshly baked breads like rye, wheat, herbed dill, and cinnamon raisin. Ham's mother had hung curtains on the front windows, red and white linen, tied back with twine. The last time a peddler had come through, Ham's father had bartered for a painting of a woman kneading dough, and he'd hung it near the front door.

"Akeela! I didn't expect you so soon."

Ham's voice startled her, and she turned to say hello but ended up laughing. Ham had his apron on, and flour smudged his face and hair. He clapped his hands, and a puff of white powder shot into the air.

Ham's face reddened as he smiled sheepishly. "Give me a moment and I'll get the bread."

Akeela nodded and turned her attention back to the baskets of bread.

"Here it is." Ham walked in carrying a small bundle. "I'll walk you to Queth's." He gestured toward the door.

Akeela flushed. "You really don't have to. I know you have work to do."

Ham shook his head. "Not really. We're done baking for the day, and it won't take long." He gave her a tender smile. "Besides, I'm in no hurry to clean up. It's a lonely job."

They walked in silence. Then Ham cleared his throat.

"Akeela? I have something I want to talk to you about."

Fairy feet! *Here it comes.* Akeela tried to keep her voice light. "What's that?"

Ham took her arm and steered her to the left. They slipped behind a stable. Akeela's heart beat so hard she felt dizzy.

They stopped, and Ham shifted the bread to his other hand. He reached out and touched Akeela's cheek. She couldn't help it. She turned away.

"You must know by now that my father has talked with Krezma."

Akeela's mouth went dry. "I know," she whispered.

Ham ran his hand through his short hair. A small cloud of flour rose and hung in the air. "I can't wait any longer. Please, Akeela, please say you'll marry me. I've loved you for so long."

Celtar, help! "Ham, we're only fifteen."

"It feels like I've loved you longer than that." Ham took Akeela's chin and turned her face back toward him. "We get along well. We've been friends forever. I'd make a good husband. Please say yes."

"I—"

Before Akeela could utter another sound, Ham kissed her. At first the kiss lingered softly, then Ham tightened his grip on her shoulder, and the kiss deepened. She shoved him away. Ham stumbled back, eyes wide.

Akeela held out her hands and tried to slow her breathing. "I can't," she gasped. "I'm sorry, Ham, I can't."

"Akeela—"

Her emotions flared. "No!"

She spun and ran all the way back to Queth's.

The bedroom door slammed behind her, and Akeela sat on the bed, shaking.

Bright movement in the fireplace caught her eye. The fire fairy she'd seen at Iari's danced in the dying embers. Akeela wiped her moist cheeks and smoothed her hair.

"Good fairy, what news do you bring?"

"Pleasant afternoon, Akeela," the fairy sang out.

"Pleasant afternoon," Akeela responded, knowing if she didn't follow protocol, she'd never hear the fairy's news.

The fairy twirled in the glowing wood, causing sparks to sparkle. "Fairies in the north woods still have the creature."

Akeela frowned. "Creature?"

The fairy flew up, drawing a small flame out of the embers. "The fairy creature from your cottage."

"Oh! Is she safe? Where is she?" Akeela slid to the edge of the bed and leaned forward.

"Safe, warm, sad." The fairy floated down. "You must tell the Guardian."

"I will when he wakes."

"We took a chance and spied on the witch," the fairy continued.

"She has a cape of fairy wings. This could be significant. The Guardian must know."

"I'll tell him."

The fire fairy raised her hands. "Blessings, Akeela." And she shot straight up the chimney.

"Blessings!" called Akeela. Then to herself she whispered, "Blessings."

After a minute of staring into the fireplace, Akeela got up and placed a piece of wood on the embers. The bark caught fire, and as the flame rose, something rose inside her. Resolve? Maybe. Sadness? Probably.

Feeling trapped? Definitely.

Then she set another small log in the fireplace. The cottage was gone, but she was still here. With some kind of job to do. Her destiny.

She added one more log. Sparks shot up, and Akeela watched them go, feeling their determination to make it out of the chimney. Krezma still considered her a child. She would prove her wrong. Akeela straightened her back. She would fulfill her destiny. If Queth was right and Celtar planned the ways of men, he also planned the ways of women.

Calm resolve filled her, and she stood.

It was time to talk to Oret.

Chapter Nine

Krezma watched Ham kiss Akeela. Dear Celtar, why hadn't she thought of this before? Since Oret had announced he was dying, she'd only been thinking of a cure, not what to do if she couldn't find one. The line of Fairy Guardians must be preserved. Stars, how could she have forgotten?

She started to walk toward the couple when Akeela pushed Ham away and ran off. Krezma stepped behind a sycamore tree and peered around.

Ham stood still for several seconds, blinking back tears. Then he turned and trudged toward the bakery. Apparently, Akeela hadn't changed her mind about him. Krezma took a deep breath and let it out. Plans still had to be made and Oret still slept, and now she had to tell Akeela about another part of her duty.

She looked at her reed basket full of mushrooms. Their earthy smell filled the air, and she could almost taste them cooked in butter. There was enough to have with dinner as well as plenty for trading. They would need supplies.

The village streets began to fill with women getting what they needed for the evening meal. They laughed and chattered as they bartered.

Krezma watched with a heavy heart. How she wished Akeela could stay and marry and have children with the young man of her choice. Without pressure or a sense of duty. Of all the places Krezma had lived, Broem was her favorite. How good it would be to live out the rest of her days here. But it wasn't Celtar's plan.

She traded Rissat some mushrooms for twine. Rissat, the village midwife, always had a good supply of twine for difficult births. Then Krezma headed back to Queth's.

Nirit bustled around the kitchen, her humming off-key as she prepared their food. Krezma dumped the remaining mushrooms into a tub and began to wash them.

"Well, blessings on you, Krezma," Nirit exclaimed. "I was just thinking of mushrooms, and we're plain out."

Krezma filled a wooden bowl and handed it to Nirit. "Mayhap we can have them sautéed in butter. With a little garlic?"

Nirit's round face wrinkled as she smiled. "That sounds lovely! Garlic and rosemary. It will be perfect with the roast chicken and mashed orange tubers."

Krezma nodded and continued her chore. She made a mental list of what was needed for Akeela's quest.

"Pleasant day."

Krezma turned at Akeela's quiet greeting. The child was obviously in need of comfort, and for the first time, Krezma would've liked to give it. But right now she had none to give. Truth be told, she was going to have to add to Akeela's already heavy burden. She'd named Akeela burden because she was only concerned for herself. She never realized Akeela would carry her own as well.

Akeela sat, picked up a fork, and tapped it on the table. "I think we need to wake Oret."

Krezma rolled the mushrooms for bartering onto a cloth. "Why is that?"

"I just think it."

Nirit sliced the remaining mushrooms. She didn't seem to pay attention to their conversation, so Krezma asked again. "Why, child?"

Akeela stared at her as though she were trying to say something without speaking. "I have news," she finally said.

"Do you now?" News and wanting to talk to Oret could only mean one thing. Akeela had spoken to a fairy. "I will have to ask Tar. You know he's been nursing Oret."

"Is he any better?"

"I have not seen him yet this morning."

Akeela folded her arms. "I have to speak to him now. If he's dying, I have a lot to learn and quickly."

Krezma nodded. "Aye, you do. We'll see him right after the evening meal."

Nirit poured the sliced mushrooms into a pan of melted butter. They sizzled and popped as they cooked. A pungent aroma filled the kitchen as Nirit added crushed garlic and a sprig of rosemary. Krezma waved toward the back door.

She and Akeela sat on the bench closest to the garden. "Now then, child, tell me what happened today with your friends."

"How — ?"

"I can see the sorrow in your eyes. And I saw you walking with Ham."

Akeela looked down at her hands, grasped tightly in her lap. "He didn't want to wait for your answer. He asked me himself."

"Did he now?"

"Yes, and of course I told him no." Akeela unclasped her hands. "But it broke my heart! I don't love him except as a friend, but I could tell he was crushed. I never wanted that to happen."

Krezma patted her hands. "I know you didn't, child. But mayhap you should not dismiss Ham entirely."

Akeela gave her a look of horror.

Krezma put up her hand. "Now, tell me what news you have."

"Oh! I almost forgot. A fire fairy came to me. She said the forest fairies are keeping the fairy creature in the north woods."

"'Tis good."

"There's more," Akeela said. "The witch made a cape from fairy wings. The fire fairy said it was significant. We have to talk to Oret."

Krezma frowned. "Yes, child. We need to make plans as well. I have already begun to gather the things you'll need for your journey."

"Me? Aren't you coming too?"

"Not right away. Tar will accompany you. Oret and I will join you as soon as we can."

Akeela's eyes narrowed. "What aren't you telling me?"

Krezma cleared her throat and stood. "Come, child. It's time for the evening meal. You will need strength. Let us thank Celtar and eat Nirit's good food, and then we'll talk to Oret."

They walked to the kitchen in silence.

Akeela knelt next to Oret's bed. The big cat sprawled over the yellow and blue patchwork quilt. He looked thinner, his breathing labored.

Tar shook Oret's shoulder. Oret opened his eyes.

"We need you awake, my friend," Tar said.

Krezma stood behind Akeela. "Time is of the essence. I saw a shooting star last night. It passed over this village. And a fire fairy brought news of the witch possessing a cape made from fairy wings. She's preparing to make a move."

A rumbling came from Oret's chest. He lifted his head, then dropped it back on the pillow. *I will do my best to stay awake.*

Akeela put her hand on Oret's side. "I have so many questions. But if you'll just tell me what I need to know for now, I'll be patient until you're stronger."

Krezma cleared her throat.

Oret wheezed and coughed. *There's not time. You have the first stone. You must place this stone on the birthmark on your hand.*

Krezma interrupted him. "Before Akeela does this, she must do something else first."

No one spoke.

"Akeela must marry and bear a child," she went on. "Or at least be pregnant."

86

Akeela's heart stopped. "What?"

Krezma, there's no time. I am dying.

"I am aware of that," Krezma said. "I'll keep working on tinctures of herbs to keep the poison from spreading. She can go on a quest to find the other pieces of the stone, but she can't place them in her birthmark until she is with child. You know this."

"What?" Akeela burst out. "What are you talking about?"

Krezma turned to her. "I'm talking about saving our world! Don't be so dense, child."

"I'm not being dense," Akeela shouted. "You want me to get married? Just who am I supposed to marry?"

Krezma stared her down.

"*Ham?*" Akeela leaped to her feet. "You want me to marry Ham? No. No! I can't marry Ham." She backed away from the bed with her hands out. "Why? Why do I have to get married and have children? Why can't I just become the Fairy Guardian? Are you married, Oret?"

Krezma, Tar, and Oret exchanged glances. Akeela's throat went dry. A feeling of dread overwhelmed her, and she sank to the floor.

I was married. My grandfather was the first Fairy Guardian. My mark appeared when he was made the first Guardian, so the Ruling Fairy knew I would be next in line. When he was killed fighting Riss'aird's army, I was already grown, married, and had a son. But I was prepared.

"What happened to your son?" Akeela asked. "And your wife?"

My wife died from sickness. My son was killed in a battle with the witch. As was my grandson. His wife died giving birth to their youngest. A daughter.

Akeela tried to take this in, but she couldn't concentrate.

"You see, child, when we realized we needed to protect the Ruling Fairy and the Fairysong from Riss'aird, the fairies and my people, the Fidesians, worked their magic in the line of a human family. Oret's family," Krezma added.

Oret nodded and coughed. *When the magic of the Fairystone senses another Guardian will be needed, a child is born with the birthmark.*

Akeela looked from Oret to Krezma. "So what does this have to do with *me* getting married?"

"Oret's line is the only one who can bear the next Fairy Guardian. It must be preserved," Krezma said. "Without a Guardian, the fairy realm will die out. Once you are the Fairy Guardian, you'll not be able to bear children."

They knew it was risky to set this responsibility on one family, but it was what they needed to do at the time.

Akeela struggled to made sense of what they were saying. "I still don't see what that has to do with me."

Krezma's eyes bore into hers. "Do you not know what we're telling you, child?"

The realization hit with a painful thrust, and Akeela stared at Oret.

You are my granddaughter.

"Great-granddaughter, actually," Krezma said.

It was for your safety I stayed away. To keep your presence hidden from the witch. But Celtar is gracious, and here we are.

Akeela tried to breathe, but she could only manage quick gasps. "I—have—family?"

Oret seemed to smile. *Yes, dear one, you have family. Krezma has been looking after you for me. I dared not reveal myself to you before now.*

Akeela leaped up. "You *knew* this?" she shrieked at Krezma. "And you never told me?"

Krezma shrugged. "I had to keep it secret. If you knew, you could've been in danger."

"I don't believe you!" Akeela wailed. "I hate you! I hate you!" She threw herself back on the floor and burst into tears.

"Come, child." Krezma tugged on her shoulder. "Get up and wipe your eyes. I will fetch Ham and Queth. We must get this done."

Akeela lifted her head. "*Now*? Today?"

"Yes, child, today."

Akeela didn't respond. All her life, she'd felt unloved, unwanted. She'd longed to be part of a family. Why hadn't she realized she must have relatives somewhere? Shouldn't she have felt it when she first met Oret?

Maybe she wasn't as special as they all thought. Maybe it

would serve them right if she failed. She almost laughed out loud. She should leave. Run away while Krezma was talking to Ham's family. No one would be there to stop her.

"What if I refuse to marry Ham?" she finally asked.

The line of Guardians will be broken. The fairy realm will continue in chaos until they die out.

"Don't be so selfish, child," Krezma put in. "You've been chosen for a noble task. Have the decency to accept it with grace."

The walls of the room started closing in on her. She trembled, trying to draw breath, but she was suffocating.

Dearest Akeela, please do not be distressed. This young man loves you. I love you. And the world needs you.

Right then, Akeela's heart ceased to feel. The cracks in the wall surrounding it came together and filled in as tight and hard as a butterfly's chrysalis. "Very well. I will do it for you—Grandfather."

Krezma strode to the door. "I will explain everything to Ham. And to Queth. Child, be ready within the hour. We must not tarry. The witch could be on her way."

Oret nodded, then coughed and groaned.

Tar stood and flexed his claw hand. "Oret needs to rest."

Wait, there's more. Oret's chest heaved with the effort of breathing. *I've received news the fountain map has been stolen.*

"What?" Krezma exclaimed. "Where? When?"

The council believes the witch has done this. It's been missing since last week.

"How could she have done that?" Krezma asked.

She had help. I don't want to believe any of my beloved fairies would do such a thing, but I cannot think of anything else.

Krezma stared out the window. "This is bad news indeed." She put her hands on Akeela's shoulders. "Make haste, child. We must act now."

Akeela followed Krezma to the door. She looked back at the great cat, and love for him swelled in her. She wouldn't let him down. With the help of Celtar, she'd marry Ham and find this Fairystone before it was too late.

"Goodbye . . . Grandfather."

Akeela went through the wedding ceremony as though she were carved from stone. Ham, obviously nervous, stammered through his vows and fumbled slipping the silver band on the forefinger of her left hand. When he kissed her, Akeela felt nothing.

"I will take good care of you," he whispered in her ear.

The guests were few. Kintcha and Mosset looked dazed; Iari and Gilron smiled like only those in love can. Anon played with his bag of stones the whole time. Queth seemed confused, but he did his duty. Celtar only knew what Krezma had told them all.

But Akeela didn't care. She'd allowed Iari to dress her in her favorite gown—a beautiful white dress with small embroidered red roses on the bodice, one Iari had been making for her own trousseau. A memory of Iari sewing the roses flitted through Akeela's thoughts and vanished.

She hadn't moved when Iari had brushed her hair and woven red rosebuds into the braid. Kintcha had given her a bouquet of roses to carry and had walked her to his waiting son by Queth's fireplace.

She ate nothing Nirit had prepared for the after-ceremony meal.

She heard none of the conversation.

She anticipated none of the joy of the coming night.

She couldn't imagine what evil thing she'd done for Celtar to choose her for a fate such as this.

Iari walked partway to the bakery with Akeela after dinner. They stopped by the lake.

"What do you mean you're leaving?" Iari's voice rose. "When?"

Akeela grabbed her arm. "Don't speak so loudly. This has to be kept secret. In two days. I can't tell you everything. But it's important I go." Akeela paused, thinking of how to tell Iari without frightening her. "It has to do with the witch."

Iari's eyes widened. "The witch from the stories? The one who's supposed to live in the Northern Province?"

Akeela nodded. "She's real. Krezma had dealings with her in the past. Before I was born."

"But why do you have to leave?"

"I have to find something that will stop —" Akeela gazed at the sunset reflected on the water. Several fairies, disguised as dragonflies, swept along the edge of the pond. Akeela wished she could point them out to Iari.

Why couldn't she? Iari had kept the secret of her spirit-sight for years.

She put her hands on Iari's arms. "Listen to me. You know I can see auras, right?"

"Yes, but what does that have to do with you leaving?"

Akeela turned her toward the pond. "See those dragonflies?"

Iari nodded.

"They're not really dragonflies. They're fairies. I can see fairies."

"Are you jesting? I thought fairies were just fantasy."

Akeela smiled. "No, they're real. Fairies are important, more important than anyone knows. Their magic sows goodness into the land. They keep evil forces at bay." She held up her gloved hand. "It's my birthmark. I have to leave because I've been chosen by Celtar to find something called the Fairystone. It will help the fairies."

"Is this why you married Ham?"

Akeela sighed. "Yes. He knows. He's coming too." Krezma was making sure there would be a child, so she insisted Ham come along. Nausea rose in Akeela's stomach and traveled up her throat. She swallowed hard.

Iari looked at Akeela with sad eyes. "Will you be back?"

"I don't know why I wouldn't." Akeela's brain screamed *liar!* "Please keep my secret. For everyone's safety."

"I will."

"I love you."

"I love you too."

Akeela walked to the bakery, taking the long way around the outskirts of the village. When she was halfway, she heard rustling. One by one, earth fairies gathered in the trees. Before Akeela could tell them to go away, they started singing. She couldn't understand their words, but the haunting music filled her being, calling to her. Leaving her feeling as though everything she wanted was *just* out of reach.

❦

"You looked beautiful today, Akeela." Ham stood in the doorway of the bedroom as though it might be a pit of snakes.

Akeela sat on the bed. She acknowledged her—husband—with a slight nod.

Ham took two steps in and closed the door. "I—I know why you agreed to marry me, even though I don't understand most of what's going on."

Akeela glanced at him and immediately wished she hadn't. He looked so lovingly at her, so vulnerable. So eager. It made her feel sick.

The bed creaked as he sat next to her. She took in a sharp breath when he ran a hand down her long, flowing hair. "Everything will be fine," he said. "I love you enough for both of us. And maybe . . . maybe you'll grow to love me back."

A tear crept down Akeela's cheek. It took all her strength not to run screaming from the room. She wiped her face. "I'm sorry, Ham."

He picked up a lock of her hair and kissed it. "I know how important it is for you to bear a child, Akeela, but I don't think one night will make a difference, do you?"

Akeela's eyes grew wide as she realized what he was saying. He smiled tenderly at her. So noble and gentle, always doing the right thing. Even as a child, Ham did as he was told. Never hurting anyone by word or deed. She hated herself for not loving him.

And she hated him for loving her.

But if they waited even one night, it would never happen. How difficult could it be? She'd grown up watching animals in the forest. She knew what it meant to mate and bear young. She turned to him.

Ham frowned slightly, even though his love radiated from every pore in his face. "What is it?"

"No. No waiting," she said. "It's too important."

"Are you sure?"

Akeela nodded.

He gathered her into his arms.

Krezma banged on the bakery door, not caring it was the middle of the night. Every part of her brain shrieked to hurry. There was no mistaking the double shooting star she'd just seen. They'd been fortunate the witch hadn't come after the first one. But if Tzmet was still awake and had seen this one, she may not wait until morning to attack the village.

Slow footsteps approached the door. A flicker of candlelight lit the window. The door opened a crack, and Kintcha peered out. "Yes?"

Krezma pushed the door open. "I must get Akeela. Now."

"Now? But 'tis their wedding night!"

"You fool! I have no time to bandy words with you. Show me where she is!" Krezma glared at Ham's father until he nodded.

Kintcha led her to the back of the bakery. He knocked on a closed door. "Ham? Ham, wake up."

"What's going on?" Mosset came up behind them.

Krezma rolled her eyes. She had no time or desire to explain things to these peasants. It would be morning in a couple of hours. More than enough time for Tzmet to completely destroy this village in her search for the enemy the double stars announced.

Ham, looking dazed, stood in the doorway.

Kintcha gestured toward Krezma. "We need Akeela."

Krezma sighed and pushed Ham out of the way. Akeela was

just sitting up in bed. "Child! Get up. Get dressed. It is imperative you leave now."

"What has happened?" Akeela clutched the quilt to her chest.

Krezma didn't bother to hide her words as she hobbled to Akeela. "A double shooting star. It has announced your presence! I know not if Tzmet has seen it, but we must make haste. Gather your things. I have all else prepared and will meet you behind Queth's house. Tar is waiting."

Akeela turned to Ham. "Krezma says I must leave now," she said as though Ham hadn't heard a thing. "She thinks the witch knows I'm here."

Ham slipped on a shirt. "It won't take long to pack. We can be ready in five minutes."

"See that you are." Krezma turned and left.

Akeela's mouth went dry. It was one thing to try to conceive a child here, but on the road with Tar? No privacy, no walls to cover her humiliation . . . she couldn't do it. "Ham? You—can't come," she stammered. "I won't be long. It's just a—ruse. To fool the witch."

Lies! Lies! her mind shrieked. But she couldn't bring Ham along.

"What?" Ham looked at her with wide eyes. "I can't come with you?"

Akeela's shoulders slumped. The weight of her decision almost knocked her down. "I won't be long. I promise."

Ham sat without speaking while she changed into traveling clothes and packed a shoulder sack. When he hugged her and whispered his love in her ear, she almost told him he could come. But the thought of them sleeping together where Tar could hear kept her from speaking the words.

Chapter Ten

Krezma and Tar loaded a cart with enough provisions to last a year. Or so it seemed to Akeela. They finished before Akeela could help, so she turned to Krezma.

"Keep your gifts to yourself," Krezma gruffly told her. "Celtar has given them to you for a reason. They may save your life someday."

Akeela shivered. Her spirit-sight might save her life? "How?"

But Krezma would say no more about it. She gave Akeela an awkward hug. "Where's Ham?"

Akeela braced herself for the lie she was about to tell. "He's on his way."

Krezma nodded and left without another word.

Thank you, Celtar. Krezma hadn't stayed to make sure.

Mule protested loudly when they set out, probably waking half the village with his braying. Stupid animal.

Hours later, Akeela trudged behind Tar. She looked back but couldn't see the village anymore. Her heart squeezed out sharp pains that needled her chest with each beat, and she fought tears that stung her eyes. It'd been hard to say goodbye to Anon. He hadn't understood. He'd kept asking, "Go with you, Keela?" then wept when she'd walked away.

But that wasn't the reason for her tears. She would never forget last night. Never.

Tar's voice broke into her thoughts. "We will stop for breakfast. And I need to check the map."

Akeela didn't say anything. She wasn't entirely sure she trusted Tar, but right now, she didn't have a choice. He didn't ask about Ham either, which was a relief.

The sky began to show the first light of dawn, throwing streaks of pink and orange into the dusky sky. Akeela rummaged through a small bag of provisions. She brought out Nirit's biscuits, a crock of raspberry jam, and dried strips of rabbit. Tar started a small fire and placed an iron pan of water on the flames. Within a few minutes, they had hot tea and sat without talking while they ate.

Akeela couldn't have spoken anyway, even if the witch herself showed up and demanded it. Last night! Oh, last night! Last night was *nothing* like she'd ever seen with the forest animals. Why hadn't anyone warned her?

Akeela sucked in a breath. She'd been violated. Violated! Ham's hot breath had seared her ear. His cries of pleasure still rang in her memory. She choked back a sob. Tar glanced her way but said nothing, so she sipped her tea and willed the terror building in her chest back down. But her mind wouldn't let go of the memories. Her body burned in every place Ham had touched her. The feeling of being invaded overwhelmed her. Why didn't anyone tell her coupling was so intimate? So *personal*?

Tar kicked dirt on the fire as Akeela returned the pan and mugs to the cart. She gave Mule an apple and climbed onto the seat. They started again, and as the cart bumped along the forest floor, Akeela's eyes grew heavy. No wonder, for she'd lain awake afterward while Ham had slept, trying to keep the building desperation at bay. She reached for a blanket, folded it for a pillow, and leaned against the side of the cart. Surrounded by familiar forest sounds, she drifted into troubled sleep.

Tzmet lifted her arms and let the soapy water run down. How she enjoyed a bath. She settled back in the metal tub. Experience had taught her to wash before conjuring a large spell. Something about being clean enhanced the magic. The enjoyment she got from bathing was a bonus.

The water grew cool. "Bring me a towel," she ordered a Hinwar. "And a cup of tea. Any kind. I don't care."

As she stepped out of the tub, her three fairies whizzed in the open window.

"It's about time. What news do you have for me?"

"The fairy council is meeting at the burned cottage," they said.

"The burned cottage? How intriguing." Tzmet wrapped the towel around her thin body. "When?"

"Sunset."

She glanced out the window at the late afternoon sun. "That gives me time to pay a short visit to that dreadful village where Oret is recuperating." Tzmet chuckled. "If I'm lucky, I'll have time to finish Oret off before I pop into the council meeting."

She walked to a granite dressing table with a large oval mirror and sat. Several jars of cosmetics, perfumes, and lotions sat to the right. A jewelry chest sat to the left.

"A fresh coat of nightshade on my nails to start, and I think violet oil for my skin. Yes. And since this is a special occasion, the death of Oret, I will indulge myself and wear my emeralds for success."

Tzmet hummed as she prepared, totally forgetting the fairies were still there. She buffed her nails and painted them with the deadly poison she favored. As they dried, she amused herself with thoughts of how she'd kill Oret.

"Should it be quick or should I prolong the deed?" she murmured to her reflection. "If I kill him right away, I can read the runes sooner, but if I take my time, I'll have so much more fun."

A Hinwar came into the bedroom carrying the dress she'd

selected, a deep-blue gown with a beaded bodice, scooped neckline, and long, fitted sleeves.

Tzmet turned and pointed to her canopy bed. "Lay it down carefully, you miserable creature. And get me something to eat. A cheese and mushroom omelet with goat's liver. Make sure the liver is properly coated with crushed *hicata* pepper. I'm in a spicy mood today."

The Hinwar left without a sound, and Tzmet whirled back to the mirror. She painted her eyelids green to match her necklace and sat back to admire herself. Movement caught her eye.

"What are you wretched fairies still doing here?"

The fairies looked confused. They didn't say a word.

Tzmet huffed. As much as she wanted these spies, their inability to think for themselves grated on her nerves. "Go volunteer to stand guard for the council so I can get close enough to listen."

"Yes, milady." They flew to the window.

"Meet me just outside the village on the southern road one hour before sunset."

The fairies hovered at the window for a moment and then zipped off. Tzmet stood and stretched. She stepped out of the towel, leaving it on the floor, and selected a sitting robe. The aroma of her meal drifted into the room, and she occupied herself shooting birds from the air with blue fire from her fingertips until the Hinwari brought it.

"There are days I amaze even myself." She took a bite of liver. The heat from the peppers made her eyes water. "Today promises to be one of those days."

Akeela wiped the sweat beaded on her forehead. She glanced at Tar, looking for some sign of weariness, but he remained unchanged. Her stomach whimpered like a hungry baby, and while she was used to walking, she ached, each step growing the pain in her most private part as well as her heart. Although she'd alternated riding and walking, the pace Tar set provided no rest. She glanced at the sky—the sun was past the midday mark.

She took a breath and clamped down on her nerves. Didn't the man have a bladder? "Tar, may we stop for a moment? I need to, well, relieve myself."

"Of course."

"And get something to eat."

Tar nodded. His face never revealed his thoughts. It unnerved Akeela, especially since his aura didn't change, and she depended on reading auras more than faces.

When she returned, Tar had started a small fire. Akeela lifted the canvas and brought out a sack. She rummaged through it and came up with two hardboiled eggs, a loaf of bread, goat's cheese, and two apples.

As she turned, she heard a sniffling sound. Mule, still hooked to the cart, grazed on sweet clover. Tar sat by the fire, looking pensive but alert. Where was the sound coming from? Akeela scanned the forest for any strange auras but only observed birds and squirrels in the trees and a skunk picking bugs out of a rotten log.

The sound persisted. Akeela set the food next to the cart wheel. She tiptoed around the side, circled Mule, and crept up the other side, straining to catch the direction of the noise. The cart moved slightly, and Akeela froze. Something was under the tarp.

A hand clamped down on her shoulder, and she screamed.

"It's me." Tar's voice, calm and quiet, penetrated her fear. "What are you doing?"

Akeela's chest heaved. "A sound . . . coming from the cart . . . something's there!"

Tar put out his hand, a gesture telling her to stay put. He stepped to the back of the cart and gripped the canvas with his claw hand. Without warning, he flung it over the side, and a small shriek came from behind the food stuffs.

"Come out!" Tar commanded.

They heard another shriek, and then a furry head peeked over the edge of a sack.

Akeela gasped. "Anon! What are you doing here?"

The little faun burst into tears. He sobbed so pitifully, Akeela forgot her earlier fear and pushed Tar out of the way. She climbed into the cart and held out her hands.

"Here, there's nothing to be afraid of. Come on, Anon. Come to Akeela."

He climbed over to her, and Akeela hugged him close.

"Anon, why are you hiding in our cart?"

Anon sniffed and glanced warily at Tar. "Go with Keela."

"Oh, Anon." Akeela helped him hop off the cart.

Tar worked at replacing the tarp. "He can't come with us. It's going to be a hard, long journey. Dangerous in places."

"What do we do? Go back?"

Tar shook his head. He walked around the cart and picked up the food Akeela had dropped. "We can't go back now. We must keep going."

"Well, we can't leave him here."

"No, but he can stay with my people."

Akeela stroked Anon's head. His arms stayed wrapped tightly around her waist. He sniffed now and then, and Akeela's heart swelled. "He can't stay with strangers. He'll be scared and won't understand. Probably run away again."

Tar set the food on a large rock by the fire. "We can discuss this later. Right now, we must eat and continue. I want to be deeper in the woods by nightfall."

"Here, Anon. Let me get you something to eat." Akeela kept one arm around him while she pulled the small bag out. "Look here. Do you want some apples and cheese?"

Anon wiped his nose. "Hungry, Keela."

Akeela smiled. "Me too. Come on."

Their small meal passed in silence. As soon as Akeela finished making her tea, Tar kicked dirt on the fire. Anon kept tight to Akeela's side, staying opposite of Tar. She held his hand and walked back to the cart.

"Up you go." He sat quietly on the seat while she put the mugs away. Then she climbed up next to him. She leaned over and whispered, "It's going to be fine. Tar is our friend."

Anon cast a sideways glance at Tar, who was pulling on Mule's reins. He didn't say a word. Mule brayed loudly, but Tar's grip was strong, and in a moment, they were past the clover patch and back on their way.

Akeela's heart was lighter now that she had a friend with her. Then she wondered what Queth would do when he found Anon missing. He'd be frantic. Fairy feet! If only she'd thought of this when they'd had a fire going. She could've sent a message to Krezma with a fire fairy. Such a simple thing, and she hadn't thought of it in time.

What kind of Guardian was she going to make, anyway?

"Oh, dear. Oh, dear." Queth wrung his hands as he paced the rug in front of the fireplace.

Krezma cleared her throat. She had more important things to worry about than a missing faun who was touched in the head. He could be anywhere. She tried to keep her voice calm. "Minister Queth, he will show up. He's probably searching the village for Akeela. He'll come home when he's hungry."

"But he's never done anything like this before. What if he's hurt? You know how people in the village treat him."

Krezma put a hand on his arm. "Aye. But surely someone would come and tell you if they found him."

Queth patted her hand. "I pray to Celtar they would."

"We also need to pray for our safety." Krezma walked to the window and glanced out. "I fear our Broem has the witch's attention. She could be here any moment. Thank Celtar she didn't come last night."

"Oh, dear. Oh, dear." Queth resumed his pacing.

Krezma gave a quick smile. "Well then, pray while you pace."

Queth put his hands together, fingers under his chin, and nodded. Krezma glanced out the window again. She saw nothing out of the ordinary, but every hair on her body tingled. She had some magic, but how could she protect a whole village? Maybe if she were younger.

"I'm going to check on Oret," she said.

Oret lifted his head and rumbled as she walked into the room. *The witch is approaching.*

Krezma nodded. "Aye, I feel it as well. Queth is praying. I need you to get a message to the fairies."

Oret closed his eyes. Krezma stood silent while he communicated his need mentally. She observed the room, taking in the fireplace, nightstand, and bookshelf. Queth's home was not fancy, and she appreciated the lack of clutter. It helped her think more clearly.

She moved surreptitiously to the window. As sure as a storm sent out clouds and wind before rain, she could feel the moving presence of her daughter.

The fire in the hearth snapped and crackled.

Hello, dear one.

Oret's voice startled her, and she spun around. He stared at the fireplace. Krezma noticed the flame a little higher than before. She peered closer. Yes, she could see the outline of a fire fairy.

Krezma, what message do you want her to carry?

"Thank you for coming." Courtesy first with fairies. "We are in dire need of your help. The witch is approaching and will be here shortly."

The fairy spun in the flames, stirring the embers. Sparks shot up, following her as she whizzed out the chimney.

Krezma turned to the bed. "That's done. Now, let's see what we can find in case of the worst. We'll need a hiding place, dear friend. She's coming for you."

***

Tzmet flexed her fingers. She continued to toy with different ways to kill Oret in the shortest amount of time as the carriage bumped along the dirt path. She could simply zap him. Surely he was weakened enough from the poisonous scratch she'd given him several weeks ago.

"Anyone else would've died sooner," she murmured. "His magic is strong, but even he cannot withstand nightshade forever."

She could tie him up and scratch him again. It would take a few days, but she could enjoy watching him grow weaker and weaker. Maybe he'd beg for mercy. She chuckled. That would be fun.

"I could hang him outside the tower window and let the ravens feast. Or maybe bind him, cover him with honey, and let the fire ants do him in." She sat up straight. "Then there's the crossbow."

Ah, yes, her enchanted crossbow. The one that never missed. The one with the poisoned arrows. She'd worked for weeks on carving a specially designed arrowhead to hold enough poison to kill three men.

She enjoyed her musings until a short whistle brought her up. "Halt!" she called.

After the lurching stopped, she pulled the curtain aside and peered out the window. The breeze ruffled her beaver's hair wig, and she shaded her eyes from the setting sun. A figure the size of a five-year-old child stood off the road, alongside an oak tree.

"I thought I recognized that whistle," Tzmet sneered. "Well, well, well. Brimridge. I wish I could say it's pleasant to see you again."

The boggart bowed. "My lady Tzmet."

Tzmet snorted. "Stop the pretense of respect. What do you want?"

Brimridge stroked his short beard. His black eyes sparkled. "My lady, I have the utmost respect for you."

"Hmm, maybe so, but you have no loyalty."

"I am loyal, wicked lady. But I also have a strong sense self preservation." Brimridge patted his chest. "However, I felt the stirrings of the great and mighty Riss'aird and thought perhaps you could use my services once again."

Tzmet studied the boggart. She disliked him immensely. He and every other boggart. All of them no taller than Brimridge, with olive-green skin, long brown hair which they pulled back and braided, piercing black eyes, and short, pointed beards. To her extreme distaste, they wore nothing except a loincloth, preferring to leave their hairy bodies to the elements. She admired their ability for moving silently through the woods and for stealing whatever they set their minds on, but that was it.

She held his gaze for several moments before she spoke. "I may have use for your services. Move your people into the lower chambers of my castle and wait for me." *Where I can keep an eye on you.*

Brimridge bowed again. "As you desire."

He slipped into the forest, and Tzmet signaled the Hinwar to begin again. Curse that Brimridge. Talking with him caused her to lose time for wreaking havoc in the village. Still, the boggarts just may come in handy. If they got out of line, her father would soon remedy that.

A slow grin spread across her lips. She loved it when things went her way.

***

Krezma shivered. Every nerve tingled, every muscle tensed. Tzmet must be sending out energy. An announcement of her impending arrival.

The fairies will come.

She turned to Oret. "But will they be enough? They feel your weakness, my friend."

Oret growled low. *It will have to be enough. She's here.*

Krezma breathed deep and let the air out in a rush. "May Celtar bless and keep you."

Oret bowed his head. *And you, dear friend.*

They walked out the door and into the street. People milled about, attending to their daily chores. Krezma had seen no need to alarm them, but she was having second thoughts as she watched girls playing jumprope in the street and boys throwing rocks at squirrels.

The wind picked up. Krezma stiffened. *Dear Celtar, her power is strong.* Fear crept into her mind. The same fear that coursed through her when she'd left Riss'aird, knowing that decision would cost her her child. She resisted the urge to laugh. *I thought I'd be able to go back and save her. If I had —*

Gasps startled Krezma out of her thoughts. Everyone stared at the sky. Krezma looked up. Her eyes widened when she saw Tzmet hovering above the village. This was something new. Tzmet hadn't been able to levitate before.

Celtar, help us!

Tzmet looked down at Oret and some old hag standing in the middle of the village. Oh, how she loved that Oret had to look up to see her. "Ah, Oret, I see you're up and about. My spies told me otherwise. But I'm glad. I really am."

Oret snarled. *I'm touched by your concern, witch.*

Tzmet smirked. "Concern, yes, but not for your well-being. I will kill you today. It will be delightful to watch you try to fight back. But first —"

She raised her hand, and blue lightening flew toward Rissat's hut. The thatched roof burst into flames, and people screamed, running in all directions.

Oret leaped forward. *Your fight is with me! Leave these people alone.*

"My fight is with anyone who isn't loyal to me and my father."

Tzmet raised her hand again. The blue fire shot to the bakery. She began to laugh but stopped short when the fire diverted into the forest. A pine tree caught and was engulfed in seconds.

"*What?*" Tzmet shrieked. She flung her hands, directing blue streaks toward homes and stables, but each one reflected off some invisible shield, igniting the trees instead of the village. She threw back her head. "Argh!"

"Cease your tantrum, witch."

Tzmet froze, her eyes darting back and forth. Then she looked down. She'd forgotten Oret wasn't alone. Astonishment filled her. "Are you speaking to me, old woman?"

The hag crossed her arms. "I am."

"How *dare* you!" She raised her hands and let loose her power, but it was once more diverted into the woods. She howled her frustration. Then she glared at the woman and Oret and smiled. "So you think you can stop me from destroying this village."

"With the help of Celtar," the hag said.

"Oh, really? Try this."

She raised her left hand and pointed at Oret. Blue fire sprang forward, the old woman waved her hand, and the fire bounced to the side as if it hit a wall. A small flame sprang up in a group of bushes near the stable. How perfectly quaint. The hag was using an old blocking spell. But she couldn't block everything. Tzmet was younger, stronger, and smarter.

Tzmet raised both arms and spread them wide. "Hah!"

Blue bolts filled the air. The old woman's hands moved quickly, like a hummingbird's wings, but Tzmet could tell she was growing weary. It was only a matter of time. Tzmet wasn't the least bit worried. She crossed her arms, the blue fire never ceasing in its intensity. The roof of another cottage burst into flames. A family ran out, the father shouting and the mother weeping. Two children ran beside them, and the smaller one tripped and fell. Tzmet aimed. The bolt of fire grazed the boy's arm before the father snatched him up.

Tzmet paused and breathed deeply. She hadn't had this much fun in ages. She looked toward the old woman and Oret. Time to finish them off. The sun was beginning to set, and she had an appointment with the fairy council. A secret appointment. A slow smile spread across her face. She raised her hands and—

Where was Oret?

As she contemplated his disappearance, buzzing filled her ears. Bees sped her way, but she was ready. A wave of her hand and several bees crashed, engulfed in flames. They shrieked, a sound that caught Tzmet's attention. They were not bees. They were fairies!

"Yes!" She cackled her delight. "Come to Tzmet, my winged foes. I'm waiting."

But the bees turned, swirling beneath her feet, forming an insect tornado. It rose toward her like an erupting volcano. Before she could wave her hands, the bees surrounded her and closed in.

Tzmet shrieked as a hundred burning stings pierced her body. Apparently, not all the bees were fairies. She allowed herself to drop. As her feet touched the ground, she leaped forward and ran into the woods. Curses, curses, curses! She paused and listened. Nothing. So the fairies were not interested in following.

Of course they weren't. They were no real match for her. She'd be back.

The sun dipped lower, casting orange and pink streaks across an azure sky. Curses again! She was going to be late. She lifted her skirt and ran all the way to the appointed spot. Oret and the village would have to wait.

Chapter Eleven

Gasps and sobs filled the air. Krezma pushed tendrils of hair out of her face. She prayed Oret had escaped safely.

Queth came alongside her. "Celtar have mercy. Look at my village."

Krezma breathed deeply. Water fairies extinguished flames in the trees. They were no longer a secret. *Maybe that is for the better.*

Queth put a hand on his forehead and surveyed the damage. "What do we do now?"

"What do you mean?"

"Will the witch return? Are we still in danger?"

Krezma shook her head slowly. "I do not know."

Rissat approached them, her face and hands blackened by smoke. "Minister Queth, please come. I was delivering a baby when the witch came. Then the fire started." She coughed and took a deep breath. "I was washing my hands in the kitchen when smoke filled the room. I tried to save them. I tried! But the roof fell —" Her voice caught, and she collapsed against Queth.

"My dear, oh my dear." Queth held her close.

A sharp pain shot through Krezma's chest. She clutched her hands and held her breath. The pain lessened and went away. "I will see to the bodies, Minister Queth. But first, I must see if any fairies are alive and need aid."

Queth nodded. "I will go to the husband. He'll need all the strength and comfort I can give him."

A breeze carried the remnant of smoke northwest. Krezma picked up her shawl, which had fallen during the confrontation, and wrapped it around her shoulders. She hurried to the far edge of the village near the pond. Several forest fairies tended their fallen comrades.

Krezma knelt. "Good fairies, may I be of assistance?"

A fairy, kneeling at the unmoving body of another, cried out, "Yes, please. We are in need of strength."

"I will do my best to bring it to you."

Krezma bowed her head. She began to hum, gathering energy from the plants and living creatures around her. She prayed to Celtar. Then she spread her hands toward the tiny, blackened bodies. Light emanated from her fingertips, reaching out and touching several, but not all, of them.

The fairies joined their voices in song. The sound rose and mingled with the rustling leaves. As the song intensified, many of the fallen fairies stirred and sat up. However, not all of them made it. Krezma dropped her hands.

The fairies helped their kin rise and began to fly into the forest. The leader hovered before Krezma. "Our thanks, good lady. And be of good cheer. The Guardian is safe and well. He will meet you at the appointed place."

Krezma's voice caught in her throat. She swallowed hard. "Thank you, and may Celtar bless you."

The fairy turned to follow the group. Some helped their friends and some carried the dead. Instead of their usual song, a silent despair filled the air, and the weight of it almost paralyzed Krezma.

Krezma trudged to Rissat's burned cottage. With the last of the tree fires out, the water fairies whizzed away. Krezma filled a bucket with water. She rinsed out a rag, grabbed a bar of soap, and tenderly washed the burned bodies of mother and baby.

"It's a boy," she whispered. Tears, unbidden, rolled down her cheeks, and she wept until she could weep no more.

Tzmet walked stiffly to the meeting place and pulled the wig from her head. Those miserable fairies had better be there. Or she'd have to do without them.

Her body bristled from the bee stings, and she longed to return to her castle and a cool bath. Sweat slid down her neck as her anger seethed. "Curse them all! I will destroy the entire village and surrounding forest. No living thing will escape my fury."

She glanced around. No fairies. Several minutes passed. Still no fairies. Her body began swelling from the bee poison, and she decided not to wait any longer.

"They can find me," she muttered. "And they better do it soon."

The sound of running water grew louder as she stalked through the forest. Yes, cool water and clay was just what she needed. Her pain was so intense, the thought of mud on her body didn't even upset her.

She parted some reeds and bent to run her hand over the bank. "Ah, yes, perfect."

Without a thought, she cast off her cloak and gown and stepped into the cool water. Immediate relief flooded her, and she soaked until she grew numb. Then she pulled herself to the side and mixed mud from the clay bank and rubbed it all over.

She closed her eyes. "I will avenge myself, oh yes. The villagers will pay. The fairies will pay. Oret will pay!"

She must've dozed off at some point because a rustling sound played around the edges of her consciousness. She fought fatigue and opened her eyes.

Three fairies hovered over a blackberry bush, their eyes darting from side to side. That irritated Tzmet. "What news do you have for me?" she snapped.

"The meeting is cancelled," the fairies said.

"*Cancelled?*"

"Because of the attack on the village," the tall fairy said. "The council went to the aid of the Guardian."

Tzmet sat up and started to rinse mud from her arms. The sun lingered on the edge of the earth, and fireflies appeared in the tall grass. She'd been at the stream longer than she'd realized.

So it was her fault the council did not meet. How ironic. "But," she said in a low voice, "I've weakened the council by killing several fairies. How unexpected. How delightful!" She turned her full attention to her allies and smiled. "Tell me, my friends. When is the next meeting?"

"We do not know," they said.

The smile vanished from her face. "Find out."

"Yes, milady."

The sun disappeared, and a pink-orange glow lit the horizon as the last rays of light streaked across the now-indigo sky. Stars began to twinkle, and Tzmet caught the scent of night flowers. She dried off with her cloak and slipped the gown over her head. The sound of water tumbling over rocks played in her thoughts, and she remembered the map.

"Wait. What have you found out about the fountains? Four fountains. The ones on the map you brought me."

The fairies looked at each other.

"Well?"

"Earth, fire, air, water," they intoned.

Tzmet stomped her foot. Blast their chorus talking! "I know what the elements are, fools! What are the fountains? What do they mean to fairies?"

The sky faded to black, and crickets began their night song. The air cooled, and Tzmet's temper fired as she waited for an answer. The key to fairies was patience, and that had never been her strong suit. She touched several reeds and ignited them so they glowed, casting a faint light on the fairies.

They glanced at each other. It seemed they communicated something without speaking. How dare they keep secrets from her! She raised her hand.

"Last chance."

The tall fairy covered her face with one hand. "I can't remember—"

Blue fired flashed, and ashes hovered a moment in the air before they floated to the ground. Tzmet's eyes became slits, and she peered sideways at the remaining two fairies. They wrapped their arms around each other, clearly shocked and terrified.

Tzmet folded her arms. "Now then, about the fountains."

The small fairy burst into tears. The other took a trembling breath.

"Yes?"

"Fountains give life to fairies."

Tzmet forgot the itching and burning of the bee stings. She took a step closer. "Really? How intriguing. Tell me where they are."

"Fountains are hidden. Earth in the desert. Water by the stream. Fire in the mountain. Air . . . air . . . I don't know!"

Tzmet stood still as the chill of the night air deepened. Still, this information was too important to let go. "How do I find them?"

"The map," the taller fairy said.

The small fairy cried out in distress. She obviously fought against giving Tzmet highly secret information. Was her potion strong enough to counter the struggle?

Tzmet took another step. She needed to take care, or she'd have to capture new fairies and start the process all over again. "Now, now, dear friends. I can see you are weary. Allow me to refresh you before you go on your way." She pulled out a small vial and thimble from her cloak pocket. "The shock of your friend's demise is too much for you. What a sad, sad accident."

The fairies took the drink. Tzmet smiled smugly as their eyes glazed and they drifted, half asleep.

"Rest. Sleep. You'll feel better in the morning." Tzmet gently scooped them into her hands. "Reach into your memory and dream of the—" Which fountain should she look for first? Yes, the one which may affect her father directly. "The Earth fountain. Yes, my lovelies. Dream and speak of the earth fountain."

The triple moons did their slow dance across the sky. Tzmet

waited patiently as her fairies began to spill their secrets. This changed her plans. She didn't need to kill Oret to weaken the fairies' power after all. There was another way. Later, she could kill Oret just for fun.

And the village? When her father rose from the ground, she'd make sure Broem was the first place he visited.

Tar stood at Mule's head and sniffed the air. "Fire. The scent of a large fire is on the air."

Akeela glanced around, her eyes darting in all directions, trying to catch sight of any aura out of place. "How far? Where is it?"

"From the direction of the breeze, I'm afraid it's coming from the village."

Akeela gasped. Anon stirred beside her, and she smoothed the blanket over his shoulders. "Are you sure?" she whispered.

Tar didn't answer. He clicked his tongue at Mule, and they started again. The sun's light flickered through the trees as it cast orange rays across the sky. Soon it would be night.

"I wonder if Krezma and Oret have left," she said.

Mule slowed to nip at an oak treeling. Tar tugged on the reins, and Mule continued walking as he munched on his find.

"If they were able, they left."

If they were able.

Akeela glanced back. Fireflies dotted the dark edges of forest. She prayed for safety and wanted her bed at the cottage.

But the cottage was no more, and she didn't know about the village.

Then she realized she hadn't thought once about Ham. She chided herself. If not for her, the village would be safe, the cottage would be safe, her friends would be safe.

For the first time, Akeela wished she were not gifted.

Krezma picked her way through her ruined cottage. She bent and lifted a singed bowl and smiled. It was Nooph's. "At least my sweet Nooph is safe."

Oret appeared in the doorway. *Your concern is a bit misplaced, my friend.*

Krezma chuckled. "Ah, but Oret, love is love, whether for a person or not. I do what I can for both."

We must not linger. Oret sniffed the air. *I'm leery of getting caught before you've had time to rest.*

"I'll not be long." Krezma pushed a charred chair away from what was left of the kitchen counter. She opened a lower cabinet door and reached in. Out came towels, a flat pan, cooking utensils, and another bowl. All miraculously untouched by the fire. She stuck her arm in up to her shoulder. "It's still here. Thank Celtar."

What's so important you would risk our safety?

Krezma held up a book and cloth bag. She tied the bag around her waist and placed the book inside her cloak. "My book of herb lore and my mortar and pestle. If enough herbs survived the fire, this will aid our cause."

Oret looked out the window at the darkness. *'Tis too dark for even me to distinguish between plants.*

Krezma stepped over a fallen roof beam. "Yes, my friend. We'll stay here tonight."

Here?

"Of course. It's the safest place. Who would think to look for us here?"

Oret lowered his head and began to purr. After a moment, he looked up and yawned. *I do not have your confidence, but I am weary beyond reasoning. I feel the poison ravaging my body.* He took a deep breath. *Krezma, it won't be long now. We must get to Akeela and Tar.*

Krezma stroked his head. "We will, my friend. We will."

As Oret slept, Krezma gazed at the heavens through an opening in the treetops. Meditating and praying were more important than sleep tonight. Tomorrow or the next would see the death of her oldest friend. She had to have strength. She had to. Thank Celtar her small labyrinth was only singed.

She began her slow prayer walk.

The thought that evil may have its way lingered in her mind, and she fought despair. If only she'd known exactly when the magic wall around Riss'aird's castle had come down. If only she hadn't had the responsibility of Akeela. Mayhap she would've been able to get to Tzmet and stop her before all this. But things hadn't turned out that way. Celtar must have a plan. She had to trust Him.

Dear Celtar, she prayed. *I ask only for what is needed and no more. Please grant my humble request.*

The crickets and tree frogs sang their night song as Krezma hummed and prayed.

The morning sun appeared much too quickly, but she gathered courage as she prepared a small meal. Perhaps the last one she'd share with Oret. A tear slipped down her cheek. If Riss'aird appeared now, she'd not be able to stand against him.

She wasn't sure she even cared.

Chapter Twelve

Akeela jolted awake as the cart ran over a tree root. She stretched her arms overhead and glanced at Anon, who still slumbered next to her on the seat. Tar walked next to Mule, occasionally tapping the animal's hindquarters with a stick.

The sun filtered through the forest. Red maple, oak, pine, and birch trees dwelt together in harmony. Akeela breathed deeply and sighed. Here she felt at peace and could almost forget her marriage night and her quest—until the memory resurfaced of Krezma's burning cottage and Oret lying weak and helpless at Queth's house.

Her stomach growled. How long had it been since breakfast? She turned and pulled out some dried venison and a crock of red berries. As she bit off a piece of meat and chewed, she heard bright, cheerful music. "Tar, do you hear that?"

Tar nodded. "It is my people. We are near the kin-tribe."

Anon grunted, and Akeela stroked his head. She'd never thought of Tar having people. He seemed so solitary except for his devotion to Oret. She bit another piece of venison. The music swelled, drifting through the leaves and swirling around the cart.

"Are they celebrating something?"

Tar cocked his head and listened. Mule interpreted his hesitation as a chance to eat and halted next to a gooseberry bush. The cart lurched to a stop, and Anon groaned and opened his eyes.

"Home, Keela?"

Akeela smiled down at him. "No, Anon. We're not home yet. Are you hungry?"

She gave the faun a piece of venison and turned back to Tar. He stood still, listening to the music, then he turned to Akeela.

"My people are celebrating a life."

"Oh, that sounds like fun."

Tar frowned at Akeela. She flushed under his gaze, feeling stupid, but not knowing what she did wrong.

"You do not understand. They are not honoring a living person, but one who has passed from this life."

Akeela felt very small. A fly buzzed around her head, and she brushed it away. "Oh."

Tar slapped Mule, and with a frustrated bray, he began his slow amble toward the music, chewing his last bite of gooseberry bush. Akeela helped Anon with the red berries, then wiped juice from his chin.

As they continued, the voices grew in intensity. Her hands trembled, and she clasped them together. The breeze shifted, bringing the sound closer, and Akeela felt such anticipation, she grew faint.

They rode in silence, Akeela's heart pounding with the beating of the drums. She was pulled toward the music and dreaded it at the same time. What kind of funeral caused people to celebrate?

In Broem, funerals were solemn occasions. Everyone wore black, and the women hid their tears behind their veils. Any sound besides Queth's voice was weeping. What kind of people were these people of the forest? Tar called them Acadians, people of the trees.

Akeela decided she didn't like them. Anyone joyful at death could not possibly be a good person.

Tar pulled Mule to a stop. "Come, watch and learn."

Akeela wanted to refuse, but curiosity got the better of her. She turned to Anon. "Be very quiet now, Anon." She helped him down. "Here, hold my hand."

They followed Tar through bushes with tiny, although startling, red flowers. Akeela brushed her hand against a bloom. Her touch released a heavy, sweet scent, and at the same time, the people began to sing.

Tar stopped at the edge of the clearing. Akeela stared at the Acadians with wide eyes. She'd never realized there were people so different from the people of Broem. These people were brown skinned and had dark, bushy hair. They all wore white tunics.

"I felt just as amazed as you when I first came across the Acadians," Tar whispered.

Akeela nodded and then remembered she was not amazed. She disliked these unfeeling people and started to tell Tar so when he continued.

"The Acadians are a people totally devoted to the earth. They also know of and worship Celtar."

"Really?" Akeela crossed her arms. The singing continued, filling the air to capacity. Many also danced. "What kind of people worship Celtar and yet celebrate a death?"

Tar flashed a rare smile. He captured Akeela's eyes with a piercing gaze. "I felt much the same when I first came across the Acadians and witnessed a funeral. But I was wrong. These people are so filled with the joy of life and the hope only Celtar gives, they choose to celebrate a passing, knowing their loved one is now free of the body and the world."

Akeela frowned. "I don't understand."

"The Acadians suffer and grapple with grief when a loved one dies," Tar said. "They have deep emotions, maybe more so than any other people I have encountered. But their faith and trust in Celtar is also deep, and they believe death is only temporary."

"Temporary?" Akeela gave a short laugh. "I've never seen anyone come back from death. How can death be temporary?" Anon pulled on her sleeve, and she started. "I'm sorry, Anon. I forgot you were there. What a good faun you are, standing so quietly."

Anon grinned and opened his hand. "Found new stone, Keela."

Akeela glanced at the stone, not really looking at it. "That's nice, Anon. Don't forget to put it in your bag." She turned back to Tar.

"Akeela, do you believe this life is all there is?"

She thought for a moment. Queth shared from the Holy Writings that Celtar gave eternal life to those who believed in, trusted, and loved Him. She'd never stopped to really think about what that meant. Still, as Akeela thought of the countless stars at night and recalled Krezma's story of the Dark Lord, she knew there had to be more.

She looked up. "No, I guess not."

"When the body dies, the spirit within is released," Tar said. "This spirit continues to live, and a believer in Celtar's spirit goes to live with Him."

"Is that what Queth meant when he said we have eternal life?"

He started to answer, but suddenly the singing stopped.

"What's happening?" Akeela whispered. She felt as though something was missing without the music.

Tar stood watching the people now gathering in a circle. They all sat except for two people—a man and a woman—young, eyes red from weeping, cheeks flushed from dancing. They wore yellow armbands over their white tunics.

Tar turned to Akeela. "They will now remember the person who has died." His voice was low. "See those people with the yellow armbands? They are the parents. This is a funeral of a child."

Tzmet gazed at her reflection in the full-length mirror. She smiled and nodded. "This will do nicely," she said to Brimridge. "I feel as though I can easily move from place to place without being noticed."

She ran a hand down the ugly brown tunic and pants. It was temporary. Stolen by the boggart, of course. And necessary. She could almost ignore the dreariness of her clothing at the thought of finding the earth fountain and gathering power from it.

Brimridge handed her something lumpy and brown. "One more thing, milady."

Tzmet looked down her nose at him. "What is it?"

"A head covering. Your baldness. You must cover your head."

She smacked the top of his head. "How dare you!"

Brimridge grinned. "I only speak the truth, milady. And you will need protection from the desert sun."

"I realize that, fool, but you don't need to be so vulgar about it."

Two Hinwari entered the bedroom. One carried a covered tray, and the other, a goblet and carafe of *caavea*. They set them on a small table next to the window and silently left.

Tzmet walked over and lifted the cover off the plate. She sniffed and smiled. "You can leave me now, Brimridge."

The boggart bowed and strode from the room.

Tzmet sighed and waved her hand in front of her face to dispel the smell of skunk cabbage mingled with sweat. Her stomach growled, and she sat at the small table. Now that the air was clear, she could enjoy her meal.

The disgusting presence of Brimridge irritated her stomach, and she hadn't missed the hungry look in his eyes when her breakfast had arrived. She had no doubt he and his family would avail themselves to all her kitchen had to offer while she was gone, but if they did their job and assisted her, she could at least feed them.

Tzmet lifted a forkful of grilled night crawlers. "To my search," she said to the open window. "And to my success!"

***

Krezma glanced back over her shoulder. "Come, Oret, we must make haste."

The big cat panted as he struggled to keep up with Krezma. *I . . . cannot . . . continue to run . . . at this . . . speed.*

"We need to arrive at the Acadian camp before sunset. I fear the witch will discover our path."

In spite of her worry, Krezma slowed. She noted the position of the sunlight filtering through the trees. Breathing a prayer for safety, she decided to stop and let Oret rest.

"Here is a stream, my friend. Let us refresh ourselves for a moment."

Oret flopped on his side, wheezing. Krezma brought him water in a large pond leaf, and he drank deeply. They rested as long as Krezma dared before setting off again.

Akeela gazed at the fire Tar had built near the cart, trying to mentally call a fire fairy so she could get news. The Acadians still celebrated, and although Tar had joined them, Akeela refused.

She understood they had faith and joy in Celtar, but to turn a funeral into a celebration was beyond her comprehension.

"Hungry, Keela."

Akeela turned to Anon. "I'm sorry, Anon. Here, let me get something from our cart."

She walked to the cart and rummaged through a sack. The light from the fire stretched toward her but gave little illumination. There must be a lantern somewhere, but in the dark, she couldn't see it.

As she drew out some dried venison, a crackling noise startled her, and she whirled around. "Krezma!"

"Yes, child, it is I. We made it, thanks be to Celtar." Krezma drew a weary breath. "Where is Tar? Oret is in need of his help. And Ham. I could use his help as well."

Akeela looked around. "Where's Oret?"

Krezma nodded toward the forest. "Out there. He walked until he could walk no more. We must get him to safety."

"Tar is at the celebration. I don't know where Ham is at the moment."

Not exactly a lie. She *didn't* know where Ham was right now.

Krezma lifted an eyebrow. "Why are you not with them, child?"

Akeela looked away. "I cannot participate in a celebration that mocks a funeral."

Krezma stood silent for a moment. "Child, there is much for you to learn, but right now, I must get Tar and Ham. I will be back." She strode off in the direction of the music.

Akeela's knees almost gave out. Krezma was going to be extremely angry when she learned Ham was not with them. She gathered venison, two carrots, and the last piece of bread and carried them to the fire.

"Here, Anon. You eat while I get us some water."

Anon happily bit into a carrot and smiled at Akeela. She smiled back and turned to peer into the forest. Somewhere out there Oret waited for help. What had happened in the village? Were Iari, Gilron, and Ham safe? Where was the witch?

The thought occurred to her that she ought to be more afraid of Krezma's wrath than the witch's right now.

***

Oret lay on his side in the bed, his breathing shallow.

The light of a small fire cast flickering shadows on the inner walls of the tree. Akeela had been amazed when the Acadians had led them to an ordinary-looking oak tree near a dried-up streambed. She'd followed them into a small ravine, bent over to walk under the roots, which had grown across, and crawled into an opening in the ground. They'd climbed roots that formed natural steps and into the middle of the oak.

Her first thought had been that it was impossible. From the outside, the oak was no larger than normal. How could there be this much room inside?

Krezma only came in to check on Oret now and then. She'd been as furious as Akeela had anticipated when she'd found out Ham was not with them, but Akeela couldn't think about that now.

Oret groaned. His aura, once brilliant, looked faded and weak. Akeela placed a hand on his side, her heart breaking. She'd finally found her family, and he was dying. Truly, Celtar must hate her.

She choked back a sob. "Dear Oret, Grandfather, how can I help you?"

You cannot. I prayed . . . I wouldn't . . . succumb . . . to the poison . . . before you completed the quest . . . but I fear I . . . cannot . . . join you.

Tears filled Akeela's eyes and ran down her cheeks. "Krezma will find a cure, I know she will. Please keep fighting."

My fight . . . is over. Yours . . . is just beginning.

Akeela blinked quickly. This couldn't be happening. She needed her family. "Grandfather—"

Listen. You must find . . . Fairystone. Must . . . strengthen . . . fairies.

"I will. I'll find the stone. I'll become the guardian. Please don't leave me."

Oret drew a ragged breath. *Pain.* He opened his eyes. They gleamed in the firelight. *I'm . . . sorry.*

"Don't be! It's not your fault."

He drew another breath. *Akeela.*

"I'm here."

A-keel-a.

Akeela leaned closer. Oret began to purr. He closed his eyes and seemed to smile. There was a pause. Silence. Then his aura flickered and went out. Akeela gasped. Then he heaved one great breath and breathed no more.

Akeela stared. "No."

The great cat lay silent.

"No."

From deep within her being, Akeela felt a trembling, as though the very earth moved at Oret's death. From within she heard many voices cry out. Fairy voices. A sob caught in her throat, and she put a hand on her chest. Part of her life, part of her heart, was no more.

Krezma entered the room. Akeela threw herself into her arms.

"Oh, my dear child. My dear child." Krezma stroked her hair. "Now is the end of a remarkable life." She paused, then in an uncustomary move, hugged Akeela close. "Dear Celtar, what are we going to do now?"

Chapter Thirteen

Tzmet wiped sweat from her brow. She shielded her eyes and gazed across the unending desert. Heat swirled up from the sand like burning incense. Then she patted Nightshade's neck and heaved a great sigh.

"If those wretched fairies gave me wrong directions, I will personally tear their arms off."

He whinnied in response.

True, they told her it would be a three-day trip toward the setting sun, and she'd only been traveling one day, but she believed she'd see something besides the glaring sun and shifting sand. And where was the oasis? She should've come across it by now.

She slid off the horse and set the backpack on the sand. She took out a bottle of water, pulled out the cork, and drank deeply. She knew she'd save time and effort if Nightshade didn't have to carry the extra weight of a saddle, but she cursed her decision to ride bareback. It was a miserable discomfort since she now felt the horse's heat as well as the sun's.

"Here, have some water." She lifted a small canvas bag to Nightshade.

After the horse drank, she put everything away, shrugged the pack over her shoulder, and pulled herself on Nightshade's back. Now that the sun was making its journey downward, she'd ride until she either saw it no more or found the oasis.

"First the earth fountain, then to find Oret. And the line of guardians will be no more!"

She gave a shout and kicked Nightshade into a trot.

Akeela watched the first forest fairy land on the log on the other side of the fire. A moment later, two more joined her. It hadn't taken long for them to begin arriving after Akeela had spoken to the fire fairy and shared the news about Oret's funeral.

The air filled with whirring wings and shimmering auras. Droplets of lights drifted down as more fairies arrived. Earth and water fairies, Akeela was familiar with. But the air fairies, clear except for their auras, were as elusive as the wind. Still, they joined the others on the branches of the surrounding trees.

The Acadians built fires to accommodate the fire fairy population. Akeela shivered in spite of the heat. Fairies settled on tree branches, gathering like birds before a storm. And a storm was coming. It loomed in Akeela's mind, breathing down her neck, gripping her heart, and she couldn't escape. Krezma hadn't said much when she'd learned Ham had not accompanied Akeela, but she'd promised they'd talk after the funeral.

The fairies leaned forward, eyes sparkling and lips smiling, looking at her as if they expected something. She wanted to scream at them to go away. She knew they expected her to take Oret's place, but how could she do that? It wasn't fair he'd died before she could know him better. There was so much more she needed to learn.

Krezma touched her shoulder. "Child, it's time. Come. Oret would not have you sitting alone in your grief."

Akeela shrugged. "I don't want to celebrate his life. I want to mourn his passing. It isn't right to sing and dance when I'm sad."

"The Holy Writings say, 'even in laughter, the heart may ache.'

It does not mean you aren't mourning Oret's death if you celebrate his life." Krezma held out her hand. "Get up. Your presence is necessary."

Akeela considered refusing. She looked around at the host of fairies who'd gathered. She was now their guardian. They were depending on her. She sighed and stood. "I will come, but I will not be joyful."

Krezma grunted. "No one has asked you to be."

The leader, Ban-ira, and the minister, Dir-mac, led the celebration. They began with a prayer to Celtar. Children sprinkled flower petals over Oret's coffin. Then everyone sang song after song. Akeela sat without taking part. She'd never lost anyone she loved to death before. Was it normal to feel so empty? So raw?

Some Acadians played instruments Akeela recognized, such as wooden flutes, shakers, and drums. Others played something that looked like a tuber. In spite of her feelings, Akeela took interest in the small brown instrument with a haunting, flute-like sound, but then sat with her head down.

When the singing stopped, several individuals talked about Oret and how he'd encouraged and assisted them. There was a pause, and Akeela raised her head. Tar stood with his eyes closed and his arms spread. The only sound was the crackling fire.

He walked to the middle of the circle, near the fire. Everyone leaned forward with eager looks. Akeela's heart beat painfully against her chest, and a small hand slipped into hers. Anon lay his furry head on her shoulder, and she hugged him close.

Tar looked around the group. Even the children grew silent. Their anticipation could be felt as they waited. Akeela wondered at this as Tar began to speak. The children in Broem had never been this attentive.

"The great wizard, Jemin, took me in when I was orphaned. He taught me the way of the bird and of the forest. We tended the wounded, such as the mighty eagle, osprey, and owl. I lived a good life with Jemin and our birds. One day I wandered far into the forest until I came to a cliff's edge. I gazed at the valley below and had a vision of flying. I have worked ever since that day to accomplish this feat."

The people murmured. Akeela's interest surged, and she forgot they were holding Oret's funeral for a moment.

"I experimented for a year, trying to make wings. I tried over and over, painting myself with the warm tar and sticking feathers in, each time a different way, but each try came to failure. Jemin nicknamed me Tar, and I have been known by that name ever since. I gave up my dream until I became a man. Then I changed my thinking and succeeded in building gliders which imitate flying."

Akeela sat up in surprise. A person could glide through the air like a bird?

"I want to lift up Oret in memory, for he helped me often during this time in my life, the great and mighty cat who saved my life and the life of my son, to accomplish my dream."

Akeela looked around. Tar had a son? She scanned the many faces, not caring if they saw her looking, but she didn't see anyone who resembled Tar. A small stab of disappointment went through her mind. She brushed it away. It was no matter to her that Tar had a son. She had an impossible quest before her. She had no time to think about anything else.

"As a young man, I wandered the forest often. I met the Acadians, and they befriended me. Out of this friendship, I met my wife, Dar-dra. We were blessed with five years and then a son." Tar paused. He placed a log in the fire. Fairies and sparks danced in the night air, and delicate humming filled Akeela's ears. The fire fairies were singing.

"One night, while Jemin was away, Dar-dra and I tended the birds while our infant son slept in the hut. The birds were nervous. I walked the area but saw nothing until I heard Dar-dra screaming. Wolves had attacked, trying to get to the birds. Dar-dra and I tried to fight them off with rakes . . . but . . . but they overcame our efforts."

The people gasped. Akeela gasped with them, caught up in Tar's story.

"The wolves were frenzied, and I knew we would die if we didn't find a way to defeat them. I don't know how long we fought. Dar-dra fell. There were too many for me, and as I fell, I prayed to Celtar to protect our son."

The singing increased in volume as the forest fairies joined in, and the people began to beat their hands on the ground. Akeela's heart beat in rhythm.

"Two wolves attacked, one leaping on my chest and one tearing at my arm. I looked death in the face. The world began to slip away, but in the dimness, I saw Oret bound over the fence. As blackness engulfed me, I heard a great roar and the death cry of the wolves. Then I saw no more until I awoke ten days later to learn my wife was gone, and Jemin, using all his magic and bird lore, had given his life to save mine."

The beating stopped, and the people swayed to the fairies' music.

"But I tell you, if it hadn't been for Oret, I'd be dead."

The people cheered and jumped to their feet. They danced around the fire and sang praises to Celtar, playing their instruments with abandon.

Akeela's spirit rose in her chest, and for a moment, she thought she might join them. Then she remembered this was Oret's funeral, and sorrow pierced her heart. She held the sleeping Anon and wept.

Krezma watched a young man sitting across the circle, almost hidden, as he gazed at Akeela during Tar's story. It was a look of wondrous recognition, and Krezma felt a warning in her soul. Someone sat next to her. She turned to see the minister, Dir-mac, looking at Akeela as well.

"Is she the one?"

Krezma nodded.

"But she is not ready, for if she were, I would not sense hesitation within her."

"'Tis true, Minister Dir-mac. She is not ready, and Oret's death will only complicate things. Especially in the fairy realm."

Dir-mac picked up a pinecone and turned it in his hand. "She is like this cone. Closed and unyielding, but with seeds of life within." He tossed it into the fire. "Under heat, the cone opens and releases the seeds. They swell in the flame and burst, burning to nothing."

Krezma nodded.

"She needs to become like the nacre seed," Dir-mac went on. "Which is tightly wrapped with pinsapo covering. When thrown in the fire, the wrapping burns away, revealing the nacre, gleaming, pure and white, and of great value. It is not destroyed by fire. Instead the fire brings out its strength."

"And the job falls to me to see this happen."

Dir-mac patted her hand. "You are not alone, my friend."

Stars began to twinkle in the darkening sky. Tzmet, exhausted to the point of exasperation, leaned forward on Nightshade. She saw the outline of palm trees and rubbed her eyes. "I must be dreaming."

Nightshade snorted and tossed his head.

The trees grew closer, and a tent and fire came into view. She laughed out loud and urged Nightshade forward. As she approached, she pulled on the reins and allowed the horse to walk into the circle of light. Three rugged, dirty men sat there drinking and apparently waiting for whatever was cooking in the pot over the fire. They looked up when Nightshade whinnied.

"Well, well, well, what do we have here?" a man with a thick mustache and protruding belly asked. "A desert spirit?"

A thin man with sallow skin, a pointed nose, and greasy hair pulled back in a ponytail shook his head. "Can't be a spirit. It's too tall and ugly."

"Not too tall for me," the third man, bald and reddish-skinned, declared.

The men laughed. Tzmet cleared her throat. She couldn't abide fools. "I want food and water."

The fat man stood. "Is that right?"

"Do you have any?"

The man smiled, revealing brown, chipped teeth. "Aye, there be food and water here."

"Whom do I speak to about getting it?"

The man rubbed his stomach and belched. "Why, that would be me, little lady."

Tzmet rolled her eyes. Of all the luck, she *would* run into the only oasis for miles, and idiots were waiting for her. Too tired to play along, she raised her hand. Blue light streaked out, striking the man and reducing him to ashes.

The other two men leaped up from their places, spilling their drinks. The short, bald man pulled a knife and brandished it before him.

"Please," Tzmet said. Blue fire blazed again, and the man joined his friend in the ash pile. She rubbed her hands. "That's better." She looked at the remaining man, the one who referred to her as ugly. He stood, trembling, eyes wide and mouth open. Tzmet buffed her nails on her tunic. "Now, about that food and water."

The man fainted.

Nightshade pawed at the sand as Tzmet slid off. She kicked the man as she walked by.

"My thanks," she said, chuckling. "My thanks."

Chapter Fourteen

Akeela remained by the fire as the Acadians carried Oret's coffin to a sacred place for burial. She stared at the flames until her eyes could take no more. She closed them and rubbed her temples.

"I'm sorry for your loss."

Akeela looked up into the smiling face of a young Acadian. His eyes reflected the fire as he grinned. Akeela started to respond when she realized his eyes were brown and not the leafy green of the forest people. His aura was also different. It was green like the others but had a tinge of blue around the edges. And he had shoulder-length hair that fell in thick strands. The other boys she'd seen had shorter, bristly hair.

She sat up. "Who are you?"

The boy bowed. "I'm Hawk. Here, I brought you a cup of saloop."

A tremor passed through Akeela. Something about this boy made her feel light, fresh, like the first warm breeze of spring. A welcome feeling, though she hadn't time to wonder why. She studied his face. "Thank you, I think. What's saloop?"

Hawk sat next to her. "It's tea made from our most sacred tree, the Laurales. You'll find it soothing."

Akeela gave a slight smile and sniffed the pungent smell wafting up from the mug. She sipped tentatively. "Interesting. I've never had anything like it."

Hawk just nodded. He never took his eyes off her face.

Her face burned. It must've been the heat from the fire. She shifted away from the flames. "Why isn't it clear?"

"We add milk and honey to it."

Akeela sipped more and cleared her throat. "Why are you staring at me?"

Hawk cocked his head, like he didn't understand.

"You keep looking at me, and frankly, it's a little disturbing." So much for the fresh feeling. She clamped down on her annoyance before she said anything else. She was a guest, after all.

"Don't you know me?" Hawk's eyes took on a pleading expression. His aura pulsed, revealing his agitation.

"No. Why would I?"

Hawk looked down. He sat silent a moment. "I've been dreaming of you all my life. I was sure, when I saw you, that you would know me."

Akeela flushed. No one had ever said something so—compelling—to her. Her annoyance slipped away. "Dreaming of . . . me? I don't understand."

Hawk's face brightened. "Yes! Your face, your voice. I know them. I've been hearing them in my dreams."

"Sapo!"

Akeela startled and looked up to see two Acadians approaching. A boy and a girl, so similar in looks they were surely related.

"Sapo!" the boy said again.

Hawk closed his eyes and groaned. "Go away."

The Acadian boy plopped next to Akeela. "So this is she, yeh?" He grinned at Akeela and wiggled his eyebrows. Akeela couldn't help but laugh.

"Aye, it's she. Now go away. You're scraping my branches."

The boy shouted with laughter. The girl pushed him off the log and sat. "Pay no mind to my brother. He's a dupeseed." She lifted her long, curly hair off her shoulders and dropped it again. "I'm

Ves-rynia, Hawk's cousin. That"—she jerked her thumb over her shoulder—"is my brother, Vorrak-ira."

Akeela didn't exactly understand the Acadian expressions, but she had a good idea what they meant. "I'm Akeela."

Ves-rynia held out her hands, palms up. Akeela look at her, confused. Ves-rynia nodded. "Here, you put your hands on mine, yeh? It's our way of greeting."

Akeela touched her palms to Ves-rynia's, relieved she'd remembered to put on her archery glove. The last thing she wanted was to answer questions about her birthmark. "How come no one did this when we first got here?"

"Things are different during a funeral celebration," Hawk said. "Then, the greeting is a bow."

It didn't make sense to Akeela, but she didn't question it. Tar had explained that the Acadians had different ways than the people of Broem. She set her mug on the ground and stood. "Our greeting is a little different." She motioned to Hawk. "Here, you stand up and hold out your hand." Hawk obeyed. Akeela touched his hand with her fingertips and curtsied. "That's how men and women greet each other. Men clasp hands and women just curtsy, but I usually hug my best friend, Iari."

Vorrak-ira jumped up. "I'll be your best friend!"

Hawk punched his thigh.

He shrugged. "I'm starved. Let's go put on some water."

Ves-rynia snorted. "First, you still have funeral clothes on. Second, you know we can't eat anything until after the burial. And last, you smell like you stepped in scat. There's no way I'm going to share a meal with you, yeh?"

Vorrak-ira brushed off his white tunic. "There's time before everyone gets back for me to change." He grinned at Akeela. "Then I'll be honored to have you a-sitting with me, yeh?"

"Sorry, she'll be sitting with me," Hawk was quick to say.

"She doesn't want to sit with a dupeseed who constantly chews bark." Ves-rynia waved her hand at her brother. "Go on, get changed *and* washed. I might save you a place." She turned and smiled at Akeela. "And she'll be sitting with *me*."

Vorrak-ira jumped over the log, kicking up some dirt. He held out his hands to Akeela. She touched his palms with hers. "Nice glove. Is that a tradition of your people, too?"

Akeela shook her head. When she didn't say anything, he shrugged and ran off, whistling.

Hawk blew air out his nose. "I'm sorry about my cousin. He can't control himself, yeh?"

Akeela smiled, again aware of how her heart reacted whenever she looked at Hawk. Ves-rynia saved her from saying something stupid.

"Akeela, come with me and we'll freshen up for the burial meal, yeh?"

"Okay."

Hawk bowed. "I'll save places."

The girls joined hands and walked to the small streambed that led to the Acadian dwellings. "I'm happy you've finally come," Ves-rynia said. "Hawk speaks of the girl with black hair and violet eyes without ceasing. I thought he was off his nut, but now that you're here, well, what can I say? Celtar must have a plan for you two, but who can tell, yeh?"

"Yeh," Akeela mumbled. She glanced back and saw Hawk still standing by the fire, watching them.

Hot winds shrieked all around Tzmet and Nightshade. Curse this sandstorm!

She huddled in a tent left by the men. It provided the only protection, other than her clothing, from the stinging sand.

Nightshade whinnied, but Tzmet said nothing. She'd urged the horse into the tent when the storm had first started and she'd gotten a mouthful of sand.

Now there was nothing to do but wait it out.

Lovely, rich aromas surrounded Akeela, and she breathed deeply, anticipating the meal in spite of her sorrow. The food, served in wooden dishes, was set in the middle of long tables.

Ves-rynia tapped her shoulder. "Here, take this leaf. Watch me."

Akeela followed Ves-rynia, scooping food into her leaf. There were tiny balls of goat cheese, seeds and nuts, red berries, a big bowl of mixed greens coated with oil, roasted kingfish, and thin brown bread. The girls walked to the great circle and sat on a log. Hawk joined them a minute later, bringing mugs of tea laced with cinnamon. He set them down and headed back toward the food table.

Akeela sat at a loss, looking at her leaf full of delicious food. Ves-rynia giggled and leaned over. "Here, watch me. Use your bread to scoop up the fish and greens."

"At home, we have metal forks and spoons," Akeela said. She tore off a piece of bread and wedged it under the fish. Using her thumb, she lifted it, grabbed some greens with her fingers, and set them on top. Then she took a bite. The spicy fish and cool greens were the perfect combination, and Akeela chewed with her eyes closed.

"I'm thinking she likes it, yeh?"

Akeela opened her eyes to see Vorrak-ira and Hawk approaching with leaves of their own.

Akeela blushed. "It's really good. I've never had this kind of fish before."

Hawk sat next to her. "Kingfish is our most abundant kind. It's also the biggest. One kingfish can feed ten people. And in spring, salmon come up our streams."

"Is it true you actually eat the meat of land animals?" Vorrak-ira asked, his mouth full of berries.

Akeela nodded.

"That's nasty. I'd rather eat scat."

Ves-rynia gave a short laugh. "Leaves. Grass. Green."

Akeela shook her head. "What?"

"It's the leaf calling the grass green," Hawk explained. "Meaning you're no different."

"Oh. But what's scat?" Akeela scooped up more fish and stuffed it in her mouth.

Hawk grinned. "Animal waste."

Akeela choked, and Ves-rynia patted her back. She turned to her brother, who was laughing so hard, tears ran down his face. "If you don't knock it off, we're going to sit someplace else, yeh?"

Hawk put his hand on Akeela's arm. "Don't go. I've waited so long to meet you. Please, let's just talk."

"Okay, but let's not talk about, um, scat." Akeela looked— really looked—into Hawk's eyes for the first time. Then she glanced down and saw the silver ring on her left forefinger. Fairy feet! She'd completely forgotten about Ham. Ves-rynia was talking, so she forced herself to pay attention. Anything to stop the pounding of her heart.

The sun began to set, and the meal passed much too quickly for Akeela. She learned Hawk's mother, Dar-dra, had been an Acadian. Ves-rynia and Vorrak-ira's father was her brother. When Tar traveled, as he often did, Hawk stayed with his cousins.

"Where do you get the material for your clothes?" Akeela asked. Acadians dressed differently than the people of her village, but their clothing was still made of green and brown cloth. The women dressed the same as the men, with tunics and close-fitting pants, and wore shoes Akeela had never seen before —leather strips attached to a sole. Ves-rynia called them strappers.

Vorrak-ira rolled up his leaf, then licked his fingers and belched. "Some no-rooter comes once a week. A peddler. We trade him nacre seeds, laurales oil, and goat milk or cheese for material and other things we need, yeh?"

Akeela frowned. "No-rooter?"

Ves-rynia set down her mug. "Someone who is not Acadian."

"Oh."

"Don't worry. We welcome no-rooters," Ves-rynia said. "If we didn't, where would that leave Hawk, yeh?"

Krezma walked up with Anon. "Here, I've had him long enough. He wanted to see you."

Akeela put out her arms. "Hello, Anon. Come sit with me. Did you have something to eat?"

"After the sweet course, you need to come to the meeting circle." Krezma glared at Hawk before glaring at Akeela. "Alone. We have plans to make and quickly."

"Of course."

Krezma left, and Vorrak-ira gave a short laugh. "What's up her trunk?"

Akeela shrugged and glanced at Hawk. He smiled, and for a moment, no one else existed. Anon's voice broke into her thoughts.

"Want dessert, Keela."

Akeela hugged him. "So do I, Anon. But I want you to meet some new friends." She turned to Ves-rynia first. "This is Ves-rynia. She's very nice."

Anon grinned. "Vessie."

Ves-rynia chuckled. "It's nice to meet you, Anon, yeh?"

Vorrak-ira wasn't as polite. "What kind of critter are you?"

Anon leaned over and grinned at him.

"Haw! He's a dupeseed if ever I saw one, yeh?"

Akeela glared at Vorrak-ira. She clenched her fists and tried to keep her voice from shaking, but to no avail. "He's a faun. And he's what we call *touched*. He can't help the way he is!"

Ves-rynia shoved her brother. "Who's a dupeseed?"

Akeela forced her anger back down. It served no purpose to alienate these people. "It's a shame more people aren't like Anon. He does nothing to hurt anyone."

Vorrak-ira had the decency to look ashamed.

Hawk stood and reached out to Akeela. "I'm ready for the sweet course. What did Anon call it? Dessert?"

Akeela smiled and took Hawk's hand. "Yes, Anon loves dessert." She turned to Anon. "This is Hawk. He's"—she realized what Ves-rynia had said about Hawk's mother, Dar-dra—"wait, you're Tar's son?"

"Guilty."

"I—oh, well, okay." She turned back to Anon. "He's our friend."

Anon examined Hawk's face. "Like Hawk," he finally said.

Hawk laughed. "That's good, yeh?"

Akeela hugged Anon. "It is."

Ves-rynia picked up her leaf and mug and waved her free hand at Akeela. "You and Hawk take Anon to get, um, dessert. I'll take our leaves and mugs and catch up with you, yeh?"

Akeela and Anon followed Hawk. It seemed to Akeela the most natural thing in the world. She rubbed her gloved hand, remembering the birthmark there, her quest, and Ham.

She'd been in Hawk's dreams. Maybe her destiny included him somehow. Akeela shivered. As much as she'd like that, it was impossible.

She was another man's wife.

Chapter Fifteen

Akeela's eyes grew heavy as the conversation droned on. Fire fairies flitted like sparks among the flames in the middle of the circle. They were the only ones left—the earth fairies and water fairies had gone long ago, and she wasn't sure where the air fairies were.

Those creatures were the most mysterious, only revealing themselves as hummingbirds at whim. Akeela could count on one hand the number of times she'd seen them. If only she could fly away with them to wherever they went. True, she'd promised Oret —Grandfather—she'd find the Fairystone, and she wanted to keep that promise. But she was so tired.

"We must be ready to leave on the morning next," Krezma said. "Time is against us, and we must move quickly."

As the Acadian leader, Ban-ira spoke for the kin-tribe. "We will provide all you need for this journey. And we can give you a good supply of nacre seeds and laurales oil for needs along the way."

Krezma bowed her head. "My thanks, Ban-ira. We could not attempt this quest without your aid."

Akeela stifled a yawn. She looked down at Anon, who'd gone

to sleep long ago. What would happen to him? She couldn't leave him, but would he be safe going along?

"My son, Hawk, will join us," Tar announced.

Akeela forgot her weariness. Her heart pounded, and she clutched Anon, causing him to stir. Hawk would travel with them! Feeling his gaze, she met his smiling eyes across the circle. Her lips curved upward, and she blushed, hoping the light of the fire would hide her feelings.

Ser-dan stood and motioned for the group to be silent. "My grandson, Vorrak-ira, will also accompany you, yeh? He is an expert with a sling and will afford protection, if needed."

Vorrak'ira punched the air.

Akeela stopped herself from groaning just in time. Instead, she held her breath and let it out slowly.

Ban-ira nodded. "Aye, it's true. Well done, Ser-dan. Vorrak-ira will also join the group." He turned to Tar. "Is this agreeable with you?"

Tar's eyes darted from Hawk to Vorrak-ira. He gave a quick nod.

Krezma sat next to Akeela and stroked Anon's head. "Now the men will pray and share a ceremonial meal. We can take our leave and prepare for sleep."

"I *am* tired," Akeela admitted, helping Anon up.

As they walked, Akeela braced herself for what was surely going to be ugly. Finally, Krezma spoke.

"Do you know what you've done, not bringing your husband?"

Akeela's throat went dry. She'd hoped Krezma would forget. "I thought you'd be able to keep Oret alive. Truly, I did."

Krezma stopped walking. "Foolish, selfish child! I know not how long it will take before the fairy realm begins to crumble. Even if you were to find all four pieces of the Fairystone tonight and become the Guardian, how long would that last? You will not live forever, and if you are not with child before you find the stones, the line ends with you."

"I'm sorry! I never meant to—I want to help—" Akeela

paused. She couldn't turn back time, but maybe she could return to the village. "I will go back to Broem and get Ham."

"I will get him myself," Krezma snapped. "As soon as you leave, I will turn back and fetch him. Unless you feel you are with child already."

"How am I supposed to know something like that?" She couldn't keep the sarcasm out of her voice. "It's not like you ever explained anything to me!"

"What are you talking about?"

Akeela faced her. "Coupling! Why didn't you tell me how much it was going to hurt? How humiliating it is? Why didn't you prepare me?"

Krezma started to speak, but Akeela kept going.

"No, no more talking. You lied to me my whole life! Why do I even wonder why you didn't prepare me?"

"It's not that way when you love your husband," Krezma whispered.

"But I *don't* love Ham." Akeela ground out the words. "And I don't love you, so go do what you think necessary. I'm only going on this quest for Oret."

Krezma gave her a queer look, between sorrow and pity. Akeela turned, grabbed Anon's hand, and starting walking.

They walked to the tree house in silence. In spite of her exhaustion, Akeela lay awake long after Krezma started snoring.

"It feels strange!" Akeela giggled as she turned around. "What does it look like?"

Ves-rynia smiled and brushed her hand across Akeela's shoulder. "It looks like what every other Acadian looks like, yeh?"

"But I've never worn pants before. I'll never get used to it."

"Of course you will. Now, let's put on some water. I'm starving, yeh?"

Akeela grabbed her glove and followed Ves-rynia through the tree roots and into the open air. She stifled a laugh as the pants brushed against her legs and was still smiling when they ran across Hawk and Vorrak-ira.

"Sapo." Hawk gave the standard Acadian greeting that Akeela learned also meant "good life." He held out his hands, palms up. Akeela touched them lightly with hers and did the same with Vorrak-ira.

Vorrak-ira snickered. "There's that glove again."

Akeela chose to ignore him. She glanced at Hawk, brushed her hand down the pants, and smiled.

Hawk tapped her shoulder. "What's the joke?"

Akeela shook her head. "Joke?"

"Aye, you were smiling."

Her cheeks burned, and she gave a short laugh. "Oh, well, I'm just not used to Acadian clothing, that's all."

Hawk's grin told her he didn't believe her.

Vorrak-ira stretched and yawned, rubbing his stomach. "Quit chewing bark and let's go. I'm so hungry I could eat a whole king-fish myself."

Ves-rynia rolled her eyes. "Wouldn't be the first time."

The foursome enjoyed breakfast together near the stream on the west side of camp. The twins' mother had prepared flatcakes topped with honey and apples. Akeela ate every bite and rinsed her hands in the icy water. The Acadian camp radiated peace and unity, yet apprehension about leaving plagued her.

Hawk grabbed her hand. "Come with me. I want to show you something."

Vorrak-ira stepped alongside them. "Is this a private party or can we come, too?"

No, Akeela thought. *You can't.*

"Uh, sure," Hawk said.

The four walked without talking until they came to a clearing. Akeela squinted at the bright sunlight. She'd gotten used to the trees filtering the light in the forest. It felt warmer, too. Then she noticed the clearing was more than just a space absent of trees. It was a circle of dirt. Nothing green grew there.

"On the other side of this clearing is a group of Laurales trees,"

Hawk said. "Celtar provided us with these amazing trees after the battle with the mud gnomes."

They skirted the clearing and walked into the shadow of the forest again. Akeela stepped over a log, marveling how comfortable the strappers were on her feet, even though it was strange to see her toes.

Hawk stopped and pointed. "The clearing we just walked around—that's where the battle took place. It's said the great Acadian warrior, Ad-vor, singlehandedly fought five mud gnomes who'd cut down trees to clear the ground for a new commune."

Akeela wrinkled her eyebrows. "What does that mean?"

Vorrak-ira tossed a small rock toward the trees. "It's where gnomes live and stink up the place, yeh?"

Akeela bit off a caustic remark. Vorrak-ira was beginning to get on her nerves.

"Well, in a matter of speaking, aye, they do," Hawk said. "They clear every living thing from an area, then bring wagon after wagon of clay and jugs of water. They dig up the ground, roots and all, and work the clay and water in. When it's good and slimy, they use it as a refuse dump."

Vorrak-ira elbowed Akeela. "A scat dump, yeh?"

Ves-rynia shoved him and hooked her arm through Akeela's. "Ignore that dupeseed. He's always been a little on the rough side of the bark."

Akeela smiled at her friend, then turned back to Hawk. "So what happened?"

"Well, after the area is rank, the gnomes move in. They make huts of sticks, straw, and mud, much like beavers do, and that's where they live. Then they drain the area of every living thing." Hawk started walking again. "It's said that Ad-vor came across these five gnomes who'd cut down trees and were working clay into the dirt. Acadians believe trees are sacred, and Ad-vor was especially passionate, so you can imagine how he felt when he saw that happening, yeh?"

Akeela nodded.

Vorrak-ira swung his arms around. "He grabbed one of the tree trunks and beat those gnomes into wood pulp!"

"Oh!" Akeela said.

"And nothing has ever grown back," Hawk said. "But the spring after that, the Acadians noticed new trees growing outside the dead area. And here they are."

They stopped before a group of trees unfamiliar to Akeela. She studied their auras, which were red and not the soft yellow of plants. They gave off a pungent smell and bore three differently shaped leaves.

Hawk tapped a trunk. A small, hollow stick protruded, and a wooden bucket sat underneath, catching liquid that dripped from the stick. "This is one way we gather oil. The other is to grind and squeeze branches or roots, but we usually don't do that unless we're desperate."

Ves-rynia picked a leaf and tore it in half. "Here, smell this."

Akeela breathed in the spicy scent. "Mm, yes, it's like the tea I had."

"Aye, we make saloop from leaves or roots." Ves-rynia dropped the ripped leaf. "And when the dried leaves are ground into powder, we use it to thicken our goulash."

Vorrak-ira rolled his eyes. "So now that Akeela knows about our sacred tree, let's go have some fun, yeh?"

Hawk crossed his arms. "Akeela needs to know about the nacre, too."

"Aw, you can be so serious sometimes, Hawk. Come find me when you lighten up, yeh?"

Akeela, Hawk, and Ves-rynia watched Vorrak-ira stalk away. Ves-rynia put her arm around Akeela. "I'm sorry for my brother. The older he gets, the more he remains a sapling."

Akeela just nodded. She didn't want to talk about him anymore. "So, Hawk, what is a nacre seed?"

"Come on. I'll explain as we walk. The pinsapo trees are on the other side of camp. You've probably seen them; they're similar to pine trees. They're green in spring and summer and turn silver in winter. The tree's seed and the nacre seed look the same on the outside—small, kind of round, and wrapped tightly in a leaf-like covering."

Ves-rynia took up the explanation. "The only way to see what's inside is to throw the pods into the fire. The wrapping burns away and reveals either a brown seed or a gleaming, white nacre seed."

"Yes, but what *is* a nacre seed?" Akeela asked.

Hawk lifted a large, low-hanging branch so the girls could pass underneath. "It's actually a type of jewel. It's smooth and round most of the time, although sometimes we find an oval."

"You use it for adornment?" Akeela asked.

Ves-rynia nodded. "Some seeds are made into necklaces, yeh? Some are used for trade, like gold coins."

"Why are you telling me all this?"

Hawk grabbed her left hand. "I want you to know us."

Akeela couldn't think of a thing to say.

They walked through the camp. Children played much as the children in Broem did, running and laughing. Women could be seen here and there, working in gardens. The men were working the larger fields.

Hawk told Akeela he usually worked alongside the men when he stayed with the kin-tribe. "Today is different, though, because we're leaving in the morning."

Akeela's peace shattered. She glanced at Ves-rynia, who was getting a basket from her mother. If only there were no witch and no prophecy and no Dark Lord. She would be content to stay with these Acadians. And Hawk.

Ves-rynia walked up, swinging the basket. "Let's go."

They walked through camp until they got to a cluster of pine-like trees. Pinsapo trees, Hawk had called them. She observed their auras, a white glow, like mist over the lake in the morning. Again, trees with auras different than the surrounding plants.

Hawk pulled a brown pod from the tree. "These are what we pick to find nacre seeds. But only pick the brown ones. Leave the green ones."

Akeela pulled off two brown pods and inspected them closely.

One gave off a soft yellow glow. The other shone with faint purple. "These are different."

Hawk and Ves-rynia looked at the pods in her hands. "How can you tell?" Ves-rynia asked. "They look exactly the same to me, yeh?"

Akeela's face burned. How foolish she was. Krezma had told her over and over again to keep her gift to herself. She fumbled to cover her blunder. "I—I don't know. They just feel different." She dropped them in the basket and turned back to the tree.

When the basket was almost full, Ves-rynia said, "That's enough," and they walked back to camp for the midday meal. Akeela felt something akin to sparks whenever she met Hawk's eyes. It was exciting and uncomfortable. She liked it and wondered if Hawk felt it, too.

As if she'd asked the question aloud, Hawk smiled at her and nodded.

Tzmet squinted at the map. The Earth Fountain should be close. Nightshade pawed the sand and tossed his head.

"Patience, my pet, patience. The journey is almost complete."

She slid from the horse's back and stood before him. The sun burned relentlessly, and Tzmet shaded her eyes. She studied the map again and pointed to the drawing of a cluster of rocks.

"That is what we need to find. Why isn't it here?"

Nightshade whinnied.

"Silence, you fool horse. I have to concentrate."

Nightshade nudged her with his nose.

"Stop it! If I don't find the fountain soon, we'll run out of water." She faced him. "Unless I levitate myself back and leave your carcass here to rot."

Nightshade gave a whinny that could've easily been a laugh, as if he knew she couldn't manage such a feat.

"Idiot," Tzmet murmured.

The hot breeze was incessant. Tzmet took off her head

covering and wiped her face. She hated to admit Brimridge had been right about her needing the wretched hat.

Nightshade grunted and started walking west. Tzmet replaced the hat and followed. "I will not walk this desert. Come back here, you miserable animal."

He responded by breaking into a trot.

"Argh!" Tzmet considered blasting him into oblivion but stopped just short of it. She needed him for the ride home. She rolled up the scroll and tucked it into her belt. "You are stew, my friend. As soon as we get back, you are stew."

The horse was soon out of sight, and Tzmet hurried to follow his prints in the sand before the breeze blew them away.

Akeela dropped two pinsapo pods into the fire. One that glimmered yellow and one that had the purple aura. She watched closely to see if there would be a different seed in each pod.

The fire licked greedily at the coverings. Akeela expected the balls to burst into flames, but instead, the edges melted away, glowing as bright as embers. Layer by layer, the covering burned away. After a minute, objects emerged from the charred remains. The pod with the yellow aura revealed a brown seed. The purple one brought forth a gleaming, white nacre seed.

Hawk picked the seeds out of the fire with metal tongs. He dropped the brown seed into one basket and the nacre into another. "We did well," he said. "There are more nacre seeds than pinsapo." He smiled at Akeela. "You must be lucky."

Akeela didn't trust herself to say anything, so she just nodded. She had picked all purple pods, guessing the pods with the yellow glow were simply plant seeds. After years of looking at yellow plant auras, when she saw purple, she knew those pods had to be different.

Hawk leaned closer, poking the smoldering pods with a stick. "Meet me at the clearing after everyone goes to sleep," he whispered.

Akeela froze for a second. Her throat constricted, but she gave a small nod. *Dear Celtar,* she prayed. *What am I doing?*

Akeela tiptoed around the clearing. Hawk's aura glowed near the laurales trees. Her heart hammered against her chest. Was this stupidity—or destiny?

She hastened her steps, and they met before the largest tree. They clung to each other, as if terrified. Akeela pulled back and grasped his arms. "Hawk, we shouldn't."

Hawk stroked her long hair, which she'd left hanging loose. "Why not?"

"We have to be up early tomorrow."

Hawk laughed.

Akeela pulled away. "Don't laugh at me."

"I'm not laughing *at* you. You just make me so happy!"

"You don't know me. If you did, I might not make you feel that way."

Hawk lowered his voice. "What's your deep, dark secret? You can trust me, yeh?"

It was Akeela's turn to laugh.

"No, really," he said. "You tell me a secret, and I'll tell you one."

Akeela felt the need to share her gift with someone. Why not Hawk? He had a secret too, after all. "I have a gift called spirit-sight. I can see a glow, called an aura, around living things. And I can see fairies, even when they're disguised."

"Interesting. Must be why you're going to be the next Fairy Guardian, whatever that is."

"I suppose."

They stood quiet for a minute.

"I'm so relieved you know," Akeela said. "It's hard to hide it all the time. Krezma has always warned me to keep it secret. She says it will save my life someday."

Hawk led her to a log. They sat. "Are you really going to be the next Fairy Guardian?"

Akeela shrugged. "Well, yes. Oret said so, and the prophecy talks about runes."

"Prophecy? Runes?"

"I have a birthmark on my hand—a circle of runes that spell out *guardian*. I'm supposed to find the Fairystone and place it in the middle." She hesitated a moment, then slipped off the glove. "See?"

Hawk leaned forward and studied the mark in the moonlight. "What happens then?"

"I don't know exactly. I become the Fairy Guardian, I guess." She shrugged again. "Okay, it's your turn. What's your secret?"

Hawk smiled. "I don't think my secret is a secret to you."

"What are you talking about?"

"This." And before Akeela could blink, he was kissing her.

For a moment, everything was still. Then something *shifted* inside the depths of her core. There was a snap, and suddenly her vision filled with shooting light. No, not exactly light. An aura. One she'd never seen before. Hawk seemed oblivious as he held her close and nuzzled her neck.

Akeela clung to him. Not out of desire, but necessity. If she let go, she'd drown in the aura. Whose light was she seeing? It was white. Silver. Golden. Sunlight and moonlight combined.

As Hawk slowly moved back, Akeela held her hands outstretched. She watched as the golden-silver light melted into her skin.

Dear Celtar! It was *her* aura! She had an aura? Her brain couldn't grasp what her eyes clearly saw.

They sat without talking for a minute. The light of the three moons cast a brilliance that trickled down through the leaves. Hawk lifted her left hand to his lips. Then he fingered the silver band on her forefinger, and Akeela remembered. She was *married*! How could she reveal this to Hawk? Face flushed, she opened her mouth to confess, but nothing came out.

Hawk squeezed her hand. "Is anything wrong?"

She should tell him. She should. But she couldn't. "Not really. I'm just a little nervous." Which was true.

He stared at her a minute, and she knew she hadn't fooled him.

But he didn't accuse her. He simply said, "We should probably go back. We leave in the morning."

"Yes, we should."

Hawk nodded, then wrapped his arm around her shoulders. Akeela sighed, closed her eyes, and silenced the voice in her head that sounded a lot like Krezma.

Neither one moved to leave.

Chapter Sixteen

Akeela tried to resist the hand that tugged her arm.

"Come on, sleepyhead. It's time to get ready, yeh?"

She opened one eye and peered up at Ves-rynia, who was already dressed and looking way too bright eyed for this ungodly hour of the morning.

Of course, you stayed out way too long with Hawk, she told herself, smiling. *But it was worth it.* She stretched and sat up. "Do I hear rain?"

Ves-rynia picked up a tunic and tossed it at her. "Aye, it's raining. A blessing of Celtar for your quest."

Akeela pulled her nightdress over her head. She slipped into the tunic, then reached for her brush. "How is traveling in the rain a blessing?"

Ves-rynia grabbed the brush. "Here, let me." She began at the ends of Akeela's hair and worked the brush in short strokes up the length. "I've watched you do this for the last two mornings. The rain is always a blessing. Our minister, Dir-mac, says it's a symbol of Celtar's cleansing and His bringing life to all."

It felt wonderful for Ves-rynia to brush the tangles out of her hair. Krezma hadn't done that since she was small. And Akeela hadn't braided it before she'd collapsed on her mat, not wanting to chance waking Krezma. It was bad enough she'd sneaked out in the first place.

She turned and looked at her new friend. "I wish you were going with us."

Ves-rynia gave her a mysterious smirk. She handed Akeela the brush and stood. "Hurry and pack the rest of your things. I'll bring food, yeh?"

Akeela pulled on pants. "Please find Anon for me. I need to see him before we go."

What was she going to do about Anon? He'd hidden himself away when they'd left the village. Would he do the same now? But she couldn't leave without saying goodbye.

Krezma had given her a large sack for her personal things. Akeela decided to leave her dresses. They'd be here when she returned. If *I come back*, a little voice echoed in her head. "I will be back," she said out loud.

Still, her tension increased with each item she put in the sack. Her brush, two tunics, one pair of pants, and the strappers—since it was raining, she'd wear her deerskin boots—and an extra archery glove. Her cloak could be placed in the cart for convenience.

Anon poked his furry head around the doorway. He looked sleepy.

"Good morn, Anon. Come, have breakfast with me."

Ves-rynia followed him in and set down a leaf of small, round cakes with red berries baked into them, some greens in laurales oil, and a generous amount of speckled green fruit roasted and cut in slices.

Akeela helped Anon get started. "Anon, I have something to tell you." He munched on a cake. Crumbs fell to the floor. "I have to go on a trip again, but this time, you can't come."

"Go with Keela." He dropped the cake. "Go with Keela."

"Anon, it's not safe. Bad people. Danger."

The little faun burst into tears. Akeela hugged him close. "Please don't cry. Hawk is coming. He will protect me."

"Go with Keela." Anon's voice was muffled against her chest.

She turned to Ves-rynia. "Short of tying him up, I don't know how you're going to keep him here."

Ves-rynia popped a piece of green fruit into her mouth. She chewed it and shrugged. "Don't know how you're going to keep me from going too, yeh?"

Akeela's eyes grew wide. "You're coming? Oh, I was hoping you would! Your father never said a thing."

Ves-rynia grinned. "He doesn't know yet."

"But—"

Akeela stopped when she heard someone enter the tree. She picked up a cake and took a bite, hoping to appear normal.

Krezma came into the room, her clothes damp. "Finish eating. We must leave and soon."

Akeela still held Anon. "Krezma, Anon will be going with us. And before you say anything, hear me out. What are we going to do? Lock him up? And for how long? You know he will try to follow."

Krezma tugged on her braid. "What you say is true. But do you realize the danger you will put him, and the group, in?"

Akeela glared at her. "I will be responsible for him."

Krezma stared back. "Child, you are the leader of this quest. It's your journey to make. I cannot tell you what to do anymore."

Akeela sat without speaking. This was the first time Krezma had acknowledged Akeela's importance. It felt . . . good. Krezma didn't say anything more about Ham, but Akeela felt the unspoken rebuke. It took away any pleasure she might've felt in Krezma's statement. She rubbed Anon's head, between his ears.

Ves-rynia cleared her throat. "If you're finished, I'll clear up, yeh?"

"Okay, Anon," Akeela said. "You can come with us."

Anon squealed, and Akeela couldn't help her smile.

Tzmet woke to something warm and sticky on her face. She tried to brush it off, but to no avail. "What the —?"

Nightshade stood above her, licking her cheek.

She rolled away. "You vile, disgusting creature! Where have you been?"

She'd followed his hooves' imprints until she could see them no more. Tired and frustrated, she'd sat in the sand and eventually had fallen asleep. Now she stood and stretched. The rays of the sun were just appearing on the horizon.

"If you want water, come here."

The horse complied, and Tzmet drew the waterskin from the pack she'd used as a pillow. She took a long drink and then poured some in the leather bag. Nightshade drank thirstily.

"Now, where are we? If you've brought us off course, I will kill you and worry about getting home later." Tzmet walked around him, looking in all directions. She rubbed the back of her hand across her chapped lips. "Curse this desert! Why didn't I find the Water Fountain instead?"

Nightshade whinnied.

"All right, all right, enough of your sass. Don't walk away from me again." Tzmet slung the pack over one shoulder and pulled herself up on the horse. She clutched the reins and kicked. "Get going, you miserable, lazy thing."

They took off in the opposite direction of the rising sun. Tzmet cursed as she bounced, vowing to never ride a horse again. But within a few minutes, she gasped.

Straight ahead was the circle of stones indicated on the map. The wretched fool horse had found it! It'd only taken two days. Far be it from her not to give credit where it was due.

Tzmet patted Nightshade's neck. "Well, done," she said. "Well done."

Akeela sat next to Anon on the cart. She tried to calm her thoughts, but Ves-rynia's father's angry voice kept going round and round in her head. Father and daughter had argued loudly while Tar hooked up Mule and finished loading the cart. In the end, Vesrynia had joined the group, but without her father's blessing.

The light rain eventually soaked through the group's clothing. Akeela pulled her cloak around Anon and shivered. They were proceeding north, toward the Undaeus Mountains, where the Kazmura's caves were supposed to be. Tar had shown her on the map, but she didn't entirely understand how to read a map. She gave in to her lack of sleep and dozed off.

Tzmet leaped from Nightshade's back and thrust her hands in the air. "I found it! I found it! Finally, the Earth Fountain is mine."

Nightshade snorted.

Tzmet rolled her eyes. "Very well, *you* found it."

He nickered.

"No, I'll not make you into stew—this time. But watch your step." Tzmet walked around the small circle. "Well, it looks as though we got here before the fairies." She yanked the scroll from her belt and unrolled it. "Let's see. Ah, here it is. When I find the circle of stones due west from the oasis, I need to recite these words to release the Fountain."

Nightshade snorted.

"I have no idea what they mean," Tzmet said. "Now, let me get on with it." She lifted her head and shouted, *"Braya reym sofring!"*

A tremor passed through the ground. Tzmet stepped back and held her breath. The sun broke the horizon behind her as the sand in the middle of the circle began to swirl.

"Yes!"

The swirl of sand rose higher, spinning, until it rose skyward. She tilted her head back. Her laughter twisted and rose with the fountain. The miserable trip had been worth it. She had to work fast, before the fairies realized she was here.

"The cape! I must get it."

Tzmet tore through the pack until she came to the bottom.

There, wrapped in black velvet, was her precious cape of poisoned fairy wings. She lifted it out and carefully opened it. The wings fluttered in the breeze the fountain made, shimmering iridescent in the rising sunlight. She whirled it around and settled it on her shoulders. Time to see if it would work as she'd planned.

"Watch, Nightshade, and see how I will personally get the advantage of those uppity fairies."

She stepped to the fountain and stretched out her left arm. It was her intention to touch the swirling sands and poison them, but as soon as her fingers came in contact with the fountain, horrific burning raced up her fingers to her elbow. She grabbed her hand and shrieked in pain. Dropping to her knees, she slowly released her hand so she could look at it.

Her fingers were blistered and swollen. The sands had taken off several layers of skin. Tzmet's eyes burned. Curses! She blinked rapidly. She would *not* be reduced to weeping.

Nightshade nickered and tossed his head. He walked to her and stood, blocking the sun, as though he knew she needed protection from the blazing heat.

Tzmet reached for the pack and pulled out the waterskin. She poured some over her burning fingers. Then she wrapped her injured hand in a piece of cloth she ripped from her tunic.

She tightened the knot with her right hand and teeth, then stood. "I will not be beaten. I will poison this fountain if it kills me!"

And saying so, she ripped the cape off her shoulders and threw it at the fountain. The sands caught it and carried it up, up, up. Nothing happened at first. Then the sands began to grow dark. A high-pitched whistle replaced the soft swish, and all at once, the fountain collapsed into a dark-red puddle. The cape fluttered down, and Tzmet caught it.

The puddle oozed into the sand and disappeared.

Tzmet stood silently for a moment. Then she smirked and turned away. "Stupid fairies." She mounted Nightshade and kicked him into a trot.

One fountain down. Three more to go.

Chapter Seventeen

Akeela drifted out of sleep. She opened her eyes, not sure where she was. The cart jolted to a stop, and she sat up. Mule brayed loudly, refusing to move.

"What is it?" she asked.

Krezma sat on a stump, her hand over her heart.

Akeela eased Anon onto the seat and jumped off the cart. "Krezma, what's wrong?"

"I'm not sure, child. I have a feeling of dread—strong, so strong."

Akeela looked around. Something felt off. What was it? She frowned as she thought. Then she fell to her knees as it hit her. "The trees. The plants. I can't see their auras. Krezma, what's happened?"

"I know not. Give me time to think and pray."

Tar shook his head. "We cannot stop. We must keep moving."

Krezma waved her hand. "Yes, yes, we'll keep going. Here, help me into the cart. I'll sit with Anon for a while."

Akeela walked next to Ves-rynia, and they clasped hands. The lack of color around the plants made Akeela dizzy. Incomplete. She glanced back at Hawk, who was bringing up the rear with Vorrak-ira, and he smiled. But she could see he was worried.

The rain slowed as they walked, and the group made steady progress until midday. They stopped for a quick meal, and at Tar's urging, began their journey again.

The sun broke through the clouds at dinnertime, and it seemed to ease everyone's spirits. Akeela sat next to Hawk during the meal. Tar had allowed a small fire. Akeela gazed at the flames, willing a fire fairy to come and give them news.

Hawk's voice broke into her thoughts. "Would you like more bread?"

Akeela shook her head. "Hawk, something is terribly wrong with the plants. I can see animal auras and everyone else's auras, but I can't see anything around the plants."

Ves-rynia frowned. "I don't know what you mean. What are auras?"

"Every living thing has an aura. It's energy, a life force. I've always been able to see them." Akeela's voice caught in her throat. She was so distressed, she didn't care she'd blurted out her secret. "What if I'm losing my gift?"

Krezma frowned. "That's enough. What did I tell you? And you are not losing anything. Something evil is afoot, I'm sure of it."

Vorrak-ira threw a piece of bread into the fire. "You're all off your nuts. This whole thing is just plain stupid. I don't know why I'm even here. I mean, I was told there would be fighting, yeh? I was ready and . . . nothing."

Ves-rynia burst into tears.

Akeela put her arms around her friend and rocked her. *Please, Celtar, send us a fire fairy.*

Tar paced near the cart. Even Mule, who was usually content to munch on whatever he could reach, shuffled and stamped a front hoof now and then. Krezma sat with her eyes closed, praying. The tension became unbearable.

The fire crackled, and Akeela glanced up. Thank Celtar! A fire fairy hovered in the flames. Akeela released Ves-rynia and moved closer. She could barely speak. "Good fairy, what news do you bring?"

"We need your help. The Earth Fountain has been poisoned."

Krezma opened her eyes. "What is this?"

"The Earth Fountain! Please. Come. Earth fairies are sick. They're dying."

Akeela looked at Krezma's white face, and her heart sank. If Krezma was afraid, what were they going to do?

"I must go to the Fountain," Krezma said. She turned to Akeela. "Child, you must continue on the quest. You must! If you fail, all is lost."

"But I—"

Krezma shushed her. "Come with me. I must gather my things. I must speak to you."

Akeela nodded. She trembled as she walked to the cart. The earth fairies were dying. Why? How could Krezma help?

"Child, listen to me well." Krezma spoke as she sorted through bags. "If the Earth Fountain is poisoned, it will spread into the ground and the plants. The only thing keeping Riss'aird's ashes in the ground is the earth fairies' magic."

Akeela gripped her hands together. "Does that mean—"

"Aye. Without the goodness the earth fairies sow into the ground, Riss'aird could soon rise from the ashes."

"What do I do?"

Krezma rummaged through a sack and brought out a small leather bag. "Here, take this. It's a mixture of my own. Make tea with it and see that everyone, especially the Acadians, drinks. It will slow the effects."

Akeela took the bag. "Effects of what?"

Krezma set the sack on the ground. "Child, think! The Acadians are tied to the earth. If poison flows through the ground, it will not only affect the plants, but also Vorrak-ira and Ves-rynia."

"In what way?"

"I know not. I only know you must be on guard."

She didn't want to ask, but she had to. "Does this mean you're not going to Broem?"

"How can I? If you had done what I asked, we wouldn't be in this predicament."

Tears filled Akeela's eyes. "I'm sorry."

"Sorry will not save the fairies." Krezma paused. "As soon as I heal the fountain, I will go to Broem."

Akeela took a deep breath and let it out. She should be more worried about the fairies, but she imagined her new friends hurting and couldn't bear it. "What about Hawk? He is half Acadian."

Krezma looked into Akeela's eyes, then rested her hand on Akeela's arm. "He may be affected. He may not. You and Tar must keep your heads. You are our only hope, child. You have to find the Fairystone." She picked up the sack.

"Will you be back?"

"If Celtar ordains it."

"With Ham?"

Krezma grunted.

Akeela clutched the bag of herbs to her chest as Krezma slipped through the trees. Trees without auras. She felt helpless, desperately foolish, and so very selfish. When she couldn't see Krezma anymore, Akeela turned toward the group. A feeling of despair filled her, but she swallowed it and took a trembling breath.

"I'll make us some tea."

Tzmet opened her eyes. Her own bedroom came into focus. How did she get here? The last thing she remembered was giving Night-shade his lead after they'd left the fountain.

She sat up, her head spinning. Moaning, she lifted a hand to her forehead. Shuffling got her attention, and two Hinwari entered the room with food and drink. Brimridge followed close behind.

Brimridge bowed. "Welcome back, my lady."

Tzmet opened her mouth to speak, but only a croak came out.

Her eyes widened, and she grabbed her throat. Sharp pain shot through her hand, and she groaned. She looked down at a clean bandage.

"You came back two days ago," Brimridge said. "We thought you were dead. Here, drink this. It will soothe your parched throat."

Tzmet glared at the boggart. She didn't trust him, but she was thirsty. She sniffed the steaming cup of tea and didn't detect anything poisonous. The first sip stung, and she coughed. The second sip felt better, and she drained the contents.

The cup clattered onto the tray.

Brimridge smiled, revealing black, rotten teeth. Tzmet wrinkled her nose and glanced away before lifting the lid on the tray. Ah, yes. Scrambled eggs with goat cheese and leeks. It seemed a lifetime since she'd eaten good food.

"My lady, were you successful?"

She nodded and lifted a forkful of eggs to her mouth.

Brimridge pulled a chair next to her bed and sat. "While you eat and are refreshed, I will tell you what has happened in your absence."

Tzmet nodded again.

He told her the boggarts had settled in downstairs, planted a garden of skunk cabbage, and fixed the loose stones in the outer wall. "We have to eat from your kitchen, of course, until our crop comes in."

Tzmet grunted.

"When you rode in two days ago and we realized you were not dead, we carried you up here. My wife, herself, tended to your hand as best she could without medicine. It is clean and covered." Brimridge leaned forward. "Can you tell me what happened?"

Tzmet dropped the fork on the tray. "I—" She clutched her throat and swallowed. "I burned it in that wretched fountain," she whispered, every word stabbing her throat. "But it did not prevent me from completing my mission."

"The fountain is poisoned?"

"Yes. Now, take this tray and leave me. I'm exhausted."

Brimridge complied. When Tzmet was alone, she turned and set her feet over the edge of the bed. She tried to stand, but her head spun and her legs shook as though she'd never walked before. Tzmet sighed and lay back down. She would try again later.

It was enough right now to know the Earth Fountain was hers.

Akeela shook out the last of the herbs Krezma had left. Six days on the road without a word from the fairies had killed all hope. Tar kept them going at a hectic pace. Ves-rynia wept almost constantly. Vorrak-ira brooded, and Hawk barely spoke at all. Akeela was numb. She had no idea how or why she kept going.

She carried two mugs to Vorrak-ira and Ves-rynia. "Here, the last of Krezma's tea."

Vorrak-ira snorted.

Akeela blinked back tears. "It's keeping whatever has poisoned the ground from killing you."

"Thank you, Akeela." Ves-rynia's voice shook, but she took the mug and sipped.

Vorrak-ira took his mug and dumped it out.

Hawk stood up. "What are you doing?"

"I can't drink one more cup of that tea. It tastes like it was made from scat."

Ves-rynia pulled on her brother's arm. "Please, don't go pickin' new shoots. Just do what Akeela says. She's our leader, yeh?"

Vorrak-ira sneered. "What kind of leader are you, Akeela? Why haven't we found the Fairystone yet? Maybe you're taking us the wrong direction, yeh?"

Hawk dove at Vorrak-ira, and the boys crashed into the side of the cart. Mule laid his ears back and brayed. Anon cried out and skittered around the cart and into the bushes.

Ves-rynia put her hands over her ears.

Akeela's numbness fled, replaced with anger. "Stop! Stop it!"

Hawk and Vorrak-ira pounded each other, ignoring everything around them.

"Tar, do something," Akeela shouted.

Tar watched the fight for a minute, then he stepped between them. He stood with his arms crossed. "Have you had enough?"

Hawk wiped blood from the corner of his mouth. He nodded.

Vorrak-ira sat on the ground, his elbows resting on his knees. "Aye, enough."

Tar pulled Vorrak-ira to his feet. "The poison is affecting you. You know this. Have some self-control."

"Aye, uncle."

The cousins embraced each other. Akeela, still trembling, walked around the cart. She found Anon rolled up on the ground, sobbing. "Oh, Anon. Come to Akeela."

He ran to her.

She held him and patted his back. "Don't cry, sweet one. Everything is fine now. Let's have some cakes and honey. You can help me take it to the fire."

The group ate without speaking. Even Anon was quiet, except for an occasional sob. Akeela stared at her feet. She felt the weight of her rash decision to talk Ham into staying in the village. It threatened to crush her. She didn't choose to be born into Oret's family, but she was, and she had a responsibility, which she'd pushed aside for her own selfish feelings.

The wretchedness of her situation took her breath away, and if she could've, she would've lain down and died.

Krezma slid from the pony she'd coaxed from a herd of wild horses with a little magic. It had taken her several days to get to the desert, and she was tired and cranky. A group of the earth fairies who tended the Fountain sat on the circle of stones. She looked around, trying to discern what had happened.

"What can you tell me?"

One fairy stood. "Seven days ago, when we arrived right after sunrise to sing and pray for Celtar's blessing, the sands did not rise up to greet us. Instead, a dark-red puddle appeared."

Krezma frowned. "Did any of you touch it?"

"No. But we did try to sing our morning song. We've tried every morning for a week."

"Obviously, that didn't work." Krezma moved closer to the circle. "Sing for me now. I must see the red puddle."

The fairies complied, and as told, a dark-red puddle bubbled up in the sand. It stank and steamed, and Krezma's stomach lurched. Then she knelt and prayed before pulling out her herb bag and bowl.

"Pray while I work," she commanded the fairies.

Chapter Eighteen

Sunrise of the seventh morning brought a cold wind. Akeela tucked the blanket tighter around Anon as he slept next to her in the back of the cart. She, Anon, and Ves-rynia shared the cart, while Tar and the boys slept in a lean-to off the side.

Akeela edged off the cart and stepped lightly to the cold firepit. She tossed on some kindling and dead leaves. Tar had left the striking stones out. *That's unusual,* Akeela thought. But she was glad for it and picked them up to start a fire. The wind worked against her, but after a few tries, the leaves began to smoke.

She knelt and blew on the kindling. A small flame appeared, and Akeela smiled. She could feel the warmth already.

They'd stopped at the edge of the forest last night. Akeela had mixed feelings about leaving it behind. She'd never been outside the woods, but not being able to see their auras disturbed her. It might be a relief to travel where there were fewer plants.

A hand landed on her shoulder, and she jumped. "Oh!"

"You shouldn't be out here by yourself." Tar's quiet voice sent shivers up her spine.

Akeela looked up. "Tar, you scared me."

Tar squatted next to her. He held out his good hand to the

growing fire. "I've been charged with your safety. Please do not put yourself in harm's way by leaving my protection."

Akeela's face burned. "I'm sorry. I just wanted to get the fire going."

"If something happens to you, where does that leave us? You are the Guardian."

"I know. I know. It won't happen again." Akeela set a small log on the fire. She felt as much a Guardian as that log. "I need to put on the kettle. I think we should take a little extra time this morning for something hot to eat. I can make porridge. It won't take too long."

Tar nodded. "While you're cooking, I will take Hawk and Vorrak-ira to collect wood. It will be scarce from now on."

Akeela and Tar stood. He turned toward the cart, but Akeela touched his arm. "Tar, will Vorrak-ira and Ves-rynia be okay?"

"I know not. But I believe it will get worse before it gets better."

"Hawk is half-Acadian. He's already somewhat affected. What if he gets like Vorrak-ira?"

Tar put the striking stones in his tunic pocket. "Hawk is strong. While the poison will try, it will not succeed."

Akeela swallowed. Fear bubbled in her stomach, and she fought to keep it in check. She was growing to trust Tar, almost like a father. A quiet, distant father, to be sure. But was he right?

Ves-rynia gave Anon a little milk while Akeela cooked breakfast. Tar and the boys piled wood into the cart. "I guess we won't be sleeping in the cart tonight," she remarked to Ves-rynia.

"Sleep in tent?" Anon asked. His upper lip was rimmed in white, and Akeela smiled as she wiped his mouth.

"Yes, sweet one, we'll sleep in a tent tonight."

"Yay!" he said.

Ves-rynia carried wooden bowls over and set them on a log. "We won't have any milk after this."

Akeela tested the porridge. "It won't be good much longer anyway."

"What will we do for food now that we're leaving the forest and the streams?"

Akeela shrugged. "Tar is a good hunter. So am I. We have food stuffs with us, and Celtar will provide what we need."

Ves-rynia sat down. She wrapped her arms around herself and rocked. "Akeela, I'm so sad. Acadians have joy. Joy gives us strength, yeh? But my joy is gone. I can't live like this!"

Akeela moved the pot to the edge of the fire, then sat next to her friend. "It must be because of the Earth Fountain. You have to remember that and fight it. Krezma will make it right. Then your joy will come back."

"Will she, Akeela? Will she be able to fix it?"

Akeela wasn't sure. "I pray she can. But you have me. I'm here for you. We'll get through this together."

Hawk came up rubbing his stomach. "I'm starved. It smells good, Akeela."

Akeela squinted up at him. "You're talking to me now?"

He grinned. "Aye, sorry about that. Trying to keep my branches bundled."

She began spooning hot cereal into bowls. To be fair, she and Hawk didn't have time to really talk because someone was always around. But although she liked how being near him made her feel, guilt racked her. She couldn't forget her vows to Ham. It was only one kiss, she reasoned. She and Hawk would part ways once the Fairystone pieces were found, and she would go back to Ham and keep those vows.

Unless Krezma came back with him before the quest was done. Akeela shoved that thought away and continued passing bowls.

They filled their jugs with water from a small stream, and Tar encouraged them to take turns washing themselves. "But do it quickly. We must keep going."

"May I see the map?" Akeela asked when the others went off.

Tar took it out of his pocket and unrolled it. "We are here." He pointed to a section marked with trees.

"Obviously."

Tar looked at her with surprise.

169

Akeela smiled. "I'm trying to lighten things. Besides, I should know something about the map if I'm going to be Guardian. Will you show me?"

Tar gave a clipped nod, and they studied the map until the rest of the group came back. Akeela felt warm inside as she helped Anon onto the cart. Tar was a man of few words, but maybe her own father could've been the same.

The sun was high when they started out. Akeela looked back at the colorless trees. *Celtar, please help Krezma fix the fountain. Before it's too late.*

Krezma sorted through her herbs. "I will try a cleansing potion first," she said to the fairies. "When I tell you, begin your song and bring forth the fountain."

The sun's heat bore down on her, and she wiped her forehead with her sleeve. True, it might be cooler without long sleeves, but that would risk a severe burn.

"I am ready."

As the fairies rose in a circle, the leader spoke the words to call forth the fountain. *Braya reym sofring!*

Krezma heard a bubbling sound. Dark-red liquid appeared in the middle of the circle. She nodded to the fairies, and they began to sing the blessing song.

As they sang, Krezma poured her cleansing potion into the puddle. It smoked and frothed. "Keep singing," she shouted.

The tainted fountain hissed and groaned. As Krezma poured, the puddle erupted. The fairies fell back, and Krezma landed several feet from the fountain. She lay dazed for a moment, catching her breath. Just as she'd feared.

She rolled over and pushed to her feet. "We need to call fairies from the other elements. Your power has been weakened."

Several fairies flew off. Krezma turned her attention to the fountain as it sank back into the sand. This had to be the witch's work. How did she know the location of the Earth Fountain? And was she aware of the others?

Tzmet sat at the open window enjoying *caavea* and honeyed nuts. Thick, gray clouds massed together and threatened rain.

She felt stronger today, although her legs still trembled when she walked. She longed to know the effects of the poisoned fountain.

Where were those wretched fairies?

A knock sounded on her door.

"Enter," she called.

Brimridge strode in as though he owned the castle. Tzmet's irritation growled in her stomach. How she hated working with boggarts. But her father found them useful, and now that he was gaining strength, it wouldn't be long before he rose. When that happened, he would want his loyal subjects near.

Tzmet set down her cup. "What do you want?"

Brimridge bowed, and Tzmet sneered at his false respect. "I'm concerned with your health. Are you back to strength?"

Tzmet studied her fingernails. He was testing her. Well, she wouldn't allow him to think she was less than her normal self. "I am," she finally said.

Brimridge nodded. "Any news of the fountain?"

Tzmet snorted. "That is none of your affair. Your job right now is to watch for spies and traitors. Once my father has risen, he will determine exactly what you and your people are to do."

Brimridge bowed again. "As you wish, my lady."

After he left the room, Tzmet let out her breath. She hadn't realized she'd been holding it. Fire and ashes! Brimridge always provoked her. She needed to calm down, or he'd get the upper hand.

Fairies from all elements arrived at the Earth Fountain. Krezma mixed another cleansing potion, stronger this time. She'd also built a small fire to accommodate the fire fairies.

"Come," she said. "I need four of you. Earth, air, fire, and water. We must bless the potion and pray Celtar will heal the fountain."

Three fairies gathered close to Krezma's bowl and began to sing and pray. The fire fairies danced in the flames, sending sparks up and into the potion.

Krezma glanced at the noonday sun. If she couldn't heal the Fountain, she didn't know what would happen. Time was running out.

Tar pulled Mule to a stop. He looked around and pointed to a group of large rocks and thick bushes to one side. "We'll spend the night here."

Akeela sighed in relief. Her feet hurt. She'd made Ves-rynia sit in the cart with Anon since the midday meal. Eyes dull and listless, her friend seemed to be fading.

Vorrak-ira, on the other hand, had grown more and more angry, mumbling to himself. Hawk stayed close to him, but Akeela feared he wouldn't be able to withstand the building rage.

Akeela longed for fresh meat. Out of courtesy to the Acadians, they'd only been eating what vegetables, fruits, and fish they could find. There must be something she could hunt and prepare for the evening meal.

Vorrak-ira threw himself on the ground and huddled in his cloak.

No, she thought. *No meat eating for a while.* She walked to the cart. "Here, Anon, come with me. We can look for stones."

Ves-rynia stirred and opened her eyes. "He can stay with me."

"I'll take him for a while. He needs to stretch his legs." She helped him climb down. They held hands and walked to the bushes. Anon must've been as tired as the rest of them, but he didn't complain. Akeela kissed the top of his head. "You stay right here while I look around."

"Look, Keela, stones!" Anon squatted down and began to pick up and examine various stones on the ground.

Akeela studied the bushes. Still no aura. But the bushes were thick and lush, resembling red berry bushes. She hoped to find some berries, but there were none to be seen.

"Akeela, stay within my sight," Tar called.

"I will."

Akeela knew Tar meant to keep her safe, but the feeling of being trapped increased. She clenched her teeth and continued to search around the bushes for anything they could use. Lifting a bottom branch, she gasped. There was a cave opening in the rocks.

Krezma stood by the circle of stones once more. She lifted the bowl with the potion over her head and nodded. The fairies spoke the words to call the Fountain. As before, red liquid bubbled up from the sand. Krezma chanted words of blessing and poured the potion slowly into the puddle. A trembling began in the ground, and smoke rose from the tainted sands.

All the fairies lifted their voices in a song of praise to Celtar.

The liquid hissed and foamed. Krezma poured out the last of the potion and stepped back. The ground shook, and she stumbled, trying to keep her balance. The wind picked up, blowing sand in her face.

Thunder crashed overhead, and the red liquid shot into the air and began to swirl. Krezma gripped her hands and prayed fervently. As she watched, the liquid changed from red to tan. Krezma fell to her knees.

A moment later, the ground swelled and moved like a writhing water snake.

"Tar, come see," Akeela said. "It's a cave. Perhaps we can spend the night inside."

Tar knelt and peered into the dark opening. "It would give us a secure shelter if it's empty."

Akeela shook her head. "I don't see any animal auras."

"Then let's move our things inside."

Almost before he finished speaking, a loud clap of thunder exploded over their heads, and the ground shook violently. Anon shrieked and covered his ears.

Akeela grabbed Tar's arm. "What is it? A storm?"

Tar pushed her toward the bush. "This is no ordinary storm. Get Anon and climb into the cave. Don't go too far back."

He dashed to the cart as Akeela helped Anon to his feet. The ground shook again and threw them to their knees. "Come on, Anon! Crawl like me." Akeela pulled on Anon, and they crawled to the bushes. She lifted the branch and pushed him inside. She glanced back and saw Tar running toward them with Ves-rynia. Where was Hawk?

"Get in!" Tar roared.

Akeela scrambled into the cave opening, where Anon sat weeping. "Anon, you have to move back. Everyone else needs to get in."

Ves-rynia appeared from under the bush. The ground continued to groan and tremble, the noise unbearable. She crawled to the side and hung on to Akeela.

Then Vorrak-ira crawled through, followed by Hawk. They pushed themselves to the other side of the cave and sat breathing heavily. Finally, Tar dove in.

Akeela held on to both Ves-rynia and Anon. This had to be connected to the Earth Fountain. What else could it be?

Then she drew in a sharp breath as a possible answer to that question forced itself into her thoughts.

Riss'aird.

Chapter Nineteen

The sudden wrenching of the earth knocked Tzmet off her seat. She grunted in pain as her hip hit the stone floor. The castle shook so fiercely, she thought for a minute the whole thing might collapse.

As suddenly as they'd started, the tremors stopped.

The silence that followed was deafening. Tzmet sat up. Her breath came in shallow gasps as she listened for any sound that would indicate what'd just happened. Then it hit her. Her father, the great and mighty Riss'aird, could've just risen from the ground. She *had* to find out. She leaped to her feet, ran to the door, and yanked it open.

"My carriage!" she shrieked.

Within minutes, she was driving south, toward the forest. If her father had, indeed, risen from the ground, he would be standing in the barren plain that stretched between her castle and the woods.

The ride seemed to take an eternity. She pulled up to the edge of the plain. Shading her eyes, she scanned the area. What was that? Was it him?

Tzmet let out a hoarse shout and slapped Nightshade into a gallop. Shimmering colors surrounded the lone figure. As Tzmet drew closer, she could see the colors were actually heat rising from the hot sand. In the middle of the heat swirls stood a man. The man raised his eyes to hers. The carriage slowed to a stop.

"Father," Tzmet said.

"Daughter."

✳

Akeela coughed as dust filtered down from the cave's ceiling.

"Are you all right?" Hawk asked.

Ves-rynia and Anon were no longer near her. "I think so. Where is Anon? I lost my hold on him."

"I have him," Ves-rynia said.

Akeela crawled toward her voice. "Is he all right?'

Ves-rynia shook her head. "I don't know. He's unconscious."

"No, oh no. Please Celtar, save him!" Akeela cried out and took him in her arms.

Tar called to them from the other side of the cave. "Vorrak-ira is hurt. He was sitting near the edge, and a large stone fell on his leg."

Akeela looked around the cave. The opening let in some light, but stones piled high in the opening. Vorrak-ira sat with his eyes closed and his teeth clenched. Tar had removed the stone and was examining his leg.

Hawk crawled over to the opening. "We need to move these rocks. There aren't that many. I can just roll them to the side."

Akeela brushed the hair from Anon's forehead. "Are you hurt?" she asked Ves-rynia.

"No, just scared, yeh?"

"Me too."

After several minutes, Hawk had the rocks moved enough for them to be able to get out of the cave. "I'll take a look around."

Anon began to stir and whimper. Akeela put her hand on his chest. "Anon, Akeela is here."

"Keela?"

"Yes, sweet one. We're still in the cave. Can you sit up?"

Anon opened his eyes and smiled at Akeela. Relieved to see him unhurt, Akeela burst into tears and hugged him tight. "Thank you! Thank you!"

"Squeeze too hard, Keela!"

Akeela and Ves-rynia laughed, and the sound echoed beyond them. Akeela glanced at Tar. "I wonder how far back this cave goes?" she asked Ves-rynia in a low voice.

Ves-rynia leaned over and whispered in her ear. "Don't even think about it, yeh?"

Hawk slid through the opening. "I don't see anything out of the ordinary. Everything looks the same, like the storm never happened. But our mule is gone."

Tar tore a strip of cloth from the bottom of his tunic. "I unhitched Mule so he could find somewhere safe. Bring in as many supplies as you can. We will rest here until we can figure out what to do next." He began wrapping Vorrak-ira's leg. "This is going to hurt."

Vorrak-ira groaned as Tar worked. Hawk pushed in the first bag of supplies. "Akeela, pull things in as I bring them."

Akeela and Ves-rynia dragged the bags in as they appeared in the opening.

Finally, Hawk came through. "I got everything but the firewood."

Tar nodded. "Now we wait."

Anon gave a cry. "Stones, Keela! Where stones?"

"Oh no," Akeela said. "Anon's bag of stones. He takes them everywhere. Help me look for them."

Hawk shook his head. "We shouldn't walk around this cave. More rocks might fall."

Anon began to wail, and Akeela held him close. "They can't be far. Please, we have to find them." She rocked Anon and whispered in his ear. "Don't cry. I'll find your stones. But you have to sit with Ves-rynia."

With Anon safely in Ves-rynia's arms, Akeela crawled around the cave. She didn't see the bag near the opening, so she moved toward the back, feeling with her hands as the light dimmed and the ceiling rose above her. "I think we can stand up back here."

"Don't go too far," Tar said.

"I won't."

Her eyes began to adjust, and she saw rocks of various sizes scattered around, some almost three feet tall. Her hand hit something soft. Anon's bag! She grabbed it, stood, and started to turn when something caught her eye. Five large rocks near the cave wall were glowing, as if they had auras. Akeela stared, trying to discern what she was seeing.

"Akeela, did you find them?" Hawk called.

"Yes, but there's something strange here."

"What is it?"

Before she could answer, the glowing rocks began to move.

Krezma lifted her head from the sand, then she sat up and brushed off her face. The ground had stopped rolling, but she could still feel mild tremors. The pony was nowhere in sight. A soft swish caught her attention. She looked up at the Earth Fountain, swirling high in the sky.

"Thanks be to Celtar!"

The Earth Fountain was healed, but was it in time to prevent Riss'aird from rising? Krezma shuddered as she thought of the consequences of his regeneration. His anger would be fierce after one hundred years of being held captive in the ground. And Tzmet, who'd surely poisoned the Fountain, would be there to greet him.

Krezma remembered the night she'd decided to escape. Tzmet was celebrating her one-hundredth birthday that evening and had invited every vile and disgusting creature to attend. When Krezma questioned her, things had turned ugly between them.

"Really, Mother, I can't do anything to please you, can I?" Tzmet glared at her reflection in the mirror.

Krezma had spread her hands and shook her head. "It's not a matter of pleasing me, dearest. I'm fearful of how these new friends might influence you. They're all reputed to have dealings with the dark arts."

Tzmet gracefully painted her eyelids with blue powder. She studied her handiwork and added a bit more to one side. "The dark arts. The dark arts! I'm sick and tired of hearing you lecture me about the dangers of dark arts. Well, I'm old enough to decide for myself, and if the dark arts are good enough for my father, they're good enough for me."

Krezma's voice died in her throat. She'd suspected Riss'aird of dabbling with evil power, but she'd never dreamed her daughter would also embrace such a dangerous and black venture. She looked at Tzmet, pleading with her eyes as tears streamed down her cheeks.

"Tears, Mother? Tears are for the weak." Tzmet stood and faced Krezma. "You sicken me. There, I said it! You are weak and powerless and you disgust me. Father and I have befriended the most powerful creatures in the universe. It's my birthday, and I want to celebrate with my friends, not with *krenda* cakes and tea."

"But—"

"Go away, Mother. If you ruin my party, I will hate you forever."

Krezma had stood silent as Tzmet swept past her and out the bedroom door. In that moment, part of her heart had ceased to beat.

She'd stayed in Tzmet's room until the party had begun. When the celebration increased in intensity, she'd slipped out of the castle and into the night. It had been the hardest thing she'd ever done. What mother wanted to leave her child? She'd left with just the clothes on her back, vowing to convince her father to send his army to rescue Tzmet.

Fairy voices raised in song brought her back to the present. She wondered about the earthquake and what it meant. It could be a result of the Earth Fountain returning to full strength. Or something Krezma dared not let herself believe.

Riss'aird had risen from the ashes.

Part Two

REVENGE

Chapter Twenty

Akeela took a step back. "The rocks are moving."

Hawk sidled up beside her. "What?"

"Those glowing rocks. They're moving!" Akeela moved closer to Hawk. She watched, wide eyed, as the largest stone unfolded itself and seemed to stand up. It stepped forward, and Akeela gasped. It was a man.

"Akeela? Hawk? What's going on?" Ves-rynia called.

The man put his hands on the sides of his head, and Akeela realized he had no ears.

Akeela turned her head. "Shh . . ." Then she looked at the strange man. Her heart beat so hard, she wondered if it could be heard. "Greetings," she said, keeping her voice low.

The man lowered his hands and cocked his head. Akeela observed his aura, pale blue, and his large, dark eyes.

She leaned close to Hawk and whispered. "He's alive. I can see an aura."

"Of coursssse I'm alive."

Akeela grabbed Hawk's arm. "Oh! I'm sorry."

The man covered his ears again. "Peasssce." He spoke in low tones.

Akeela remembered how her laughter had echoed earlier. If these people lived in the caves, it would stand to reason they spoke quietly. The noise would be unbearable. She stepped forward and lowered her voice. "I'm sorry again. Do you live here?"

"Yesss."

Akeela's heart leaped. "Are you the Kazmura?"

"Yesss."

The other rocks behind him moved forward, revealing four more of these strange cave men. Each one looked almost exactly alike: gray skin, no hair, and large, dark eyes. They wore grayish clothing, tunics, and no pants. Their fingers were long and thin with black nails.

Akeela nodded to Hawk. "Let the others know." Then she turned back to the cave men. "We needed a place to hide, and we didn't know you were here. The map showed us a diff—"

"You mussst come with usss."

"But—"

The man reached out and grabbed her arm. "Come."

An unnatural chill filled Akeela at his touch. Her arms and legs stiffened. Akeela opened her mouth to scream, but no sound came out.

The other men walked around them. They signaled to Hawk and the others to follow them. Hawk started forward, his face angry.

Tar's voice stopped him. "No, Hawk."

Hawk stood with his fists clenched at his sides. "Let her go."

The man holding Akeela nodded. "Yesss. Come with usss."

Hawk pointed behind him. "We have a hurt man. I need to help carry him."

"Yesss."

"It's okay, Akeela," Hawk said. "I'm right behind you."

Akeela wanted to say that gave her precious little relief, but she couldn't utter a word, and this was no time for sarcasm. She cleared her throat, trying to indicate she would not scream. The man stared at her a moment, then let go. Akeela shivered and rubbed her arms. Warmth crept back into her body, although she wasn't entirely sure she'd be all the way warm ever again. At least, not in this cave.

Ves-rynia walked up with Anon. Akeela handed him the bag she still carried. "Stones!" he cried.

The men covered their ears. Akeela bent to whisper in his ear. "We must speak softly, Anon." He looked at her with confused eyes. How could she help him understand? Akeela thought for a moment. "It's a cave whispering game, Anon. Can you whisper to me?"

Anon grinned. He loved games. "Whisper."

Tar and Hawk approached and stood on either side of Vorrak-ira, holding him under his arms. His leg was wrapped snugly.

The darkness grew thick as they walked farther into the cave. The man in the front and the man bringing up the rear carried something that gave off faint light. Akeela couldn't see a flame, but something in the lanterns glowed. If not for the light of everyone's auras, she wouldn't have been able to see anything. She could only imagine how the rest of the group felt.

They made slow progress, feeling their way with their feet. Akeela prayed as they traveled into the depths of the earth. She'd never thought of being able to travel underground like this. The air grew cool and damp.

After the better part of an hour, light grew ahead. Not too bright, but lighter than the lantern thing the cave men carried. They all gasped when they entered a huge room with stone layered in pinks, oranges, and whites. The massive walls sparkled in the faint light of many lanterns that glowed without fire.

The man in the front held up his hand. "Ssstay here."

He walked across the great room, stopped at a large gray boulder, and picked up a small stone. He began to tap on the rock. A minute later, shuffling carried to them. Person after person walked almost silently into the room. Men, women, and children—each with gray skin and large, dark eyes. They spoke not a word, and the eerie silence was more disturbing than angry shouting.

Then a man wearing a thin crown, encrusted with shiny, clear stones, came into the room. Akeela almost laughed at the absurdity of such a beautiful piece of jewelry on such a gray, drab man.

He walked, holding his head high, until he stopped before a large stone seat. Akeela hadn't noticed it before because her attention was on the people. The man held his right hand out, palm up. Then he made a fist and turned it over. The people repeated the gesture. Then they sat.

The man with the crown turned to Akeela. "I am the Mikado of the Kazsssmura. Uplandersss are not welcome here. Kazsssmura live in sssecret. You cannot be allowed to leave."

Ves-rynia gasped. Akeela looked back at Tar, who was slowly shaking his head. She had to do something. As their leader, the Fairy Guardian, she had to. She stepped forward. "Please listen. I tried to tell your men. We needed some place to hide when the storm started."

The people murmured.

The Mikado raised his hand to quiet them. "The earth movesss often. Kazsssmura keep rocksss in order. Keep them from shifting too much. Uplandersss have brought big earth shift to Kazsssmura. Many die."

"We didn't cause the earth shift," Akeela pleaded. "An evil Dark Lord may have risen from the ground. We don't know for sure if he did, but we did nothing to cause the earth to move."

"Dark Lord isss uplander?"

A trap. What could she say to make them understand? She looked back at Hawk.

He held up a finger and stepped forward. "We mean no harm to the Kazmura. We are on an important quest. One that will defeat the evil uplander."

The Mikado frowned.

"We need your help," Akeela begged. "We've been looking for you."

"What will you give usss?"

"Give you?"

A man leaned over and said something in the Mikado's ear. The

Mikado sat back, his fingertips touching. "Kazsssura love ssstory. You tell usss good ssstory."

Akeela's confidence faded. "What kind of story do you like?"

The Mikado grinned, an expression that made Akeela squirm. "All kindsss."

"I have a story." Hawk's low voice settled over the cave people.

The Mikado actually chuckled. "A good ssstory? Yesss, I will allow one good ssstory before you go to deep pit."

"Wait—" Akeela started.

"Peasssce!" The Mikado's raised voice, while still almost a whisper, felt like a trumpet blast. The people put their hands to their heads.

Hawk began slowly. "In another time, a dark time, there lived an evil uplander called Riss'aird."

Hawk wove his way through the story of Riss'aird and the great spell. Akeela listened raptly, amazed at this side of Hawk. Judging by the looks on their faces, the Kazmura were also caught up in the tale.

When Hawk finished, Akeela held her breath as she watched the Mikado. He frowned for a moment. Then he smiled and lifted both hands, twisting them back and forth quickly. The people did the same. Then the Mikado walked to Hawk. He held out his palm as before, making a fist and turning it over.

Hawk did the same. Then he held out his hands, palms up, in the Acadian way. "Touch your hands to mine."

The Kazmura leader hesitated. Akeela reached out and touched her hands to Hawk's. She nodded to the Mikado. He imitated Akeela.

"Sapo," said Hawk.

"Sssapo," the Mikado repeated.

Akeela wanted to weep in relief. She held her breath until the urge passed. Hawk looked at her and raised his eyebrows as if asking what to do next. Yes, she was the leader!

She gave Hawk a look of thanks and turned to the Kazmura leader. "Mikado, we need your help."

He gave her the greeting gesture. "We help good ssstory tellersss."

Akeela smiled. "Our supplies are still near the cave opening. We need to help our friend who is hurt. And mostly, we need the stone the fairies gave you for safekeeping."

The Mikado cocked his head. "Many wordsss. Firssst, help friend." He waved two Kazmura over. "Take them to healing poolsss."

Tar and Hawk helped Vorrak-ira up and followed the men.

The Mikado frowned. "Evil man. Risss'aird. Make earth shift. We help defeat him."

"Thank you," Akeela said.

"Sssupplies sssafe. No worry. Come, we make planssss." The Mikado turned and walked toward the tunnel he'd arrived in. "Come. Make planssss."

Akeela, Ves-rynia, and Anon followed him through the tunnel. It was lit by glowing objects, thin and stringy. Akeela looked closely and discovered spiders spinning glowing webs.

"Amazing," she whispered to Ves-rynia.

The Mikado's voice echoed through the tunnel. "Come. Make planssss."

Akeela wanted to tear her hair out. The Mikado talked about making plans, but so far he'd had Ves-rynia tell him three Acadian stories. Anon had curled up in a corner and had gone to sleep during the second one.

As Ves-rynia finished, whispering and shuffling came from outside the small room. Tar entered, ducking his head as he came through the doorway. "Vorrak-ira is doing well. The healing pools here are incredible."

Akeela smiled in relief. At least one of their problems was solved.

Tar sat on a rock next to Akeela. "What plans have you made?"

The Mikado lifted his hands. "Good ssstories. Make plansss after ssstories."

Tar glanced at Akeela. She nodded, afraid to say anything that might change the Mikado's mind.

"Pleassse, give me good ssstory."

Tar shifted in his seat.

The Mikado tapped his fingers on the arms of his rock chair. "Give me ssstory of your handsss."

Akeela drew in a sharp breath. Tar didn't like to speak of the horrible incident where he'd lost his wife and his hand.

Tar bowed his head. Then he looked the Mikado in the eye. "We have a book of Holy Writings. In it is written, 'There is no love more pure than a man who would give up his life for his friends.' One dark night, my friend did that for me."

Akeela relived Oret's funeral as Tar recounted the wolves' attack and how Oret had saved him from certain death. Great sorrow swept her again as he told how the wizard, Jemin, had used bird parts and all his magic power to heal Tar and give him another chance at life.

The Mikado was silent long after Tar finished. Akeela felt almost hollow as she waited for his response. So tired and hungry.

Finally, the Mikado spoke. "I learn much from your ssstories. You are people who love dirt and plantsss. You love ssstrength and wisssdom. You are faithful friendsss. But what can Kazsssura get in return for help?"

Akeela frowned. "You are helping defeat an evil uplander."

The Mikado laced his long fingers together and nodded. "Yesss, evil uplander."

"What kind of reward do you want?" Tar asked.

"Sssomething we like. Sssomething that hasss value to you."

Akeela listed all their supplies in her head. Surely the Kazmura didn't want dried meat or fruit. They had no need for firewood. And the clothing they carried would be too large. What was left?

Nacre seeds.

Akeela glanced at Tar and took a breath. "Mikado, we carry

something I believe your people will like. It's a type of stone called a nacre seed."

The Mikado's eyes lit up. "Nacre ssseed. Yesss. Bring nacre ssseed to me."

Tar left with two Kazmura to get the seeds. The Mikado sat with his eyes closed as the minutes went by. Akeela checked on Anon. She squeezed Ves-rynia's hand. Finally, they heard the shuffle of feet, and Tar entered the room carrying a small basket covered with a cloth.

The Mikado opened his eyes and held out his hands. "Give ssseeds."

Tar shifted the basket from his good hand to his claw hand. "I will show you a nacre seed. You will let us know if you will help us. After we work out an agreement, I will give you the nacre seeds."

The Mikado's eyes narrowed. He stood and waved the two Kazmura men who'd accompanied Tar out of the room. "Show ssseed."

Tar slipped his hand under the cover and brought out a gleaming nacre. He handed it to the Mikado, who snatched it and turned his back. He stood that way, examining the seed, for several seconds. Akeela's heartbeat rang in her ears.

Finally the Mikado faced them. "Kazsssmura will help you."

Akeela let out her breath. The Mikado had learned about them from their stories. Now he saw they would keep their word and give the Kazmura something they treasured. "Can we make plans now?" she asked.

"Yesss. Make planss. Give more ssseeds."

After several hours of bartering nacre seeds, it was decided Tar would be allowed to retrieve the rest of their supplies. Two Kazmura would accompany them, leading the way to the hiding place of the Fairystone piece. The Mikado ran his fingers through the basket of seeds, having haggled with Tar for the whole thing.

Akeela learned more about patience that night than she ever had in her whole life. The Kazmura leader would not be hurried into anything. Later, she pondered everything that had happened since she'd left Broem.

"Be careful what you wish for," she told Ves-rynia as they ate a meal of boiled fish wrapped in some kind of plant the Kazmura grew in underground lakes. "I wanted to leave Krezma and have my own life, and now I'd give anything to be back in our cottage, tending the garden or picking strawberries."

Ves-rynia squeezed her hand. "But then we wouldn't have met, yeh?"

Akeela nodded. She looked up as Hawk, Vorrak-ira, and Tar entered the small room they'd been given to sleep in.

Tar squatted. "We must talk quickly," he whispered. "Before we are overheard. Be especially quiet so our voices don't carry." The boys sat.

Akeela set aside the remnants of her dinner and wiped her hands on a cloth. "What's wrong?"

"The Mikado thinks we gave him all our nacre seeds," Tar said. "It must not be known we have more."

Everyone nodded. "How are we going to carry our supplies?" Hawk asked.

Tar glanced at the door before he answered. "The Kazmura have small carts for moving dirt and rocks. They are made of some kind of metal."

Akeela held up a hand. "Where did they get metal carts?"

Tar shook his head. "I know not. They could've made them or perhaps bartered for them. I suspect they've had bad dealings with uplanders in the past. It's probably the reason they dislike us so much."

"How do we know we can trust them?" Ves-rynia asked.

"The Fairy Council trusted them," Akeela put in. "Or they wouldn't have given them a piece of the stone."

"I don't know," Hawk said. "But what choice do we have? I mean, we're underground with no light or directions."

Vorrak-ira laughed. "You're entirely off your nut, cousin."

Tar leaned forward. "Is your intention to get us killed?"

"Aye, let them try to chop down our branches. I'll be ready for 'em." He started to laugh again but stopped when they heard footsteps outside the room.

Akeela crawled over to sit next to Anon, who was still sleeping. She frowned as she looked at his peaceful face. She feared the days ahead. Krezma had taught her Celtar would always be with his people. He would take care of their needs. Akeela tried to find faith. So much depended on her. But nothing stirred in her soul.

A Kazmuran man stood at the doorway. "Pleassse, get sssleep. We leave after firssst meal."

Akeela shook out her cloak. She and Ves-rynia settled on either side of Anon. Tar made his bed near the door. Hawk and Vorrak-ira lay at the girls' feet. No one said a word. Akeela stared at a glowing spider making its way across the ceiling. It left a faint, thin trail behind. A lowly spider had more freedom than they did.

She felt Hawk's hand on her foot and smiled. If Celtar had truly called her to an almost impossible mission, he hadn't left her to do it alone. There was some comfort in that.

As she prepared to sleep, Akeela pulled her cloak tight and reached over to rub Anon's head. Only time would tell if Riss'aird had risen. Thoughts of Oret filled her mind as sleep claimed her. She'd promised him she would not fail.

The quest would continue tomorrow.

Chapter Twenty-One

Tzmet waved her hand over the simmering pot and took a quick sniff. Her nostrils filled with the spicy aroma of garlic, *hicata* pepper, and dark vine. She hiccupped, turned her head, and sneezed.

"Curse this wretched brew!"

Since her father had risen from the ashes and she'd brought him back to the castle, he would allow no one to wait on him. For seven days, Tzmet had kept vigil outside his room until he'd finally called. What he did during that time, she had no idea.

Tzmet sneezed again. She'd never been able to tolerate dark vine, but her father loved it, demanding his favorite soup as his first meal.

Two Hinwari stood in the shadows near the kitchen door. Tzmet snapped her fingers at them. "Bring me some red wine, you miserable, lazy creatures!"

They turned toward the cellar and shuffled down the stairs. A whistle caught Tzmet's attention, and she looked up as Brimridge entered the room. He tossed a cloth bag onto the large table near the fireplace.

"What is that?"

The boggart leader bowed. "My lady Tzmet, this is the muskrat you asked for."

Tzmet arched her eyebrows and lifted the edge of the bag. "You uncivilized cockroach! Why isn't this skinned and cleaned?"

"Didn't the great and mighty Riss'aird give explicit instructions that only you were to prepare his food?" Brimridge's black eyes sparkled with obvious delight.

Tzmet pressed her lips tightly.

Brimridge took a step closer. "Make sure you use a sharp knife, my lady."

"Get out! Get out, you vile, disgusting, poor excuse for a servant!"

The Hinwari came up from the cellar as Brimridge bowed and left the kitchen.

Tzmet pointed at one Hinwar. "Set down the wine and stand by the door. I want to know immediately if anyone comes near this room." She turned to the other Hinwar. "You, come here and skin and clean this muskrat. And do it quickly!"

The Hinwar complied, and Tzmet poured a glass of wine. She took a sip.

"As if I'd actually do something as revolting as that."

The Hinwar worked without showing emotion. In short order, the muskrat was ready. Tzmet, warmed by the wine, slid the strips of dark-red meat into the simmering broth.

She smiled and stirred the soup. "I don't mind cooking. Really. It's worth having my father back."

Tzmet moved to the counter and arranged some green onions and a loaf of bread and butter on a tray. She set a goblet and spoon to the right of the bowl.

"When the soup is ready, I'll pour it into a crock, and you'll carry it behind me," she said to the Hinwar by the door. "And you —" She turned to the other. "Clean up that bloody mess and spread some lemongrass on the table to cover the smell."

Tzmet walked regally to her father's room. She was the daughter of the risen and mighty Dark Lord, a Sultana. Her days of cooking and waiting on him, while honoring, of course, wouldn't last long. She was more than ready to take her place at his side.

❧

Akeela found a strip of cloth in her pocket and tied back her hair. She glanced at the weary group sitting on the cold, damp earth in the dark. Their Kazmura guides, Rig and Dok, were preparing another meal of fish wrapped with some kind of green leaf in a hot spring, so the lanterns were next to them. Akeela and the group sat in the shadows, waiting on the cave men. Who knew how far they'd traveled? They'd walked the winding trails for at least seven days, stopping for a midday meal, an evening meal, and a few hours of sleep. It seemed a lifetime since they'd seen the sun or breathed fresh air. The damp stone and musty smell would never leave her memory. If she ever got out.

Anon's voice pierced the silence. "Hungry, Keela."

Akeela put her finger to her lips. "Remember, Anon, whisper." She knelt next to him. "The Kazmura are preparing our meal. It won't be long now."

"No fishes, Keela. Want apples and cheese!"

Akeela hugged him. "Me, too, Anon, but this is all we have."

She glanced at the Kazmura guides, who still had their backs to the group. It wasn't right that they forbid them to use their own supplies. Dried rabbit and venison along with carrots, apples, and cheese were in the cart they pushed along the dark trails. Although the cheese was likely moldy by now.

Hawk sat next to them. Akeela tugged on his sleeve. "We need to ask about using our own food."

"I don't think it'll do any good. They're posturing for us. Throwing their weight around. Being bullies. Those kinds of people are hard to reason with."

Akeela shook her head. "Poor Anon just doesn't understand. I'm afraid if I can't give him something different, he'll really have a fit."

"We're at their mercy, Akeela." Tar said. "I'm an excellent tracker, but even I cannot hope to lead us out of these caves."

"And if they get angry or upset, what will happen to us?" Ves-rynia asked.

Akeela's eyes narrowed. "If Anon has a fit, they will definitely be angry."

Vorrak-ira snorted. "Maybe I'll have a fit, yeh?"

"Okay, I'll ask again." Hawk stood and brushed off his pants. He paused a moment, then walked over to the Kazmura.

Ves-rynia and Vorrak-ira watched.

Rig, the apparent leader of the two, turned. "Meal almossst ready. You sssit."

"I want to ask again about using our food supplies," Hawk said. "You must understand that Anon can't comprehend our situation. Surely it won't hurt to give him something different."

"Mussst have Kazsssmura food," Rig said. "Uplander food no good."

Vorrak-ira jumped to his feet. "Kazmura food no good. I'm getting something for Anon. For all of us!"

"Vorrak-ira, please don't," Ves-rynia pleaded.

"I will not listen anymore. If Anon wants apples and cheese, he should be able to have apples and cheese, yeh?"

Vorrak-ira took two steps toward the cart and collapsed. Akeela gasped, and Ves-rynia leaped to her brother's side. Tar stood and flexed his claw hand.

"Sssit and wait for meal," said Rig.

Akeela's anger grew. "What did you do to him?"

Dok tossed a small stone in the air. He grinned and turned back to the hot spring. Akeela's face burned, and she clenched her hands. The temptation to scream almost overpowered her, so she took a deep breath.

Hawk slipped next to her and put his hand over her mouth. "Don't," he whispered.

Hot, burning tears ran down Akeela's cheeks and over Hawk's hand. She trembled with the effort of calming down. Ves-rynia cradled Vorrak-ira's head in her lap.

Anon pulled on Akeela's leg. "Want apples and cheese, Keela."

Akeela pushed Hawk's hand away. "Okay, Anon. Akeela will get them for you."

Hawk grabbed her arm. "Akeela—"

She pulled out of his grip. "Trust me. I have an idea." She said to Anon, "Sit here like a good faun and be very quiet. If you make noise, I won't be able to get your apples and cheese."

Anon sniffed and put his head on his arms. Akeela patted his head as she moved toward the cart. She nodded to Tar, who still stood alert. Her heart hammered as she anticipated the feel of a rock against her head, but she reached the cart without incident.

Hawk talked to the Kazmura about the leaves that grew in the cave lakes. Without glancing back, she slipped her hand into a bag. It contained clothing. She felt around for anything that could be an apple. As she pushed through the bags, a faint glimmer peeked out of one. The nacre seeds. She pulled out one gleaming stone-like seed and kept it tightly in her palm. After rolling the bag closed and pulling another over it, she located the food stores and brought out an apple.

"Ssstop!" Rig's voice, while a whisper, had the effect of a shouted command. Akeela froze. Then she turned around. The small cave man strode toward her, his face angry in the low light.

Akeela held out her hand. The nacre seed gleamed white in her palm. Rig's eyes widened, and he reached out for it. Akeela pulled her hand back. "I don't think so, Rig. If you want this stone, you'll have to give me something for it."

Rig glanced back at Dok. "You ssstay with food. Rig handle uplander girl."

Dok nodded and turned back to the hot spring. Hawk remained with him.

Akeela licked her dry lips. She gave a timid smile as Rig faced her again.

He pointed to her hand. "You want uplander food for glowing ssstone?"

"Yes, I do. But you must keep it a secret. It's the only one we have left." Akeela hated telling a lie, but if he suspected there were more, they'd soon be without any.

Rig thought a moment. Then he crossed his arms. "Rig will allow ssstrange boy to have uplander food for glowing ssstone. But no one else."

"Thank you." She handed him the seed.

He snatched it out of her hand and slipped it into his tunic. "If more want food, mussst give more ssstones."

"But—"

Rig nodded, his smile as cold as the air. "More ssstonesss."

Akeela waited until he walked to the hot spring before she pulled out the food bag and selected dried rabbit and a carrot to go with the apple for Anon. Her mouth watered when she smelled the meat, and she swallowed hard before giving Anon his meal.

Hawk squeezed her shoulder, and the group ate their leaf-wrapped fish in silence.

Riss'aird sat in his bed, propped up with several thick pillows. He dipped his fingers into a bowl of scented water, dried them on a cloth, and waved his hand, indicating he was through with the meal.

Tzmet removed the tray and set it on a stand outside the door. She pulled on a cord, then turned to face her father.

"The boggarts have taken over the lower rooms." She spread her skirt and sat. "I've found them helpful with cleaning the court-yard and barracks, which are now ready for your armies."

Riss'aird nodded slightly. His long, white hair gleamed in the firelight. His eyes were no longer dark as before the disastrous spell. Now they were pale blue. His face was sallow, his cheeks sunken without the covering of a beard. Surely it wouldn't be long before he was his robust self. She would make sure his meals were particularly appealing.

When he finally spoke, his voice had none of its former strength. "You have changed as well, daughter."

Tzmet's face flamed as she realized he knew her thoughts. "It has been many years, my father."

"So it has."

"Your strength will return," she insisted. "I'll gather the herbs needed to feed your blood. It will not take long."

Riss'aird looked over his room, his gaze lingering on each wall. Tzmet's eyes followed his, taking in the rich tapestries and carved wooden trim circling the room. Evil runes, etched deeply into the wood, spelled out many curses over his enemies. The tapestries told the stories of his conquests. Tzmet had woven them herself during the long days, months, and years of waiting for him to rise.

But the longer she sat there, the more she wanted to leave and take refuge in her own room. She desired a hot bath and something to eat. Her father hadn't dismissed her after she'd brought his evening meal. She'd sat by his side as he ate, her own stomach begging for food. She wondered, for a brief moment, if it was a good thing, this change in her life.

Finally, she could stand no more. "Father . . ."

Riss'aird's pale eyes rested on her. A tremor of fear shivered through her, but she lifted her chin. "If you have no need for me tonight, I would retire to my room."

He nodded, and Tzmet rose to leave.

"Daughter."

Tzmet paused with her hand on the doorknob. She turned. "Yes?"

"I hope your loyalty to me has not changed along with everything else."

Tzmet's heart leaped into her throat. "It has not."

"Good."

When he said no more, Tzmet curtsied and slipped out the door, forcing herself to walk calmly to her room.

Chapter Twenty-Two

Krezma, though weary, stepped lightly over a rotting log. She could hear the Acadian kin-tribe gathering together for the evening meal. What a relief. Her long journey from the desert was at an end. She could now go to Broem and bring Ham to Akeela. If they went on horseback, they'd quickly catch up.

"Sapo!"

Dir-mac strode toward her, holding out his hands and smiling.

"Minister Dir-mac, it's good to see you." Krezma touched her hands lightly to his palms.

Ban-ira called his greeting from where he sat at the fire. Krezma and Dir-mac joined him and accepted mugs of steaming saloop from a young girl.

Ban-ira leaned forward, his face expectant. "Tell us all, Krezma. We've been anxious to know what happened."

Krezma sipped her tea. She set the mug on the ground and folded her gnarled hands. "I arrived at the Earth Fountain to find it had been poisoned."

Several Acadians gathered as she related her story. They listened raptly, murmuring as Krezma's tale unfolded.

"I was successful in healing the fountain," she said, finishing her story. "And I advised the Fairy Council to set guards around it so this does not happen again."

Dir-mac nodded. "That is good. We are thankful it's over. The poisoning of the earth affected us deeply, robbed our joy. Many became angry, and we fought among ourselves."

"I fear it is far from over, Minister," Krezma said. "I'm not sure, but it's possible the Dark Lord, Riss'aird, has risen from the ashes. If this is true, we must prepare ourselves for violent and wicked times."

The people gasped and began talking at once. Confusion and fear grew evident, but Ban-ira raised his hands to quiet his tribe. "We will hold a special prayer cluster tonight, when the moons rise, to beseech Celtar for guidance and protection. This is not the time to pull apart but to band together."

Krezma picked up her mug and sipped as Ban-ira and Dir-mac took stock of what supplies they had.

The children would gather stones for slings, and women would make and store food supplies. Their homes in the trees were undetectable, so they would be safe. And the gliders Tar had made were still in the surrounding trees. They could be used for escape, if needed.

The people agreed a prayer cluster would be wise, although Krezma could still sense their insecurity. Even she felt unsure. If Riss'aird had risen, things would go from bad to worse quickly.

After praying, Ban-ira gave orders. As the Acadians went off to begin working, Krezma stretched her arms above her head. "I could use a good night's sleep."

Ban-ira stood and helped her up. "Come, friend. I'll show you where you can rest."

Krezma's fatigued body welcomed the sleeping mat in one of the Acadian tree dwellings. She closed her eyes and thought of Akeela and the group, offering a quick prayer for safety before falling into deep slumber.

"I don't like it," Akeela whispered to Hawk.

Hawk shrugged. "I don't either, but it's helpful to have something different to do. Everyone's nerves are on edge."

Akeela glanced at the group watching Rig and Dok play a game with small stones. "Rig and Dok can't be trusted."

"True, but this is a nice diversion, yeh?"

"I suppose."

Hawk took her left hand and squeezed. Even though it gave her a pleasant, tickly feeling, the pressure of his grip pushed the silver band against her flesh, reminding her of what she was hiding. She slipped her hand from his.

The group gave a silent cheer by raising their hands and shaking them as taught by the Kazmura. The game they played, simply called "Stones," consisted of two players, who drew a circle in the ground and placed their stones within. Using a larger stone, the first player dropped it into the pile and would keep any of the smaller stones that rolled outside the circle. The game went on until all the stones were gone, and the one with the most stones won.

Something in Akeela's mind flashed a warning. True, the group seemed to enjoy watching the new game, an innocent diversion, but Akeela couldn't shake the feeling that something wasn't right.

Her head snapped up at Anon's eager voice. "Play with stones?"

Rig and Dok looked at each other and grinned. Rig pointed at Anon. "Ssstrange boy want to play? Have ssstones?"

Anon shook his cloth bag. "Yah."

Rig gestured with his hand. "You sssit here. I teach you game."

Akeela stepped forward. "Anon, I don't think this is a good game for you. It looks terribly difficult."

"Want to play, Keela."

Hawk put his hand on Anon's shoulder. "I'll help him. It'll be fine."

Vorrak-ira agreed. "It's just a game, yeh? Let the little sprout have some fun. C'mon, Anon. Plant your trunk by me."

Akeela looked at Hawk. He shrugged. Rig's sharp whisper

broke in. "Game not hard. Sssee, we show ssstrange boy how we teach sssmall Kazsssmura."

Akeela glanced at Tar, who stood watching and flexing his claw hand. Surely he'd step in if needed.

Anon practiced with Vorrak-ira's help. Akeela relaxed as time passed. She looked at her friend's faces. Everyone seemed less tense. The Kazmura guides were generous with their stones and allowed Anon to keep his small bag. It was the first time in many days that Anon smiled happily. After a while, she started dozing off and leaned against the cave wall.

Ves-rynia brought a blanket and sat next to her. "The men can take care of Anon, yeh?"

Akeela yawned. "But he's my charge."

Ves-rynia handed her the blanket. "Rest. Dream of sun and fresh air. I'll join you in a minute, yeh?"

Akeela wrapped the blanket around herself and fell asleep before Ves-rynia came back. She did dream. Visions of home—Krezma baking *krenda* cakes, making strawberry jam, and tending the garden—filled her with peace. She tasted rabbit stew and felt grass beneath her bare feet. Fairy songs filled the air as Hawk grabbed her hand and together they raced to the stream. The stars began to twinkle, and the softness of her quilt and pillow caressed her as she settled for rest. But a sound interrupted her sleep. She tried to ignore it, but it didn't stop. Voices were rising. Someone was weeping.

She opened her eyes, trying to remember where she was. The damp smell of stone and dirt reminded her that she wasn't home but deep within the ground. She sat up and rubbed her eyes, trying to adjust to the dim light.

Anon sat before Rig and Dok, hands outstretched. "Give stones!" he pleaded.

Rig passed Anon's little bag to Dok. "You lossse ssstones in game. No give back."

Anon's voice rose. "Give stones!"

The Kazmura guides covered the sides of their heads. Rig's

voice, while still low, pierced the air. "Sssilence, ssstrange boy! Or Rig make you quiet."

Anon wailed, his cry echoing through the cave and waking everyone. Akeela stood, letting the blanket fall. "What's going on?"

Anon ran to her and buried his furry head against her. "Want stones!"

Rig pointed to him. "Uplandersss sssleep. Ssstrange boy come to usss and want to play game."

Tar and Hawk stepped into the lantern light. Akeela turned to them in anger. "You went to sleep and left Anon alone with them?"

Hawk rubbed his head. "What?"

Her anger built. "How could you?"

Tar flexed his claw hand. "Akeela, no one left Anon alone. After several games, I had Hawk settle Anon next to you."

"I did," Hawk said. "We all lay down to sleep. Anon must've gotten up later."

Akeela pulled Anon's clutching hands away from her tunic and knelt. "Did you get up to play the game while we were sleeping?"

Anon sniffed, rubbing his nose. "Want stones," he whined.

Akeela took him to Ves-rynia. "Here, Anon, you sit with Ves-rynia. I'll get your stones." Ves-rynia put Anon on her lap and wrapped the blanket around them both. Akeela patted his head. Then she faced Rig and Dok. "I want Anon's stones back. You know he doesn't understand. It wasn't right for you to play the game with him alone."

Rig crossed his arms. "Win ssstones fair. No give back."

Hawk and Tar came up beside Akeela. She barely noticed them. "I'm not asking you. I'm telling you. Give Anon his stones back."

Dok shook the bag. "Not right to give ssstones back. We win. Keep ssstones."

Hawk stepped forward. "You *will* give Anon his stones back, or I'll take them from you."

Tar stood next to his son, his golden eyes fierce. "And I will help him."

Rig glanced at Dok. He glared at Akeela and raised his chin. "Challenge."

Akeela blinked. "What?"

"Challenge. You play Rig and Dok. If you win, give back ssstones. If we win, keep ssstones."

Hawk pointed at Rig. "I accept your challenge."

"No."

Everyone looked at Akeela.

"No, *I* accept the challenge. Anon is *my* responsibility."

Rig stared at Akeela for a moment. Then he signaled Dok, who handed Anon's bag of stones to Akeela. She snatched the bag and held it tight. Then Rig stooped down and redrew the circle, which had gotten scuffed.

Dok brought another bag from his tunic and dumped the stones in the circle. He glanced up at Akeela. Her mouth went dry, and she hesitated. What if she couldn't win Anon's stones? They were his precious possession. What would she say to him? How could he understand?

Rig's impatient voice startled her. "Put ssstones in ssscircle!"

Hawk squeezed her shoulder, and she opened the bag and poured out the stones. Anon gave a little cry, and Ves-rynia shushed him.

Rig nodded. "I begin."

Tar held out his claw hand. "No. I will begin."

Both Kazmura narrowed their eyes. Rig made a slight hissing sound. Tar didn't move, his eyes fixed on the cave men. Glancing at Tar's claw, Rig finally dropped the large stone. "You begin."

Tar held the stone over the circle. "Who went first when you played Anon?"

"He did." Dok was quick to answer.

Hawk shook his head. Tar's smile made Akeela shiver. She thanked Celtar he was on their side and prayed for favor to win Anon's stones back.

"Then Akeela will also go first."

Rig nodded. Tar dropped the stone, and Akeela jumped at the

sound of impact. She knelt and gathered the stones that rolled outside the circle. There were five. "What do I do next?"

Hawk explained the rules, and the game started. It was not hard to learn, but she never knew which way the stones would roll. Still, her love for Anon kept her eyes sharp and her hand steady. The pile in front of her grew. So did the pile before the Kazmura. When the stones were gone from the center, they counted their winnings.

"Twenty-five," Rig announced, his voice sure and strong.

Akeela counted the last stone. "I also have twenty-five." She looked at the Kazmura guides. "What happens now?"

Rig smiled. "Play again."

Tar shook his head. "No. No more games. Akeela will keep her pile of stones, and you will keep yours."

Rig blinked. "Not the way game isss played. Tie meansss play again."

"No." Tar's voice rose a little above a whisper.

No one spoke or moved. Akeela's heart beat so hard, blood pulsed in her head. They were in a precarious position. If they played again, she would lose. Somehow, the Kazmura would find a way to win.

Finally, Rig said, "You keep ssssstones. We keep ssstones."

"Thank you." Akeela kept her eyes lowered as she gathered her pile and quickly stuffed them into Anon's bag. Her whole body trembled, and she forced back tears. Anon squealed with delight when she handed him the bag.

"What's going on?" Vorrak-ira's sleep-laced voice drifted over Anon's joyful chatter.

Everyone chuckled, and Ves-rynia reached over and punched her brother. "Go back to sleep, you dupeseed."

Akeela pulled Anon close under the blankets. He held his bag against his chest. "Go to sleep now," she told him. "And don't get up without me, okay?"

"Yah."

Akeela didn't know how long they slept, but when she opened her eyes, it was almost pitch black. "Oh!" She sat up and looked around, trying desperately to catch a glimmer of light—besides the faint glow coming from the auras of those who hadn't pulled the blankets completely over themselves. Anon mumbled something in his sleep, and Akeela pushed off her blanket and snugged it around him.

Where were the lanterns? When Rig and Dok left to catch fish, they never took both lights.

Akeela felt around where she thought Hawk had settled last night. Her fingers brushed against a blanket, and she grabbed the foot underneath. "Hawk," she whispered. "Hawk, wake up!"

Hawk's aura appeared when he sat up and the cover fell off.

Akeela scrambled to him and threw her arms around his shoulders. "Hawk, something's wrong. The lanterns are gone. Rig and Dok. I don't hear them. I can't see their auras."

"Akeela, wait. They must be here somewhere."

Akeela thought of last night's game and remembered the dark look on Rig's face. She shook her head. "Why did they take both lanterns? They've never done that before."

"What happened to the light?" Tar's voice broke into their conversation. Akeela could see his aura's outline from across the room.

Ves-rynia's voice came from the right. "Where is everyone? I can't see a thing."

"Keela?" That was Anon's frightened voice.

Akeela crawled to him. "It's all right, Anon. I'm here."

Anon clung to her arm. "Dark, Keela."

"Yes, Anon, it's dark." Akeela shivered. She couldn't see the cave walls, but they closed in, almost suffocating her as a terrifying thought ran through her head.

The lanterns were gone. And that could only mean one thing.

The Kazmura were gone as well.

Chapter Twenty-Three

"Blood worms and swamp grass!" Tzmet screeched. "Why are the chairs on top of the table?"

Shuffling and giggling came from behind heavy drapes that covered the north windows of the castle's great room. Tzmet's eyes narrowed as she crept toward the sound.

With one sweep of her arm, she wrenched the curtains aside. "Ah-ha!"

Two small goblins tumbled onto the floor. They held their sides and roared with laughter. How did goblins get into the castle? Tzmet's anger filled her beyond all reason, and she lifted her hand to annihilate them when a voice behind her spoke.

"Daughter."

Tzmet whirled around, choking on her emotions. "Father, you're up."

Riss'aird stood in the doorway, his face expressionless. He nodded at the now-silent goblins and waved them away. They scampered around him. One looked back and stuck its tongue out at Tzmet.

"Father, I—"

"Make the rooms in the west wing ready."

Tzmet curtsied. "Yes, Father. Who are we expecting?"

The corners of Riss'aird's lips rose. "My goblin servants."

"What? But, but . . ." Tzmet sputtered. Goblins living in the castle? Surely she'd heard wrong. There would be no peace, no order with goblins. They had no respect for anything or anyone. They loved practical jokes and turning things upside down.

Riss'aird's smile dropped. "Is there a problem, daughter?"

Tzmet lifted her head. "Yes, Father. Goblins *in* the castle? You see this room? That's just a sample of what'll happen. I know you need them, but the boggarts have the barracks ready. Surely they can stay there."

Riss'aird stood silent.

"They have no loyalty," Tzmet continued. "Why, after the spell went wrong—"

"Indeed, daughter. I've been wondering where you were and why you didn't get caught in the backfire?"

Tzmet licked her lips and gave a short chuckle. "I wanted a charm to give luck and make sure the magic's direction would not stray. I thought I had time to gather dark vine to braid in my hair."

Riss'aird's eyes went to her bald head. She reached up and touched her scalp. "As you can see, I did not escape unscathed."

"I see."

A loud crash sounded from the west wing. Tzmet gritted her teeth. Obviously, the goblins were already making themselves at home. The days ahead would be filled with pranks, trickery, and deceit. To say nothing of hair. Black, wiry, disgusting hair everywhere as the goblins shed all year round. She suppressed a shudder.

Riss'aird's even voice penetrated her thoughts. "I am retiring to my room now. Bring me the evening meal."

Tzmet brushed off her skirt. A few hairs fell to the floor. Striding to the kitchen, she screeched orders to the Hinwari. Then she yanked on a rope which hung near the door, sat at the table, and poured herself a goblet of red wine.

In a minute, Brimridge appeared at the doorway. "You rang, my lady?"

Tzmet drummed her fingers on the table.

"My lady?"

"Quiet, fool! I'm thinking."

The more Tzmet thought, the less she liked the idea. But what else could she do? Her father's decision to bring goblins into the castle forced her to this revolting option. She cleared her throat.

"Brimridge, tell me true. Are you loyal to me?"

The boggart leader shifted. He looked around the kitchen before answering. "Why, yes, my lady Tzmet. We are loyal to you and your father."

Tzmet pounded her fist on the table. "Wipe that irksome smile off your face and speak the truth, if you can. I must know if you are loyal to *me*."

His eyes narrowed. "What has happened? You have no reason to question my loyalty."

Tzmet didn't trust Brimridge. She despised him. But she needed him. Of all the disgusting creatures her father had called to his side, the boggarts were the least repulsive. Still, how much should she say?

As little as possible.

"My father has moved goblins into the west wing of the castle." Tzmet took a sip of wine and waited.

Brimridge chuckled. "How is that a problem?"

"How is it not a problem?" Tzmet snapped. She waved her hand. "Leave."

The boggart bowed and left the room without question. Tzmet knew he suspected she wasn't sharing all with him. Of course he suspected. She would've had she been in his place. Curse him and those wretched goblins. Although he'd be on alert now. She smiled as she realized they had an alliance against the goblins without her having to commit to anything.

Tzmet arranged her father's tray with cutlery and a vase of swamp roses. "Still, I may need to tell him more," she murmured as she folded the cloth napkin. "But I shall have to be careful not to let down my guard. Even though he's helping me, he's still a boggart."

Akeela held Anon as he wept. The other three spoke at once, their voices reverberating off the cave walls.

Tar's voice finally rose above the others. "Stop talking! We must calm down and make a plan."

Vorrak-ira snorted. "What kind of plan can we make? We're totally blind, yeh?"

"So what you think we should do, sit here and wait to die?" Ves-rynia asked.

"If I could use my sling, I'd feel better," Vorrak-ira retorted. "I came for protection, and I haven't been able to do anything!"

Ves-rynia gave a short laugh. "And what would you do then, sling a rock at our guides? We'd be in the same predicament we are now, yeh?"

"Stop arguing." Tar's voice was harsh. "We're not going to simply sit here. What good would that do?"

"Maybe we can feel our way by putting our hands on the walls," Hawk suggested.

Akeela saw Tar shake his head. If only they could see auras as she did. It'd be easier to communicate.

"I don't know, Hawk," Tar said. "We could try. It'll be slow going, and we'll have to make sure we don't lose anyone."

"Walk through these caves with no light and no way of knowing if we're going the right way?" Vorrak-ira sounded incredulous. "That's not much of a plan."

"Do you have a better one?" Ves-rynia asked.

Everyone started talking again, and Akeela watched their auras pulse and glow. Hawk moved closer to Vorrak-ira, and their auras touched. Where the lights joined, the bright blending startled Akeela and she gasped. If they'd not been in complete darkness, she would've missed it.

"Everyone, listen! I have an idea." She gave Anon a little hug. "Krezma told me someday my gift would save my life. Well, our lives are in danger right now. We can't see because there's no light, and we don't know which way to go."

Vorrak-ira sighed. "Tell us something we don't know, yeh?"

"I'm trying to tell you I can see your auras. They get brighter when you're closer to another person."

"So you're saying—" Hawk's voice sounded urgent.

"I'm saying that if we stand close to each other, your auras will make enough light for me to see." Akeela shrugged. "At least enough light for a few steps at a time."

"Let's try it," Tar said. "Akeela, locate each person and bring us together."

"Maybe we should tie ourselves one to another," Hawk added. "That way we're sure to stay close."

Everyone agreed, and Akeela placed them in a tight group. The glow lit up the area enough for her to find rope in the cart and food for everyone. They ate quickly, and in spite of the situation, Akeela enjoyed dried venison and apples as she never had before.

Tar decided it would be easier to leave the cart, so they took the most important things and divided the bags. Akeela insisted Anon be tied to her. Behind Anon was Hawk, then Ves-rynia, Vorrak-ira, and Tar.

Akeela took a deep breath. She could only see about two steps in front of her, but there was only one tunnel, so only one way to go. She took a deep breath. "Here we go."

Tzmet poured over the map with the fairy writings. She pounded her fist on the table. Rat's teeth! Where were her spies? Now that the Earth Fountain was hers, she wanted to move on to the next.

"The Water Fountain, I think," she said. "Yes, the Water Fountain. And I'll bring back water for my father to drink. Surely it will boost his energy."

The raven squawked and flapped its wings.

"Silence, you fool bird. And lay me some eggs or I'll pull out all your feathers."

The raven fluffed the mentioned feathers but didn't make a sound.

Tzmet ran her hand over the map. Once again, the niggling thought came that maybe she should've left things the way they were. She looked up at the sound of footsteps, and Brimridge strode in. He stopped next to her chair and gave a quick bow.

"Well? What is it?" Tzmet ground out the words.

"My lady Tzmet, your father has need of you."

Tzmet flushed. She was getting tired of being at his beck and call, not much more than a slave. What could she possibly do that the goblins could not? Finding and poisoning the Water Fountain was surely more important than anything else.

"My lady?"

Tzmet's eyes narrowed. "Did he say what he wanted?"

"No, my lady." Brimridge smiled, stroking his beard. "But the goblin leader is with him."

"Argh! I hate goblins." The words were out before she could stop them. In frustration, she stood and flung her hand out. "Leave!"

He turned to leave but paused. "One more thing. I found two small goblins coming out of your bedroom, just a short time ago."

"*What?*" Tzmet shrieked.

"Now, my lady, it's best not to keep the mighty Riss'aird waiting." Brimridge left the room and chuckled as he walked down the hall.

"Bloodworms and fireweed! If those goblins have touched a single thing of mine, I will personally pulverize them." She closed her book of spells and lugged it to the large cabinet. After locking it, she dropped the key into her skirt pocket. "My father can wait another minute. I'm going to check my room first."

The raven squawked.

"Get to laying those eggs!"

Chapter Twenty-Four

Her room was in a shambles. The bedcovers were strewn across her breakfast table, the vanity chair was on top of the bed, and her jewelry box was upside down on the dresser. The closet door was open, and every dress she owned lay in a heap on the floor. Tzmet's anger boiled as she picked up an onyx earring.

No more. She would demand the goblins leave today.

She whipped down the hallway and flung open her father's bedroom door. Riss'aird and the putrid goblin leader, Sleg, were sitting at a small table and looked up in surprise.

Pointing at Sleg, she said, "You and your heathens have to leave today. I'll have no more of your accursed pranks!"

Riss'aird folded his hands on the silk blanket that covered his legs. "Daughter?"

Tzmet trembled with anger. She should've paid attention to her father's tone of voice, but at the moment, she didn't care. "They have been here a mere three days, and my castle has been turned upside down." She crossed her arms. "I cannot stand it anymore."

Sleg picked up his tall, pointed hat. "I will take my leave of you now, Mighty One." He bowed to Riss'aird, placed the hat on his hairy head, and strolled past Tzmet. She sneered at him, and he turned and winked.

Before she could respond, Riss'aird spoke. "Come in and shut the door."

Tzmet watched the goblin until he turned a corner. Then she closed the door and turned around. She opened her mouth to speak, but he held up a finger.

"It seems you've forgotten who the owner of this castle is."

"I . . . well . . . I have no idea how long I slept after the spell backfired. It's just been me for fifteen years, Father, and I—"

Riss'aird waved his hand. "Indeed, daughter, but I am here now."

Tzmet dropped into a quick curtsey. Unreasonable fear filled her mind, and all she wanted to do was to go back to her room and clean up. "Please forgive me. I won't forget again."

She turned to go, and Riss'aird's voice stopped her. "The goblins are here at my request, daughter. You will treat them as guests."

She set her lips and looked away.

"Is this a problem?"

Tzmet took a breath. Riss'aird was her father. Surely he would understand. She lifted her chin and looked him straight in his icy-blue eyes, ignoring the trembling in her legs. "The problem I have is all the upset and havoc they bring. Why, just this morning two of those wretched goblins completely destroyed my bedroom!"

Riss'aird smiled.

Tzmet's temper snapped. "Father! How can I continue with my plans to poison the fairy fountains if I have to clean up after those vile, smelly, hairy creatures?"

His eyebrows lowered. "Peace, daughter. I will not have you speak to me in such a manner." He clicked his fingernails on the table. "I will order the goblins away from your room, but you will see to it they have everything they need."

Tzmet nodded once. The ornately decorated walls felt as though they were closing in. She struggled to take a deep breath. "And what do they need?"

Riss'aird leaned forward, his face void of expression. "The goblins are the only creatures willing to handle the transvariant process. Unless you would like the honor."

Tzmet's stomach dropped to her knees. She shook her head.

"So we understand each other?"

She nodded.

"And you will make sure they have all the necessary items?"

She nodded again.

Riss'aird gave a cold smile. "Go and clean your room, daughter."

He didn't need to tell her twice. She whirled, yanked the door open, and fled down the hall.

<hr />

Akeela pushed her foot forward, cautious about stepping out of the light of their auras. Desperation almost overwhelmed her. At least she could see a little; she could only imagine how everyone else felt.

The damp darkness seemed to seep into her skin, and she fought panic with each step.

She reached out to touch the cave walls and realized she could feel both sides with her fingertips. Glancing up, she saw a single, glowing spider scoot across the ceiling. The tunnel was growing narrower and the ceiling lower, but it was also heading up.

One step at a time, she told herself. Anon gripped her waist tightly, and she reached back to rub his furry head.

"Hungry, Keela," he said.

"Just a little farther, Anon."

Ten more steps.

The tunnel continued to close in.

Ten more steps.

Akeela could now feel both sides without having to stretch her arms all the way out. *Dear Celtar, help us.*

Tzmet stormed into the great room, intending to finish her plans to find the Water Fountain. She'd just cleaned up a goblin mess in the north hallway and was in no mood for more tricks.

She snapped her fingers at a Hinwar. "Get me something to eat! I have a long trip ahead of me."

Thoughts of destroying another fairy fountain pushed the goblins' tricks out of her mind, and she fingered the key in her pocket. But before she could pull it out, something caught her eye. Sticking out from under the dining table was a slender branch of dried dark vine. She frowned and stooped to pick it up. Several black hairs floated to the floor. Blast! Wretched goblins. She flew to her cabinet and jammed the key in the lock.

"Snakeroot and marshflies! I'll kill them! I'll kill them all!"

The cabinet, usually so organized and neat, was a wreck. Bowls crashed to the floor as she opened the doors. Herbs lay scattered on every shelf, and parchments were crumpled into balls. Her precious map was torn in two, one half on the top shelf and the other on the bottom. Her potion bottles had tipped over, and if not for the corks, would've emptied their contents everywhere.

Tzmet whirled at the sound of footsteps approaching.

Brimridge stood at the doorway, his eyes wide. "I heard your scream, my lady. Our goblin friends have paid you a visit, I see."

"Your astuteness astounds me. What do you want?"

Brimridge bowed. "Only to serve you."

The raven squawked, and Tzmet folded her arms. "Silence, you confounded bird! I have to think." She began to pace. "So you want to serve me. You can start by moving my cabinet into my bedroom. It's off-limits to the goblins. I have my father's word."

"As you wish," Brimridge murmured. He stroked his beard and gave a slight smile before turning to go.

Tzmet strode across the room and grabbed the boggart's arm. "What's so funny, you putrid piece of swamp grass?"

Brimridge's black eyes glittered in the candlelight. "My lady, do you really think Riss'aird is concerned with your personal belongings? If he were, he would've made sure this room was protected since it contains so many important things."

Tzmet opened her mouth to retort, but Brimridge interrupted.

"Listen, my lady. The goblins are here only for the transvarient process, which you and I would be forced to do otherwise. My people are not willing. You are not willing. This gives us something in common."

The aroma of her meal being prepared slipped into the room, and her stomach growled. She dropped Brimridge's arm and glared at him. He met her stare with unflinching eyes.

"Fine," she said, grinding out the word. "Stay. Have a meal with me. We can talk about an . . . alliance."

Brimridge bowed again. "Yes, my lady."

Tzmet put up a hand. "A *temporary* alliance!"

"Yes, my lady."

The feeling of a trap closing persisted as she and Brimridge worked out their alliance. But the roast pig was excellent, and the wine made their negotiations bearable. Tzmet sat alone after the meal ended and considered their plan.

"I believe this will benefit me," she said to the raven, who only ruffled its feathers in response. "And I'll have less worry when I'm on my trip to the Water Fountain." She took a sip of wine and smiled. "Those goblins are in for a surprise."

The sun cast its first rays on the highest tower of the castle as Tzmet checked her bag of supplies. The magically repaired map was rolled and placed in the front along with her mixture of herbs and the fairy wing cape. She'd packed extra waterskins and several days' worth of dried muskrat and flatbread.

As she entered the stable, Nightshade whinnied and pawed at the ground, anxious to be off.

"Easy, my pet," Tzmet said. "Our adventure will begin soon, and you'll have the chance to stretch your legs."

She led Nightshade out of his stall. The morning air was crisp, and Tzmet breathed deeply. If luck, weather, and good roads stayed with her, she should arrive at the Water Fountain in three, maybe four, days.

Brimridge met her at the castle gate, looking mighty pleased.

Tzmet frowned. "I hope that look of delight is not because I'm leaving."

"Oh, no, my lady." Brimridge bowed and stroked his pointed beard. "I came to inform you of the tragic accident."

Tzmet put a hand on her hip. "What are you talking about, fool? I don't have time for games."

Nightshade nickered in agreement.

Brimridge chuckled. "No games, my lady. You see, two young goblins apparently decided to wander into forbidden territory. Fortunately, they were quick, or they would've lost more than their fingertips."

Tzmet smiled. She looked at her hand, stretching out her fingers. "Oh my. That must've hurt."

"Indeed, my lady."

"I suppose they won't be so quick to enter my bedchamber again."

Brimridge bowed again. "No, my lady."

Tzmet leaped onto the horse's back. She heard murmuring and turned. All the boggarts filed into the courtyard, Brimridge's wife in front. Many held bouquets of swamp grass, which was in the flowering stage. Brimridge nodded, and those with the vilely fragrant flowers stepped forward and cast the bouquets in front of Nightshade, who tossed his head.

"Farewell, my lady," Brimridge said. "Farewell and success!"

Tzmet nodded and urged Nightshade forward. As he stepped on the swamp grass, the sulfurous odor wafted up, and Tzmet tried not to gag. She held herself high, as a Sultana should. If not for the urgency of finding the fountains and poisoning them, she never would've allied herself with boggarts.

Would her bedchamber and cabinet of precious herbs and spells be intact when she returned? They'd better, or she'd beat the boggarts with their own swamp grass.

Chapter Twenty-Five

Krezma held a mug of saloop and stared into the fire. Dawn was just breaking, and the first rays of the sun filtered through the trees. Minister Dir-mac sat silently beside her as the rest of the Acadian camp slumbered, though it wouldn't be long before they stirred.

"I have stayed too long," she finally said.

Dir-mac set his mug on the ground and rubbed his hands. "It has only been two days."

Krezma nodded. "Yes, two days, but much can happen in that time. I cannot leave until I get news, though. It would be even worse to go the wrong way after I leave Broem."

Daylight increased and with it, animal activity. A squirrel wandered into the circle of logs. He sniffed the ground, his head darting here and there. Then he stopped and began to dig furiously. After several seconds, he came up with an acorn and scampered off.

Krezma had to smile. Something about the animals behaving normally gave her peace. She'd just started to relax when the small fire threw up sparks, jolting her back to reality and the danger they were all in. A fire fairy danced in the flames.

Krezma leaned forward. "Good fairy, what news do you bring?"

"Blessings, Krezma!" The fairy lifted her hands and spun around. Then she settled to stand in the embers. "The news is dire. Two of our fire fairy spies were able to get into the witch's castle. Riss'aird *has* risen from the ashes!"

Krezma put a hand to her throat. "I feared this. What else have they learned?"

"Evil creatures are gathering at the castle. Although they quarrel among themselves."

"I see." Krezma paused to take a breath. "Thank you, dear one. I can prepare to leave once you give me the location of Akeela and the group."

The fire fairy spun up from the embers. "We have lost the Guardian."

Krezma looked up, her heart beating hard against her chest.

Dir-mac put his hand on her arm. "What is it?"

Krezma leaned forward. "What do you mean, lost her?"

"We have not seen her or any other member of the group since the quake."

"What is the opinion of the Counsel?" Krezma asked.

"The Ruling Fairy believes the Guardian and her companions have gone into hiding, although we know not where they might be."

Krezma nodded. "I thank you for the news, although it is distressing. May Celtar bless you."

The fairy whizzed up out of the flames and disappeared in a spark.

Krezma turned to the minister. "I must prepare to leave. What we feared has happened. Riss'aird has risen."

Dir-mac gasped.

"And Akeela is missing," she went on. "We must not panic. I will find her."

"Of course," Dir-mac said. "Of course. Let's get you supplies, yeh?"

"My thanks. And you must inform Ban-ira so he can get the Kin-tribe ready."

Krezma would only allow half an hour to prepare. She couldn't waste any more time. The Acadians would have to get themselves ready. She needed to get Ham and then find Akeela.

It's funny—she lifted the bag to her shoulder—*that I should be searching for the child when I spent the last fifteen years wanting to be rid of her.*

Desperation filled her as she walked in Broem's direction. No more wasted time. The group had left ten days earlier. That was ten days closer to whatever Riss'aird had surely planned.

Akeela's shoulder brushed the side of the cave, and the stone's chill seeped through her tunic. If it got any narrower, they'd have to go back.

"This is crazy," Vorrak-ira said. "I can feel the sides on both shoulders, yeh?"

Ves-rynia's voice came from behind Hawk. "Did you really have to point that out?"

"I'm only speaking the truth, yeh?"

Tar spoke up. "Bickering is not going to help. We have to keep going."

"Aye, what do you want to do, sit down and die?" Ves-rynia asked.

Vorrak-ira stopped, causing everyone in the group to stumble. "Nay, I want to sit down and eat. I'm starving!"

The tension broke, and everyone laughed.

"You're a dupeseed," Hawk said. "How can we sit when the tunnel is so narrow?"

"I dunno," Vorrak-ira said. "But I *am* hungry."

"We need to keep going," Akeela said. "I can feel the air moving a little up ahead. Maybe it will open up some."

"Cold, Keela." Anon's voice sounded thin.

"I know, dear. We're all cold. But we have to keep walking.

Can you be a brave faun?"

Everyone started shuffling along again, and Akeela tried to feel optimistic. But while mostly blind, hungry, and without direction, how could she get through this? As despair crept over her, Anon began humming.

It reverberated off the walls and surrounded the group like a fuzzy blanket. Akeela joined in and then Tar, Hawk, and Ves-rynia. Vorrak'ira remained stubbornly silent. About the third time through the song, Akeela's hands slipped off the walls into nothing.

She stopped and called out, "Stop!"

What should she do? The group was depending on her. She closed her eyes and took a breath. "Okay, everyone, we have to be careful because I can't feel the walls anymore."

"Try one side," Tar said. "Move us in a group so you can have more light."

Akeela nodded. Then she smiled. Why nod when no one could see? But habit was habit. "Yes, let's move to the left."

When the whole group was out of the tunnel, Akeela moved them into a circle. Their auras touched and shone like a beacon.

"Okay, don't move. I need to look around."

"What can you see?" Vorrak-ira asked.

"Be quiet," Ves-rynia said. "You're scraping my branches."

Akeela looked around the cave. Even though the group's auras gave off light, it was still difficult to see details. "I wish we could light a fire. We're in a room of some sort, but I can't see if there's another opening."

Everyone groaned. "If we have something to burn, I could light a fire," Tar said. "I still have the striking stones."

Vorrak-ira laughed. "Anyone see any trees underground?"

Hawk hit him in the head.

"What?" Vorrak-ira asked.

Tar put out his hands in a gesture of peace. Akeela smiled because even though they couldn't see each other, the group still shook their heads or moved their hands. She wished they could all see auras.

"Let's sit and eat now that we have room," Tar said. "Then we can talk about what to do next."

Everyone sat, and Akeela struggled not to let tears fall. If only she hadn't found that cave for them to hide in. They were in this situation because of her. She handed an apple to Anon. "Here, Anon dear, you take this, and I'll find you some dried rabbit."

Anon clutched the apple. "Want light, Keela. Can't see."

"I know, I know," she said. "I'm trying to get us to the light."

Ves-rynia lifted one of the bags. "This bag is almost empty. Can we put the rest of the food into another bag and burn this? Maybe it will give us enough light to see where to go next."

"We can try," Tar said. "Akeela, will you get the bag and give it to me?"

Ves-rynia pulled out the remaining apples and held out the bag. "Here. There are three apples left. Who has the other food bag?"

"I do," said Hawk. "Pass them to me."

Akeela took the empty bag and gave it to Tar. She could almost feel everyone holding their breath as Tar struck the stones. The sparks startled them, and they laughed nervously. But the bag didn't light. Tar tried several times with no success.

"It's no good," he finally said. "I need something for the sparks to catch on."

"Like what?" Vorrak-ira asked. "No trees, no pine needles, no leaves. What are we going to do now, yeh?"

"Leaves! My bag has dried herbs," Akeela said. "Will they do?"

"They might." Tar sounded excited, which was strange coming from Tar.

Akeela felt through her bag and wrapped her fingers around the cloth that held Krezma's dried herbs. She'd packed them in case they were needed for cooking. Now she'd gladly eat stew or roasted pheasant without any flavoring at all. She handed the herbs to Tar, who placed them in a pile on the bag.

"Please, Celtar, let this work," Ves-rynia prayed.

Tar struck the stones. Nothing. He struck them again. The sparks flashed and caught the herbs. He leaned forward and blew gently over the pile. It started to flame, and everyone cheered, their voices echoing off the walls. Anon put his hands over his ears.

The difference the small flame made was amazing. Everyone looked at each other and smiled. Tar pulled up a section of the bag and held it in the fire. It caught, and everyone cheered again.

Tar fanned his hand over the flames. "Akeela, we need to look around quickly. I fear this won't last long. The bag's edges have caught, but they're not flaming, they're smoldering. We only have until the herbs burn out."

They were, indeed, in a small room. A large stone mound stood in the middle, reaching up to the ceiling, and on the wall beyond it were two openings.

"What do we do now?" Vorrak-ira asked.

Anguish filled Akeela as she stared at the two tunnels. If she chose wrong, they would all die.

Tzmet pulled on Nightshade's reigns. The edge of the forest stood before her, but she was hungry. "We'll rest here and refresh ourselves," she said to the horse.

Nightshade tossed his head and whinnied.

"Don't reveal our position, you dolt. I don't wish for those wretched forest people to know we're here."

Tzmet slid from the horse and adjusted her clothing. She'd chosen the pants and tunic once more, even though they were hideous. She led Nightshade to a cluster of rocks.

"I think we can chance a small fire."

It didn't take long to get the fire going, and she spread the map out before her while the rabbit she'd caught roasted on a stick. According to her map, the water fountain was located southwest of her castle in a lake on the forest's edge. Finding it shouldn't be too difficult. She leaned back on a large rock and closed her eyes.

She awoke with a start. At first, she didn't know where she was. A whiff of smoke drifted past her, and she coughed. The fire! The map! With a shriek, she leaped to her feet. The rabbit was a black lump, and the map was in flames.

"Curses and blast!" She stamped out the burning map. "You

wretched, no good, poor excuse for a horse! Couldn't you have warned me?"

Nightshade snorted and pawed the ground.

Tzmet lifted the map by a corner. Fortunately, only one edge had caught, and the majority of the map was still readable. Her stomach growled, and she rolled the map, stuffed it into the bag, and plopped on the ground. "I suppose I can eat what I brought, but you're on your own."

Nightshade tossed his head.

As she reached into her sack for some dried muskrat, thunder cracked overhead, and the heavens let loose. Nightshade whinnied and shook his head.

"Be quiet, you miserable beast," Tzmet growled, "and get under those trees. It shouldn't last long."

But the rain poured all night and all the next day.

Tzmet urged Nightshade on, and they sloshed through mud and puddles. "I will not allow a little water to stop me. And besides, we are less likely to be seen. Why, those wretched forest people are most likely huddled in their homes waiting for it to end."

Nightshade nickered in response.

"No sass from you, or you'll see the inside of my cooking pot."

The rain continued as Tzmet slogged her way closer to the lake on the other side of the forest.

❧

"Two tunnels," Akeela whispered. "How do I choose?"

"Let's move closer," Tar said. "Hawk, help me move the bag before the herbs go out." He lifted the corner and dragged it across the room with Hawk's help. Then Hawk picked up the striking stones and a food bag.

Akeela stood. "Anon, hold my hand. Ves-rynia, will you and Vorrak-ira get the other two bags?"

They stood facing the two tunnels. In the dim light, the tunnel on the left sloped up and the other, down.

Vorrak-ira laughed. "What's so hard about this, yeh? I'm for going up and out of here."

Everyone murmured in agreement. Tar waved his hand over the barely burning bag to keep the flame going, but to no avail. The fire went out, and they were thrust into endless dark once more. Anon began to wail.

"Hush, dearest!" Akeela hugged him. "We'll all move together again. I can see enough for all of us. Please, Anon, it'll be all right."

Anon sobbed against Akeela's chest. "Want light, Keela."

"I know, I know. We'll find light." Akeela reached over and pulled on Ves-rynia's arm. "Come on, everyone. Get tied together again."

As the group positioned themselves in the same order, Akeela studied the tunnel openings in the dim light of their auras. The left one would take them up, which was the way they wanted to go. But it didn't feel right to her.

"We're ready, Akeela," said Hawk.

"Give me a minute," she said. "I don't want to make the wrong decision."

Vorrak-ira snorted. "What's the problem? Up and out. Let's go, yeh?"

Akeela looked at their frightened faces, then she glanced at the smoldering bag. Something moved. She peered closer. It was smoke. White fingers of smoke drifted away from the bag and into the tunnel opening on the right.

Akeela had an idea. "Tar?"

"Yes?"

"I can see the smoke from the bag. It's drifting into the tunnel on the right. I think we should go that way."

"Yes," Tar said. "Smoke will drift with air currents."

"And if there's air moving, it must be coming from outside," Hawk said.

Akeela nodded. "Let's go then."

"Nah, that tunnel leads down," Vorrak-ira snapped. "We want to go up. I'm *not* going back down."

Ves-rynia and Hawk tried to persuade him, and their voices

grew louder. Finally, Tar shouted, and the sound reverberated off the walls. Anon squealed in fright.

"Vorrak-ira, you have to go where the group decides," Tar said. "We have to stay together."

"I didn't hear anyone agree," Vorrak-ira said, his voice heavy with sarcasm. "Akeela decided and told us. Why can't we decide, yeh?"

"You're about as useful as a run-off," Ves-rynia said. "I agree with Akeela."

"So do I," said Hawk.

Vorrak-ira gave a short laugh. "Sure you do. But what about Anon? He gets a choice. Hey, Anon, do you want to go up and out or back down?"

Anon's arms tightened around Akeela's waist.

"Don't scare him. He doesn't understand."

"He understands more than you know," Vorrak-ira sneered. "Come on, Anon. Which way do you want to go?"

"Want to go with Keela," he said into Akeela's tunic.

"Up or down, Anon?" Vorrak-ira's voice rose in anger.

"Want to go with Keela!" Anon shouted.

Tar interrupted them. "That's enough. We need to get going."

"Besides, even if Anon said up, you're still outvoted," said Ves-rynia. "So quit standing around like a piece of scat. Let's go."

Vorrak-ira mumbled to himself but argued no more. The group started their slow shuffle as Akeela led them into the tunnel on the right, where they started a downward trek.

Tzmet stood at the edge of the lake. The sun had yet to make an appearance, but the storm clouds had dissipated, and the horizon had thrown off the cloak of night. The first of the mourning doves began their haunting call as she studied the map, which was burned exactly where the fountain should be.

"This is ridiculous. How am I supposed to find the fountain with this wretched map?"

Nightshade nickered. He began to walk south, along the water's edge.

Tzmet slapped her thigh. "Get back here, you miscreant!"

Nightshade ignored her and kept going.

"Argh! You useless, disobedient, senseless horse. When I catch you, you're done. Through. Ashes. *Do you hear me?*"

Nightshade broke into a trot.

Tzmet ground her teeth and rolled up the map. She slid it in the bag, heaved the bag on her shoulder, and started after the horse.

"Stupid animal. Did the same thing to me in the desert —" Realization hit her like a bolt. "Like the desert! Wait. Wait! You blasted brute."

The sun broke over the horizon as Tzmet arrived, panting, at the lower part of the lake. Nightshade stood staring at a waterfall.

"You aggravating, idiotic, bloody pain in my —"

Nightshade whinnied, and it seemed to Tzmet that he laughed at her. She sat on a large boulder and tried to catch her breath. She had to move quickly to beat the water fairies' morning ritual. But where exactly was the source of the fountain? She pulled out the map and blew across the burned part. Yes, there was the lake, but the waterfall was gone. She could make out lines rising in an arc out of what looked like a cloud. A rainbow? On the lake. How was this possible?

Nightshade snorted, and Tzmet glanced up. The force of the water hitting the lake forced clouds of mist to rise at the base of the fall. She looked at the map again. That could be what the drawing represented, but where was the rainbow? Before she could come up with an answer, the sun rose above the trees. The light refracted through the mist, and in a moment, colors danced in an arch, revealing a perfect rainbow.

"Yes! Stand back, Nightshade." The horse complied, and Tzmet tipped her head back and thrust her hands in the air. *"Braya reym sofring!"*

Tzmet braced for the fountain to burst forth from the lake. Instead, the waterfall stopped flowing. She stared at the dripping pile of rocks. Where was the fountain?

Chapter Twenty-Six

Krezma paused to catch her breath. She'd pushed herself to keep a quick pace, and it was now telling on her.

"I am not as young as I used to be," she said under her breath.

She had not yet reached Broem but hoped to by lunchtime. Thankfully, the rain had ceased during the night, and the new day promised to be pleasant.

"I may as well break my fast," she said aloud to no one.

She longed for a cup of tea but didn't want to take the time to build a fire and find a large leaf to boil water. She must get Ham and find Akeela.

Before it was too late.

After eating a strip of dried rabbit and a handful of red berries, she took note of the rising sun's position. The group, if they stayed their course, was heading northeast from the Acadian camp, so as soon as she got to Broem and Ham packed a few things, that's the direction they would head.

With a stretch and a groan, she stood and began walking.

Tzmet stared at the cave now visible behind the fall. Could the fountain be inside? The Earth Fountain had been so large and so easily seen. She took a step toward the water's edge. The distance to the cave was not long, but she didn't relish the thought of wading across the lake. How deep was the water?

"Nightshade," she said over her shoulder. "Come here and make yourself useful."

The horse moved to her side. She took a handful of his mane and pulled herself up.

"Let's go."

He took a few steps into the water and stopped.

Tzmet kicked his sides. "Move, you lazy creature!"

Nightshade waded in farther. A few feet from the cave, the water rose a little above his midsection, and he refused to take any more steps. Tzmet kicked and kicked, but he only tossed his head and wouldn't budge.

"Argh!" Tzmet slid off his back and into the water. Her feet touched the sandy bottom, and she lifted her chin and propelled herself forward. After a few steps, the ground disappeared from beneath her. Before she could take a breath, she went under. She came up choking and splashing. "Useless, stupid animal!" she screeched. "If you value your life, you won't move a muscle. Wait for me."

She took a deep breath and plunged under the water, reaching the rocks at the base of the cave in a few seconds.

The sun appeared above the treetops as Tzmet pulled herself out of the water. She dropped the bag and wrung out her tunic. Then she pulled out the soaked fairy wing cape and gave it a good shake. "This had better still work."

But she didn't see anything that resembled a fountain. This puzzled her, for the waterfall had ceased to run when she'd uttered the magic words, and she expected the Water Fountain to be revealed. As she stood pondering, a trickling sound caught her attention, so she moved into the cave and found a puddle, about five or six hands wide. In the center bubbled a small fountain.

Surely this couldn't be what she was searching for. "Stupid, mindless fairies. They must've given me a defective map."

No sooner were the words out of her mouth than the sunlight broke in through a hole in the cave ceiling and shone directly on the fountain. It gleamed as bright as polished silver, and Tzmet had to shade her eyes. For a moment, she couldn't move.

"Sun, moon, and stars! The cape. The cape!"

She darted to the front of the cave where the poisoned fairy wing cape lay in a heap.

"Blast!" She snatched it up. Any minute, the wretched water fairies would be here. She had to move now.

Whirling around, Tzmet hugged the cape to her chest. She approached the shining fountain, held her breath, then reached out to toss the cape. Suddenly, she yanked it back.

"How could I forget?"

Tzmet went back to the bag and pulled out an empty water-skin. She filled it with water from the fountain and smiled.

"If I'm right, this will strengthen my father."

She turned her attention back to the cape and lifted it once more. With a flick of her wrist, she sent the cape spinning. The fairy wings fluttered and sparkled in the sunlight, and the cape drifted over the tiny fountain of water. The water bubbled under it for a moment. Then all movement stopped, and Tzmet pulled the cape back. The ray of sunlight still shone through the opening, but instead of silver, the puddle of water now gleamed a dark red.

Tzmet smirked, stuffed the waterskin and cape back into the bag, and nodded. Time to go home and report her success. Satisfaction filled her. She had no doubt Riss'aird would be impressed.

A sound broke into her thoughts. Water began to run down the cave opening.

"Nightshade!" she screeched and ran for the cave entrance.

Before she could climb over the rocks and leap into the lake, the full force of the waterfall returned, and she was swept down, crashing against large stones. She grasped at a rock and held on with her fingertips as the water blasted her face and surged up her nose. She screamed and let go. Sharp pain burst on the side of her head, and everything went black.

＊

Akeela's feet ached as she trudged along the tunnel. While she could stretch out her arms and feel both walls, at least they weren't closing in. The path continued downward, and she prayed fervently she hadn't chosen the wrong way.

Vorrak-ira grumbled continually under his breath, and Anon whimpered from time to time. Once Ves-rynia tried to get everyone to sing again, but the echoes grew loud and harsh, so they stopped.

"Isn't it time to rest?" Vorrak-ira asked.

"We should go a little farther," Tar answered. "We haven't been walking that long."

Vorrak-ira snorted. "Who gave you a crown of leaves?"

"Vorrak-ira, stop," said Ves-rynia.

"We need to keep going," added Hawk.

Akeela stopped and turned around. "Hey, everyone—"

But before she could continue, Vorrak-ira reached around Ves-rynia and shoved Hawk, who fell into Anon, taking Ves-rynia with him. Anon immediately began to cry.

Akeela shouted, "What are you doing?" and hugged Anon tight the same time Tar cried, "That's enough!"

No one said anything for a moment while the sound echoed and died off. Anon sobbed against Akeela's shoulder. Vorrak-ira stood looking down as Hawk helped Ves-rynia up. Tar gripped his shoulder, as though he thought Vorrak-ira would run away.

Akeela took a deep breath. What she wouldn't give for fresh air. "Listen, I think the path is changing. It feels like we're not moving down anymore."

"I agree. That's why we need to keep going," Tar said.

Vorrak-ira pulled himself out of Tar's grasp. "Why didn't you say something? Here we are, walking in the dark, trusting you when we can't see a thing, yeh?"

Akeela's face flushed. "I'm sorry, please forgive me. I just want to get us out of here."

"It's fine, Akeela," Hawk said. "If Vorrak-ira had been paying attention instead of scraping his own bark, he'd have noticed too."

"Aye, let's go," said Ves-rynia.

They started walking again, and Akeela was sure they were now heading up. She thanked Celtar, and for the first time in days, felt optimistic. Relief flooded her, and she said over her shoulder, "We *are* going up!"

"Finally," grumbled Vorrak-ira.

Akeela smiled. Everything was going to work out. All they had to do was keep going. Then she looked up. Not again! Another set of tunnels stood before them.

"Oh, no." She stopped.

"What is it?" Tar asked.

"Another set of tunnels. And I don't have any more dried herbs to light. Maybe we could —"

But before she could say anything else, everyone's auras went out.

Krezma scooped water in her hand. The sun's heat bore down on her back, and she wiped sweat from her forehead. Funny, the water didn't refresh her thirst. *I'm too old for this.*

Resting by the stream at the forest's edge seemed like a good idea, so she stretched out in the shade of an oak and closed her eyes. But rest was not to be had, for as soon as she started to drift off, voices raised in alarm.

"What's going on?" She struggled to her feet.

A group of five forest fairies hovered in front of her. One flew forward. "Please, Krezma, you must come. Something's wrong with the water."

It had to be Tzmet's doing. "How long?"

"Since the sun rose," the fairy answered. "We've searched the forest for you all morning."

Krezma wrestled with continuing to Broem or going to the fountain. She was so close to the village! But what damage had this done to the water fairies, and what would be the result? She must attend to the Water Fountain before something worse happened. Then there'd be no need for Akeela's husband at all.

Krezma turned and walked away from Broem. "Let's go."

Krezma looked down at the dark-red puddle. Just as she'd thought. Tzmet had poisoned the Water Fountain. A dozen water fairies lay outside the cave on rocks, their strength draining away. On the sand at the edge of the lake, hundreds of earth fairies gathered, waiting for Krezma's instructions. Fifteen more hovered at her sides. Five small fires burned near the cave entrance, each holding three fire fairies, and she felt the presence of air fairies, although she had no idea how many had come. Krezma hoped it would be enough.

Dear Celtar, give me success. Then, straightening her back, she walked to the cave entrance. "Sing, dear ones. Sing!"

As the fairies lifted their voices, Krezma crushed several herbs between her fingers and let them fall into the poisoned water. She murmured a healing prayer and poured in a drop of the nacre oil Dir-mac had given her.

The water steamed and hissed. A stench of rotting plants and stagnant water filled the cave, and Krezma coughed. But she didn't move. *This must work!* She added another drop.

Without warning, the water shot up and out the opening in the cave ceiling, then collapsed with a splash. Krezma held her breath. A few moments passed in complete silence. Then the ground trembled, and the fountain began to bubble. Krezma watched as the red color faded and clear, fresh water could be seen.

She picked up the small bag that held her herbs and nacre oil and moved slowly to the cave opening. "It is done."

The fairies cheered and gave thanks to Celtar, but Krezma's thoughts were of her daughter. How had Tzmet found the fountains? She must've had help, but who? Never before had Krezma known fairies to betray each other, and no one except fairies, Oret, and herself knew the location of the Fairy Fountains.

"Thank you, Krezma."

Krezma turned and smiled at the water fairies. "Your strength will return. Rest here where it's safe. I must leave you."

The water fairies huddled together and closed their eyes. Krezma looked once more at the bubbling fountain. Then she walked out and climbed carefully over the slippery rocks. She eased herself into the water, holding the herb bag high, and turned to float on her back. When she reached shore, she slipped her dress on over the still-wet tunic and motioned for the earth fairies to come near.

"We must think ahead," she said. "Tzmet has poisoned the Earth Fountain and now the Water Fountain. I know not if she realizes we have healed them, so we must assume she'll look for the others."

A male fairy, one of the Ruling Fairy's Warriors, stepped forward. "We must protect the other fountains!"

All the fairies murmured agreement.

Krezma held up a hand. Things were dire, indeed, for the Ruling Fairy to send one of her warriors. No time to dwell on that, though. "Yes, yes. We must. But listen to me. Tzmet could not have figured this out on her own, so great care is needed. I believe we must go to the Fire Fountain next. The Air Fountain is the safest of all because it moves from place to place."

"Agreed," the Warrior said. "I will gather more warriors and meet you at the Fire Fountain."

Krezma nodded and turned her attention to the fire fairies. "You must warn the others. Alert the council! I will leave directly. The journey will take three days, and I fear Tzmet has the advantage."

"How do you know?" one of the fire fairies asked.

Krezma pointed to the hoofprints in the sand, leading away from the lake.

Chapter Twenty-Seven

Tzmet groaned and tried to open her eyes. Excruciating pain pounded in her head. Where was she? What'd happened? She tried to speak, but only a rumble came from her throat, and her chest felt like Nightshade was sitting on it. She blinked against the light.

"My lady, welcome back," said a rough and slimy voice.

Tzmet groaned again. "Brimridge."

"At your service, as always."

Akeela stood, stunned, in the inky blackness of the cave. *There has to be light!* But no light could be seen. A deep, consuming fear rose in her, and she could no longer stand. Kneeling on the stone floor, Akeela tried desperately to see something. Anything.

"Akeela?" Hawk called. "What's wrong?"

No one else knew she was as blind as they. How could she tell them? What could she say? She didn't even know what'd happened. Never in her whole life had Akeela seen such complete darkness. There was always an aura to light her way.

Tar's voice came next. "Akeela?"

"I'm here," she said.

"What are you waiting for, yeh?" Vorrak-ira grumbled. "Pick a tunnel and keep going."

Akeela didn't trust her voice. Anon's hand slipped into hers. She tried to muffle a cry by hugging him, but there was no hiding any sound in the caves. The gasp reverberated off the walls and echoed away.

"What in the name of Celtar is going on?" Tar asked.

"There are two tunnels," Akeela finally got out.

Vorrak-ira snorted. "Aye, so what's the problem? Pick one and get walking."

"Akeela, what's wrong?" Hawk asked again.

"I—" She clung to Anon. She couldn't be blind. Maybe if she rubbed her eyes. Blinked hard. Shook her head.

"Akeela?" Tar's voice went up a notch.

"I'm blind! I can't see," she blurted.

Everyone began to talk at once. The echoes tossed the words around and together in a jumble. Anon began to cry.

"Everyone, be quiet!" Tar shouted.

Talking stopped, and echoes dissipated. Anon's sobs were muffled against Akeela's chest. Akeela fought the urge to join him. It seemed as though she could *feel* the darkness. Despair welled up and overwhelmed her.

"I can't see," she said. "I saw the tunnels and then suddenly your auras went out."

"Here, let's get closer," Hawk said.

"Don't you understand?" Akeela cried. "I can't see *anything*!"

The group moved, and then Hawk's fingers brushed her shoulder. She grasped his hand and wept. She was the leader. How could she lead if she couldn't see? Someone pulled Anon away, and Hawk lifted her to her feet. "Listen, we'll figure something out," he whispered. "Even if we have to feel our way along the wall."

"Aye, let's try that," Ves-rynia said, her voice shaking.

"It's either that or sit here and die, yeh?" Vorrak-ira mumbled.

"We die?" Anon's frightened voice broke in.

Akeela gripped Hawk's arms. "No, Anon, we're not going to die. We're going to pray that Celtar will lead us out. Tar?"

Everyone stood with their arms around each other, and Tar prayed. Akeela trembled as Tar's voice, laced with fear, begged Celtar for assistance. If Tar was afraid, what hope did they have? When the prayer ended, no one spoke for a moment. Then Tar cleared his throat. "I think we should move closer to the wall and feel along until we find one of the tunnels."

Akeela nodded. She opened her eyes and stood. Something shimmered in the darkness.

"Ready?" Hawk asked.

Akeela grabbed his arm. "Wait. Wait, I see something!"

This got the group talking again. Akeela squinted. Yes, something glowed faintly to the right. "Shh. I still see it. Here, everyone, stay tight and move closer."

They inched their way along the wall.

Akeela kept her eyes fixed on whatever it was. "It's still there."

Vorrak-ira grunted but didn't comment.

After several minutes, Akeela felt the tunnel opening. She peered up at glowing strands and noticed they stretched into the tunnel. Then something moved, and Akeela stepped back.

"What is it?" Ves-rynia said.

Akeela looked again and smiled. "It's a glowing spider like we saw with the Kazmura! Tar, what do you think? A spider, even one like this, would keep closer to the surface. To trap insects."

"I think you may be right."

"Thank Celtar!" Akeela took a deep breath. "Well then, let's keep going."

Once again, they crept along, feeling the wall as they went. Akeela lost track of time, but her confidence soared as she saw other spiders the farther they went.

"I can see them now," Ves-rynia exclaimed. "Can anyone else?"

"Yes," Hawk said. "I was so busy concentrating on walking, I didn't think to look up."

Everyone laughed. They quickened their pace, and Akeela prayed her thanks over and over again.

"When we get out of here, the first thing I'm going to do is sleep in the sun," Vorrak-ira said.

"I want to see flowers," said Ves-rynia.

"I'll even eat roasted rabbit, if Akeela gets one," Hawk said. "I'm pretty sick of fish, cheese, and apples."

Akeela glanced back at the group. She gasped. "I can see shadows!"

They stopped walking.

"So can I!" Ves-rynia's voice was full of relief.

"I can too," said Hawk.

"What are you saying?" Vorrak-ira asked.

No one said anything at first, then they all burst out cheering and laughing. Anon squealed when Akeela hugged him tight.

"We must be near an opening!" she exclaimed. "Come on, everyone. Let's go!"

They pushed forward eagerly. The light grew until they could see each other clearly. Tar untied the ropes holding them together. They grinned at each other. Hawk moved to Akeela and ran a finger down her cheek.

"We have to keep moving while there's still light," Tar said.

But as the light increased, the narrower the tunnel became, forcing them to form a single line once more.

"I think the ceiling is lower too," Hawk said. "I can feel it with my fingertips."

Anxiety replaced joy, but at least they weren't in the dark anymore. Akeela clenched her jaw and kept going. Soon it was apparent Hawk was right. She, Anon, and Ves-rynia could still move normally, but Hawk, Vorrak-ira, and Tar had to stoop over.

After a few minutes, Akeela bumped her head. With each step, while the light grew brighter, the ceiling grew lower. Finally, everyone dropped to their hands and knees. No one spoke, as if talking would force them back. Just about the time Akeela was sure they'd have to turn back, she rounded a corner and saw a large room. There was an opening in the ceiling where sunlight shone on a stalagmite in the center of an island. A crevice yawned before them and all around the island.

At the same time, her birthmark started to grow warm.

"Oh no!" Akeela said, pushing the strange sensation aside.

"What? What is it?" Vorrak-ira asked.

Akeela stepped forward to let everyone out of the tunnel. She crept to the edge of the crevice and kicked a stone in. Everyone looked, wide eyed, at each other when the stone finally hit bottom, almost a minute later.

"Look." Hawk pointed to an opening on the other side. "See the light in that tunnel? That has to be the way out."

"Aye, but how do we get across?" Ves-rynia asked.

"Over here," Tar called. "I found something. A bridge."

A bridge. Akeela let out her breath. Thank Celtar! A bridge.

The group rushed over to Tar. They stared at what Tar had called a bridge. Three worn ropes stretched to the island, one for someone's feet and one on either side for handholds.

"What? Where's the bridge?" Akeela asked.

"That's our bridge." Tar pointed.

Vorrak-ira laughed. "Those frayed ropes? Are you off your nut?"

Tar frowned. "Do you have a better suggestion?"

"And what do we do if there's not another *bridge* on the other side?" Vorrak-ira went on.

No one spoke. Akeela looked around the room. Even though the light was low, she could see rock layers in the walls. The stalagmite in the center of the island reached almost to the ceiling. Akeela tilted her head. Something like an aura glowed on top.

Vorrak-ira wandered to the other side of the room while the rest of the group contemplated the rope bridge. "Snap my branch!" he exclaimed. "Look here. I think, if we're careful, we can walk along the edge and get to the other side, yeh?" And to prove his theory, he began to shuffle sideways along the wall. It was slow going, but he made it and waved from the other side of the crevice.

Hawk clapped. "I'll help Anon. Let's go."

Akeela walked to the rope bridge. "I can't."

Everyone turned to look at her.

She held up her hand to show them her now-glowing birthmark.

"See the top of that stalagmite? It's holding the second stone."

Krezma sat straight in the saddle of the horse she'd bought from a farmer, using the nacre seeds from Dir-mac. The chestnut mare, Lily, had seen better days, but with some loving care, good food, and a nacre-oil rub, she'd perked up and seemed happy to carry Krezma.

They'd only been traveling two days, yet Krezma's feeling of urgency increased, and she pushed Lily to walk far into the evening. They rested after the triple moons descended and the night grew dark.

"Only one more day," she told the mare. "Especially if you pick up the pace."

Lily snorted and tossed her head, but she broke into a slow trot at Krezma's urging.

The Fire Fountain lay southwest of Tzmet's castle, and Krezma knew if she didn't keep going, she wouldn't make it in time. What would she say when she saw her daughter again? Did Tzmet think of her? Remember her? Did she resent being left? Krezma had tried to find a way to rescue her daughter after Riss'aird's spell backfired, but the dark magic's residue prevented her from getting close to the castle. For almost a hundred years, she'd tried and tried, but nothing could penetrate the magic wall.

In order to find a way through, she'd begun studying as much of the dark arts as she dared. The allure was great, and she'd almost succumbed. If not for Oret and Tar finding her wandering in the woods, half crazy and sending out wave after wave of magic pulses, she would've given herself to the evil that seemed so beautiful.

Tar had knocked her unconscious, and when she woke up, three days later, she was surrounded by fairies. The Ruling Fairy herself had blessed Krezma, and after many days of ministering, the fairies' power had healed her. The desperation had released her. She'd sworn to serve and protect them, and while she'd never given up hope of finding Tzmet, she'd kept her vow.

How ironic, then, that she was likely coming face to face with her daughter after all this time, but not to save her. Protecting the fountains was the only way to keep evil from overcoming the world until Akeela found the Fairystone. As far as Krezma could tell, Tzmet didn't know about Akeela, or she wouldn't be concentrating on the fountains. When Krezma found her, would she have the strength to stop her?

"If only I'd found a way through the wall."

Lily whinnied as if to say, *Everything will be all right.*

Krezma gave a short laugh. "What do you know about it, hmm?"

In answer, Lily tossed her head and trotted faster.

Chapter Twenty-Eight

"You're pulling our leaves," Vorrak-ira called from the other side of the crevice. "I find us a way around without having to use that rotten rope bridge, and you say you can't?"

Akeela looked back at the group. "I'm sorry, but I have to get that stone."

"Are you sure it's the right stone?" Vorrak-ira sounded like a petulant child.

Akeela held up her hand again. "I'm sure!"

Ves-rynia came up and hugged her. "Ignore him. How can we help you?"

"Can you fly me over and back?" Akeela gave a short laugh, and Ves-rynia chuckled with her.

Tar knelt to inspect the ropes, his face grim.

Hawk stooped next to him. He tugged on the bottom rope and shook his head. "I don't know, Akeela. It's old."

Akeela crossed her arms. "How else am I going to get across? I have to get the second stone."

No one spoke. Akeela glanced up at the glowing stone and down at the crevice. If the bridge broke while she was on it, she had no doubt the quest would end. She couldn't fly. And the distance was too far to jump.

Vorrak-ira waved from the other side. "I'm great with a sling. I could knock it off."

Hawk shook his head. "Someone would still have to cross over and get it."

"Or it might fall into the crevice," Ves-rynia said.

Tar stood. "I have an idea. How much rope do we have left?"

"What are you thinking?" Hawk asked.

"If we tie all the rope we have together and fasten one end around Akeela, we could pull her to safety if the bridge breaks," Tar said.

Akeela's mouth went dry. "That's a good idea. I think."

Hawk put out his hands. "Wait. I still don't want Akeela going across there. She's too important. I should be the one to go."

"That rope bridge wouldn't hold you for two steps," Akeela argued. "I'm the lightest, except for Anon. And this is my responsibility."

"Akeela's right," Ves-rynia said. "If she falls, we'll need your strength to help pull her up."

"And what if there's more than one stone on top?" Akeela asked. "Only I can see the aura."

"More stones?" Anon asked.

"Yes, sweetie," Akeela said. "I have to get more stones."

"Yay!" he cheered.

"Hawk, I need your help with these ropes," Tar said. He lifted three coils. "I found these in one of the bags. If we tie them with the rope we used to keep ourselves together, we should have enough."

They worked swiftly, testing each knot. Akeela's stomach jerked each time Tar yanked on one. He started to wind up one end. "Here," he said to Hawk. "Take the other end and tie it around Akeela's waist."

"Do you need me to come back?" Vorrak-ira called.

"Nay," Tar said. "I'm sending Ves-rynia and Anon over. You wait with them."

Hawk put his arms around Akeela's waist and circled the rope. Her heart pounded as his breath tickled her neck. The sudden memory of Ham's hot breath in the same spot flashed, and she grabbed at the rope. "It's too tight."

"I am taking no chances," Hawk said and surreptitiously kissed her cheek. He tugged on the rope one more time. "I want you to come back to me."

Tears filled Akeela's eyes. Ham's face floated before her. His declarations of love. His passion on their wedding night. Her ears rang and her pulse pounded as she remembered. What would Hawk's reaction be when she told him she was married? He would hate her. She should've told him right away.

Again, she wished there was no quest. No Dark Lord. If only they could leave these caves and stay wherever they found themselves. If only she'd met Hawk before. But she couldn't forget her promise to Oret or her wedding vows. And the fairies were depending on her. If sorrow could kill a person, she'd be dead already. She looked deep into Hawk's eyes and touched his cheek. Then she turned to Tar.

"I'm ready."

Tar put his good hand on the bridge. "Hold on to both sides and do not look down. Stay focused on the other side."

Akeela nodded, her breath catching in her throat.

"Step lightly and evenly. Keep your movements smooth."

"I will."

"May Celtar grant you success."

Success? She wanted to laugh. Celtar would probably let her fall to her death, and why not? She may be the Guardian, but she was a liar. Celtar wasn't in anything false. She knew that from Krezma. Akeela gripped the ropes and stepped out. The bridge shuddered and began to sway. Liar that she was, she begged Celtar for help anyway.

"Keep going. Smooth and light," Tar said. "I have the other end of the rope."

Akeela put one foot in front of the other, counting the steps and staring at the stalagmite on the island. The silence bothered her.

She wanted to tell someone to talk to her, but she was so scared, she couldn't find her voice.

Twenty-one, twenty-two, twenty-three.

If only she knew how much farther. It was hard to judge the distance in the dim light.

Thirty-five, thirty-six, thirty-seven. She could see the end of the bridge now. Her jaw hurt from clenching her teeth, but she couldn't stop.

Forty-nine, fifty.

She struggled up the last part of the bridge and collapsed. Thank, Celtar! Her breath came in short gasps.

"Akeela, are you all right?" Hawk called.

She sat up and brushed herself off. "Yes."

"Akeela, listen," Tar said. "There's not enough rope for you to climb the stalagmite. Vorrak-ira is going to try to knock the stone off the top without making it fall into the crevice."

Akeela looked at Vorrak-ira, who raised his sling in the air. She remembered his father saying he was good—no—excellent with a sling. Well, he wasn't good at anything else but eating, so it might work.

"Are you sure?" she asked. "I can untie the rope, climb the stalagmite, and tie myself back up again."

"No!" Hawk shouted.

Tar shook his head. "Keep the rope on, Akeela. We are not taking any risks with your safety. If something happens and you can't get the rope back on, we may not be able to get to you."

Fine. She didn't want to climb the rock structure anyway. It was damp and slippery. So now it was up to Celtar to grant them success. Queth used to say Celtar was the greatest of all the gods. If he was on their side, they couldn't lose.

Akeela sighed. *Forgive my unbelief,* she prayed. *Please help us!*

Vorrak-ira stepped back from the edge of the crevice. He put a small stone in his sling, stared at the top of the stalagmite, and nodded. "Get ready to catch it!"

"How will I know which direction it's going to fall?" Akeela asked, trying not to sound too sarcastic.

Vorrak-ira snorted. Then he swung the sling around his head three times and let go. The small stone sailed across the crevice, skimmed the top of the stalagmite and dropped into the darkness. Some pebbles tumbled down and Akeela looked up in disbelief as the glowing stone fell right at her. She caught it, still not believing Vorrak-ira had actually done it.

"Victree!" Vorrak-ira did a little dance, then took a bow. "Happy, my lady?"

Akeela didn't trust her voice, so she simply nodded. There would be no living with him now. One more reason for this quest to end quickly.

"Now, let's get you back," Tar said. "Just like going over, step smooth and easy."

The stone glowed pale yellow in her fingertips. It felt warm. Interesting. The first stone had been white and cold. Akeela clenched it in her left hand. She pulled the small bag with the first stone from under her tunic and slipped the second stone in. A slight rush filled her head. A moment of dizziness passed, then all was normal. She took a deep breath. It was time to get out of the caves.

Ves-rynia had moved Anon to the other side of the crevice with Vorrak-ira. She waved. Akeela set her jaw and stepped back onto the rope bridge. Her heart hammered as she counted steps once more.

Forty-five, forty-six, forty-seven.

Almost there. In an instant, a snapping sound filled the cave. The bridge trembled and fell out from beneath her feet. She screamed once, reaching for Hawk, whose terrified face vanished as she plunged into the dark crevice. Her body slammed into the rocky cliff and jolted to a stop. At first, the pain wasn't bad. Then it grew until it was so intense, she almost fainted. The rope around her waist cut into her sides and slid up to her underarms.

"Akeela! Akeela!"

Hawk's voice sounded far away. She tried to answer, but nothing came out. Her right shoulder and arm were on fire. The pain took her breath away.

"Akeela! Akeela!"

Everyone was shouting, and the sound reverberated off the rocks. Akeela held on to the rope with all her strength. "I'm here," she whispered. Then she coughed. "Here."

"Is she dead?" Vorrak-ira called.

She really hated Hawk's cousin. "I'm here," she managed a little louder.

"Hang on, we're going to pull you up," Tar said.

Akeela felt the first tug on the rope, whispered a prayer for Celtar to forgive her, and promptly passed out.

A buzzing sound filled her ears as her eyes fluttered open. What'd happened? Her hand brushed something cold and rough. Rocks. They were still in the caves. That's right. The rope bridge. Someone tugged on the rope under her arms. Pain shot up her arm, and she couldn't suppress a moan. Apparently she was still alive and being rescued. If the pain didn't kill her first, she just may get out of this infernal cave.

Hawk groaned as he grasped the rope. Akeela tried to help by pulling on the cliff side, but that just caused more pain. Tar and Hawk's combined breaths came in short gasps as they slowly, hand over hand, pulled her up. She sucked in air when one tug bumped her against the rocks again.

"Take it easy, okay?" she muttered.

"Sorry!" Hawk sounded desperate.

Tug after tug. She must be near the top by now. Ves-rynia sang softly with Anon. Vorrak-ira had the decency to keep quiet, though he did offer to come over and help. Tar told him to stay with Ves-rynia.

Akeela's head finally appeared at the edge of the crevice, and she could see Tar and Hawk's feet. She lifted her left hand and gripped the edge.

"Hawk, put your hands under her arms," Tar said, his voice strained and weak.

"Can you hold her if I let go?"

"Yes. Do it."

"Grab my hands," Akeela said. "I can push up with my feet."

A single drop of sweat trailed down the side of Hawk's face as he edged closer to Akeela. He held tight to the rope, inching his hands along as he moved.

Tar planted his feet, tightened his grip, and leaned back. He nodded.

Hawk begged Celtar out loud for help, held his breath, and knelt. He let go with one hand and hooked his left arm under hers. Then he let go with the right and grabbed her other arm. She cried out as searing pain shot through her right shoulder and down her arm. Tar dropped the rope and threw himself down next to Hawk. Together, they pulled Akeela up and over the edge. She lay on the ground and wept, lightheaded with pain but so very thankful to be alive.

Hawk brushed her hair back. "Akeela, can you hear me?"

She nodded, trying to stop sobbing.

"Where are you hurt?" Tar asked.

"My right shoulder and arm. I hit the rocks when the bridge broke."

Hawk hugged her and stroked her hair.

"I want to go home," Akeela cried against his shoulder.

"I know," he whispered. "I do too."

"Is the stone safe?" Tar asked as he and Hawk helped Akeela sit up.

Akeela nodded and winced. "It's safe."

Tar gently examined her wounds. "Nothing's broken." Murmurs of "Thank Celtar" surrounded them. "You'll have a bad bruise for a while, but we were fortunate."

They inched their way to the other side, and Anon trotted up to Akeela. He threw his arms around her. "Go home now?"

Akeela hugged him with her left arm. "Yes, Anon. We're going to get out of this cave now."

"No like caves anymore."

Everyone chuckled. Akeela took him by the hand and walked

toward the tunnel where dim light lit the way. "I've had enough of them too."

The light grew brighter as they moved along the narrow tunnel. Hawk walked right behind Akeela and Anon. "I'm keeping you close from now on," he whispered in her ear.

She gave him a sad smile, knowing once Krezma and Ham caught up to them, there would be no more Hawk in her life.

The air moved as Akeela turned a corner. There, right in front of her, was a small opening. "There it is! It's small, but I think we can get out."

"Well, don't put down roots," Vorrak-ira said. "Let's get out of here, yeh?"

Akeela crawled out, favoring her sore arm, and breathed deeply. Sunlight knifed through her eyes, and she gasped.

One by one, the group emerged, then huddled together.

"I can't open my eyes," Ves-rynia cried. "It's too bright."

Akeela mumbled her agreement.

Tar spoke up. "Rest easy. Our eyes will adjust. Stay together until we can see."

Vorrak-ira snorted. "Where would we go, yeh?"

"I want to sit in the grass," Hawk said.

Ves-rynia laughed. "I want to hug a tree."

Akeela lifted her face. "It's wonderful to feel the sun's warmth again. I'm so cold. I didn't think we'd ever get out."

The group grew silent. They clasped hands and waited. After a minute, Anon began to sing a song about planting seeds. Akeela smiled as memories of the Planting Festival filtered through her mind. Home. How far away were they? She missed the stone cottage and hunting and the smell of baking bread. She'd even be glad to see Krezma again. If only the quest was done and she was back home.

Then she remembered Ham. Her mouth went dry. She'd forgotten she was a married woman. Again. How was she going to tell Hawk? Akeela shook her head. Not now. Now they had to figure out where they were and what they were going to do next.

She blinked twice. "It's getting easier. Try opening your eyes."

They all looked around, eyes in slits.

Akeela blinked rapidly, her eyes tearing up. "Blink your eyes. It helps."

Tar motioned to the boys. "Let's check our supplies." They emptied the bags on the ground.

"I'm starved," Vorrak-ira said. "What do we have left?"

Akeela looked at the small pile. "Three apples, two carrots, and one loaf of bread, which is probably stale." She picked up a linen-wrapped package and opened it. "The cheese is moldy."

Tar pulled out a small knife. "Here, we can cut that away. And we can divide the rest."

Hawk built a fire while Tar prepared the food. Ves-rynia found the pot and sent Vorrak-ira off to locate a stream. Hawk insisted Akeela rest. Fine with her. She led Anon to a grassy patch and sat with him. She helped him count stones and group them in colors. She shivered. It would be a long time before the nightmare of the caves left her. Especially with the chill in her soul that threatened to be permanent.

Vorrak-ira came back with fresh water, and they all watched it boil. The hot tea and small meal of apples, carrots, cheese, and bread felt like a feast. No one spoke, even after they'd eaten. As the sun began its descent, the fire crackled and threw sparks high.

Akeela started. Could a fire fairy have found them? She peered closer. Nothing. She sat back and looked at the trees. Then she brought herself up. "Everyone! I can see auras. The trees and plants and grass. I can see them again!"

Ves-rynia clapped her hands.

"Krezma must've been successful," Hawk said.

Vorrak-ira blew air out his nose. "Aye, but what happened to make our auras go out?"

Akeela stared into the fire again. "If only a fire fairy were here to give us news."

"We haven't been out of the caves that long," Ves-rynia said. "Let's give it some time, yeh?"

Without warning, a harsh voice broke the stillness of the evening. It was a language unknown to Akeela, but there was no mistaking the meaning. They all came to their feet and turned toward the sound. A small, bearded man stood frowning at them. He wore a brushed-leather tunic and a dark-green shirt and leggings. A wicked-looking curved knife was tucked into his belt, and his hands were covered with huge kidskin gloves. A black and tan dog, almost as tall as the man, growled, baring his teeth.

Akeela's heart dropped.

They'd escaped the caves only to trespass on dwarf territory.

Chapter Twenty-Nine

Tar took a step forward. To Akeela's surprise, he stooped, and he and the dwarf embraced, clapping each others' backs soundly. Then he spoke dwarfish.

Akeela grabbed Anon's hand and pulled him close. She didn't know a lot about dwarves, but they had a savage reputation for guarding their land. They kept to themselves, only allowing the occasional peddler in to barter for the salt they mined. When Akeela had repeated a story she'd heard in the village about dwarves eating people who trespassed on their property, Krezma had dismissed it as a children's tale. "Dwarves are solitary. They don't need or want interaction with others," she'd said. "But that doesn't make them cannibals."

Tar interrupted her thoughts. "This is Ode Janmar Axegrinder of the Se'Vrawd Tribe—salt dwarves. Oret and I saved him from drowning once when he'd fallen into a stream while practicing with a war axe."

Ode Janmar snorted. "I would've gotten meself up, ye feathered rascal," he said in the common language. "I just needed more time."

Akeela studied the dwarf, knowing she was staring, but she

couldn't help herself. Ode Janmar Axegrinder looked as she expected: short, stocky, and bearded. His dark eyes glittered in the firelight from under bushy brows. His long hair was braided down his back, and a band of leather with circular metal links kept the curly wisps out of his face.

To her surprise, and from what she could see through his bushy beard, he was actually smiling. Before she could speak, Tar began to introduce the group.

Ode Janmar nodded to each person as Tar gave their names. When he got to Anon, the dwarf frowned. Akeela's defenses rose, and she put her arm around Anon's shoulders. The dog took a step forward and wagged his tail.

Anon wiggled out of Akeela's grasp. "Doggie!" He stretched out his hand.

Akeela cried, "Anon, don't!" the same time Ode Janmar shouted, "Fin!" But the touched faun and the huge dog greeted each other as if old friends. Anon giggled as the dog licked his face.

Ode Janmar shook his head. "What do ye know? Crazy dog." Then he turned to Akeela. "I welcome ye because I trust Fin. He be as good a judge of character as any dwarf."

Akeela didn't know what to say, so she simply smiled.

Tar put his good hand on the dwarf's shoulder. "Old friend, we are in desperate need of help. According to our map, your people have something we're looking for." Then he explained their mission and Akeela's destiny.

Ode Janmar stared at Akeela with respect and wonder. "Well, I be. Oret's granddaughter? Ye are doubly welcome!"

"My thanks." Akeela glanced at the rest of group, who stood silent. Even Vorrak-ira. "Sir Axegrinder—"

"Me name's Ode Janmar," the dwarf interrupted. "Don't be giving me any airs."

Akeela flushed. "Ode Janmar. Can you help us?"

He studied her face. "I will help ye as best I can. But I cannot speak for me clan."

Tar slapped the dwarf's back. "We'd be grateful for food and a warm bed."

Vorrak-ira spoke up then. "Aye, I'm tired of sleeping on the ground, yeh?"

Everyone murmured their agreement, and the dwarf whistled to Fin, who hadn't left Anon's side. "Follow me, for evening is upon us. I'll put ye up for tonight."

As if in response to his words, the sun's final rays faded, and the stars grew brighter. Akeela looked up. "The moons are closer than when we first went into the caves."

"Which is why we need Ode's help," Tar said.

No one spoke as they followed Ode Janmar Axegrinder. But when they stopped at a cave opening, Vorrak-ira gave a cry of dismay. "You're skipping acorns, yeh? We're not really going back into a cave, are we?"

"This is me home," Ode Janmar said. "If ye like, ye can sleep outside. Just don't go into the lower field at night." He pointed to a field to the cave's left. "There be evil spirits which'll take ye away."

Tar shoved Vorrak-ira toward the opening. "Fool. Get inside."

Ves-rynia giggled, and Akeela rolled her eyes. She held Anon's hand and followed Vorrak-ira. As they got closer, Akeela could see the cave opening was covered by a wooden door. Light glowed from the small, square window in the middle.

At least there's light. I couldn't go back into the dark.

The cave was surprisingly warm and dry. Ode Janmar had carved a fireplace in the wall, and a rough-hewn table and four chairs sat in the middle of the room. The floor was covered with a braided rug. Akeela couldn't tell its color in the dim light. Shelves to the right of the fireplace held a few mugs, plates, and bowls, and on the other side of the fireplace, several stools were stacked together.

"If ye would, Oret's granddaughter and the other lass, please take the chairs," Ode Janmar said. "The rest of ye can sit on the floor."

Vorrak-ira groaned. "I knew it."

Hawk punched his cousin's arm.

Ode Janmar stared at Vorrak-ira, his face unreadable. After a few awkward seconds, he continued. "I'll go fetch the evening meal."

"I'll go with you," Tar said.

Ode Janmar lifted two lanterns from a peg. He took a stick from a basket, placed the end in the fire until it caught, and lit the wicks from the flame. Then he handed one to Hawk along with a jug. "Take this and go to the back of the cave. Fresh water in a small stream be there." He and Tar moved to the door. "And ye can wash up. Soap and towels in the cabinet near the bed. But ye'll have to share, I'm afraid."

The door closed, and Akeela shook her head. It was like waking up from a distant and not-so-nice dream. "Thank you!" she called.

Vorrak-ira snickered, earning him another punch.

"I'll walk back and check everything out," Hawk said. "Stay here."

"I'm coming too, yeh?" Vorrak-ira said. "The girls will be fine here."

Akeela nodded. She was only too happy to sit and rest. Ves-rynia reached over, clasped her hand, and gave her a sleepy smile.

The fire crackled and sent out such warmth, Akeela started to nod off. Ves-rynia had already fallen asleep, her head resting on her arm. *So different from the other cave,* Akeela thought. She looked to see what Anon was doing, but he wasn't in the room.

"Anon?" she called.

Nothing.

She stood. "Anon?"

Nothing.

Ves-rynia opened her eyes. "What's wrong?"

"Anon's gone!" Akeela's voice shook. "But he has to be here. I would've heard the door open."

Ves-rynia sat up. "He's here, Akeela. He must be."

"I wonder if there are other lanterns," Akeela said, her fear rising. She walked to the door to check when Hawk and Vorrak-ira came back.

"What's wrong?" Hawk asked.

Akeela clutched his arm. "Anon, he's gone!"

Vorrak-ira set the jug on the table. "Don't go diggin' up your roots. The little sprout is sleeping on the bed."

Akeela stood without moving. Then she began to cry. Deep, wrenching sobs shook her body, and she gripped Hawk's shoulders to keep from falling to her knees.

"Akeela? Akeela! Stop. It's all right," Hawk said. "Here, Ves, take the lantern."

But Akeela couldn't stop. She wailed her distress — the discovery of who she was, marrying Ham, the devastating wedding night, leaving home, meeting and falling in love with Hawk, the dark caves, almost dying, ending up in dwarf territory, Anon missing. She couldn't take one more thing.

Hawk pushed her into a chair. Ves-rynia rubbed her back. Akeela cried on and on. Finally, Hawk gave her a little shake. "Stop, Akeela. This isn't good for you."

Akeela took deep breaths, working to calm down. Her eyes felt as though they might fall out, and she pressed her fingers to them. "I'm-all-right-give-me-a-minute," she gasped.

"Why don't you show her where Anon is?" Ves-rynia asked.

Hawk nodded. "That's a good idea. Here, Akeela, come with me. Anon's right here."

He led Akeela to Ode Janmar's bedroom. A linen curtain hung, pushed to the side, across an alcove. Hawk lifted the lantern, and Anon was sound asleep on a bed covered with furs.

Akeela drew a shaking breath. "I think I'll lay down with him for a little while."

"That's fine," Hawk said.

Akeela stretched out next to Anon. Hawk leaned down and kissed her. She took one deep breath and fell asleep.

Chapter Thirty

Tzmet rapped her fingernails on the table. Brimridge sat at the other end of the long table, stuffing his face with Tzmet's uneaten lunch. Miserable wretch. If she didn't need his help, she would've sent him and his disgusting family away long ago.

A loud belch broke the silence.

"Sorry, my lady." Brimridge wiped his mouth. "I quite enjoyed that. Your Hinwari are most excellent cooks."

Tzmet snorted. "I thought all you boggarts ate was skunk cabbage."

Brimridge pushed the dish away. "Cabbage is the mainstay of our diet, but we don't mind straying from it at times." He belched again and patted his stomach. "Especially when goat liver is prepared so well."

Tzmet wiped a few black goblin hairs from the map in front of her. Putrid beasts! Just this morning, she'd caught two young ones trying to open her locked bedroom door. She grinned and took a sip of wine. They'd think about their actions every time they tried to sit down.

"More wine, my lady?"

Tzmet startled and looked up to see Brimridge standing next to her with the carafe in his hand. "No, no more," she said. "I need to concentrate."

Brimridge slid into the chair at her elbow. He leaned forward, gazing at the map. Between his body stench and the garlic from the livers, Tzmet wanted to gag. But she wouldn't give him the satisfaction. She needed to know exactly where she was going—and she wanted to leave early in the morning—so she turned away from him slightly and tried to concentrate.

"Don't you have something to do?" she finally asked.

Brimridge's eyes crinkled as he smiled. "I only live to serve you, my lady."

Tzmet rolled her eyes. Idiot. She turned her attention back to the map and ran a finger over the Earth Fountain and then the Water Fountain. The symbols for each one weren't exactly the same, but there was something similar to the shape. If only she could figure it out.

A soft musical sound drifted in the window, and Tzmet looked up. Ah, her fairy spies. "You'd better have information for me."

The fairy pair lit on the top of the map. They looked pale and sick, as they had ever since she'd fried the tall one. She'd increased the potion's strength, but the horror remained with them, even though they couldn't remember. At least she didn't have to watch her tone of voice anymore.

"We have," they said in unison.

Tzmet sat back in her chair. "Well?"

The little fairy trembled and sat. This one needed to be watched. Even though she was small, she struggled against the spell. The taller fairy stepped forward. "The council met, but the new Guardian still has not been found. Fire fairies are searching every fireplace."

That caught Tzmet's full attention. "What do you mean, searching every fireplace?"

"Fire fairies live in fire," the fairy said. "They send messages and bring news."

Tzmet glanced at Brimridge. "Really? How interesting. Tell me, my friends, can these fire fairies live in *any* fireplace?"

The fairy nodded. "Any fire or embers."

"In *my* fireplace?"

The little fairy jumped to her feet. "No, no!"

"I do not think so," the tall fairy said.

Tzmet slammed her fist on the table. The fairies fell over, and the map slid to the floor. "Lies!" she screeched. "Those miserable, wretched fairies must've been spying on me ever since the magic wall went down."

Brimridge put his hand on her arm. "My lady, be calm. There is a simple solution."

Tzmet glared at the boggart leader.

"You must not make any plans in a room with a fire," he said.

The fairies clung to each other, their eyes wide with fright. Tzmet thought about Brimridge's suggestion. It made sense. Still, she felt violated. How dare they sneak into her home and watch her. She was more surprised by that than the news of a new Guardian. That she expected.

She leaned over to pick up the map and stopped to stare. The map had landed sideways. Tzmet peered at the symbol of the earth fountain. Then she looked at the water fountain. Snake eggs! It was the same symbol, but turned to the side a quarter. How had she missed this?

"Argh!" She snatched the map and smacked it on the table. She wiped her hand over it, searching every symbol and sign. There, just to the south of the castle. The symbol for fountain. And next to it a small shape that could be a flame. "There's one. See? The symbol is the same, only in a different direction."

"Nicely done, my lady," Brimridge said. "Shall I prepare for your trip?"

Tzmet waved her hand as she gazed at the map. "Yes, yes! You know what to do. I want to leave right after sunrise."

Brimridge bowed and left. Tzmet waited until he was gone to turn her attention back to the fairies. They still sat, arms around each other.

She smiled. "My friends, please forgive my outburst. I am fatigued. Please tell me more about the council meeting."

The tall fairy shrugged. "Air fairies assist the search for the new Guardian."

"Air fairies? And where do they live? In the air?" She chuckled at her own joke.

The fairies shook their heads. "We don't know," the little one said. "We've never seen them."

Tzmet raised her eyebrows. "Really? You expect me to believe you've never seen your fairy sisters? Hah!"

"They're invisible," the tall fairy said. "Some can see them, but we never have."

Tzmet thought about this. If the air fairies were invisible, it was then possible the fountain was also invisible. How would she be able to find the wretched thing?

The tall fairy continued. "When any fairy finds the new Guardian, we are to send word through the fire fairies and then stay to protect her."

"Her?" Tzmet barked. "The new guardian is a *girl?*"

The small fairy cried out, as if in pain.

Tzmet got up and began to pace. All this time, she'd thought the next guardian would be a man. Oret was a man. She certainly never would've choosen a girl. Girls were silly and weak. She gave a short laugh. "This is too delicious. Stupid fairies. A girl will be no match for me." She turned to the fairies. "My thanks. You may go. I expect to hear from you the moment you find the new guardian."

As the fairies whizzed off, Tzmet sat and dipped a finger into the wine goblet. She watched the red liquid drop back into the cup.

"A girl," she whispered.

Akeela opened her eyes. It was dark except for the dim light of a lantern, but she was warm and wrapped in furs. That's right—they were out of the caves and with a dwarf. Tar's friend.

A small sound came from her left. Anon slept beside her. She gazed at him a moment, watching him breathe. Then she heard voices.

"Still sleeping," Hawk said. "But I know they'll be hungry. I should wake them."

"Give them a little more time," Ves-rynia said. "The meal isn't ready yet, yeh?"

A strange voice broke in. "The little one, he's different, aye?"

The dwarf. What was his name again? Ode Janmar. Akeela kept listening, although she should probably let them know she was awake.

"Akeela calls him *touched*," Hawk said. "I don't know any details, but she loves him very much, and he returns the feeling."

"Aye, he's likeable, even though he's a dupeseed," Vorrak-ira said.

Akeela shook her head. *Nice impression he's giving the dwarf.*

Ves-rynia spoke next. "Who's a dupeseed?"

Akeela chuckled silently. Then she smelled roasting meat, and her stomach pinched. *That's enough eavesdropping.* She needed to wake Anon and get something to eat. And no more crying. She was as sick of feeling weak as she'd been sick of the caves.

She pushed the curtain aside. "Hello? Come on, Anon. Dinner."

Fin got up from the fireplace, stretched, and ambled over to Anon. Akeela went to Ode Janmar, who was roasting hares.

"That smells good," she said. "We haven't had anything but plant-wrapped fish in the caves and a small stale meal before you found us."

Vorrak-ira wrinkled his nose. "Aye, the fish was good at first, but after a while, it was like eating scat."

"I'll not be knowing what that means, but ye are welcome to my table. And I'll not have any more criticizing of the poor wee faun." Ode Janmar poked the fire. "Fin and me, we try to treat others with respect."

Hawk kicked Vorrak-ira under the table. Ode Janmar brought bowls and mugs, and Ves-rynia poured water. When she got to the last mug, Ode Janmar held up his hand.

A few gasped. Ode Janmar had taken off his gloves, and the hand he held up was withered and curled. Any suspicion Akeela had drifted away. The man knew what it was like to be an outcast, and it made him compassionate, if a bit defensive.

Ode Janmar lowered his hand and nodded at Akeela. Then he turned to Ves-rynia. "I'll be having ale, lass."

Ves-rynia glared at her brother. Vorrak-ira actually looked chagrined.

"Have ye had a good rest?" Ode Janmar asked as he placed a loaf of bread in the middle of the table.

Akeela smiled. "Yes, thank you, sir."

Ode Janmar grunted. "Me name's Ode Janmar."

Anon grinned at the dwarf. "Ode. Hi, Ode. Have dinner now?"

"Sure enough, little buck. Ode will take care of ye. Come, get a bowl."

The dwarf helped Anon fill his bowl and led him to a low stool by the fireplace. A thought began to grow in the back of Akeela's mind. If the dwarf had compassion toward weaker creatures, perhaps he would keep Anon with him until the quest was done.

Akeela glanced at Hawk. The look on his face was pure joy as he stared at her. Then he gave her a reassuring smile and turned his attention to the food. Everyone, even the Acadians and Tar, ate the rabbit meat. Ves-rynia giggled with the first bite. Vorrak-ira grimaced as he lifted a piece to his mouth, but after tasting it, he sat up straight and chewed with delight.

Tar clapped Ode Janmar's shoulder. "No one roasts a hare like you, old friend. Too bad Oret couldn't be here."

"Aye, Oret was a good friend, even though he preferred milk to ale with his food." Ode laughed and raised his mug. "To a good life!"

Tar joined him in the toast.

Akeela got up from the table and sat on the floor next to them. "I'm a little confused how we got here. If I remember right, dwarf territory is west of Broem. We were heading north when we found the caves."

Ode Janmar nodded. "'Tis true, lass. Appears your guides brought ye the wrong way."

Vorrak-ira snorted. "And who is surprised by that, yeh? Those Kazmura were a bunch of turn leaves."

Ode Janmar stroked his beard. "Aye, that they are. They're thieves as well. Caught them more than once stealing salt from our mines."

"You *know* the Kazmura?" Akeela asked.

"Aye, we know of them. Aside from their thieving ways, we have not had contact with them."

Tar spoke up. "Still, according to Oret, a piece of the Fairys- tone was given to the dwarves for safekeeping."

Ode frowned. "I'll not be knowing about that. 'Tis the council ye need to be speakin' to."

Everyone sat silent. Then Anon piped up. "Ode, Fin like roasted bunny."

The dog responded by shaking his head, flinging spit on the table and in Vorrak'ira's face.

"Aw! C'mon, Fin!" he cried. "Give my leaves a rest!"

That broke the tension, and everyone laughed.

Ode Janmar grunted. "Aye, he does. But don't be giving him too much, little buck."

Vorrak-ira pointed at Ode Janmar with a piece of meat. "We Acadians don't eat the meat of animals unless we can't get fish, but I had enough fish in those caves to last me two lifetimes!" He shoved the meat in his mouth, chewed, swallowed, and belched.

Ves-rynia shook her head. "Please forgive my brother. He's such a sapling."

Vorrak-ira snorted.

Akeela smiled and reached for her mug. She met Hawk's eyes across the room. The love on his face would've made her heart sing —if she wasn't carrying such a secret. There was no telling when Krezma would arrived with Ham in tow. She had to tell Hawk before that happened. It was only fair to him, and she wasn't going to break her vows.

But it would break her heart beyond repair.

Chapter Thirty-One

Akeela leaned over the stream outside the cave and rinsed her face. Her eyes were still swollen from yesterday's weeping, and the cold water felt good. She sat back and looked around. Ode Janmar's cave was situated at the beginning of the Undaeus Mountain range.

As Ode Janmar Axegrinder had told her, he was just what his name implied. He made an ax called a handhew, which was valued among the clan because it held true when thrown. When Akeela had asked why he lived by himself, he'd shrugged and said, "I have no use for others giving me the eye on account of me hand."

"Don't you miss your home?"

Ode shrugged. "Home is where me and Fin be."

Home. A sharp attack of homesickness hit Akeela. She missed Iari. And the cottage. In a strange way, she also missed Krezma. How she wished the old woman were here now to accompany her to the dwarf council. Krezma wouldn't be afraid, and she'd know exactly what to say. Akeela had no idea. Desperation grew as the minutes went by.

"Greetings, chosen one!"

Akeela looked up at the sound of the small voice. Three water fairies hovered in front of her. Thank Celtar! Perhaps she could get a message to Krezma.

"Blessings on you, good fairies." She gave the standard, polite response fairies enjoyed so much. "Have you any news for me?"

One water fairy came closer. "The witch poisoned the Water Fountain, but Krezma healed it. She wishes to come to you, but she must protect the Fire Fountain."

Akeela nodded. "Yes." She knew Krezma was doing what needed to be done, but oh, how she'd like for Krezma to put her first, just once. Then she flushed in shame. How selfish! Krezma *should* protect the Fountains. Krezma was doing her duty. As should she.

Akeela's heart pounded as she remembered she was supposed to be trying to get pregnant while searching for the Fairystone pieces. But she'd talked Ham into staying at the village, so that was impossible. And she only had two pieces. And she didn't know if the dwarves would give her the third piece.

Then there was Hawk. She wasn't blind or stupid. She knew how he felt. She felt the same way, except she shouldn't. Couldn't. It was wrong, and she'd made vows. The pain in her heart was a sharp as the pain in her shoulder. She ran her fingertips over the bruise and let herself hear the love in Hawk's voice once more.

The fairies waited, as though expecting her to say more. Akeela couldn't make sense of what they might want.

Finally, one fairy said, "Have you any news for us?"

Of course they wanted news. Krezma would expect something. "I—" she started to say, but nothing came to mind.

She didn't care to recount the experience in the caves, and what could she say about the dwarves?

"Well," she started again. "I guess you could let Krezma know where we are and that I'm going to meet with the dwarves about getting the third piece of the Fairystone."

The fairies whispered among themselves. The first one turned to Akeela. "We will take this news to Krezma and the Fairy Council."

They whizzed off, their auras leaving a shimmering blue-green trail behind them. Akeela stood and brushed off her tunic. She'd better get back to Ode Janmar's cave. It would soon be time to leave for the settlement.

Akeela clutched Hawk's hand as the dwarf leaders talked among themselves in the next room.

That couldn't have gone more wrong.

She'd tried to put on a strong front, but the unsmiling faces and sharp stares from under bushy eyebrows unnerved her. She'd stammered and stumbled over her words and felt more like a child than a Guardian.

Hawk squeezed her hand. "Relax. I think it went well. They may have looked stern, but I could sense they have great interest and even sympathy for you. Especially when you told them about the Kazmura guides leaving us."

"I wish I could ask Ode Janmar what he thought," Akeela said. "I wonder why they wanted him in their meeting?"

"I'm sure they want his opinion of us," Hawk said. "We did spend time with him."

Akeela could still hear the rise and fall of their voices. They must help, they *must!* She got up and walked to the window. The Se'Vrawd settlement looked no different than any other village might, busy with children playing and women bartering.

The dwarf leader, Tanchor Battlefury, had explained the importance of salt in their lifestyle. Besides trading their different types of salt, they also used salt in their worship, for decorating their homes, and for sickness. Their lifestyle was precious and balanced.

"Hawk," Akeela said without turning from the window. "Is it right, asking these people for help? Their lives are untroubled."

Hawk got up and stood next to her. He watched the dwarves going about their business before answering. "If we can't get all the Fairystone pieces and you can't become the Fairy Guardian, their lives will surely be troubled, yeh?"

Akeela nodded. "I wonder if we should've brought the rest of the group with us. Maybe they could've influenced the dwarves."

Hawk chuckled and put his arm around Akeela. "Aye, can you imagine the influence Vorrak-ira would have?"

Before Akeela could respond, the door to the side room opened, and the dwarves came out and sat at the table.

Tanchor gestured to Akeela. "We have decided."

Akeela took a deep breath and stood in front of them.

Tzmet paced as she ranted. "I've caught goblins trying to break into my bedroom five times this week! They keep stealing spices from the kitchen. I can hardly sleep because of the ruckus every night. And there's hair everywhere."

Riss'aird's lips turned up in a slight, amused smile. "Indeed?"

"Yes, and if I can't concentrate on preparing my potions and destroying the Fairy Fountains, it will all be for nothing!"

When her father didn't respond, Tzmet stopped pacing and stood before him. He sat at the table next to the window, as he usually did after breakfast, studying charts and maps. Of what, Tzmet had no idea.

She wanted to stamp her foot. What was wrong with him?

He kept to his room, only allowing her and the wretched goblin leader in. He never walked around the castle or went outside to talk to the boggarts, who'd come back specifically to serve him. They did more to serve her. Which wasn't a bad thing—just not normal.

She put a hand on his arm. "Father, I must say this. Something is wrong."

Riss'aird looked at her hand. She quickly removed it. A sick feeling of fear stirred in her as he turned his attention back to his charts and books. She pushed the feeling down and tried again.

"Brimridge and his family are waiting for your orders. They've made repairs to the stables, which are now suitable for your army."

"Excellent."

"The sooner the goblins get men for the Transvarient process, the sooner they can leave."

Riss'aird's ice-blue eyes bore into hers. She couldn't breathe for a moment, and she couldn't look away. "I—I," she choked out. "I only meant, when everything is done, we'll have peace. We can reign without interruption."

Riss'aird closed the book he'd been leafing through. Tzmet saw the title—*Spells Gone Wrong: Antidotes and Power-Releasing Potions.*

Her throat tightened. "Father?"

"Yes, daughter," Riss'aird said. He ran his hand over the cover. "I am powerless. When the spell backfired, it also swept away my magic."

Tzmet swallowed. Impossible! She must've heard him wrong. "Magic . . . gone?"

"So I have just said." Riss'aird rubbed his forehead. "This knowledge must not leave this room."

Tzmet shook her head. "No, no, of course not! I would never. No, Father. You can trust me."

Riss'aird sighed. "Then do something to get my power back."

"I have just the thing, Father!" Tzmet clapped her hands. "I brought back water from the Fairy Fountain before I poisoned it. Surely there's a magical quality that can help restore your power." She rushed to the door. "I'll get it and be right back."

Fear, shock, and joy filled Tzmet as she ran down the hall to her bedroom. How could this have happened? And why didn't she sense it in the beginning? Those vile, thieving fairies. It had to be their magic that rendered Riss'aird powerless, therefore the water from the Fairy Fountain would surely bring it back.

Tzmet darted into her bedroom, unlocked the cabinet, and grabbed the large vial holding the precious water. She held it to the sunlight. The water was clear and bright. Surely now her father would return to normal. And she would make it possible.

She hurried back to his room.

"Here, Father." She held up the vial.

Riss'aird nodded. "Very good. Now, take a drink."

Tzmet stared at him in disbelief. "You don't trust me, Father?"

"I have learned to be careful," Riss'aird said. "After all, you survived the spell unscathed. I did not."

Tzmet's breath left her. How could he question her loyalty? She'd worked for years to make a way to bring him back. And she'd succeeded! She started to protest when he held up his hand.

"There is no reason to refuse my request, is there?"

"No, Father," Tzmet said. "But I want you to have the full effect of the water. If I drink some, it may not be enough for you."

"I am willing to take that chance."

Tzmet met his eyes. If only she were able to see some kind of affection. Some sign he was pleased with her efforts. She pulled out the cork and lifted the vial to her lips, never looking away from him.

The ice-cold water hit her stomach with a jolt. She took in a deep breath as a surge of energy filled her body. "Oh!" she gasped. Then she laughed. "It feels wonderful!"

Riss'aird looked bored. "Give me the vial."

She handed it to him. The refreshing liquid made her feel as though she could fly around the room without restraint. Yes, magic was there, and with only one sip. The whole vial would surely restore Riss'aird's power.

He drained the container and set it on the table.

"Well?" she asked.

Riss'aird stared at the empty vial for a moment before throwing it across the room. It smashed against the fireplace. Then he turned to her, the expression on his face accusing and angry.

"But—but," she stammered. "I felt it! There was magic in that water."

"I wonder, daughter, why you could sense fairy magic and I only tasted plain water." Riss'aird's voice was low and dangerous.

Then, before she could react, he reached out and grabbed her wrist. She fell to her knees, crying out in pain.

"And now, you will find a way to restore my power." He took her jaw in his other hand and forced her to look up. "I will not stand for any more failures."

She collapsed on the floor as he released her. She lay sobbing as he turned back to the table, picked up the book, and opened it.

"Get out."

Tzmet crawled to the door. She pulled herself up, brushed goblin hairs off her skirt, and took a breath. Down the hall, footsteps approached.

Before she could walk away, Sleg turned the corner.

"Have a nice visit with our father, did we?"

Tzmet raised her throbbing head and walked away with as much dignity as she could muster.

The goblin leader's laughter followed her all the way to her bedroom.

Chapter Thirty-Two

"We cannot help ye."

Tanchor Battlefury's words punched Akeela's heart as her gaze swept over the dwarf council, looking for a sympathetic face. She must've heard wrong. Perhaps she didn't convey the danger strongly enough.

"Tanchor," she said, turning her attention to the dwarf leader. "Please. You must understand what will happen if I don't complete my quest."

Tanchor made a rumbling sound. "Lass, this Dark Lord ye mention. We'll not be knowin' if he's the threat ye say." The other dwarves nodded. Only Ode Janmar sat silent.

"But—"

Hawk stopped her with a hand on her arm and stepped forward. He bowed his head to the council. "Mighty dwarves. I have always heard it said your people were quick to help those weaker than yourselves. Why has this changed?"

The largest dwarf stood, his dark eyes flashing in anger. "What is this ye say?"

Tanchor reached out his hand in a gesture of peace. "Sit ye

down, Bracken Bearbane. The lad is not questioning your strength." He turned to Hawk. "Are ye?"

"I am not."

The dwarves shifted in their seats, and after a strained moment, Bracken sat. He glared at Hawk while Tanchor spoke.

"What are ye sayin', lad?"

Akeela breathed a prayer. She was acutely aware if Hawk aroused the dwarves' anger, things could get violent and fast. Along the wall behind the Council were tapestries depicting various battle scenes. One, quite graphic, showed a dwarf hewing the head off a warrior elf. Akeela shivered and looked back to Tanchor.

"I'm wondering what has changed," Hawk said. "I recall stories my father told about the dwarves. He's a good friend to your own Ode Janmar Axegrinder."

Ode Janmar looked troubled, but he still said nothing.

Bracken leaned forward. "Ode Janmar would befriend an elf."

The other dwarves mumbled in agreement.

"He thinks because he has a shriveled hand, that somehow makes him less worthy," Bracken continued. "He has separated himself from the clan. Aye, 'tis true yer father is a friend to him, but who is he to us?"

Keron Saltcutter, the overseer of the mines, stood next. "'Tis all I can do to keep those thievin' cave people from my salt! I cannot leave the mines without enough workers."

The priest motioned to quiet the council. He turned to Akeela. "Ye are a good lass, and I wish we could be helpin' ye, but 'tis also true that ye do not serve the goddess, Khewra."

"Why should that matter?" Akeela asked. "We don't require someone to worship Celtar before we help them."

Eli smiled. "Ye know nothing about our religion," he said, as if to a small child. "And 'tis hard for outsiders to accept. But we must obey the diktats of the goddess."

Tanchor nodded. "Aye, lass. We are bound to keep what the diktats state, and part of that be keepin' ourselves from other religions."

"But we're not asking you to do anything like that. We're only asking for the third piece of the Fairystone and a few of your warriors." Akeela's voice rose. Hawk squeezed her hand. She yanked it away. "If Riss'aird rises from the ashes, it will affect you. The salt mines. Your clan. Don't you see this?"

Bracken slammed his hand on the table.

"Peace, Bracken," Tanchor said. "Ye must remember the outsiders do not know our ways."

Akeela fought breaking down and weeping in front of these uncaring, rock-headed dwarves. Why had Celtar brought them here if they wouldn't give up the third piece of the Fairystone? It seemed their only friend was an outcast, and he said nothing in their defense.

Hawk stepped forward and gently moved Akeela behind him. He took a protective stance, which should've touched her heart, but for some reason, it annoyed her. Before she could move away, he spoke to the council. "We thank you for listening to our pleas."

How polite he sounded. Akeela wanted to smack the back of his head.

Tanchor nodded.

"We will take no more of your time," Hawk continued. "If the council would give us permission to stay a few nights longer with Ode Janmar so we can make plans, we would be grateful."

Akeela started to protest, but Hawk glanced at her and mouthed, *No.*

The council stood together, as if they'd received a silent command. One by one, they bowed to Hawk and Akeela.

Tanchor raised his hands. "Ye are welcome to stay outside the village with Ode Janmar Axegrinder. And may ye find favor with the god ye serve."

Hawk took Akeela's arm and steered her to the door. When they stepped out into the bright sunlight, Ode Janmar closed the door behind them. Akeela started to say something, but Hawk shook his head. "Wait," he whispered. "They're probably listening."

Akeela tried to push down her anger at Hawk's stepping in.

This was her charge! But she didn't want the dwarves to think they disagreed, so she walked back to the cave in silence.

Vorrak-ira gave a snort of disgust. "What a bunch of dupeseeds! They're all off their nuts. I think we should head back home, yeh?"

Akeela said nothing as she paced in front of the fireplace.

"I hate to agree with my brother," Ves-rynia said from the bed, where she played with Anon and his bag of stones. "But perhaps it would be best to get help from our father and the kin-tribe."

Hawk shook his head. "I don't think that's a good idea. We still need the stone."

Akeela stopped pacing. "What do you mean?"

"I don't know about everyone else, but I'm hoping they'll change their minds."

Vorrak-ira laughed. "You go ahead and trust them, cousin, but the whole lot of them are scraping my branches."

"What should we do next, then?" Ves-rynia asked.

Everyone looked at Hawk. "We'll talk with my father when he gets back from hunting with Ode Janmar. He always has solid plans and rarely loses his breeze."

Akeela's hackles rose. "I hope you're going to include me in this discussion."

"Whoa! What's up your trunk?" Vorrak-ira laughed.

Hawk gave her a puzzled look. He couldn't be that dense, could he? She cleared her throat. "I was talking with the dwarf council, and all of a sudden, Hawk took over and ended the meeting."

Vorrak-ira guffawed. "Now that's what I call picking new shoots!"

"Akeela," Hawk said in a tight voice. "Many of the dwarves were growing angry. I just wanted to protect you." He looked hurt.

Akeela had to relent. A little. "Fine, but find a way to warn me next time, okay?"

He grinned. "Okay. Now, I think we should gather supplies for the trip home."

"How can we leave without the Fairystone piece?" Ves-rynia asked.

Vorrak-ira laughed. "Maybe we should steal it."

Hawk shook his head. "We don't know where the dwarves keep it."

"I thought you said the dwarves would change their minds," Akeela said.

"They might, but it doesn't hurt to get ready, yeh?"

Akeela resumed pacing. Hawk cleared his throat. When she looked up, he jerked his head toward the door. He wanted to talk. Fine, she did too. It would be easier to tell him about Ham when she was aggravated. She followed him outside.

"I don't understand you, Akeela," Hawk said. "I'm trying to help you!"

Akeela raised her eyebrows. "By taking over my job?"

Hawk blew air out his nose. "I'm not taking over. We can't depend on anyone but ourselves. And sure, there's a chance the dwarves will help. I could see hesitation, even in Tanchor."

"Then why pack?"

"I don't know," he answered. "Just in case?"

Akeela laughed.

He grinned. "Did I miss something?"

She wiped her eyes. "Celtar must have a great sense of humor. Why else would I have been chosen to save everyone? It's impossible! I can't even convince a bunch of dwarves to give me what I need to save the world." She walked away from him. "Have you been watching the moons? They're getting closer. Time's running out, and I still don't have the Fairystone."

"Akeela, don't walk away!" Now *he* sounded angry.

She turned and looked at him. "Why not?"

She drew in a breath. This was the moment. She knew it. Time to reveal who she really was. A married woman. Her cheeks burned, her heart pounded, and she prayed she'd be able to say it. She opened her mouth to confess when he reached for her.

"I know this isn't a good time for this, but I can't help it."

He took her right hand in his, pulled off the glove, and turned her palm up. He traced her birthmark. She trembled but didn't pull back. All the anger she felt toward him vanished.

"I love you, Akeela," he whispered. "I don't want to be without you ever. When you fell in the caves and I thought you might be dead, part of me died with you. My father will say we're too young, and maybe we are, but your face filled my dreams before I even knew you. And now that I know you, I'm sure." He hesitated, then drew in a ragged breath. "When this is all over, will you marry me?"

Akeela gaped at him. Marry him? She wanted to respond, but no words came. Marry him? Marry him? Yes, of course she would marry him! She started to say that when he took her left hand to draw her closer, and she felt the pressure of the silver wedding band.

He lifted her chin and kissed her. Her aura radiated between them as before.

"Oh ho!"

Hawk let go so quickly, Akeela almost fell. He grabbed her, and they turned. Tar and Ode Janmar stood about ten feet away. Ode Janmar held two rabbits in one hand.

His dark eyes twinkled as he elbowed Tar. "Ye have more problems than ye thought, me friend."

Tar's eyebrows lowered. He handed the pheasant he held to Hawk. "Take the bird and prepare it for roasting." Then to Akeela he said, "Come with me."

Hawk picked up the pheasant and followed Ode Janmar.

Akeela offered Tar a small smile. "What's wrong?"

Tar walked away. Akeela paused, then trailed him to behind Ode's cave. They stood silent for a moment.

"Akeela, what are you doing?" Tar finally asked.

She looked at her feet. She knew what Tar meant and wouldn't insult him by faking ignorance. "I was going to tell him. I was! But then . . ." She couldn't finish.

"I'm not your father, but your grandfather was my best friend, so I'll speak as I know he would."

Akeela nodded.

"Celtar hates falsehood. He values integrity and honor," Tar said. "Hawk is my son, the only part of his mother I have. I will not allow you to mislead him. And I will hold you to your responsibility to Oret and to all of us."

Akeela nodded again, filled with shame.

He put his hand on her shoulder. "You are young, I understand that. But you've been chosen for a great honor. You need to get yourself together."

"I will," she whispered. "Please give me a little more time. I'll tell him. I promise."

"Good. Let's get inside and prepare the evening meal. Celtar will guide us."

Akeela and Ves-rynia worked on a bowl of greens at the counter while Ode Janmar roasted the pheasant and rabbits outside. The mild evening air drifted through the open door, bringing the scent of the fire with it. Her hands shook as she tore up more greens to add to the bowl. Hawk would hate her when she told him, and she couldn't blame him.

"Let's add a little nacre oil to the greens," Ves-rynia said.

Akeela shrugged. "Sure."

Anon had spread some of his stones on the table. "Have new stone, Keela. Ode give me."

Akeela smiled. The dwarf seemed taken with Anon. She thanked Celtar for Ode Janmar's kindness, but she felt guilty because she'd neglected Anon the past couple of days.

"Let me see."

Anon brought her the strangest rock she'd ever seen. It was clear, like water, and carved like the head of a wolf. "It's nice, Anon." She handed it back. "Make sure to put it in your bag so you don't lose it."

"What was that?" Ves-rynia whispered.

Akeela rubbed her forehead. Why did everyone think she knew everything? "I don't know. Something Ode Janmar gave him. It's nothing."

"It be salt!" Anon said.

The girls stared at him. Akeela put her hands on her hips. "I think you've been hanging around Ode too long."

Anon grinned. "I be a dwarf."

Akeela and Ves-rynia chuckled and turned back to their preparations. As Akeela wiped her hands on a cloth, the thought popped in her head again that she could leave Anon here with Ode Janmar while she finished the quest. He'd be safe. The dwarf seemed to really care for him.

Questions and doubts. That's pretty much what she had—besides guilt. And fear, which had tripled since Tar had called Hawk outside as soon as she'd entered the cave.

Vorrak-ira set a pitcher of water on the counter, causing her to start. He shouted with laughter. "Didn't mean to rattle your branches!"

Ves-rynia shoved him. "Get some mugs and put them on the table."

"Who died and put you in the top of the tree?"

"Just do it!"

Vorrak-ira snickered, but he got the mugs. "Whatcha got there, little sprout?" he asked Anon.

"Stones," Anon replied. He dropped the last one in his bag and pulled the string. Holding it tight to his chest, he trotted back to the bed and yanked the curtain across.

Akeela glanced out the door. What was taking Tar and Hawk so long? Was Tar telling Hawk about Ham? He said he'd give her a chance. Maybe he'd changed his mind. Her heart leaped. If only she'd been honest from the beginning, she wouldn't be here now. She carried the bowl of greens to the table.

"Cousin! Off playing while we're working, yeh?"

Vorrak-ira's voice made her turn around. Hawk followed Tar into the cave. Tar took the hunting gear to the back of the cave.

Hawk smiled and winked at her. At least he didn't look angry or upset. She gave him a small smile and hated herself a little more.

"Who be hungry?" Ode Janmar bellowed as he carried the roasted meat to the table.

***

"Ode tell story?" Anon asked when the meal was done.

Ode Janmar lit a pipe with a stick from the fire. He puffed and blew smoke into the air. "After the meetin' today with the Council, I be thinkin' of an old story."

Akeela took the kettle with *caavea* beans off the fire. "Shouldn't we make plans?"

Ode Janmar nodded. "Aye, lass. That's why I be tellin' ye this story." Anon slid his stool close to Ode Janmar and snuggled up to his side. Ode patted his head. "I'll be tellin' ye the Legend of Undryn."

Akeela poured *caavea* for herself and Tar. The Acadians preferred tea, which Ves-rynia prepared. Ode Janmar kept his mug of ale; Anon had water. There was no cream available to cut the *caavea's* bitterness, so Akeela sipped slowly.

Ode Janmar began.

"Undryn be a warrior, the greatest warrior of all the dwarves. He'd hewn so many enemy heads, his belt be so full of notches there was no room for more. One day, he heard a challenge issued. He turned to fight and saw another warrior, unfamiliar to him. He knew not if the warrior be dwarf, elf, or some other creature. They fought, equally matched, until both fell to the ground in exhaustion."

"I would've liked to see that, yeh?" Hawk said.

"Undryn offered his hand in friendship and respect first. The warrior accepted. But when they removed their helmets, Undryn saw the warrior be a woman! And an elf. Atana be the daughter of the Elven King, Artor. But instead of hatin' each other, Undryn and Atana fell in love. But they be outcasts because dwarves and elves be mortal enemies."

Vorrak-ira snorted. Ves-rynia punched his arm.

"No one knew what happened to them until a great famine filled the land. This be three hundred years ago. The dwarves were slowly starvin' to death. They had plenty of seed to plant, but there be no water.

"In the mountains, the elves were also feeling the effects of the famine. They had plenty of water from the mountain snows and streams, but they had no seed to plant.

"One dark night, Undryn came to the dwarf village council. 'I have a proposal,' he said. The council was eager to hear until he told them his plan. 'We will never partner with the elves!' the head of the council roared. 'Then ye will die,' Undryn said."

Dwarves are no different today, Akeela thought.

"On the same night, Atana went to her people in the mountains with the same proposal and was met with the same reaction.

"But the mothers of both dwarves and elves decided to accept the help of the other in order to save their wee children. Undryn stole seed from the dwarves' supply, enough to plant many gardens. Then he and Atana and women from both groups worked to build an irrigation system to bring water down the mountain and to the gardens they planted. It be a hard job, but when the women worked together, the work went quickly."

"I be quick!" Anon declared. Everyone chuckled.

"The men be furious, but once they saw the plants growing, and their stomachs be cryin' for food, they gave in. Elves and dwarves worked together—something completely unknown to have happened before or since.

"Because of this, both races be preserved, and once the famine was done and food be plentiful, they went their separate ways. Undryn and Atana left, never to be seen again. But it is believed in times of great trouble, Undryn and Atana will come back and help their people once more."

Ode Janmar sat back in his chair and took a long drink. Anon had fallen asleep, so Akeela went to put him in bed.

"I'll take him," Hawk said. He lifted Anon and carried him across the cave. Akeela followed.

Akeela tucked the furs around him. "What did Tar say to you?"

Hawk set the bag of stones on the table next to the bed. "He cautioned me, said we were too young, and you have a quest. He shook my branches a little, said you had something to tell me."

Fairy feet! She had to tell him now.

Futilely wishing for more time, she closed her eyes and took a breath. "I—"

"Come on, you two," Vorrak-ira called. "It doesn't take that long to put the little sprout to bed, yeh?"

"I'll tell you later," she whispered, thanking Celtar for the interruption.

Akeela walked to the fireplace and poured more *caavea* into her mug to warm it up before she sat at the table. She had a reprieve, but for how long?

Vorrak-ira was shaking his head. "So you told us a nice bedtime story. What's the point?"

Ode Janmar puffed on his pipe. "Ye are always the difficult one, aren't ye?

Ves-rynia laughed.

"Don't ye understand the meanin' of the legend?" Ode looked right at Akeela. "Can't ye see how ye might use this to sway the Council?"

Akeela ran the story through her head. "I should meet with Tanchor again and ask him to help me like Undryn and Atana helped the dwarves and elves?"

Ode stared at her. "Have ye learned nothin' about dwarves, lass?"

"Well, they're stubborn and strong and proud," she said. "They love their salt. They work hard. They don't like outsiders."

"Aye, that be true. We be proud."

Akeela pondered. Proud. The dwarves were proud. That was it! "A challenge! I need to challenge them. Call them out in the name of Undryn." She leaned forward. "Is that right?"

Ode Janmar chuckled. "Aye, lass. And I'll help ye know what to be sayin'. There be no one who knows more about Undryn than meself."

Vorrak-ira gave a short laugh. "Why's that?"

Ode Janmar lowered his pipe and tucked his hair back to reveal slightly pointed ears. "Undryn be me great, great, great grandfather."

Ves-rynia clasped Akeela's hand. "Undryn and Atana are your ancestors, yeh?"

Ode nodded.

Akeela squeezed Ves-rynia's hand. "Queth often said Celtar puts his people where he wants them. And here we are!"

For a moment, hope surged. Even though Rig and Dok had deserted them, they'd come out in the perfect place to get the help they needed. A comforting warmth grew in her heart.

No one stirred for a long moment. The fire crackled, and Fin whined in his sleep from his place on the hearth.

Finally, Tar spoke. "Between the spirit of Undryn and Atana in Ode Janmar and the spirit of Oret in Akeela, I believe our chances have just improved."

Chapter Thirty-Three

"My lady, sit and eat your meal," Brimridge said to Tzmet. He had included himself in her mealtimes lately and ate whatever the Hinwari prepared with gusto. At first, Tzmet felt annoyed. But now she welcomed his company. What was happening to her?

"Silence, fool. You are not my father. Restrain yourself from telling me what to do."

Brimridge put down his fork. "And how is the great and mighty Riss'aird? Ready to conquer the world?"

Tzmet stopped pacing and stood at the window that overlooked the swamp where she'd picked the dark vine so many years ago and had somehow escaped the spell gone wrong. How many times since then had she picked plants and herbs for her many spells? How many hours had she spent working on plans to save her father? How many dreams of ruling by his side? It sickened her.

And she was scared to death.

"Brimridge," she said, not turning away from the window. "Whom did you come back to serve?"

"Why, my lady, my people and I came to serve you and your father."

Tzmet ran a finger across the windowpane. "And do you still feel that way?"

"Of course. Why do you ask?"

Why did she ask. What a question! If the fool was observant, he'd know what was going on. Tzmet turned away from the window. Brimridge sat at the table staring at her with his beady, black eyes. She wanted so much to have someone to confide in. To talk things over with. Since the magic wall had come down, she'd only had the Hinwari to talk to. Which was a joke. They didn't respond. They couldn't talk. Deep longing rose in Tzmet, and she sat and picked up her fork.

"Listen to me and listen well," she said. "I'm going to trust you."

Brimridge stroked his pointed beard and nodded.

Tzmet hesitated. How much should she tell him? Not everything, certainly. And she didn't want to appear weak. Curses! She hated feeling afraid.

"Things are not going as I expected," she said.

Brimridge pushed his plate away. "Indeed?"

"Yes, you idiot!" she snapped. She stopped, closed her eyes, and took a deep breath. *Be calm. Be in control.*

"Now," she said. "Remember how things were between my father and myself before the spell. How close we were. How he adored me and gave me anything I wanted."

Brimridge's mouth twitched as though he were trying to keep a straight face.

"Do not laugh at me, you lunkhead!" she shrieked.

Before Brimridge could react, she horrified herself by bursting into tears. Bloody swamp grass! She clutched the edge of the table and tried to catch her breath. After a minute of wretched sobbing, she calmed and took a sip of her wine. Averting her eyes from Brimridge's ugly face, she continued.

"As I was saying, my father and I had a close relationship. Something I'm sure you boggarts know nothing about. But since he's come back, it's—different. I do not know him. He doesn't seem to trust me. I feel—"

Brimridge put his hand on top of hers.

Tzmet felt the tears forming again. She snatched her hand away. "I don't want your pity, you loathsome, smelly creature."

"What do you want, my lady?"

His voice was gentle, even friendly. Tzmet's anger drained away. "I am afraid of him," she whispered. "And I am . . . lonely."

She felt his surprise. They sat without speaking until a Hinwar came to clear their plates. The long shadows of the setting sun began to filter through the windows.

"Bring us tea and cake," she said.

Brimridge cleared his throat.

Tzmet raised her head and looked at him. She'd said it, and there was no going back. Well then, she would see what she would see.

Akeela stood before the Dwarf Council. She tried to picture Oret as she prepared to plead her case again. She'd promised she would complete the quest. His blood ran in her veins. And even greater than that—she was a child of Celtar, and he'd placed her here.

"Tanchor and respected members of the Council," she said. "I'm here to ask you to reconsider helping me. After spending some time around your people, I can see you are hardworking and loyal."

The dwarves nodded and smiled. Bracken Bearbane growled, but he didn't say anything. Akeela's mouth went dry even as she felt encouraged.

"I know in great times of trouble, the warrior, Undryn, will rise again to help his people."

Bracken jumped to his feet. "What do ye know about Undryn?"

The other dwarves mumbled in agreement.

Tanchor raised his hands. "Peace, Bracken. Ye know who she be staying with. Ode Janmar be the only one who can relate the legend."

Bracken frowned, staring at Akeela, but he sat.

"Now, lass, why do ye bring up our most beloved warrior?" Tanchor's voice sounded friendly, but something in his eyes told Akeela to tread lightly.

Akeela cleared her throat. She didn't dare glance at Hawk or Ode. That would make her appear weak. "I'm asking you, in the spirit of Undryn, to help me."

Tanchor's voice was low and deadly calm. "How can ye, an outsider, ask for help in the spirit of Undryn?"

"How can you, in the spirit of Undryn, deny me?"

Bracken roared and scrambled over the table. He drew his handhew and ran at Akeela. The other dwarves jumped up. Tanchor beat his fists on the table and bellowed, "Bracken!"

Bracken grabbed Akeela's arm. Instead an enveloping fear, anger rose in Akeela. She lifted her chin and hoped her frown was as intimidating as his. "Undryn and Atana worked together!" she shouted. "They saw the greater need and did the right thing!"

"What?" Bracken barked.

He held the small but fierce-looking weapon high.

"Undryn and Atana saw the need to help even their mortal enemies," she said quickly. Her heart felt as though it would burst out of her chest. "I am not your enemy. My people are not your enemies. Please! If Riss'aird rises, he will make the elves look like your best friends. I only need one small stone. You don't even have to send warriors yet."

Ode Janmar stepped up. "Aye, Bracken. Do ye not see the truth in what the lass says? I'm not the warrior me grandfather was, but his spirit lives in me. I be seein' the rightness of helping Akeela and her friends."

The priest, Eli Saltpraise, came to stand next to Akeela. He put out a hand to lower Bracken's weapon. "I be studyin' old writings since ye first came to us, lass, and I can verify what ye say about the Dark Lord. 'Tis true that if he rises from the ashes, he be causin' trouble. But I not be knowin' if his trouble will come our way."

"Undryn didn't know if helping the elves would bring trouble your way, but he helped anyway," Akeela whispered. She kept her eyes on Bracken, who looked less red in the face now.

Tanchor stood and raised his hands. "Ye be using the name of our most beloved warrior, lass, to shame us. But I will not force any of me people to help. If they wish to assist ye, I'll not be stoppin' them."

The room grew silent except for Bracken's footsteps as he marched out the door. Akeela tried to hold on to the hope she'd started with, but if she couldn't rely on the leader of the dwarf warriors, who would help her? She felt Hawk's hand on her shoulder and lifted her head.

Ode Janmar nodded. "Ye can depend on me, Akeela. I'll go with ye."

Keron Saltcutter spoke next. "I'll not be a warrior, but I know the salt mines. Ye will be needin' weapons, and I be makin' the best salt bombs."

Akeela gave a small smile and nodded.

Tulor Alewerks cleared his throat and stood. "I be no fighter, but me eldest son is. I'll be asking him for ye."

"Thank you," Akeela whispered.

The priest came and clasped her hands. "'Tis true our goddess speaks against minglin' with other religions. But she also addresses mercy to those weaker. I will pray for yer success."

Akeela's eyes filled with tears, and she couldn't speak. Three dwarves. Only three! But maybe, just maybe others would see and do the same. Before she could leave, the door flew open and slammed against the wall. Bracken Bearbane strode in, followed by twelve fierce-looking warriors.

"This be all I can spare," he said, his voice clipped. He put his hand on the first dwarf's arm. "Here be me second-in-command, Krin Clubhand. He be takin' charge of any fightin' ye need."

Krin nodded.

Akeela thought she saw a twinkle in Krin's eyes. He obviously looked forward to battle. "I'm happy to have you," she said and turned back to Tanchor. "We still need the third piece of the Fairy-stone. According to our map, it's here somewhere."

Tanchor looked at Eli. "We need to be asking Khewra about this matter. While we be doin' this, me dwarves be getting ready to accompany ye."

Bracken smacked his fist on his palm. "Aye, we be meetin' ye at Ode Janmar's cave then. He be sharpenin' our axes before we leave."

Ode grunted. "Ye best bring 'em startin' today so I be havin' enough time."

Hawk pulled Akeela out the door while the dwarves spoke to Ode. "You did it," he said, hugging her.

She resisted the urge to let him hold her and stepped back. "We did it together. Celtar is good."

He gave her a curious look but said nothing. They hurried back to Ode's cave to let the group know what had happened.

"Here, my lady," Brimridge said from the doorway to the great room. "I've prepared your supplies."

Ever since she'd confessed her feelings to him last evening, Tzmet felt edgy. She hated showing any weakness. *Feeling* any weakness. And she'd done both. Rat's teeth! She had a job to do: poison the Fire Fountain. And she needed to focus.

"Yes, yes," she snapped. "Put my bag on the table and see to Nightshade."

Brimridge set the bag next to the map she was studying. "My son is seeing to your horse."

Ugh. His son. The thought of boggarts breeding more boggarts turned her stomach. She tried to keep her eyes on the map, but when he stood without saying more, she finally looked at him. He bowed his head and gave her a sly smile.

"I caught the same two goblins by your bedroom door just moments ago," he said. "Apparently, their memory is short."

Tzmet snorted.

"The funny thing is, they're the same two who've been caught stealing our skunk cabbage."

"Really?"

"Lucky for me I was not alone," Brimridge continued. "Two of my best men were there. I was feeling generous, so I told them they could have a bit of fun."

"And?"

"I won't bore you with the details, my lady, but I believe they won't be sneaking into our gardens for skunk cabbage. They have most certainly lost their taste for it." He chuckled. "And if their curiosity for your bedroom continues, they will lose their taste for anything else."

Tzmet couldn't keep the smile from her face. If she wasn't careful, she may actually start to *like* Brimridge. "Yes, well, the little cretins had it coming." She rolled up the map. "Now, if you'll leave me, I want to eat before I leave, and I want to sit alone."

"But, my lady, we have a farewell feast prepared for you." Brimridge bowed and gestured to the door.

"What? Eat with you? *All* of you?" Tzmet's eyes bulged.

Brimridge stepped closer and put his hand on her arm. "My lady, it would honor us."

Tzmet was at a loss for words, something that typically didn't happen. Eat with the boggarts. Why would she want to do such a disgusting thing? Her stomach growled. For over fifteen years, she'd eaten alone. But for the last couple of weeks, Brimridge occasionally ate at her table. And it wasn't disgusting. In fact, she found herself enjoying the conversation after she'd gotten over the initial shock of his bad table manners.

Eat with the boggarts. She let out a chuckle.

"My lady?"

She looked up into Brimridge's hopeful, ugly face. "I will eat with you and your family. Just this once."

Brimridge bowed. "Thank you, my lady." He turned to go.

"I will not have even one sliver of skunk cabbage touch my plate."

"Yes, my lady."

"And I will not sit with your—er—children."

"Yes, my lady."

"Make sure the plates and utensils are clean."

"Yes, my lady."

"And the meat is thoroughly cooked."

"Yes, my lady."

"Well, what are you waiting for? Tell them I'm coming!"

"Yes, my lady."

Brimridge closed the door behind him, and Tzmet sat back in her chair. What would her father say if he knew? He ate with that obnoxious Sleg. What could be more disgusting than that? And the boggarts had prepared a feast for her. Just for her! She didn't see the goblins doing that for Riss'aird.

She stood. Very well. A feast before her mission could only bring good luck, and she didn't want anything going wrong. After she poisoned the Fire Fountain, only one Fountain remained.

And once all the Fountains were poisoned, nothing would stand in her way.

Tzmet reached into her bag of herbs and selected two mint leaves. She belched and almost gagged on the strong garlic and *hicata* pepper fumes that rose from her stomach.

Curse those wretched boggarts! Just because she enjoyed garlic and pepper was no reason to flavor every dish with them.

Nightshade snorted and shook his head.

"Don't be smart with me, you sorry excuse for a horse." Tzmet chewed on the leaves, hoping for some relief. "Just keep going. I want to reach the Fire Fountain before sunrise."

She kicked his sides, and Nightshade broke into a trot. The jostling didn't help her stomach, but she'd stayed too long with the boggarts. Time was of the essence. Still, the evening had not been entirely revolting.

The frog legs in garlic butter had been tender, the muskrat filets done to perfection—even though the crust of garlic and pepper overpowered the meat—and the skunk cabbage salad had smelled so delicious, she'd given in and eaten some.

A group of five boggarts, one who claimed to be Brimridge's cousin, had provided music for the feast. Tzmet wasn't familiar with the songs, but they didn't screech like banshees, so she tolerated it.

By the end of the meal, she'd felt pleasantly full and warm, so she'd accepted, with grace and tact, a bouquet of swamp roses from the children. She'd clutched it in her arms, its sweet scent rising up and making her stomach recoil, then tossed them on the ground when she was out of sight.

"Putrid, sickening things! I don't know why I took them."

Nightshade whinnied.

"Does the word 'stew' mean anything to you?" she snapped. "Just keep going and get me to that fountain."

Nightshade tossed his head and leaped forward.

❧

Akeela knelt at the stream and rinsed out the wooden bowls for dinner. Nervous anticipation welled up in her. How she longed for Oret's advice. Even Krezma would be able to help. Still, the promised dwarf warriors gave her confidence.

Tomorrow she'd take a quick tour of the salt mines, as a courtesy, and the day after that, if they were successful in getting the third piece, they'd leave for Fedestia, where the fourth piece was located.

Then she had to be pregnant before she placed the stones into her birthmark, so they had to get back to Broem. Where Ham waited. Unless Krezma was on her way with him.

She had to tell Hawk she was married. Tonight.

A familiar, musical sound broke into her thoughts, and she looked up. Two earth fairies flew straight toward her. She smiled and called out a greeting.

"Greetings, Akeela," they said in unison. "The water fairies told us of your location, and we've come to help."

❧

Tzmet stared in disbelief as the fairy wing cape burst into flames and flared all the way to the ceiling of the cave. After a moment, the ashes floated down all around her.

She'd called up the Fire Fountain in the same way she had the others. Tossed the cape into the Fountain in the same way. Never had she imagined the wretched thing would burn up. The sands hadn't harmed it. The water hadn't ruined it. What had gone wrong?

"Argh!" she shrieked. She threw her hands in the air and stamped her feet.

"Cease your temper tantrum."

Tzmet whirled around to see an old woman standing next to a large rock. Great swamp flies! It was the hag from the peasant village. How had she gotten here? Why was she here? Tzmet sputtered and stuttered, not getting a word out in her frustration.

The hag shook her head. "Some things never change. You always did give in to your anger."

Tzmet opened her mouth, but still no words came. The Fire Fountain continued to swirl and burn behind her, and her temper rose with the heat. She took a step toward the hag and lifted her hand.

The hag chuckled. "Have you really forgotten me, Tzmet?"

"Forgotten you?" There, her voice was working again.

But who was this hag and how did she know Tzmet's name? Indeed, she seemed to *know* Tzmet. This was confusing, but she refused to show it.

"Of course, it has been over a hundred years," the hag continued. "And you'd just come of age when I left."

Tzmet couldn't stand the heat of the Fountain anymore and walked deliberately from it and past the hag. When she felt cooler, she turned. "You're talking nonsense. I don't know you. I don't want to. I'm leaving now."

She'd taken three steps when the hag's words stopped her.

"I am your mother."

Tzmet stood with her back to the hag. She silently ordered her feet to keep walking, but she couldn't move. A pain started in her gut and worked up to her heart.

"My mother is dead."

"Is that what Riss'aird told you?"

Tzmet's body stiffened.

"Tzmet, I left the night of your hundredth birthday. We quarreled. I knew the only way to save you was to leave."

Tzmet turned then. She gave a short laugh. "That makes no sense."

The hag took a step toward her. "I tried and tried to get back to you. After the spell Riss'aird cast was turned back, I couldn't get through the magic wall."

Tzmet folded her arms. Her fingers itched to release blue fire and blow this uppity hag into oblivion. But something stopped her. Something about the accent. Not the same as her father's but still familiar.

A pleading look came over the hag's face. "I never meant to leave you for so long. I knew you'd somehow survived. A mother knows."

That was enough. No more. Tzmet lifted her hand and fired into the ceiling of the cave. The rocks glowed blue and started to crumble.

The hag took a step forward, reaching for her. Tzmet leaped back as the ceiling collapsed. When the dust settled, she was completely sealed off from the fountain and the hag.

The ride home was filled with memories she thought she'd suppressed. A little girl dancing with her mother. Drinking tea and eating *krenda* cakes. Walking the labyrinth. Practicing spells with her father.

And the quarrel on the night of her birthday.

The pain in her heart grew.

Nightshade must've sensed her mood because he made not a sound all the way back to the castle.

Krezma coughed and waved her hand to dispel the dust. That couldn't have gone more wrong. She'd known Tzmet wouldn't exactly be happy to see her, but she hadn't expected such *hatred*.

Feeling defeated, she sank to a rock and sat with her head down. What should she do first?

After a minute, the Fire Fairies arrived to bless the fountain, singing as they flew around and around in the flames. At least Tzmet hadn't poisoned this one. If Krezma hadn't gotten there first and set a protective charm in place, things would have been worse. Without the Fire Fairies to carry messages and bring news, their fight against Riss'aird was futile.

She really had expected news about Akeela by now. It was as if she'd vanished off the surface of the earth. Off the surface!

That was it! Krezma stood. "Dear ones, it is even more important to find Akeela and see if she's found the pieces of the Fairystone yet. Stop looking for her in obvious places and go underground. Anywhere you can find a flame!"

Chapter Thirty-Four

Hawk looked up as Akeela approached Ode Janmar's cave. She smiled and waved, and he started to smile back but then stopped.

"Hawk! Hawk!" Akeela called. "Guess who found me?"

"I see," Hawk said, staring at the fairies. He took the bowls from Akeela.

"You can see them?" Akeela asked. "How is that possible?"

"That's a good question," Hawk said.

The small fairy looked stricken. The taller fairy grabbed her hand. "The Council gave us permission to be visible. So we could help the Guardian."

Akeela beamed at them. She was so thankful to have them here. Besides Anon, they were a part of home. "We're working to get the third piece of the Fairystone from the dwarves, then we can go south for the fourth piece."

"The witch! The witch!" the small fairy squeaked out.

The tall fairy shushed her. "The fourth piece of the . . . Fairystone?"

"Yes, I'm on a quest to find the pieces," Akeela said. "Weren't you informed?"

"No!" the small fairy exclaimed.

"Yes, I was," the tall fairy spoke over the small one. "We have orders, remember? We have to find the Guardian and help."

Akeela looked from one fairy to the other. They were acting strange. Not like the ones from home. Maybe they were from another part of forest. A part she hadn't been to.

"And I'm thankful for that," Akeela said. "Do you know where in Fedestia the fourth piece is being held?"

The tall fairy hesitated. "The fourth piece . . . has been . . . is being held . . ."

"The witch! The witch!" the small fairy cried out again.

"Yes, it's at the witch's castle!"

That didn't make sense to Akeela. "Are you sure?"

"Yes," the tall fairy said.

"That can't be right," Hawk said. "What about our map? It says the fourth piece is with Krezma's people." His voice was light, but Akeela frowned.

"What's wrong?" she asked.

He hesitated as though he searched for the right words. "How did the fourth piece get to the witch's castle?"

The fairies looked at each other. Akeela didn't understand Hawk's attitude. It was like he didn't trust the fairies. Although he had a point. She turned to the fairies.

"The Council revealed it to us," the tall fairy finally said.

"Why didn't the Council reveal this to Akeela?" Hawk asked.

Akeela put her hand on his arm. "Hawk. It's fine. When could the Council have told me? We were underground for a long time. No one knew where we were."

Just then Ode Janmar came out the cave door carrying a string of fish. His eyes grew wide when he saw the fairies flying by Akeela. "Well, I'll be. Your fairies finally find ye?"

"Wait, you can see them, too?" Hawk's voice rose.

Akeela nodded. "They're going to help me find the fourth piece of the Fairystone."

Hawk grunted. "I'm going to get wood for the fireplace, yeh?"

"I thank ye," Ode said.

Hawk grunted again and stalked off. Akeela watched him, confused. What was going on?

***

Akeela looked up when the door opened. Hawk stepped in, glanced her way, and walked to the fireplace. He dropped an armful of wood on the floor, making everyone jump. He looked grim. Something about that annoyed Akeela. Why did the fairies make him angry?

Tar and Ode Janmar came in then — Tar carrying a platter of the cleaned fish and Ode carrying another armful of wood.

"Dinner be ready soon," Ode said. "I be frying it crisp with smoked salt for ye tonight."

Akeela smiled. "That sounds delicious, Ode Janmar." She looked at Hawk, who was poking embers with a stick. Her annoyed feeling turned to concern.

Ode Janmar handed his wood to Hawk. "Here, lad. Build me up a good, hot fire. 'Tis needed to properly fry fish."

While Ode busied himself with the fish, Akeela and Ves-rynia set out clean bowls and mugs. Vorrak-ira sat in the corner across from the fireplace, brooding. Fin had long taken the responsibility of Anon, not willing to leave him for long. He lay next to the faun, looking content. Anon stacked sticks Ode Janmar had carved flat. He spent as much time building them up and knocking them down as he did sorting his stones.

Ode glanced over and seemed pleased with how much Anon loved the sticks. "'Tis a favorite pastime of our dwarflings." He handed Anon another cloth bag to put them in.

Anon squealed with delight and ran to show Akeela. "Look, Keela! Anon have two bags!"

Akeela smiled. The next instant, her heart lurched, and she caught her breath in almost a sob.

Ves-rynia touched her hand. "What's wrong, Akeela?"

"I don't know." Akeela squeezed her friend's hand. "I guess I'm just nervous."

"I am too," Ves-rynia admitted. "But it's just a tour of the salt caves. You won't be with the Kazmura, yeh?"

Akeela nodded.

Ves-rynia hugged her. "Celtar brought us this far, yeh? As long as we keep our roots entwined, we'll be all right."

The fried fish with smoked salt and roasted white tubers with onions and tomatoes were delicious. The thick, brown bread with salted butter was a perfect complement to the fish, and Akeela even had half a mug of ale at Ode Janmar's suggestion. It was a dinner worthy of a king, but Akeela felt as though it was her last meal. Only the two fairies hovering at her shoulders gave her comfort.

Hawk sat silent for the most part, only grunting or giving short answers when necessary. The atmosphere in the cave was guarded, at best. Only Anon didn't seem to notice anything wrong. Between bites, he chattered about his new stones and how high he'd stacked the sticks and how many bunnies he'd seen by the stream.

When the meal was complete, Hawk stood and cleared his throat. "Akeela, come outside with me. Everyone, please excuse us."

No one spoke as Hawk strode out the door. Akeela smiled weakly at Ves-rynia and followed him, the two fairies close behind.

Hawk stood at the edge of the lower field, which gleamed in the moonlight with an almost ethereal glow. Akeela approached him with caution. This was a side of Hawk she'd never seen, and it scared her.

For a long moment, Hawk said nothing. He stared at her, his face shadowed so she couldn't see his expression. Akeela's senses tingled, and the feeling of dread increased. Maybe he no longer loved her. Her face blanched at the thought. That would be good, though. Then he wouldn't care that she was married.

Her heart flipped in her chest.

Hawk looked at the two fairies, and his eyebrows lowered. He turned his focus back to Akeela. "I'd like to talk to you alone."

Akeela nodded. "It's all right, dear ones. We'll not be long. Please wait for me by the stream."

"We must stay with the Guardian!" the tall fairy exclaimed.

"I'm safe with Hawk," Akeela said. "Please go wait for me."

The small fairy looked terrified, but the tall one pulled on her arm, and they flew off.

Akeela turned to Hawk. "They're gone."

Hawk grabbed her shoulders. "Akeela, listen to me." His face was earnest, and his eyes bore into hers. "Something's not right with those fairies. I can feel it. I can see them. Ode can see them. This is wrong, wrong, wrong!"

"Are you saying they're not telling the truth?" Akeela crossed her arms and frowned.

Hawk shook his head. "I don't know. Maybe."

Akeela took a step toward him. "Maybe? Maybe? Either you think it or not."

Hawk touched her cheek. "Akeela, what's wrong? Don't you trust my instincts?"

"Your instincts are wrong." She kept her voice level and cold. "There are no bad fairies. I know. I'm the Fairy Guardian."

Hawk pulled back his hands and clenched his fists. "Not yet, you aren't."

Akeela gasped. "I-I-I . . . you! Oh!"

She turned and ran blindly into the field. As she entered a group of white lace flowers, her arms tingled. She skidded to a stop, turned, and looked at Hawk. Spots of white light rose from the ground. A chorus of voices rose in song, light and airy. The light grew and filled her senses. Pure joy filled her, and she took a deep breath and gave herself to it.

Tzmet poured over her book of spells. She hadn't been able to concentrate since talking with the hag at the Fire Fountain, and her level of stress increased with each passing minute. It wasn't true. Her mother was dead. It was a beastly trick.

"It isn't true," she said. "It can't be true. My father would've told me."

There was no time to ponder it. She had a job to do. If she didn't find a way to restore her father's power, she didn't know what would happen.

And that terrified her.

A tap sounded on the door, causing the raven to squawk. Tzmet started and dropped her goblet of wine. It crashed to the floor, spilling red liquid like blood.

"What *is* it?" she screeched.

Brimridge stepped in the great room. "Pardon, my lady." He bowed. "I have the herbs you asked for."

Tzmet watched the wine creep across the floor. Her heart beat in her throat, and she willed her body to calm down. Spells like this needed study. To rush it could mean disaster.

She waved her hand. "Come in, come in. Put them here on the table."

Brimridge complied and sat in the chair next to Tzmet. "My lady, what happened at the Fire Fountain? You've said nothing except that you lost the cape. But I can tell there's more."

Tzmet rang for a Hinwar. "This mess needs to be cleaned."

"I thought we'd become friends," Brimridge said. "How can I help if you won't talk to me?"

Tzmet rapped her fingernails on the table. The setting sun shot orange rays through the window and onto the opposite wall. Two Hinwari appeared in the doorway. She pointed to the one on the left.

"You, clean up this mess." To the other she said, "You, get working on the evening meal. I want a snapper pie. Make sure there's enough brandy in the gravy. Use leeks instead of onions. No garlic." She reached over, grabbed the herbs, and pulled out a stalk of rosemary. "Here, take this. Use some in the pie along with a small amount of swamp grass."

Brimridge chuckled.

Tzmet ignored him. "While that is baking, bring me—us—a platter of cheese and fried night crawlers and more wine. My father will have a bowl of venison broth and greens."

Brimridge didn't speak as the Hinwari went about their business and Tzmet turned back to her book. She could feel his eyes on her, like tiny gnats buzzing in her ears. She slammed the book shut. He said they'd become friends? Fine.

"A hag who claimed to be my mother was at the Fire Fountain."

"Really? It was Krezma?"

Tzmet glared at him.

Brimridge held up his hands. "My lady, I'm not doubting you. What would you have me do?"

A Hinwar entered with a carafe of wine and two goblets. When it left, Tzmet looked at Brimridge and raised an eyebrow. He scrambled to his feet and poured the wine. Tzmet fought the urge to smile. She looked at him with what she hoped was a serious and condescending expression.

"The hag, whoever she may be, is not important. What I need to do is finish the potion I've started for my father."

"What about the Air Fountain?"

"According to the map, it moves. And I've lost the cape, so I couldn't poison it even if I found it. Therefore, I'm turning my attention to the spell I think will help my father."

Brimridge sipped noisily from his goblet.

Tzmet cleared her throat. "What you can do is assist me. I have everything ready, but this is a long spell, and I don't have time to put it to memory. So I will read, and you will add the herbs and other necessary items."

"Aye, my lady. I'll do anything you need."

Tzmet nodded. After the evening meal, she and Brimridge would put everything together and take it to Riss'aird. And when his power was restored, she'd be back in his good graces.

Tzmet tapped on Riss'aird's bedroom door and entered. "Father, I believe I have a potion that will restore your power."

She nodded to Brimridge, who followed her, carrying a goblet as though it were a snake.

Riss'aird and Sleg looked up from their game of *Grifnoc*, a stupid game of strategy the goblins had brought with them. Who cared about capturing an imaginary enemy's flag?

"Excellent," Riss'aird said. "Bring it to me."

Tzmet took the cup from Brimridge and walked regally to her father. She presented it to him with a curtsey. Riss'aird waved his hand over it and sniffed. He nodded to Sleg, who took the cup and peered into the contents. Tzmet held back a snort. What did this abominable goblin think he knew about potions?

Sleg handed the goblet back to Riss'aird and nodded.

"Father—"

Riss'aird held up a hand. He lifted the goblet to his lips and drained the contents. His head snapped back, and the floor trembled under their feet. Tzmet gave Brimridge a triumphant smile.

Riss'aird slowly lifted his head. He closed his eyes and sighed.

Tzmet stepped forward and took the goblet from his hand. "Father?"

"Leave, daughter."

"But, Father, how do you feel? Is your power back?"

Riss'aird cupped his hands. A spark appeared. Then another. Then several snapped and crackled. A ball of light flashed and rose in the air. Tzmet clapped her hands, delighted. Surely now her father would be pleased with her.

Then the light went out.

Riss'aird turned pale eyes on her. "As you can see, you were not entirely successful. Now leave."

Tzmet's face flushed. "I can make another cup. Now that I know—"

"Do not bother yourself," Riss'aird said. "I'll handle it from here."

"But—"

Brimridge pulled on her sleeve. He bowed to Riss'aird and

steered her toward the door. In the hallway, he put a finger to his lips and shook his head.

Tzmet pushed him aside and swept down the steps. She strode into the kitchen and threw the goblet into the washbasin.

"My lady, do not be distressed," Brimridge said. "He will give you another chance. He was only posturing for the goblin."

Tzmet couldn't speak.

If she did, she'd cry, and that would be the worst thing she could do.

Chapter Thirty-Five

Hawk watched Akeela slide to the ground. He ran into the field. They'd been warned to stay out of the lower field at night, but he was not leaving Akeela. When he stepped into the field, Hawk stopped. He could feel a presence. A magical presence.

Interested.

Watching.

Desperation rose in Hawk, and he took a step forward. The feeling of being watched stayed with each step. His eyes swept the moonlit field. If only he could see auras, he'd know exactly where Akeela was.

A breeze picked up and rustled through the tall grass and flowers. Hawk saw a flash of white out of the corner of his eye. He turned and edged toward it. The invisible eyes kept watching. As he got closer, he realized the white was the lace flowers that grew only in this field.

"Akeela?" Hawk whispered.

His toe bumped into something soft. He dropped to the ground and reached out. There she was. He pulled her to him and brushed her hair from her face, which glowed in the light of the moons. She was breathing.

He gave her a little shake. "Akeela? Wake up."

When she didn't move, he stood and carried her out of the field. A stray cloud passed overhead, and the world went dark. Hawk made his way to Ode Janmar's cave by the light of the fireplace through the front door window.

Tar opened the door at Hawk's call. "What happened?"

"I don't know," Hawk said. "She ran into the field and collapsed."

Ode Janmar set down his mug with a bang. "The lower field?"

Hawk laid Akeela on the bed. "Aye, the lower field. I know we were warned to stay away from it at night. I didn't know she'd run away from me like that."

Ves-rynia sat on the edge of the bed and put her hand on Akeela's forehead. She looked up at Hawk and smiled. "You two been crushing leaves, yeh?"

Hawk felt his face flush. "Aye. Well, not really. Just a little. I didn't mean to upset her. She can be so stubborn!"

Ode Janmar put his hand on Hawk's shoulder. "Tell me, lad, where did ye find her?"

"By the lace flowers."

Ode growled. "That be bad. The Moon Dancers be out at night in the lace flowers."

"What are Moon Dancers?" Ves-rynia asked.

Vorrak-ira and Anon came in the cave. Hawk turned and waved them over to the table. He didn't have the patience to deal with Anon right then, and the faun wouldn't understand why Akeela wasn't waking up.

"Moon Dancers be spirits," Ode Janmar was saying. "I've never seen them meself, but I heard tell of them who interrupt their dancin' and be spirited away."

Ves-rynia's eyes were wide with fright. "How do we get Akeela back?"

Ode Janmar slowly shook his head.

"What are you all chewing bark about?" Vorrak-ira called.

Ves-rynia went to the table and sat next to Anon, who was happily setting up the carved salt animals Ode had brought him.

She smiled and patted his head. "Anon, I have something to tell you."

Anon looked up and grinned. "Vessie. Have bear and rabbit and doggie."

"Aye, I see them. Listen, Anon, Akeela is sleeping. We need to let her sleep, so no trying to wake her up, yeh?"

Vorrak-ira leaned on the table. "What's happening?" he whispered.

Ves-rynia put a finger to her lips.

Anon looked up from his toys. "Anon have snack?"

"What would you like, dear one?" Ves-rynia asked as she busied herself at the counter.

Hawk held Akeela's cold hand, feeling helpless and stupid. If he'd kept his thoughts to himself, Akeela wouldn't be in this situation. And that made him wonder where the fairies were. They'd vanished after he and Akeela had argued.

"Ode Janmar, is there another entrance to your cave?" He didn't want the fairies to find another way in.

"Aye, but it be difficult to find." Ode jerked his thumb over his shoulder. "If ye follow the cave past the stream, ye'll end up near the mines. It be quite a piece from here. Are ye worried about something?"

Hawk strode to the door and peered out the window. The cloud had moved away, and the moons illuminated the world again in silvery light. He saw no signs of the fairies, and he couldn't sense their presence. If they overheard him, they'd be on alert.

Tar came to stand beside him.

"Father," Hawk said in a low voice. "Something's not right about the fairies who came to Akeela yesterday."

"Are you sure?"

Hawk nodded. He knew his father would believe him, but what could Tar do about it? They needed someone who could communicate with fairies, and he only knew two people who could do that. Krezma was nowhere around, and Akeela was lost in the Moon Dancer realm.

Dear Celtar, what do we do now?

Tzmet paced the balcony. The stench that rose from the goblin army made her sick. Putrid things. She should feel anticipation. Instead, dread took over, and she couldn't stand still.

"My lady, please do not distress yourself," Brimridge said. "All will be right when the mighty Riss'aird's army is complete."

"Shut up! Shut up!" Tzmet screeched. "I don't need your patronizing words."

Brimridge bowed. "My pardon. I'll leave you alone now."

Tzmet stopped and leaned on the balcony rail. "Wait."

"My lady?"

Sleg blew a horn, and the army fell silent. Riss'aird walked out and stood next to the goblin leader. He raised his hands. "My friends, this day will see the rebuilding of my great army!"

The goblins roared in response.

"I will personally reward each one of you if I am satisfied with your efforts," Riss'aird continued. "And once my army is complete, the world will kneel at your feet!"

This drove the goblins crazy. They butted heads and punched each other as they cheered. The sound was deafening. Tzmet should've felt as excited as the goblins, sickening as they were, but her heart sank. She turned to Brimridge.

"My pardon, Brimridge. I would keep our friendship intact."

Brimridge nodded.

"I have an idea," Tzmet said. "Come with me to the great room."

Hawk sat by Akeela's side all night. He prayed and wept and begged her to wake up. She never moved. By morning, he was spent. What would they do if she never regained consciousness?

She was the only hope for the fairy realm. And without fairies, they could not defeat Riss'aird.

He felt a hand on his shoulder and looked up to see Ves-rynia.

"Sapo, you look tired. Did you not sleep?"

Hawk shook his head. "Nay, I couldn't."

Ves-rynia set a tray with a mug of water and a small towel on the bed. "Here, come eat. You'll need your strength, yeh? I'll sit with Akeela."

She tugged on Hawk's arm, and he grudgingly got up. "My thanks."

His cousin nodded as she dipped the towels' corner into the water. He watched her dribble some on Akeela's lips. It ran off the side of her face onto the pillow.

"Sit ye down," Ode Janmar said as Hawk approached the table. "There be biscuits and honey and salted pork. Eat up!"

"Where's my father?" Hawk asked as Ode Janmar handed him a mug of *caavea*.

Ode shrugged. "Ye know yer father. He be comin' and going in his own way. I'm sure he be back soon."

Hawk wrapped both hands around the warm mug. Was Akeela cold? Hungry? He wanted to shout his frustration and anger — with himself, with Riss'aird, with Celtar. Even, if he was honest, with Akeela herself.

Ode Janmar set a platter of steaming, salted pork strips on the table. "Best ye eat before that Vorrak-ira comes back. I never did see anyone eat as much as that boy."

Hawk grinned. "Aye, he sure can eat. Where's Anon?"

"With the boy." Ode Janmar filled a mug of *caavea* for himself and sat. "The wee faun wanted to take a walk before breakfast."

Hawk ate because he was hungry, but he didn't want to linger long away from Akeela. He had to figure out a way to wake her. Without her, they were lost.

He was lost.

Tzmet heard the first group of goblins come back at midday.

Brimridge walked to the window. "It looks like Sleg was successful. I count at least twenty men."

"It's been three days," she said. "I should think they've had ample time to get what we need."

"Indeed." Brimridge glanced at her and turned back to the window. "Do not forget, there are two more groups of goblins yet to return."

"Don't be sarcastic, fool. They have their job; we have ours." Tzmet pushed her plate to the side and picked up a goblet. She sniffed, wrinkled her nose, and downed the contents. Ever since the goblin army had marched out, she and Brimridge had tried several potions for increasing magic power. Riss'aird had refused each one, even though Tzmet had tried them all and found success. She'd tried to convince her father the potions were working, but he'd waved her away.

"Easy, my lady," Brimridge said with a grin. "If you keep going, you'll be the one with all the power."

Tzmet gave a short laugh. "If you keep going, you'll be the one who finds himself out in the cold. Remember who you serve, boggart."

Brimridge burst into laughter.

She set down the goblet and belched. "The impudence."

"Yes, my lady," Brimridge said between chuckles.

"Idiot." Tzmet pressed her lips together to keep from smiling. She really did like the smelly leader of the boggarts, even though she had no idea when that had happened.

Two Hinwari entered the room silently and removed the midday meal dishes. A third brought a fresh carafe of cold mint tea. Tzmet waited until they left the room before going on.

"Really, Brimridge, if my father were to realize we have an alliance, there would be trouble for you."

Brimridge poured the tea into porcelain cups. "And not for you?"

"Of course not." Tzmet sipped her tea. "I am his daughter."

"Hmm."

"What's *that* supposed to mean?" Tzmet snapped.

"Just that . . . you cannot be sure," Brimridge said. "Even you cannot be sure."

Tzmet opened her mouth to retort, but no words came. She set down her cup. Curse the boggart! He'd hit a nerve. Deep down, she was more worried than she wanted to admit. No use pretending to herself, although she'd never admit it aloud.

Riss'aird's bell rang, startling her. She glared at Brimridge, then hurried to her father's bedroom. Sleg, dirty and bloody, stood proudly next to Riss'aird. He winked at Tzmet. She ignored him. If he wanted to breach etiquette by appearing before her father before washing, then let him take the consequences.

Riss'aird's eyes looked colder than usual. "Bring us wine and food, daughter."

Tzmet swallowed and curtsied. "Of course, Father. Do you have a preference?"

"No."

Tzmet curtsied again, forcing herself to smile. "Right away, Father."

"There has to be something we can do!" Hawk stood at the end of the bed. Akeela still hadn't moved. Ves-rynia continued to dribble water into her mouth. Sometimes she succeeded, sometimes not. When Anon had realized Akeela wasn't waking up, he'd curled up next to her and wouldn't move unless someone picked him up to eat or wash or relieve himself. Then he trotted back as quickly as he could.

Ode Janmar had consulted with Eli Saltpraise, the minister, but Eli had little to no knowledge of the Moon Dancers. He'd assured them he would pray and offer sacrifices of the best salt to Khewra.

Tar had no answers. Hawk wanted to rant and rave against Celtar. Why was He allowing this to happen? Why didn't He help?

Had He abandoned them?

Hawk stopped pacing and stared down at his sleeping love. What would happen if Akeela never woke up?

Tzmet gagged and lost her dinner into a bucket next to the wash-basin. The kitchen reeked of rat's blood from the preparations for the transvarient process. After all three groups of goblins returned, they now had a total of fifty human males in the dungeons. More than enough to annihilate anyone they wished, once the process was complete. Riss'aird preferred strength instead of numbers, and his preference had served him well in the past.

"Easy, my lady." Brimridge handed her a wet rag. "Your Hinwari have removed all the brains and have started on the hearts. It won't be long now."

Tzmet wiped her mouth with the rag. How totally humiliating. She wanted to sink into the floor. Where was her strength?

She let Brimridge help her stand and accepted a mug of water from him. When the room stopped spinning, she walked as calmly as she could manage to the open window. The sun had just set, casting a few rays of deep pink upward. Soon the moons would rise. Another few days, and all three would be full. Tzmet took a deep breath of fresh air. Her thoughts raced. How different things had turned out than what she'd pictured all the many years she'd planned to raise her father's ashes from the ground.

The Riss'aird she remembered laughed. He included her in his plans. Doted on her. Gave her gifts. Loved her. What had happened?

Brimridge's hand rested on her shoulder, and she chuckled. How ironic. The being she'd despised had turned out to be her only friend. And the father she'd longed to have back was the one person she wished never to see again.

"My lady?"

Tzmet turned to face Brimridge. "Is all ready?"

"It is."

"Very well." Tzmet lifted her chin, smoothed her skirt, and walked to the table where the prepared rats lay in a heap. She accepted two brass bowls from a Hinwar and held her breath as she quickly scooped the brains into one bowl and the hearts another. The battered bodies she placed in a canvas bag.

"Brimridge," she said. "Would you do me the honor of accompanying me to the dungeons?"

"Father, the transvarient process has begun," Tzmet said with a bow.

Riss'aird and Sleg sat the table, as they usually did in the evenings, playing cards or *grifnoc*. This night proved no different. Tzmet wondered why she was never asked to play. Not that she would spend any time with the putrid goblin leader.

"Excellent." Riss'aird set his cards down face up. "I believe I have won again, my dear Sleg."

Sleg gave a slight smile that Tzmet took to mean, *I let you win, fool.* She seethed inside, wishing to see the uppity goblin put down in such a way to completely humiliate the whole goblin race. Perhaps her father would love her again if only the goblins would go away.

Riss'aird cleared his throat.

"Father?"

"Bring champagne, daughter. It's time to celebrate."

Tzmet fairly flew down the stairs and into the kitchen. "Get three glasses!" she screeched to a Hinwar. "Brimridge, help me carry everything."

After fetching a bottle from the cellar, Tzmet and Brimridge carried the champagne and a tray of bread, soft cheese, and leeks, as well as a bowl of olives and a platter of smoked fish to Riss'aird's bedroom. Tzmet graciously poured the sparkling wine and handed a glass to Sleg and her father. She turned to pour herself a glass when Riss'aird spoke.

"That will be all, daughter."

She looked up in surprise. "Father?"

"You may go."

"But—but . . ."

Riss'aird pointed from her to the door. "You. May. Go. Now."

Sleg smirked behind his glass as Riss'aird turned his attention to the platter of delectables. Tzmet stood still for a moment. Her father's words sank in, and she turned and walked, as if in a trance, into the hallway.

As she was closing the door, Sleg congratulated Riss'aird. She could hear the clink of their glasses.

"My lady?" Brimridge had waited outside the room.

Tzmet walked past him and into her bedroom. She shut and locked the door behind her. Everything looked the same, but Tzmet felt as though the world had suddenly shifted, as though she'd somehow gone through an invisible doorway and stepped into exactly the same world, but in a stranger's body.

She walked to her vanity and sat. After a moment, she looked up and gazed at her reflection. Who was this strange woman with dark, haunted eyes? She looked like the daughter of the great and mighty Riss'aird.

But Tzmet had no idea who she was.

Part Three

REBIRTH

Chapter Thirty-Six

Silver light.
  Floating, twirling, singing.
  Enveloping.
  White, lacy flowers bending in the breeze.
  Calling, sinking, praying.
  Reaching.
  "Rest, Chosen One. Rest. The time will come when you will do battle. Celtar has ordained this time of refreshment for you. For you are weary and in need of strength."
  Colors blending, auras dancing.
  Water, fresh and sparkling, filling.
  Rest, rest, rest.

Hawk covered his face with his hands and prayed. He begged, pleaded, and demanded Celtar to wake Akeela. He bargained and threatened. Finally, exhausted, he dropped his head onto the side of the bed and wept.

For three days, they kept vigil over Akeela. Anon grew more

desperate every day and could not be coaxed to eat. Ves-rynia never gave up trickling water into Akeela's mouth. Ode spent most of his time in the temple. Tar, when he wasn't pacing in front of the fireplace, hunted and cooked, even though appetites were slim.

And Vorrak-ira, well, Hawk had no idea how he spent his time. He hadn't come near Akeela after the first night. Hawk didn't care. All that mattered was waking Akeela.

"Hawk?"

He lifted his head at Ves-rynia's voice but didn't look at her.

"I need to tend Akeela. You go outside and get some fresh air, yeh?"

Hawk stood painfully, his legs stiff and tingly after being cramped for so long at Akeela's bedside. He shuffled to the door. The sunlight stunned him for a moment, and he lifted a hand to shade his eyes. The warm breeze caressed his face. His chest hurt from crying, and he was almost dizzy with despair.

And he was thirsty.

Cold water dripped from his cupped hands as he drank. Then he splashed his face, sat down, and put his feet in the stream. Several fish swam by. As he stretched his arms above his head, he felt a presence. *Their* presence. The fairies he didn't trust.

"Where is the Guardian?" they asked, hovering just out of Hawk's reach.

Hawk was surprised. He thought fairies only communicated with Akeela or Krezma. Desperation did funny things to people — and fairies, he supposed.

"Why are you talking to me?" he asked.

"Where is the Guardian?" they asked again.

So they didn't trust him, either. Hawk smiled. "Can't you sense what's happened to her?"

The fairies glanced at each other. "We can't leave the Guardian," the tall one said.

Hawk stood, and the fairies drew back in alarm. He shrugged. "Well, she's left you."

The fairies gasped, their eyes wide. "Where did she go?" the small one cried.

Hawk cocked his head and crossed his arms. "Does the name Moon Dancers mean anything to you?"

The fairies looked at each other, confused. The little one looked like she wanted to burst into tears. Good. Let them worry.

"Go away. I don't want you here." Hawk turned his attention back to the stream. He felt them leave and gave a harsh laugh. A dragonfly flew past, and he wondered it if was a water fairy in disguise. And how would he know? He wondered if he could talk to a fire fairy. Akeela said they were the ones who carried messages and news.

But what kind of news could he give? *I'm sorry, but your Guardian is dying.*

***

Lingering, longing, searching.
"Do not struggle, Chosen One. Be filled."
Warmth, peace, joy.
Rest, rest, rest.

***

Hawk heard loud voices and opened his eyes. He'd been dreaming Akeela was lost in some strange fairy world. He stretched and pulled his feet, now ice cold, out of the stream. It must be time for the midday meal.

Five dwarves stood at Ode Janmar's cave door. Tanchor, the leader, and Bracken Bearbane, Eli Saltpraise, and two other dwarves Hawk recognized but couldn't remember their names. Tar was with them, his brow furrowed and his mouth grim.

Tar's good hand was clenched. "We cannot do this without your help."

Bracken had a dangerous look on his face, but Tanchor raised his hand. "We know ye be needin' help, but our goddess has spoken."

Eli gazed at the ground, shifting from foot to foot as though the ground was hot. Ode Janmar was nowhere in sight. This couldn't be good.

"We must be obeyin' what Khewra says through our priest," Tanchor continued. "Ye be followin' yer own god. Do ye disobey?"

Tar shook his head. "Nay, but sometimes we misunderstand Celtar's will because our own desires get in the way."

"Are ye callin' us liars?" Bracken roared.

Hawk decided to keep quiet.

Tanchor and one of the other dwarves pulled Bracken back. Tar made no move, but his face flushed. Not much rattled Tar, and Hawk watched in amazement.

Tar turned to the priest. "Do you not ever experience this?"

Eli continued shuffling from side to side.

"It has nothing to do with telling the truth," Tar went on. "I believe you. I'm only saying you may not be clear in your understanding."

Bracken growled, and the other dwarves shook their heads.

Eli put his hands together as if praying. He glanced at his brethren and cleared his throat. "Aye, well, this bears thinkin'. If it pleases ye all, I can read the salt crystals again."

Tanchor nodded. "Aye, we'll do this for ye, but we'll also be abidin' by the outcome. There be no more talkin' about it."

Tar bowed his head. "My thanks."

Hawk decided to make his presence known then. He strolled around the side of the cave and called a greeting.

The dwarves turned to leave. Tanchor nodded at Hawk, then turned back to Tar and said, "Remember, we will obey the goddess, no matter the outcome."

Tar remained silent as the dwarves took their leave. Hawk stood beside him. The sun had moved from the midday mark, and he was famished.

"Let's get something to eat," he said. "I want to check on Akeela too."

Tar nodded.

Inside the cave, Ode Janmar sat on a stool near an open window. He was deep into carving a small piece of wood.

"There're be stew on the fire," Ode Janmar said without looking up.

Hawk looked over at Akeela. Ves-rynia shook her head. He sighed and dipped squirrel stew into a wooden bowl. Three days had gone by. How much longer would Akeela be able to survive without food? The little water Ves-rynia was able to dribble into her mouth couldn't be enough to sustain her. Even though it'd only been a couple of weeks since she'd come out of his dreams and into his world, he couldn't imagine life without her. Couldn't bear the thought of her body in a box in the ground.

He took a spoonful of the stew and swallowed. Then he poured the rest back into the pot.

"But, Father, I'm trying every spell in my book!" Tzmet knelt to wipe up the potion Riss'aird had knocked to the floor. She blinked back tears.

Riss'aird leaned back on the pillows and sighed. "Daughter, I ask so little of you. And I have given you ample time to research and study spells."

Tzmet set the wet cloth in a metal bowl. Her hands trembled, and she clenched them at her sides. "I'm working every minute, truly I am! I don't understand why the potions do not give you power. When I test them on myself, I can feel it working."

"Indeed?"

"Don't you believe me?" The question was out before Tzmet could check herself.

Riss'aird gave her an icy stare.

"I'm sorry, Father." Tzmet curtsied. "I'll work harder. I'll try new spells. Mayhap, if the potions increase my power, I can be of better help to you."

She waited while Riss'aird appeared to consider this. The sun had set, and Tzmet grew weary. She'd done nothing but work on spells all day, only stopping for the midday meal. Tzmet and Brimridge had been sure this latest attempt would have an effect.

"I accept your proposal," Riss'aird finally said. "Build yourself up as much as you can. When you find the strongest potion, bring it to me."

Tzmet curtsied again. "Yes, Father."

Riss'aird waved his hand. "Leave."

"Yes, Father."

Brimridge sat at the kitchen table with only one candle lit. Tzmet almost didn't see him when she entered the room.

"My lady," he said. "Were you successful?"

Tzmet slammed the bowl on the counter next to the sink.

"I see." The boggart leader stroked his pointed beard. "And have we been kicked out of the castle?"

"No."

"Are you going to tell me what happened?"

Tzmet sank onto the bench and ran a hand across her bare head. How long had it been since she'd worn one of her beautiful wigs? There hadn't been an occasion to dress up or do anything fun since her father had returned. And now everything she did to help him failed.

"I wish he'd never come back," she whispered.

Brimridge looked at her in amazement. "What did you say?"

Tzmet banged her fist on the table. "You heard me, you smelly rodent! And if you breathe a word to *anyone*, I will personally shave your beard and cut your throat."

Brimridge started to laugh. He laughed so hard, he grabbed his sides and tried to catch his breath.

Tzmet sneered, her lip curling. "I see nothing amusing, you putrid, obnoxious . . . boggart! I should put you all out tonight."

"My—lady—" Brimridge gasped and stuttered. "I'm not laughing at you. I'm relieved you finally said it."

"What do you mean?"

"Here, let me light more candles and get you something to eat. Then we can talk."

He got up, lit two candles, and set one on the table. The other he took with him into the cellar. Tzmet sat, stewing in her thoughts until he returned with a tray laden with bread, hard cheese, cold sliced muskrat, and two stalks of sage leaves. After he poured her a glass of wine, he retrieved a crock of oil, a plate, and a knife and set it before her.

Tzmet's stomach cramped, and she forgot her anger. "This looks good."

"My lady, allow me to prepare your meal." Without waiting for an answer, Brimridge sliced the bread and cheese. He poured oil on the bread and layered the cheese, meat, and sage leaves on it. Then he topped it with another slice of oiled bread, cut it in half, and set it on the plate.

"What am I supposed to do with this, fool?" Tzmet wrinkled her nose as she inspected the strange thing before her.

Brimridge smiled as he prepared another for himself. "We call it a hand-meal. You pick it up and eat it all together. Watch me." And saying so, he sat, picked up the hand-meal, and took a bite.

"That is vulgar." But Tzmet was too hungry to fix anything else, so she picked up the hand-meal, sniffed it, and took a small bite. Sun, moon, and stars, the thing was actually good! She took another bite, and oil ran down her chin.

Brimridge's black eyes twinkled in the candlelight. "You're welcome."

Tzmet grunted and took another bite. The boggart must've put some kind of spell on her, she decided. A few weeks ago, she would've blasted him into ashes for being so rude and familiar with her. She took a sip of wine and realized she didn't care. She was fond of the nasty little man and his family now and wished with all her heart Riss'aird would go away and leave them to live in the castle in peace.

Brimridge interrupted her thoughts. "My lady, I have a thought. What would happen if you continued to increase your power? Your father doesn't want any more potions—well, at least until you find the strongest. Why not simply prepare them for yourself?"

Tzmet contemplated this. If she increased her power and her father remained weak, she may be in a position to make her wish come true. She giggled.

"My lady, what are you thinking?"

Tzmet smiled. "I'm thinking I need to do exactly what my Father said."

Chapter Thirty-Seven

Krezma studied the area around the cave before she stepped out of the forest. The sun cast its first rays into the sky. She noticed the position of the setting moons and prayed once more to Celtar for help.

If Akeela were not able to complete the quest before the moons came together, all would be lost.

Still, Celtar had not abandoned her. If He had, she wouldn't have stumbled across the two fairies who told her Akeela's whereabouts. She was so relieved to know where Akeela was, she shoved aside the thought that something wasn't quite right.

Krezma glanced around and decided not to wait any longer. She must see if Akeela had succeeded in finding the other three pieces of the Fairystone. Now that Riss'aird had risen from the ashes, he would waste no time putting an army together.

She rapped sharply on the door. After a minute, the door opened a crack. "Who be ye?"

"I am Krezma, Akeela's, uh, friend."

It sounded strange to her ears, calling herself Akeela's friend. But really, what else could she say? She was not related. The person at the door walked away, and Krezma waited.

After several moments, the door yanked opened, and Tar, who looked as though he'd aged ten years, greeted her.

"Krezma! Thank Celtar! Come inside."

She stepped in and let her eyes adjust. A dwarf was pouring water into a kettle near the fireplace. Other than that, Tar seemed to be the only person there.

"Where's Akeela?"

Tar gestured with his claw hand. "Sit. I would speak to you."

Krezma's eyes narrowed, but she sat. The optimism she felt vanished. She knew Tar well enough to know he'd be straightforward. He related all that had happened after she'd left. As the story went on, Krezma's stress rose, and her shoulders hunched. When he finished, she could barely reach for the mug of *caavea* the dwarf brought. She wrapped her hands around it.

"Krezma, this is our host." He nodded at the dwarf. "Ode Janmar Axegrinder. He was also a friend to Oret."

Krezma smiled. "The dwarf he rescued from drowning?"

Ode grunted.

"Aye," Tar said. "And he has been a faithful friend to us."

"Well, let me see what I can do for Akeela." Krezma stood. "Please take me to her."

Tar pointed to a curtain. Krezma pulled it back and saw Akeela, looking as though dead, with Anon and a huge dog curled up at her side, Ves-rynia sitting on the floor with her head on the bed, sound asleep, and Hawk propped up in a chair, snoring. The pallor on Akeela's face struck dread in her heart.

She was looking at Akeela's death face, and the sharp stab she felt took her breath away. Not even when she'd left Tzmet that fateful night had she felt this level of pain.

She gently shook Ves-rynia's shoulder. "Child, forgive me, but I need to sit next to Akeela."

Ves-rynia rubbed her eyes. "Krezma?"

"Aye."

"Thank Celtar you've come. Mayhap you can wake her, yeh?"

Krezma squared her shoulders. "I will try."

She sat on the bed and put her hand on Akeela's forehead. No fever. Then she lifted Akeela's hand and looked at the birthmark. It gave off a faint glow. A good sign. A sign that meant fairy magic was somehow involved.

Hawk stirred and woke. "I'm dreaming, yeh?"

Krezma put her hands on Akeela's cheeks. "Nay, I am here."

"How did you find us?"

She continued to ponder what was needed for the best way to try to wake her.

"Krezma?"

"Eh?"

"How did you find us?" Hawk asked again.

"Two earth fairies told me."

Hawk sat up. "Those fairies! I don't trust them. Something about them didn't feel right."

Krezma waved a hand at him. "Indeed? I know of only good fairies. What are you saying?"

"I'm saying, with these fairies, something wasn't right. I shouldn't be able to see them," Hawk exclaimed. "Even Ode could see them!"

"This is bad news." Krezma continued to check Akeela as she talked. "If somehow these fairies are serving the Dark Lord, it won't be long before he knows our whereabouts."

Anon opened his eyes and stared at Krezma a moment before sitting up. The dog lifted his head and looked at Krezma with sleepy eyes. That animal would have to leave.

"Krez! You help Keela?" Anon cried.

"I'm going to try. Hawk, bring me a bowl of hot water."

Ves-rynia, who'd been sitting to the side, came to the bed and helped Anon down. "Come here, sweet one. Let's go have something to eat, yeh?" She took his hand. "Fin, come."

The dog stretched, then ambled behind them.

Krezma opened her bag of herbs, selected several, and placed them in the steaming bowl. A pungent smell filled the area. She asked for a towel, and Hawk brought it. Then she moved the steaming bowl onto the bed near Akeela's face and covered both the bowl and Akeela's head with the towel.

Ode Janmar came to stand next to Hawk. He nodded and said, "I saw this type of thing done meself. Twill infuse the herbs into Akeela, even though she can't drink."

Krezma moved her hands in a circle above Akeela and murmured words of power and bidding. She prayed, no, *begged* Celtar to intervene and wake Akeela. After several minutes, she lifted the towel.

The water had cooled, and Akeela's face appeared flushed, but still she slept.

"Try again," Hawk pleaded. "Please! Try again!"

Krezma shook her head. "Nay, if it didn't work this time, it will not work. But I won't give up. I have other methods to try."

For the rest of the morning and well into the afternoon, Krezma tried every potion, herb, and oil she had knowledge of and could find. Akeela slept on. Finally, she tied her bag closed. Resignation filled her soul.

"That's it. I know of nothing else to do but wait on Celtar's will."

Hawk, who'd not left her side, begged her not to stop.

Krezma sighed and turned to him. "I'm tired, young man. I know of nothing else to do. Now, get me something to eat. After I rest, I'll send word to the Fairy Council." She paused. "And I believe her husband should be here in case she really is dying, but there's no time to fetch him."

Hawk choked. The blood drained from his head, and he gave it a small shake.

Krezma gave him a curious look, but he turned his head. He couldn't have heard right. The old woman had to be shaking his branches.

But he couldn't stop from asking, "Akeela is married?"

"Aye, as I have said." Krezma's eyes narrowed. "What business is it of yours?"

Hawk slammed the door on his emotions. "It's not." And he walked from the bedroom without looking back.

Resting, floating, dreaming.
Colors swirling, music singing.
Calling.
"Awake, Chosen One. It is time."
Bright light . . . sunshine so warm . . . fading . . .
"Wake up."
Feels so peaceful . . . safe . . . filled . . . must I come back?
"Return, Chosen One. I am waiting."
Rising . . . up . . . up . . . up . . .

Akeela's eyelids fluttered. She felt soft, light, as though she were not entirely solid. A cocoon of silvery white enveloped her body. Was someone calling? She wanted to ignore it and keep floating, but the voice penetrated the mist.

"Chosen One, come back."

Voices. Singing. Many voices. They compelled her, and she could sleep no longer. She opened her eyes. A being came into focus. The first thing Akeela noticed was the aura, silver with a gold edge. The being, a type of fairy unfamiliar to Akeela, looked as though she floated underwater. Her dark hair flowed around her head, and the skirt of her blood-red dress swelled and fell in an invisible current. A ringlet of stars circled her forehead, and her skin shimmered with an iridescent glow. Her pink wings had six sections, with ripples along the edges.

Akeela sat up to find she floated with the fairy. Even though she didn't know where she was, she felt no fear. She smiled at the woman. "Am I dead?"

The fairy being floated closer, and Akeela realized she had no eyes. Just black pools where eyes should be.

Several balls of light gathered behind her. More followed until one large mass of light hovered all around. The lights faded to reveal thousands of tiny, pure-white fairies with silver auras. This seemed natural to Akeela, and she welcomed their presence.

They sang, and Akeela felt rather than heard it. It refreshed her as though she stood under a gentle waterfall. She wanted it to never end. But a small buzzing sensation in the far recesses of her thoughts kept the perfection from totally taking over.

Akeela, granddaughter of Oret.

The lilting voice echoed in her mind. Akeela turned to the large fairy.

I am Rowena Rayenath, Queen of the Moon Dancers.

The queen's voice was like a song.

Akeela bowed. "Your Majesty."

We brought thy spirit here to prepare thee for what lies ahead. You do not know how important you are.

Akeela tried to make sense of this. She was important?

Fairy Guardian.

The words hit Akeela like a slap. Fairy Guardian. The quest! Hawk!

Peace, Chosen One. I am here to confirm the knowledge thy grandfather taught thee. If you do not complete the quest, our realm will disappear. Then all will be lost to darkness.

Akeela's heart raced. How long had she been here? "Please, Your Majesty, I am willing. But I need to get back to my friends."

I will restore thee in time. You are the one chosen to become the next Fairy Guardian. The Guardian is the co-bearer of the Fairysong, which sustains life for all fairies. When the Fairystone is complete within thee, a bond forms between thee and the Ruling Fairy. She is the source of the Fairysong and the bearer of life for fairies. All four elements meet in the Fairysong. It is powerful and will defeat the Dark Lord.

Akeela tried to imagine being more powerful than Riss'aird. What would that look like?

When thy grandfather died, the bond was broken. The Ruling Fairy is now dying. If you do not complete the quest before the end of my moons' conjunction, she will perish. You have two pieces. The third lies in the crown of the dwarves' goddess. You must pass their test.

"Test? What kind of test?" Akeela asked. "Where is the fourth piece?"

The fourth piece is hidden from me, but I can give thee this piece of wisdom: thy faith will carry thee through. The Queen drifted closer and placed her hands on Akeela's head. *Now go. I bless and commission thee. Return and complete the quest. We have refreshed thee and have brought one to aid thee. She is waiting for thee now.*

The Moon Dancers flew around Akeela—faster, faster—enveloping her at first and then becoming part of her. Their song caressed her spirit until they vanished. Although Queen Rowena began to fade, the black pools of her eyes remained steady on Akeela's face.

"Will I see you again?" Akeela called. But within a moment, empty space was all around her, deep blue and cold. A mist drifted up from below, and Akeela closed her eyes.

When she opened them, Krezma smiled down at her.

"It's about time, child."

Chapter Thirty-Eight

Akeela paced as the Dwarf Council talked in the next room. They'd all seemed impressed at what they called her "vision" of the Moon Dancers. She'd tried to convince them it was real—not a vision—but they'd laughed at her. She'd clamped down her anger and had insisted they allow her to have the stone. She felt it was enough to change their minds about helping, as well. How could it not? Queen Rowena had blessed and commissioned her.

An hour later, the door opened, and the Council took their seats. The priest, Eli Saltpraise, smiled at her.

"We have discussed the situation in full," Tanchor began. "And we be willin' to help ye on one condition."

Akeela stood silent. Confident.

Eli stood and spread his hands. "After prayin' and askin' Khewra for wisdom, she has answered: 'Sacrifice to me, and I will give ye the stone in my crown.'"

The dwarves shifted and grunted. Tanchor looked from side to side and frowned.

Akeela's mouth went dry. She licked her lips. "I'm not sure what you mean."

"'Tis a simple task," Eli said. "Ye need to go into the mines and gather the purest salt, bring it to the temple, and lay it at Khewra's feet."

"But Celtar forbids any worship to another god," Akeela said.

Bracken leaned forward and grinned. "Then ye'll not be gettin' the stone."

The dwarves nodded, and Akeela stood without speaking. Sacrificing to their goddess was out of the question. There had to be another way. She glanced at the council and knew reasoning with them would be futile. *Celtar, help me know what to do!*

The longer she stood, the more restless the dwarves became. They shifted in their seats and twisted their beards. Finally, the priest spoke. "What be your answer, lass?"

"I'm asking Celtar for wisdom," she said. "Surely I have time for that."

"Aye, ye do."

"Thank you."

She closed her eyes and focused. Waited for an answer. The dwarves whispered among themselves, and she tried to ignore it, but to no avail. She had to give them an answer. She could ask to consult with her group, but she wanted to make this decision herself. She was the Guardian, after all. Or would be.

Celtar, please!

Then she had a thought. If she simply went through the motions of getting the salt and bringing it to the temple, she wouldn't have to mean it. It wouldn't be a real sacrifice. The dwarves would be satisfied, and she'd get the stone.

She looked at Tanchor without blinking. "I will do it."

Tzmet pushed her book of spells away. "This is insane. How will I know when I've found the strongest spell?"

Brimridge poured hot *caavea* into a mug and handed it to her. "My lady, do not distress yourself. Your power is increasing, and the goblins have begun the transvarient process. It won't be long until the fairies are eliminated."

342

"Hmph," she snorted. "Give me the cream, you dolt."

A Hinwar entered the room and set a breakfast tray next to Brimridge. He lifted the lid off the platter, and steam rose, bringing with it a savory aroma. Tzmet sipped her *caavea* while Brimridge dished out their food. She felt torn about the whole situation with the goblins, the whiptail army, and the fairies. True, she'd dried and eaten her share of the revolting things, but there was no need to deal with them now that her father had regenerated. If she hadn't been so keen to raise her father from the ashes, she probably would've ignored them.

Brimridge slid a plate to her. He'd heaped plenty of scrambled duck eggs and white tubers with leeks on it. Tzmet smelled herbs and a little *hicata* pepper. A seemingly perfect meal, but instead of feeling good about it, she was annoyed. Brimridge shoved forkful after forkful into his mouth while Tzmet pushed hers around the plate. She nibbled a little, and it was delicious, but not satisfying.

"Brimridge." She set down her fork. "What do you think will happen once the transvarient process is complete?"

The boggart leader chewed, swallowed, and slurped from his mug. Then he belched and wiped his mouth with the back of his hand. "What you do mean?"

"Don't be so dense! With things the way they are, do you think my father will really have me at his side?"

Brimridge pondered this. Tzmet cursed and jumped up from the table. She walked to the window and watched a goblin stroll across the courtyard. The ache in her stomach grew.

"Don't answer that," she said as two more goblins followed the first.

"My lady," Brimridge said.

Tzmet put up her hand. "I'll keep working on stronger spells. But I wonder if I hadn't lost my fairy wing cape, if that would've been some help."

"Perhaps you can make another?"

Tzmet glared at him.

Brimridge chuckled. "It was just a suggestion."

"I have a suggestion for you," Tzmet retorted.

343

"Now, now, my lady," Brimridge said. "I'm your friend, remember?"

Tzmet sat back down. "Are you? Well, I'm going to say this once, *friend*. I don't know what my father's planning, but I don't trust him." She picked up a piece of bread and tore it in half. "And if I find out you have betrayed me, I will kill your entire family."

Brimridge cleared his throat. "My lady Tzmet, I take quite a bit from you, and I take it with grace. But I'm going to say *this* once, *friend*. I will not sit here while you threaten my loved ones."

The blood rushed from Tzmet's face, and she clung to the table. Her throat closed, and she struggled to get the words out. "I—can't—do—this."

"Do what, my lady?"

Tzmet grabbed her mug and gulped the contents. She took a deep breath. "I can't be my father's servant. I will not! Brimridge, are you truly my friend? If you are not, tell me now, and I'll leave the castle. I'll leave all my potions for you to strengthen my father. I'll never be seen again."

Brimridge sat silently, staring at his empty plate. Tzmet flushed with embarrassment. Cursed emotions! What was she thinking? Never before had she felt so frightened, not even after she'd woken from the spell-gone-wrong and found herself alone.

Two Hinwari came in and began to clear the table.

"Get out!" Tzmet shrieked. She clenched her fists and fought to keep herself together. Brimridge had obviously deserted her. Well then, she'd show no weakness. She'd do as she'd said: pack her things and leave. She pushed back from the table.

Brimridge lifted a hand, his finger pointing up. "Wait. I have a plan."

Tzmet arched her eyebrows. "A plan?"

"Indeed, my lady. Now you listen to me because I'll only say this one more time. I am your friend. It wasn't so in the beginning, for either of us, but now that we know each other better, I find I actually like you."

Tzmet snorted.

Brimridge grinned. "Even when you're cranky."

"Quit your rambling and tell me this plan, you idiot." Tzmet sat and smoothed her skirt, working not to show relief or pleasure. The twinkle in Brimridge's eyes said she hadn't fooled him, but somehow, that didn't bother her.

"Well, my lady. You've been working hard to mix potions to restore your father's power, and they aren't working as you'd like."

"Your observant powers astound me, fool. Get to the point."

Brimridge settled back in his chair. "You alluded to something the other day. Without coming out and saying it, I understood if you continued to mix and sample the power potions, your power would become greater than Riss'aird's. My lady, your power is already greater! He has little. Why are you so afraid of him?"

Tzmet's heart leaped. She studied her fingernails. "I am not afraid of him."

It was Brimridge's turn to snort.

"Curses and fireweed! He's my father." Tzmet crossed her arms. "I do not know what you boggarts teach your children, but I respect my father. That's different from fear."

"Respect works both ways, my lady," Brimridge said. "My plan is this: If you find Riss'aird has, indeed, betrayed your trust, you should not hesitate to use your powers to stop him. Then you can take his place. You're smart. You can rule."

Tzmet was shocked. Take her father's place? No, she couldn't. Could she? If she did, she wouldn't destroy every living thing. She'd force them to bring her offerings. She had the boggarts and the Hinwari to serve her in the castle. Servants bringing gifts would be a marvelous addition. She smiled.

Brimridge stroked his pointed beard. "I have a taste for something sweet. What do you say?"

"Whatever."

They sat without speaking until a Hinwar brought them a platter of sliced green apples, a brick of soft goat cheese, and a crock of honey. Brimridge spread some cheese on the apple slices, drizzled them with honey, and slid a plate to Tzmet.

Chapter Thirty-Nine

❧❧❧

"You're going to what?" Ves-rynia screeched.

Everyone began talking at once. Anon, who misunderstood what the excitement was about, began to laugh and dance, causing Fin to bark and nip at his hooves. Ode Janmar tried to calm his dog, but Fin wouldn't obey a single command.

Akeela climbed onto a chair. "Listen!" she shouted. "Please, listen!"

The noise faded, echoing against the cave walls. Anon looked surprised when Akeela raised her voice. He stopped singing, sat on the floor, and leaned on Fin's back. Hawk lifted his eyebrows, and Vorrak-ira looked mildly impressed.

"Thank you," Akeela said. "I know what this sounds like, but I've thought about it. I'm not really going to sacrifice to their goddess. I'll put salt at her feet, aye, but only to get the stone. It won't come from my heart."

Tar frowned. "I don't feel right about deceiving the dwarves."

Akeela stepped down from the chair. "I have no desire to deceive them, but I don't know any other way to get the stone."

"Sneak me in. I'll get the stone for you, yeh?" Vorrak-ira said. "It'll be easy as shimmying up a tree."

Ode Janmar shook his head. "Ye are a fool, boy. I may not be liking what the council decided, but I'll not allow ye to desecrate our temple or the goddess."

Everyone began talking again. Akeela looked at Hawk, who just frowned. Krezma sat across the room on the edge of the bed. She'd remained silent, which Akeela thought strange, so she left the group and sat next to her.

"Don't you have anything to say?"

Krezma tugged on her braid and didn't speak right away. Then she coughed. "Child, I cannot tell you what to do. You must decide. I have taught and guided you for fifteen years. If you cannot think for yourself now, you are not ready to be the Guardian."

Akeela looked at the floor. Fairy feet! Krezma had spoken to her as an adult. Sure, she still called Akeela "child," but what mattered was her tone of voice. And she was giving Akeela encouragement!

Akeela straightened. "Will you come with me tomorrow?"

"I will."

The group still argued and talked about what Akeela should do. They didn't seem to notice she'd left. She turned to Krezma. "I have something to tell you."

Krezma raised her eyebrows.

"I'm sorry about Ham—" Akeela couldn't go on.

"I know, child." Krezma gave her a slight smile. "Mayhap it was wrong of me to force you into this marriage. Yet it is done. What you need to do now is get that third stone. Time is running out."

Akeela nodded. She'd get the stone. Then she'd tell Hawk about Ham. A shiver passed through her chest. Which would be more difficult?

There was no question about it. She looked at Hawk, who returned her gaze with a cool expression. She didn't understand his aloofness, but she didn't have the energy to face him right now. She'd speak to him after she got the stone. Akeela prayed he'd see her true feelings. She hoped he'd understand and not be angry.

There was a better chance for the sun to stop shining.

Krezma pressed her hand. "Come outside with me, child. I want to tell you a story."

That wasn't what Akeela wanted to hear. She wanted Krezma to tell her she was doing the right thing. But she followed Krezma out the door.

They walked to the edge of the field, keeping away from the lace flowers. Akeela waited for Krezma to speak.

"Where do I start? Well, child, you know some of my past. Let me tell you the rest. Where I followed my heart with disastrous results."

Akeela's own heart jumped, but still she said nothing.

"It was my one hundredth birthday. My father gave me a coming-of-age party, and the King of the Northern Province sent his steward's son. I met Riss'aird that night and was quite taken with him." Krezma chuckled. "Ah, the young and foolish heart. My father forbade me to see him. 'He is one of the Mal'fiks,' he said. 'They are an evil people.' I would not believe it. When Riss'aird sent word to me through a raven, I ran away to him. You know what happened between us. I will not recount it again."

Akeela nodded, fascinated by this side of Krezma. "Your family must've been important for the king to attend your party."

Krezma smiled. "Yes, they were. My father *was* the king of our people, the Fidesians. We are a people of truth and protection."

"That's why you took care of me."

"Before I decided to leave Riss'aird's castle," Krezma went on, "I sent a letter to my father, telling him everything I knew. That I suspected he was delving into dark arts. That I believed he had the King of the Northern Province murdered. When I was sure they'd received it, I went to Tzmet. It was *her* one-hundredth birthday. Life can be funny sometimes, can it not? We quarreled and I left, planning to go back and get her."

"That must've been hard," Akeela said.

"Indeed, child. But it was harder to go home. By then, my father had been killed in a battle, and my sister sat on the throne as queen in my place."

That startled Akeela. "You would've been a queen?"

Krezma gave a hearty laugh and put her hand on Akeela's shoulder. "If you could see your face. You can never tell by looking at a person, can you? I would've been a queen if not for my foolish heart."

"What happened when you went home?"

"When my father received my letter, he met with the Fairy Council. Together they came up with a plan of defense against Riss'aird, which was implemented after my father was killed. As you know, I joined the fairies. Combining fairy magic, Fidesian magic, and a strong human line, we transformed the first man into the Fairy Guardian. Everyone knew Riss'aird was conjuring a disastrous spell, so the fairies began to sow good magic into the earth. Fortunately, when Riss'aird's spell went wrong, the Mal'fik race was eliminated, except for Riss'aird, whose ashes slept in the ground."

"What kept him from being completely destroyed?" Akeela asked.

Krezma shrugged. "My daughter also survived. Who can know why? Even though a great wall of magic prevented me from entering the castle, I tried to break through. I refused to entirely learn the dark arts, which may have gotten me through. I saw the results of that wicked force even though I studied it, trying to understand what'd happened. Thank Celtar Oret and Tar found me before I was lost to it."

Akeela's heart wept for Krezma. "Can you go to her now?"

Krezma didn't speak for a moment. "I have seen her. We met at the Fire Fountain."

"And?"

Krezma walked back toward the cave. "She has no love for me. But I do not wish to discuss my troubles. Now you know about the bond between the Guardian and the Ruling Fairy. Without this bond, all fairy life will pass away."

Akeela fell in step with her. "And that is why I'm doing this."

But would Celtar understand that? Queth had taught them not

to give any form of worship to another god. If she didn't mean it in her heart, would it still be worshipping another god?

No, I'm doing the right thing. It's what has to be done.

🦗

Akeela gazed in awe at the great domed ceiling of the salt mine. Torches on the walls illuminated white, pink, and red bands of salt. Crystals sparkled in the light like sunlight on a stream.

"Dear Celtar," she whispered.

Celtar's name echoed faintly around the room. Hesitation grew in Akeela's heart, but she set her jaw and walked to the center of the room. Keron placed three more torches in the rings on the walls. Tiny balls of light scattered as the salt crystals reflected the torches' glow.

Akeela took a deep breath. "It's beautiful. I wish I had better words to describe it, but, really, it's beautiful."

Keron's eyes twinkled. "Aye, that it be, lass. Come. I'll show ye how to extract the salt."

Akeela carefully scraped only the pink band of salt as Keron instructed. "Keep yer mind clear of all but the salt. See how it be catchin' the light, how it feels in yer hand. Salt be the gift of Khewra to preserve and flavor."

The longer it took, the heavier Akeela's heart grew. Finally, the small crystal bowl was full.

Keron nodded. "Before ye leave, I wish to show ye one more thing."

Just let me do this, Akeela thought. But she followed the dwarf down a tunnel and into another room. Keron lit a torch next to the doorway. The glow revealed shelves with crystal bowls and cups of many shapes and sizes.

"Salt be not only for eatin' and worship. It also be for beauty." Keron picked up a bowl similar to what Akeela held. "This bowl and the one ye be holdin' be made of salt."

"Salt?" Akeela's surprise and admiration was genuine. "You made all these things out of salt?"

"Aye, lass." Keron set the bowl back on the shelf. He gestured to the roof. "And that, too."

"Oh!" Akeela's eyes widened. Then she gave a quiet chuckle. "That explains the Mikado's crown." Hanging from the ceiling was a large crystal chandelier. She'd only seen one other chandelier, and that one hung in the house of worship in Broem and was made of metal. Guilt and doubt stabbed her heart, partly for admiring the items made for the dwarves' goddess, and partly for the deception she was about to take part in. The dwarf council trusted she was really going to offer a sacrifice to their goddess. They believed she meant it.

Keron touched her shoulder. "Come, lass. It be time."

***

Tzmet drained the bitter contents of the mug. She shivered and set it on the table. Before she could speak, power coursed through her veins, and she jumped to her feet. Then she sat back down.

"My lady?" Brimridge stood on the other side of the table. "What happened?"

Tzmet stood again. Another shiver ran through her body. She opened her mouth to speak, but nothing came out. Lightening and thunder, the feeling was delicious! This was one potion she was not going to share with her father.

The tingles and sparks subsided, and she cleared her throat. "I think we got it this time."

Brimridge grinned. "Excellent, my lady. Shall I mix more for Riss'aird?"

Tzmet slapped the table. "Fool! Have you forgotten the plan?"

"No, I have not forgotten the plan. Just checking to make sure you haven't changed your mind."

"Idiot." Tzmet sat. She rapped her fingernails on the side of the mug. "But mix up a similar potion. We don't want my father to think we've given up."

Brimridge bowed. "Yes, my lady."

"And get those lazy Hinwari to fix me a platter. I'm famished.

All this extra power makes me hungry."

"Yes, my lady."

"And have your wife lay out the cream satin," Tzmet continued. "I'll wear the rubies with it. That should please my father."

"Yes, my lady."

"And make sure she washes her grimy, skunky hands before she touches my things!"

"Yes, my lady."

"And Brimridge?"

"Yes, my lady?"

"My thanks."

Brimridge nodded. "Yes, my lady."

Tzmet curtsied and entered Riss'aird's chambers. She set a goblet before her father and waited. The sun was setting and casting vivid colors and deep shadows in the room. She used to love coming here at sunset and sitting with her father while he studied his books, sometimes reading aloud to her. They would often share a meal when the sky grew dark and the stars began to appear. But she couldn't dwell on the past. Things were not the same, and neither was she.

Riss'aird raised an eyebrow and looked up at her.

"Father, this is my latest try."

"Indeed."

"Yes, and I believe I'm close to accomplishing the restoration of your mighty power." Tzmet didn't mind lying, she did it all the time, but she couldn't shake the feeling her father didn't believe her. Still, she kept her composure and smiled.

Riss'aird lifted the goblet and drained the contents. His eyes widened, and he coughed. Tzmet smirked inwardly. Let him accuse her now of not helping him. The potion was weaker than she'd made for herself, but it was strong enough for Riss'aird to feel the increase of power. She curtsied again as she took the goblet from him. But before she could say anything, the bedroom door opened, and Sleg strode in. He glanced at Tzmet and nodded. She turned to leave.

"Daughter."

Tzmet forced what she hoped was a pleasant demeanor on her face and turned back. "Yes, Father?"

"Stay. I wish you to know what Sleg has to say."

Ugh. As if she cared.

Sleg bowed, showing her the first bit of respect ever. "Yes, please stay. I have good news."

His oily voice made Tzmet sick, but she nodded, brushed a few black hairs from a chair, and sat. *Just play along a little longer,* she told herself. *Just a little longer.*

Sleg assumed a pompous air. "My lord Riss'aird and Lady Tzmet, let me be the first to announce the beginning of your whip-tail army is complete. At least, as many as survived the process."

Riss'aird clapped lightly. "Excellent, my dear Sleg. Excellent." He turned to Tzmet. "We will send the army out tomorrow morning as a test. Where shall we send them?"

He sounded so much like the old Riss'aird, Tzmet let down her guard. She smoothed her dress. "I'd like to see the uppity villagers of Broem come under your rule first, Father. After that, it matters not."

Riss'aird nodded to Sleg. "Have your experts draw up a map for the army."

"As you wish, mighty Dark Lord." Sleg strode to the door and gave Tzmet a sly wink. But before he could step into the hall, Riss'aird put up a finger.

"And have your warriors ready. I want them to accompany the whiptails. You know how confused they can be at first."

Tzmet bit the inside of her cheek to keep from giggling at the look on Sleg's face, but she couldn't resist winking back at him. So the goblin leader didn't admire Riss'aird as much as he seemed to. The nasty liar. Well, she'd deal with him and his disgusting creatures later. What mattered now was being at her father's side. Relief flooded her as she smiled at Riss'aird.

Maybe things were going to work out after all.

Chapter Forty

Akeela followed Keron Saltcutter through the tunnels. Every now and then, they'd pass a salt crystal candelabrum, which held two candles. And every now and then, the flames reflected on the salt crystals in the walls, illuminating the tunnels with sparkling light.

Akeela tried to calm her mind, but thoughts and doubts swirled in her head and pounded in her heart with every step she took. A flicker in the last candle caught her eye.

A fire fairy danced in the flames. "Akeela! Riss'aird's army is gathering. They march on Broem in the morning!"

"Oh!" Akeela put a hand to her mouth. Keron didn't seem to notice, because he kept walking. She leaned closer to the torch. "Are you sure?"

The fire fairy twirled, causing the candle to burn brighter. "Our spies are sure. We even lost one while gathering this news."

Akeela's heart throbbed. How many dear fairies would be lost before this was done? Anger, fear, hesitation all bubbled up inside. And determination. She *must* get the third piece of the stone. "Thank you, dear one. Please let the fairies know I'm about to get the third piece of the Fairystone. I'll let Tar know this news."

The flame popped, and the fairy disappeared. Akeela hurried

along the tunnel to catch up with the dwarf. She'd get the third stone, but she still needed the fourth. The safety of Broem and her friends—and husband—depended on it.

She boldly stepped forward in spite of the anguish building in her heart as she thought about leaving Hawk when this was over and done. She'd made a promise. She'd taken vows. She'd do her duty.

But no one could make her love it.

*

The temple was a place of beauty. The high ceiling held three salt crystal chandeliers. Twelve candles burned brightly on each one, reflecting through the clear, crystal-like arms. Teardrop-shaped salt crystals hung from each arm, and strings of salt crystal beads draped from arm to arm. Woven tapestries depicting Khewra's conquests and provision hung between each window. The small windows, square at the bottom and round at the top, were adorned with salt crystal beads. While the chandeliers were clear, the salt crystals in the windows were shades of pink and red. Thick, dark-red carpet covered the floors.

The statue of the goddess, made entirely of smoked salt, loomed at the end of the center aisle. Bowls of incense burned at her feet, and braziers of fire illuminated the altar. Akeela breathed in the spicy scent. It reminded her of worship at home, which brought sharp doubt once again to her heart. Music played, filling the room with a sense of reverence. Akeela peered up at the crown. The third piece of the Fairystone glowed with a blue aura.

Khewra's stoic face and sightless eyes seemed to look right through Akeela. She swallowed and took a step. An incessant beat echoed in her head, and she wished the drummers would stop playing. Then she realized it was her pulse pounding.

Eli stood behind the altar. His ornate robes were almost identical to Queth's. Akeela couldn't meet his eyes. The Dwarf Council stood on both sides of the goddess, their faces as serious as

Khewra's. She wished Krezma could walk with her, but she'd only been allowed to stand in the doorway.

Akeela took another two steps. Her hands trembled under the bowl's weight. It hadn't felt quite so heavy in the mines. She struggled to take a deep breath and glanced at the priest. He stood as silent as his goddess.

Two more steps. The salt shifted in the bowl, and she tightened her grip.

She was now halfway to the altar. An invisible hand pressed on her chest, and the pounding in her ears increased with each step. The goddess's lifeless eyes bore into her heart.

She tried to pray as she walked, but she could only focus on breathing. She was almost there when words from the Holy Writings came to her mind.

"Do not bow down or worship another god."

But I'm not. I'm not! It's not real. I'm only pretending.

Another step.

I'm only pretending.

Another.

It's not real.

Akeela stopped.

Eli frowned and gestured her forward. Akeela looked from him to the bowl in her hands. She touched the grains of salt. *They* were real.

"No. I can't do it."

Some of the dwarves mumbled, others clenched their fists. Bracken gave her a wicked smile. Her mouth went dry, but she held her head high.

Eli waved the dwarves back. "What are ye doing? Do not disrespect the goddess by yer anger. Be givin' the girl a chance." He turned to Akeela. "'Tis fine, lass. Bring the sacrifice."

"I can't," Akeela said. "My god, just like yours, forbids worship of any other god. I thought I could set the salt on the altar and not mean it in my heart, but I can't."

And she poured the salt on the floor.

A creaking sound came from the goddess. Bracken Bearbane

roared and started to tramp toward Akeela. But before he reached the aisle, the ground rumbled. As everyone watched, the statue's knees cracked, and the goddess fell forward, scattering incense and crushing the altar. Eli jumped out of the way just in time.

Akeela watched in amazement as the stone in the crown fell out and rolled down the aisle. It stopped at her feet. The dwarves gasped. A warm feeling grew in her stomach, and she picked it up.

She trembled as she felt Celtar's approval and held out the stone. "My god has given this stone into my hand. Celtar will not yield his glory to another!"

The dwarves began talking at once. Akeela felt a hand on her shoulder and turned to see Krezma's concerned face. "Come, child. It is best to get you out of here."

"No. I will not run as though I did anything wrong." Akeela turned back to the dwarves. "Do you agree to let me leave with the stone?"

"Nay!" Bracken roared as he charged her.

Krezma pulled Akeela's arm, but Akeela anchored her feet to the floor. Her head snapped back as Bracken struck her cheek. Chaos broke out. The other dwarves argued. Some ran to her, others shouted at the priest.

Bracken grabbed Akeela's arm and pulled the stone out of her hand. He shoved her to the floor and placed his foot on her chest while Krezma shrieked and beat on his back. The sound was deafening. Akeela grasped Bracken's boot, trying to ease the weight, but she couldn't budge it. Panic rose as black spots formed on the edges of her eyesight.

She wheezed and began to feel faint. *Celtar, help!*

"Stop, Bracken! Stop!" Eli shouted.

Several dwarves pulled Bracken away and shoved him to the ground. Akeela gasped and coughed as Krezma helped her stand. Eli took the stone from Bracken and hung his head. Then he brushed dust from his robes. He nodded to Tanchor and the council. They released Bracken, who stood with his arms crossed, scowling.

"Ye will wait outside while I pray," Eli said to Akeela. "When I have Khewra's answer, I will tell ye."

Akeela and Krezma walked to the door without looking back. When they got outside, Akeela's knees gave out, and she sank to the ground.

Krezma grinned down at her. "Well, child, you are full of surprises today."

Akeela nodded. "To myself as well. How long do you think it'll take the dwarves to give me an answer?"

Krezma shrugged. "All in Celtar's good time."

Akeela was called in an hour later. Eli stood in front of the dwarf council, who were lined up in front of the fallen goddess as though they thought Akeela would do more damage. They all frowned, including Bracken, but she didn't sense hatred or anger. Curious.

Eli pointed to the sacrificial bowl that now held the stone. It was in the same place Akeela had left it, but the salt on the floor was gone. "Ye can have the stone. Khewra be angry with us for not helping ye, so she be givin' ye the stone herself."

Akeela took the bowl. "Thank you." She wanted to say, *Celtar had nothing to do with it?* but she'd better not take any chances.

Tanchor stepped forward. "We still be sendin' the warriors who volunteered to help ye. Ye just need to tell us when ye'll be leavin'."

Akeela bowed her head. "I'm grateful for your help. We'll leave in the morning."

"Me men will be at Ode Janmar's cave after the mornin' meal," Tanchor said.

Vesrynia hugged Akeela. "Praise Celtar! I'm so relieved. We've been trying not to pull off our leaves, yeh?"

"If you came back without the stone, we were ready to get it ourselves," Vorrak-ira said.

Hawk shoved him. "I'd like to see you take on those dwarf warriors. They'd break you into twigs."

Vorrak-ira laughed. "Aye, they probably would."

Akeela smiled. Oh, how she wished she could go back to the Acadian kin-tribe with Hawk. But she wouldn't disgrace Ham, or herself, by not returning to the village.

While Ves-rynia and Vorrak-ira talked over preparations with Tar, Akeela tapped Hawk's shoulder. "Will you come outside with me? We have to talk."

He nodded and followed her out. Akeela sighed and watched a bee go from flower to flower. It was doing what Celtar had created it to do. Just like her.

"So talk to me," Hawk said.

Akeela turned to look at him. His beautiful yellow aura held a darker edge today. "I have something to tell you. You won't like it."

"Is it the fact you're married and lied about it?"

Akeela gasped. "I never lied about anything! How did you find out?"

"Krezma said she should send for your *husband* in case you were dying." Hawk's voice was unnaturally quiet.

Akeela shivered. "Let me explain."

He shrugged.

"You need to know something about the Fairy Guardian," she began. "All the Guardians come from my family line. Not every generation will have the mark, only when the fairy magic senses another Guardian is needed. It's usually when a Guardian grows older."

"But Oret wasn't old," Hawk said.

Akeela nodded. "But he was dying. The fairy magic must've known I would be needed. That's where the problem comes in. See, since I'm the next Guardian, I need to be married—well, pregnant—before the transformation happens."

Hawk grunted.

"Once I become the Fairy Guardian, I can't have children," Akeela went on, trying not to let Hawk's disdain overwhelm her.

"Because Oret was dying, Krezma made me marry. Well, I agreed to do it, but there was no other way."

Hawk took a step back. "So you got married. When?"

"The night before I left the village with Tar. I convinced him—Ham—to stay and wait for me." Akeela's eyes filled with tears. "I'm sorry, Hawk. I wanted to tell you so many times."

Hawk took another step back. "Do you love him?"

Akeela shook her head. "No! Yes. No, not like that. Not like . . . you . . ." She paused. "He's been my friend since childhood. And he was willing."

Hawk closed his eyes. "What happens now? Are you with child?"

Akeela hung her head. A breeze caressed her face, a sweet scent with it. She took a deep breath. "No, I'm not with child. I have to return to Broem and hope I can find the fourth piece of the Fairystone before I get there. If I don't become the Fairy Guardian, I can't defeat Riss'aird."

Hawk gave a frustrated, sharp sob. "Why didn't you wait until you *found* the pieces of the stone? If you had, *we* could've gotten married!"

"I know! Don't you think I know?" Akeela cried.

They held each other, weeping, telling each other of their love, over and over.

Finally, Akeela pulled back and wiped her cheeks. "That's enough. As much as I wish otherwise, it's done. I have to keep going. Riss'aird won't wait until I find the stone, get pregnant, and become the Guardian."

Hawk glanced up at the moons. "What happens if you become the Guardian before you have a child . . . ?"

"I will be the last Guardian."

Chapter Forty-One

Akeela hugged Ves-rynia. "May Celtar bless your journey and bring us together again soon. I love you."

"I love you too," Ves-rynia replied. "As dear to me as a sister, yeh?"

Akeela wiped tears from her cheeks. "I wish I could've told you. I never meant to hide it. There just didn't seem to be a good time to tell everyone."

Ves-rynia lifted her shoulder sack. "I know. But you know how thick-barked boys can be. Especially my brother. He'll have to drop his leaves and grow new ones. Don't worry."

Don't worry. How was she going to do that? Hawk said he still loved her, but he'd distanced himself. And now he was leaving to enlist the Acadians' help.

Vorrak-ira glared his hate at her. Ode Janmar said nothing. If Akeela had words to effectively explain, she would. If she had more time, she'd even argue with Vorrak'ira.

But her job was too important.

Celtar must be with her, or he wouldn't have delivered the third piece of the stone into her hand. She trembled at the memory. His presence had felt so real. He was real. Her destiny was real.

She wanted to laugh and cry and sing, and at the same time, her despair over losing Hawk cut deep. Yet she was doing the right thing. She didn't need Krezma or Queth or anyone else to tell her that.

Why did doing the right thing feel so desperately horrible?

Ves-rynia's voice broke into her thoughts. "Will you come out and see us off?"

"Aye. I'm right behind you."

Rising sunlight filtered through the trees.

Ode Janmar had secured horses for everyone, and Hawk was already astride the black gelding. Vorrak-ira glanced her way, snorted, and pulled himself onto the chestnut.

Akeela looked down at her boots.

They were the ones she'd been working on when Ham's father had asked Krezma's permission for Ham to marry her. And they were the ones she'd now wear to return to him.

Hawk's eyes flickered her direction, but he said nothing. Vorrak-ira snorted again and kicked his horse into a walk. Ves-rynia smiled at Akeela before following her brother.

Anon came up behind Akeela and slipped his hand into hers. "Bye, Vessie. Bye, Hawk."

"You be a good faun," Hawk said.

Anon grinned. "I like your horsie."

Akeela wanted to say something. Anything. Hawk looked at her then.

Despair welled up when he nudged his horse forward. She swallowed it and watched him go across the field and into the woods. The trees seemed to come together, and with a swish of his horse's tail, he was gone.

Tar gestured to the door. "Come. We have our own plans to finish."

Akeela nodded but didn't move. Anon called for Fin, and the two trotted to the stream.

Krezma stood in the cave's doorway, holding a mug of tea. "Here, child. And have something to eat. You're going to need your strength."

Akeela took the mug and sat at the table. Tar and Ode Janmar were already talking.

"Cutting across the plain be the quickest way," Ode said. "We be in sight, but going through the forest be takin' too long."

"I agree." Tar flexed his claw hand as though the thought of battle excited him.

Akeela shivered. Tar was battle ready. So were Ode Janmar and the dwarves. Yet she was defenseless without the Fairystone.

Krezma set a plate of bread and cheese on the table. "While you prepare for battle, Akeela and I will pack provisions." She turned to Akeela. "Child, eat something. Now."

Akeela picked up a piece of cheese but couldn't convince herself to put it in her mouth. The end of her world was coming. Who could eat at a time like this? She got up and joined Krezma by the fireplace.

"I'll eat later. After we're ready for the trip."

Krezma grunted. "As you say." She picked up three waterskins. "Take these to the stream and fill them."

Akeela took the skins. "Only three?"

"Aye, three. I'll not be coming with you."

"What?" Akeela startled. "You have to come with us! What am I going to do without you?"

Krezma wrapped salted meat in thin cloth. "You don't need me. You have Tar and the dwarves. You've been blessed by the Moon Dancers, and you have the favor of Celtar."

"But—"

"I must go to my daughter before it's too late." Krezma stuffed the wrapped meat into a sack. "I must try one more time."

Akeela sank to the hearth. She'd forgotten about Tzmet. Of course Krezma would want to go to her daughter. "I'm sorry."

Krezma shook out a towel. "Sorry for what? There's nothing to be sorry for except for taking so long to prepare. Have I taught you nothing?"

Akeela smiled at the familiar gruff tone that used to make her feel small and unwanted. It all made sense now. Had Krezma been soft with her, she would've never gotten through all she had so far.

"Very well. I'm going to the stream. Just don't leave before I get back."

Krezma grunted and kept at her task.

$$\ast$$

They left before dawn. Akeela and Krezma's goodbyes were short. Krezma, after all, was not known for sentiment.

The only thing Akeela felt bad about was leaving Anon, but he had to stay this time. He seemed happy enough to stay with Ode Janmar's sister and her family last night, but he probably didn't understand Akeela was going. Leaving him again. Akeela had been surprised when Ode Janmar suggested Anon stay with his family. He'd never mentioned a family. But they'd taken Anon in and shown him their pet rabbits, and Anon was in heaven.

At least he'll be safe. He'll be alive.

Akeela shifted her shoulder pack. According to Tar, they'd reach Broem in two days if they kept a fast pace. She was disappointed they couldn't use gliders, but there simply weren't enough for everyone. And it was important the Acadians get to Broem first to alert the people and set up defences. Thank Celtar for providing horses. Their *nacre* seeds and oil were gone, but two peddlers were very happy.

Akeela clenched her jaw. Five hours of hard riding until she'd know her fate. Five hours until she'd know if she—or any of them —even had a fate.

$$\ast$$

Tzmet fastened the last buckle of Riss'aird's leather breastplate. Her heart pounded with what felt like fear. But she should fear nothing. She was going into battle with her father, even though he didn't have all his power. She was the one with the power now.

"How does that feel, Father?"

Riss'aird flexed his arms out, across his chest, and out again. "It will do."

Tzmet poured wine into a chalice. She handed it to Riss'aird, then poured one for herself. She lifted her glass. "To our success!"

They both drank, and Tzmet took special delight that her father hadn't invited Sleg to join them this time.

Tzmet glanced at Brimridge, who stood by the door as though he might flee at a moment's notice. She frowned at him before turning back to her father.

"Brimridge will ready your horse while his wife helps me with my armor. Our supplies are in the kitchen. We can be on our way within the hour."

Riss'aird gave her an icy smile. "I would have you stay here and prepare the dungeons for more prisoners. We surely will bring men to supply our army and women for slaves."

"But Father! I have a great desire to see Broem destroyed. You've no idea the trouble those peasants have been."

Riss'aird laughed. "What you desire has no meaning. The only desires to be met are my own."

Tzmet's anger wouldn't let her back down. "I worked alone for fifteen years to bring you back. I kept this castle in working order with just those wretched Hinwari. I've waited on you hand and foot without any thanks. I'm going to Broem with you!"

Riss'aird strode across the room and slapped her.

The impact knocked her to the floor. Pain shot through her jaw, and she rubbed it. Brimridge squeaked and slipped into the hall. Her cheek burned, but more than that, anger churned in her heart. She stood, brushed off her skirts, and faced her father.

"I am going to Broem," she said calmly.

Riss'aird raised his hand.

Tzmet raised hers. "No, Father. You cannot intimidate me anymore."

To her surprise, Riss'aird chuckled.

He raised his other hand, looked at the ceiling, and muttered a spell. Before Tzmet could blink, all the power inside her welled up. There was a moment's hesitation, then she shrieked as searing pain erupted throughout her body.

The power grew and grew until she thought she'd explode.

She cried out once when, as suddenly as a flash of lightening, all her power was ripped from her.

Everything went black.

Chapter Forty-Two

The Acadian gliders made no noise as they flew over the treetops toward Broem. The village came into view, so peaceful and unsuspecting, and Hawk couldn't help but shiver. These villagers were gardeners, bakers, fishermen. Not warriors. But then, neither were the Acadians.

One by one, the gliders landed in the village center.

A large man wearing robes stepped out of the gathering crowd, clearly flustered. "Oh dear, oh dear. Celtar bless and protect us! Who are you?"

Ban-ira walked up to the man. "Sapo! I am Ban-ira, leader of the Acadian kin-tribe. We are here to warn you and offer help."

The man gave them a cautious smile. "I am Queth, minister of Celtar and leader of Broem. Warn us?"

Dir-mac joined Ban-ira. "I am Dir-mac, also a minister of Celtar."

The men nodded to each other.

"Enough ceremony," Ban-ira said. "An army is coming this way. An evil army led by the risen Dark Lord, Riss'aird."

The people shifted nervously.

Queth fanned himself with his hand. "Oh dear, oh dear! Are you quite sure?"

A red-faced young man dusty with flour and wearing an apron spoke up. "How are we to know this is true?"

Queth turned to the young man. "Ham, be still. I have just remembered the strange man who came with Akeela, the man with the claw hand. He and Krezma mentioned Acadians."

Ham's face turned eager as he stepped forward. "That was Tar. He took Akeela with him. Where is she? Where's my wife?"

Hawk's heart jerked. So this was Akeela's husband. He looked at this boy called Ham and tried to feel hatred for him, but he couldn't.

Hawk called him a boy in his mind, but Ham was no younger than himself. Still, Hawk could only think of him as a boy—it was obvious Ham had grown up indulged and protected. It was a good thing Hawk was there. Someone would have to protect Akeela, and this baker could no more do that than grow leaves.

"Have your women and children barricade themselves within their homes," Ban-ira was saying. "The men will need any weapons you can come up with. We will give you our protection."

The people immediately went into action. Women screamed for their children. Men ordered their families home. Little children cried. Older children were more interested in the gliders.

"Please, don't panic," Ban-ira shouted.

But no one heeded him.

Dir-mac spoke with Queth while the people ran around them. In a few minutes, the center of the village had cleared except for the men. The Acadians looked at each other. Hawk could sense fear among them, but also determination. He looked to his grandfather. Ban-ira nodded, and Hawk signaled his group.

The young men gathered around Hawk. "Do you have your nacre seeds? Are they notched?"

They nodded.

"Let's gather our branches and get going, yeh?"

Vorrak-ira put his arm around Hawk's shoulders. "Aye, cousin. Let's give that army of scat something to chew on, yeh?"

"What are you going to do?" Ham asked.

Hawk turned to Akeela's baker husband. He was still red-faced but calmer. Hawk wanted to say something mean. Something to hurt the boy. But he couldn't. Ham loved Akeekla, and it was that love that stayed Hawk's tongue. They both loved the same girl. And she deserved better than for them to be at odds.

"We're going to plant a wall of protection around the village," Hawk said.

Ham frowned. "But you said the army was coming now. How can you grow a wall in time?"

Vorrak-ira snorted. "We're Acadians, you dupeseed."

Hawk punched his cousin's arm. "Acadians have the power to make things grow quickly. Trust me, we'll have the wall ready."

"Do you need help?"

Vorrak-ira gave a short laugh. Hawk punched him again. "Nay, you'd best prepare for any fighting. I can't guarantee the wall will keep the army out, yeh?"

Ham nodded but didn't go.

Hawk pushed his exasperation down. "You have another question?"

"I, well, I was wondering about Akeela." Ham shifted from foot to foot. "See, she left so quickly. I wanted to come, but she said she wouldn't be long. But it's been so long."

Hawk worked up a smile. "She's been through a lot. We've seen danger, but Celtar has kept us safe." He hesitated a moment. "You might find she's changed some."

Ham looked startled. "Changed? In what way?"

Vorrak-ira snickered.

Hawk put out his hand. "I don't have time to tell you all. We were lost underground and came out in dwarf country. Thank Celtar, the dwarf who found us was my father's friend. Akeela is coming with a group of dwarf warriors."

"Aye," Vorrak-ira put in. "That would change anyone, yeh?"

Ham nodded slowly.

"Please, prepare what you can," Hawk said.

He watched the boy cross the village green. Ham had great

love for Akeela. Hawk's face flushed, and he was torn between envy and hate. He fought to suppress it.

Vorrak-ira shoved him. "I can make it so he's outside the wall, yeh?"

"Nay," Hawk said. "Let's get going. We have a lot to do."

Hawk and his group left the village and began to place the notched *nacre* seeds in the ground around the whole village. Queth and Dir-mac moved to each spot behind them, praying. As they moved on, three earth fairies, not bothering to disguise themselves, hovered over each seed.

Ban-ira gave more orders to the villagers. "You must stay inside the village. Anyone caught outside will be left outside. There will be no way back in once we begin."

Hawk stood with the villagers as the rest of the Acadians began to walk around the village. Someone came up beside him. He knew it was Ham before he spoke.

"Why aren't *you* with your people, making the wall grow?"

A fair question, but it annoyed Hawk. "I'm not fully Acadian. My father was married to an Acadian woman."

Ham looked at the Acadian men. "Where are the women?"

"They stayed back to protect the children," Hawk said.

Ham nodded. He opened his mouth to speak, but then pointed. "Look!"

Around the village, vines were sprouting up from the ground and twisting together as they rose.

Krezma gripped the handles of the glider. Blast Tar for hiding gliders wherever he went. If she wasn't so desperate to get to her daughter, she wouldn't have taken a glider for anything. Tar had instructed her and had even hooked an extra line for her to "sort of" sit, plus a safety line so she wouldn't lose the blessed contraption, but she fully expected to die before she reached the castle.

Thankfully, she hadn't had to climb a tree. It was enough to trek up the side of the mountain over the salt mines, but it took all her courage to leap off the cliff. There was a terrifying moment when the glider dipped before it caught the air currents and lifted her back up. If it weren't for the air fairies who accompanied her, Krezma would've panicked.

She couldn't judge how long she'd been in the air, because she couldn't read the position of the sun. But suddenly she caught sight of the castle, and in less time than she'd expected. Now, what had Tar said about landing?

The ground rushed up, and Krezma closed her eyes. Thank Celtar for the air fairies' help. They created a back breeze, which helped her land gently and without injury. She thanked them, fumbled with the lines, and released herself. It felt awkward walking in pants and a tunic, but it would've been difficult to use the glider in her skirt. She approached the castle's door with some trepidation, but the stillness convinced her the army had left. She hoped Riss'aird had gone with them.

Krezma looked around the courtyard and saw some movement in the slave quarters. Then she caught the aroma of skunk cabbage simmering. Boggarts. So Brimridge and his family were back.

The kitchen door stood open, so she went in. Other than a stretched fairy standing silently by the table, Krezma saw no one.

She walked quickly upstairs, intending to go to Tzmet's bedroom, but voices stopped her. She turned and slunk to Riss'aird's room, hugging the wall. When she peered around the doorway, she saw Tzmet on the floor and Brimridge and his wife kneeling over her.

Stars! She rushed into the room. "What happened?"

Brimridge looked up, his eyes wide. "Krezma! Is it you?"

Krezma knelt. "Aye, I'm here. What happened?"

"I don't know. Tzmet argued with Riss'aird. They raised their hands, as if they were going to engage in a magical exchange. Riss'aird spoke some kind of spell, and Tzmet collapsed."

Please, Celtar, don't let her be dead. Krezma put her hand on Tzmet's chest and closed her eyes. "She's alive, but we must work quickly."

"I've been reading her book of potions," Brimridge said. "From the symptoms, it looks like Riss'aird has taken her power. My wife was just bringing me the ingredients for a revival spell."

"Good," Krezma said. "What do you have?"

Brimridge spread out the herbs and oils. Krezma added a few things from her pouch, and they made a drink and a poultice.

"Here," Krezma said to Brimridge's wife. "Hold up her head. Brimridge, take that cloth and put it under her chin. I'll drip the potion in her mouth."

It took longer than Krezma wanted, but they got most of the potion down Tzmet's throat. Then Krezma put the poultice on Tzmet's chest.

"There's nothing to do now but pray and wait."

Brimridge sent his wife to prepare a meal. "I'm glad you came," he said to Krezma. "I fear I wouldn't have been able to save Tzmet."

Krezma grunted. "She's not saved yet."

"She has a better chance now."

"Brimridge, why are you here and not with Riss'aird?"

The boggart grinned. "It's a long story."

Krezma grunted. "What else can we do while we wait?"

Brimridge told her everything that had happened since he and his family had come to the castle. Krezma listened with growing amazement. When she'd lived here, the boggarts served only Riss'aird and stole anything they could. They lied, cheated, and caused general mischief. Now they were friendly and helpful. She wondered at the change.

They shared the morning meal, since Krezma had eaten nothing. She changed the poultice for the third time and closed her eyes. When she opened them, the sun was high in the sky. She sat up in a panic, but Tzmet remained unchanged.

Please, Celtar, give me another chance with my daughter!

Brimridge entered the room with a food tray. As he set it on the table, Tzmet stirred, groaned, and opened her eyes.

Krezma held her hand. "Tzmet, can you hear me?"

Tzmet groaned again.

Brimridge leaned over her. "I see she's not dead."

"Idiot," Tzmet rasped.

Brimridge grinned. "Back to normal too."

Krezma helped Tzmet sit up. She gestured to Brimridge for a goblet of hot water. After crumbling some dried herbs in it, she stirred and lifted the spoon to Tzmet's lips. Tzmet kept her eyes on Krezma's face as she sipped the tea.

"That's good," Krezma said. "We have to build your strength."

Tzmet blinked. "What happened?"

Brimridge knelt next to her. "Krezma believes Riss'aird has taken all your power, my lady. I was trying to revive you when she came to the castle. She saved your life."

"Indeed?"

"Yes, indeed," Krezma said. "Can you take the cup? You should drink it all while it's hot."

Tzmet hesitated but took the goblet. "You're the hag who claims to be my mother."

Krezma nodded and glanced at Brimridge.

"She is, my lady," he said.

"Why did you come here?" Tzmet asked.

Krezma stood and stretched. "I wanted to try one more time to talk to you."

Tzmet sipped the tea. "I suppose I should thank you, but with all that's happened, I'm not sure I want saving." She handed the cup to Brimridge. "I've had enough. Help me to my room. We have to stop Father."

Krezma and Brimridge lifted her and walked her down the hall. Krezma pondered the situation. She had to get through to her daughter. Convince her of the truth. After Brimridge left, she helped Tzmet out of her dress and into another.

"I used to brush your hair every day. I'd bring you *krenda* cakes and milk."

Tzmet's eyes widened, but she said nothing.

"We argued the night of your birthday party," Krezma went on. "I wanted to come back for you. I tried to come back—for seventy-five years. But the spell wouldn't allow it."

"I was asleep for that long?" Tzmet asked. "I couldn't leave the castle for fifteen years after I woke up."

Krezma clutched Tzmet's hand. "Do you believe I am your mother?"

Tzmet looked away. "Yes. But this changes nothing! You abandoned me, and now my father has abandoned me."

"Daughter, listen to me. There is a difference between my leaving and Riss'aird's leaving. I wish I had time to explain it all to you, but I don't. Riss'aird and his army are on the move. Do you know where they're headed?"

Tzmet looked at their hands, which were still clasped. "Broem."

Chapter Forty-Three

Hawk walked the village's perimeter. The hedge of thorn-crusted branches rose high above his head. Thank Celtar for the earth fairies' magic. Combined with the Acadians' gift, the plants grew twice as quickly and twice as strong. He tried to see through to the outside, but the vines had woven themselves too thick.

"Good day."

Hawk turned to see Ham standing with a young man and girl. Hawk nodded.

The girl stepped forward. "I'm Iari. Akeela's best friend."

"She's mentioned you," Hawk said.

Iari's face was earnest. "When will Riss'aird's army get here?"

"I don't know."

The other boy held out his hand. "I'm Gilron. How long will the wall hold?"

Hawk clasped Gilron's hand, which was strong and callused. "I don't know."

Gilron considered that. "We'll be ready. You think we're weak, don't you?"

Hawk shrugged.

"We're not," Gilron said. "My father is the blacksmith. We can

377

handle weapons. And many farmers have fought off wild animals such as mountain lions and bears from our flocks. We're not helpless."

"I'm happy to hear that." Hawk grinned, then sobered. "But you're going to need all the help you can get if Krezma is right about the army."

The Acadians sat in a group to eat the midday meal. Vorrak'ira grunted when Hawk joined him.

"Aren't my leaves good enough for you now?" he said when Hawk sat. "Or would you rather sit with your new friends?"

"Don't go digging up your roots," Hawk said. "I was only being friendly."

Vorrak'ira laughed. "Friendly? With the enemy?"

"What are you talking about?"

"Akeela's dupeseed of a husband." Vorrak'ira leaned over and whispered, "You should've let me put him outside the hedge, yeh?"

Hawk shoved his cousin. "Are you off your nut? We're here to help these people, not get them killed."

"Don't you love Akeela?"

"Aye, I love her! And that's why I'm going to do what I can to help her friends. Even if one of them is married to her."

Vorrak-ira sneered. "You sound like your father."

Hawk smiled and stood. "Thank you." He walked away, leaving his mouthy cousin silent.

But before he got ten steps away, he heard what could only be the footsteps and snarling of Riss'aird's army.

Tzmet watched her mother pour a mug of *caavea*. She felt strange, like another person had invaded her body. A person who didn't hate her mother. A thousand curses on her father for making her believe Krezma had deserted her! A thousand more for making her believe he loved her. She felt empty and humiliated.

And angry.

"Mother."

Krezma looked up.

"Father left after the army did, so he will arrive after they do." She took the mug from Krezma and set it on the nightstand. "It's not a big army. We were testing the whiptails to see if the transvarient process had worked properly before making more."

"What are you thinking, daughter?"

Tzmet smiled. "I'm not totally helpless. I have in my possession a crossbow. It's enchanted and doesn't miss. Ever."

Krezma frowned and put her gnarled hand on Tzmet's. "Daughter, murder is never right. No matter how just you believe the cause. Vengence belongs to Celtar."

Tzmet pushed Krezma's hand away. "Then I'll go myself. Brimridge and his people are loyal to me. They'll help."

Krezma sighed. "Nay, you'll not go alone. I will accompany you. But I must be allowed to try to speak with him. And we will not bring the weapon."

"You cannot order me!" Tzmet shrieked. "I'm not a child, and I'll not be treated like one."

"Then stop acting like one," Krezma retorted. "Wanting to kill Riss'aird makes you no better than he. Do you think he thought you were alive when he left?"

Tzmet's reply died on her lips. Rat's teeth! It was true. Her father had thought he'd killed her. And he'd felt no concern. No remorse. He'd simply ripped the magic from her and left. Pain stabbed her heart, but she replaced it with calm determination.

"Very well, Mother. I'll leave it. We can try to talk to him, but you listen to me." Tzmet leaned forward. "He isn't the same man. When he rose from the ashes, part of him stayed behind."

Krezma nodded. "Can you be ready to leave within the hour?"

"I can."

Krezma left. Tzmet pushed away the tray, got out of bed, and dressed herself in the ugly brown pants and tunic. Curse the weakness in her legs! She had to be strong for her task.

After opening her closet, she pushed her beautiful gowns aside, reached to the back, and brought out a plain, wooden box. She lifted the lid and brought out the crossbow, no bigger than her shoe.

"There you are, my beauty. Careful now, careful." She lifted the enchanted arrow, its tip wrapped in cloth. "No need for more than one. You never miss, do you?" Tzmet chuckled. She placed the bow and arrow into a cloth bag and tucked it safely inside her tunic. "There. No one will be the wiser until it's too late."

The people of Broem were calm until the snapping sounds began. Hawk's grandfather and the village minister shouted for everyone not to panic.

Ban-ira called, "They are only testing the wall. It will hold."

Branches breaking could be heard all around the village. Hawk closed his eyes. The sword he carried felt heavy in his hand, and he prayed for Celtar to help them. In the middle of his prayer, he sensed someone next to him.

"I've been praying, too, but I don't know if Celtar is listening," Ham said. "Tell me the truth, Hawk. Are we going to die?"

Hawk shrugged.

"If we're going to die, I would know something." Ham looked straight at Hawk. "Do you love Akeela?"

Hawk's mouth went dry, and he could only nod.

Ham looked down and then back up again. "Does she love you?"

"I—"

"I thought so. When we talked earlier, and you shared some of what you'd both gone through, I knew."

"Listen, Akeela has not dishonored you," Hawk said. "She was coming back to you after the quest."

Ham gave a bitter smile. "She'll be with me, but her heart will stay with you."

Ham's pain washed over Hawk. "I'll protect you. My father has trained me to fight. I'll make sure Akeela has a husband to come back to."

Ham's eyes filled with tears, and he clasped Hawk's hand. "You're a true friend. But I will fight with the men of my village."

Then he walked away, leaving Hawk feeling like a sapling in the mud.

Suddenly, the snapping and creaking stopped. Hawk looked at the hedge. What was happening out there? The Acadians and people of Broem stopped talking. Shuffling could still be heard outside the wall, but then a different sound started, like crackling.

Hawk looked at his grandfather. "What are they doing now?"

Then he smelled smoke.

Akeela and the dwarves stood at the edge of the forest. Broem was surrounded by a wall of thorns, and Riss'aird's army was busy setting fire to it. She turned to Ode Janmar.

"What do we do? There are so many."

Ode Janmar put a hand on his braided beard. "Ye'll not have to worry. They don't know we be here. And Bracken be sure to have a plan."

Akeela looked at the rest of the dwarves. She was glad Bracken had decided to come with them, but fifteen dwarf warriors and Ode Janmar against a hundred goblins and at least twenty-five of whatever the other creatures were didn't make for success in her mind.

Resisting the urge to touch her still-tender cheek, she tried to remain calm when Bracken approached her.

"I see the village be protected for now. While the goblins be busy with trying to burn down the wall, I be placin' my men around them. The best thing for ye to be doin' is to stay out of sight."

Akeela nodded. She wasn't foolish enough to think she could defend herself. But there must be something she could do to help. The fire caught her attention. If the wall burned, the village would be in grave danger.

"I'll move back into the forest and contact the fairies. There's a lake on the other side of the village. Maybe the water fairies can help."

Bracken nodded and strode back to the dwarves. They began to move around the edge of the forest behind the army.

Ode Janmar put his hand on Akeela's arm. "I be stayin' with ye for protection. Bracken's orders."

Akeela laughed. "So Bracken does care after all."

Ode grinned. "Nay, he be thinkin' ye're in the way, and I can't fight with me hand. But he doesn't know I still be an expert with the handhew." He opened his vest to reveal twelve handhews tucked inside pockets, six on each side.

"And I have the salt bombs Kerin Saltcutter made." Akeela lifted a bag from her horse's saddle. "And the launcher." Out of her pocket, she pulled a piece of carved, split wood that had a net between the split.

"We be set," Ode Janmar said. "Now, best ye be callin' the fairies. The fire be gettin' higher."

Akeela tugged on her horse's reins and led him back into the forest. She sat on a stump and concentrated, then she whispered into the breeze, "Dear fairies, come to me!"

Five earth fairies flew in from the trees. "Guardian, we've been waiting for you to arrive," one said.

Akeela clasped her hands. "My village needs help. Please ask the water fairies."

"As you command, Guardian."

They zipped away, and confidence filled Akeela. Surely Celtar would give them favor! She turned to Ode Janmar. "That will take care of the fire. What do we do next?"

Ode pointed up. "Climb. I saw me a good spot in this old oak tree where we can release the salt bombs. Bring all the bags with ye."

Akeela picked up the first bag and staggered. It felt like a sack of rocks. And, in a way, it was. It took all her strength to raise it over her head for Ode to take the rest of the way up the oak. As she lifted the fifth and last bag, Akeela heard a rushing sound. She turned to see a column of water rise over the wall and crash down. The fire went out with a hiss, and people cheered. She shoved the bag at Ode Janmar.

"Look," she said. "The water fairies did it!"

Ode grunted. "I be seein'. Now get ye up this tree. I can't protect ye down there."

Akeela climbed up after the dwarf. The trunk had grown divided, and the branches created a natural seat in two places. As they settled in, the goblins began to chop away at the burnt hedge.

"Oh!" Akeela gasped. "Look at them. Should we start the bombs now?"

Ode Janmar shook his head. "Nay, we wait. Bracken will lead the attack."

Just then, Bracken and the other dwarves roared out of the forest, swinging huge battle axes. They caught many goblins by surprise, and heads flew. Akeela couldn't take her eyes off the battle. Once they realized what was happening, the goblins began to shout, and the other creatures with them faced the dwarves.

Akeela had never seen anything like them. They stood hunched like old men, had legs and arms like men, but with long, thin tails. Their heads and faces were hideous, swollen and blotched. They opened their mouths to reveal fangs, and a yellowish liquid dripped from their lips. "Whiptails," she whispered in horror.

"What's that?" Ode asked.

"Riss'aird's army. Tar told us about them. Riss'aird somehow combines men and rats. They use their tails as whips and their saliva burns. We have to warn Bracken!"

"By the goddess!" Ode Janmar shook his head. "Nay, lass. Bracken and the others be knowin' how to defend themselves. I'll not leave ye."

Akeela looked out over the fighting. Axes met goblin swords, and tails whipped and beat against leather tunics, both sides snarling and roaring their hatred. She'd never seen such violence, not even between natural forest enemies.

"Hand me a bomb," Ode Janmar said.

Akeela complied, and Ode placed it in the launcher, drew back his arm, and flung it. It sailed over the battle and hit the side of a goblin's head. The goblin shrieked as its skin burned and melted away. Akeela's eyes widened. Ode had never said what the bombs did. She turned and lost her breakfast.

Ode patted her back, reached in the bag, and flung bomb after bomb. Akeela averted her eyes. She shuddered as nausea passed through her stomach again. True, the goblins and whiptails were their enemies. They'd surely kill the villagers, or worse, take them captive. They needed to be stopped. But her instinct was to save, not destroy.

"Now that be trouble," Ode Janmar said.

Akeela looked to where he was pointing.

The goblins had broken through the wall.

Chapter Forty-Four

Hawk watched the older men push through the broken part of the wall. The villagers carried pitchforks and sickles, sledgehammers and rakes. The Acadians had slingshots and long, thin blades. Fear was on all their faces, but also strength. Ban-ira had given orders for the young men to stay back until needed.

"I'll not sacrifice the young men," he'd said. "You're our future."

Vorrak-ira came up next to him. "This strips my bark. I say we get out there and uproot some goblins, yeh?"

"We'll get our chance," Hawk said. "And you may not like it as much as you think. Now, pay attention to your job. We have to keep them from getting in."

"Just let them try." Vorrak'ira raised his slingshot.

The wall had been breached in two places. Hawk and three village boys, including Gilron and Ham, stood watch at one opening. Vorrak-ira and his group stood at the other.

The whiptails used their tails to take the men off their feet. The villagers and Acadians fought valiantly, although they were not trained fighters, but the small group of dwarves did more damage than Hawk could've imagined. Still, screams of agony came from both sides. The men were burned with whiptail saliva, and the whiptails and goblins were pelted with salt bombs.

"We need to get out there and help, yeh?" Vorrak-ira called from his position at the other opening.

Hawk didn't answer, but the villagers and other Acadian youth grumbled. Someone put a hand on his shoulder. He turned to see Gilron holding an ax.

"I don't like your cousin much, but I agree with him. I've been chopping wood and pounding metal since I was eight summers old, and I've been watching the dwarves use their axes. My father is out there. My place is with him."

"What about Iari and your place with her?" Hawk asked. "What about the future of your village?"

Ham joined Gilron. Several other village youths stood behind them, all holding tools. "This is our village, not yours," Ham said. "We're grateful for your help, but we want to defend our homes."

Hawk saw their determined faces and knew the feeling. He had people out there too. He looked over at his cousin. Vorrak-ira lifted his fist in the air.

"Very well," Hawk said. "But not all of us. We need someone here to keep the goblins and whiptails from entering the village."

Sounds of battle grew louder.

"I'm going. You can't stop me," Gilron shouted.

A salt bomb sailed over the hedge. Everyone ducked.

Ham's face paled, but he stood his ground. "I'm going too."

Most of the young men stepped forward. Hawk was impressed. They were afraid, but they were going to fight. Pride and courage filled him. "Let's do it."

He made sure the two who stood at the openings had some kind of weapon. Most of the villagers had axes, and a few brought bows and arrows.

The boys surged out of the village, whooping. The smell of burning flesh and blood permeated the air, but they pressed on.

Hawk heard something rising above the clang of battle. It sounded like a mighty wind, but the trees were still.

Hawk scanned the sky. A shriek tore all around him. The

dwarves, goblins, and men on the battlefield ceased fighting, but the frenzied whiptails continued to advance. Suddenly, a dark cloud burst out of the forest.

Fairies, now visible, sped through the trees, singing. Bees, flies, and beetles followed. The sound was deafening. What were they doing?

The storm of insects swarmed the battlefield, and the fairies' song rose above the goblin's shrieks. The dwarves and men pulled back.

"Come on!" Vorrak-ira shouted.

The boys pushed forward. Hawk ran through and tripped over a man's body.

The whiptails ignored the bugs, even though the crazed insects attacked them viciously. The goblins shrieked and batted at them, but to no avail. The dwarves pressed on, which encouraged the young men to do the same.

Hawk tried to shout over the noise. "Watch out for the tails!"

He jumped back just in time as one of the whiptails nearly took him off his feet. Many of the boys fell, injured. Hawk swung his sword and cut off a whiptail's arm. Another approached, snarling and spitting. Saliva hit Hawk's forearm, burned a hole in his shirt, and began to eat at his skin. He stumbled back. Pulling a small knife from his boot, he flung it. It embedded itself in the whiptail's shoulder, but the crazed thing kept coming.

Hawk took another step back and tripped over a body. He lifted his sword, but it offered little protection. Just as the whiptail was about to leap on him, it collapsed. Vorrak-ira grinned and pulled his sword out of the creature's back.

"Taking a nap?" he asked Hawk. "That's a good way to get your bark stripped."

Hawk allowed his cousin to help him up. "Not funny."

Vorrak-ira gestured. "Looks like we're winning, yeh? Come on, cousin. Let's get in on the action."

Before Hawk could answer, his heart trembled. The ground was still, but the air buzzed with power. Everyone, even the whiptails, stopped fighting and turned. There, hanging in the sky like a vulture ready to attack, was a figure in a black robe.

Riss'aird.

The goblins cheered. Riss'aird raised his hands, and blue lightening flew in every direction, hitting men and even goblins and whiptails. Pandemonium erupted as everyone scrambled for cover. Something burned across Hawk's back as he dove behind a dead whiptail. He rolled away when his hand hit the blood. It burned as much as the saliva! Some of the Acadians and villagers made it back into the village. Others tried to hide in the forest. The dwarves had pulled back at first sight of the Dark Lord, but Hawk could hear them fighting the goblins within the trees.

Riss'aird laughed. The sound lingered like thunder, and Hawk's courage faltered. His arms and legs grew weak. Watery. He lowered his sword, as did all who held weapons. The whiptails roared and stamped their feet. A sense of hopelessness started in his fingertips and surged through his body. He gasped for air. Then Krezma and another woman galloped out of the woods.

The woman behind Krezma reined her horse into a skid and shouted, "Father! Stop!"

Akeela and Ode Janmar watched Krezma ride out of the woods. When the woman with her addressed Riss'aird as father, Akeela gasped. "That's Krezma's daughter."

Ode Janmar looked at Riss'aird and the women. "I be havin' a bad feeling. This could be a trick."

"And Krezma is in on it?"

"Nay, that's not what I be meanin'," Ode said. "Stay here. I be going to talk to Bracken. Do not leave this tree."

Akeela nodded. Ode climbed down, and she turned her attention to Tzmet. She was taller than Krezma, no resemblance that Akeela noticed, but then she was too far away to see clearly. The purple aura was there, but it was edged with a purple so dark, it almost appeared black.

Tzmet was afraid of her father.

Before Akeela could ponder this, Riss'aird laughed again. Akeela took a good look at him—he had no aura. What did that mean? Every living thing had an aura. Was he a spirit? The Moon Dancers were spirits, and they had auras.

Then Krezma approached Riss'aird. Two earth fairies hovered near her shoulders. Even at this distance, Akeela knew they were the fairies Hawk hadn't trusted. She wanted to laugh.

I knew it! I knew they were good!

>

Krezma stepped around Tzmet, who was still sitting on her horse. A deep, searing fear shook her body as she walked toward her husband. The smell of blood and burned flesh sickened her, but she was thankful for the fairies who accompanied her. She prayed as she walked, but she had the feeling her prayers went no further than the inside of her head.

She stood before Riss'aird, who was still floating. Mild surprise crossed his face, and he eased himself to the ground. Krezma swallowed. Then she lifted her head and took a step forward.

"Husband, cease your attack on this village." Her voice shook, but she kept her head up and looked him in the eyes. "These people have done you no harm. Leave them be."

Riss'aird crossed his arms. His icy smile stabbed Krezma's heart. She was looking at a person without a soul.

"Wife, have you come back to me? As you can see, our daughter has lied to me and betrayed me. She has, most likely, lied to you as well."

Krezma shook off the chill. "I've come back, but only to talk reason with you."

"Indeed." Riss'aird gave a short laugh. "Reason? The only reason for living is domination. I am worthy of loyalty. Those who cross me will die."

She tried to glimpse some humanity in his eyes, but they were cold, unfeeling. She began to weave power around herself for protection, even though Riss'aird showed no inclination of attack. "Please, Riss'aird. There must be some way to convince you to let us live in peace."

Without warning, Riss'aird shot a single bolt of blue fire at her. Thank Celtar she'd heeded the inner warning to protect herself. Still, the fire knocked her down and took her breath away. Stars, but it hurt!

She struggled to her feet. "Husband—"

Riss'aird roared, "You are not my wife!"

The blue fire blazed once more. Then Tzmet pushed her aside, and she was on the ground again. Riss'aird's blue fire struck Tzmet instead and threw her several feet away. She lay still. Riss'aird grabbed his shoulder and went down on one knee. A small arrow stuck out, just above his heart. With his attention on that, Krezma crawled to her daughter and cradled her head.

"I'm—sorry." Tzmet gasped. "Thank—you—Mother."

"I forgive you, daughter. Celtar can forgive you. He longs to forgive you! Ask his forgiveness while you still can," Krezma said.

"I—I—"

Krezma put two fingers on Tzmet's forehead and ran them gently down her cheek. "May Celtar bless and keep you," she whispered.

Tzmet drew one ragged breath and breathed no more.

Krezma hugged Tzmet's body to her own. She wanted to cry out in anguish, but she couldn't. She couldn't.

She glanced at Riss'aird, who pulled out the small arrow and threw it on the ground. He stood. "And now . . ."

Krezma cringed, but the fairies who'd come with her were shaking their heads and rubbing their eyes, as if coming out of a deep sleep. They flew straight up and back to the forest. As they flew, they screeched, "Guardian! Guardian!"

The men, goblins, and whiptails seemed to wake up too. They bellowed and stamped their feet, then charged the still-stunned men.

Riss'aird turned to follow the fairies.

They were flying straight toward an old oak tree.

Chapter Forty-Five

Akeela heard the fairies coming before she saw them. What were they doing? They'd surely give her hiding place away. In a panic, Akeela began to climb down the tree. Riss'aird was coming for her. A scream escaped her lips before she could check it.

A shadow passed overhead.

Tar, flying in on a glider, made straight for Riss'aird, who was focused on following the fairies. He slammed into Riss'aird's chest, and they tumbled to the ground. Tar leaped up and pushed the glider on top of Riss'aird, then drew a sword and slashed at the cloth and ropes.

"Celtar, help!" Akeela shrieked as she clung to the tree trunk. The fairies flew around her. "Go away! Go away! You're going to get me killed!"

"Guardian!" they cried.

In desperation, Akeela batted them out of the air. They fell, weeping, and hit the ground.

Riss'aird fought his way out of the tangle, stood, and tossed the wreckage in Tar's face. Then he lifted his hands, and the ground shook. Akeela climbed the rest of the way down and ran to a hollow sycamore with enough room inside for five men. She dove inside and watched from an opening in the trunk, unable to tear her eyes away.

Tar and Riss'aird faced each other. Both had murder on their faces. Riss'aird laughed and shot blue fire at Tar. Tar reflected it off his sword. If only she had the power of the Fairy Guardian! She shouldn't be hiding. She should be out there, doing her job. But how? She only had three pieces! She prayed with all her might for help.

Riss'aird fired bolt after bolt. Tar blocked each one, although Riss'aird increased his speed. No way could Tar keep this up.

Men continued fighting whiptails. The gentle forest people and farmers were almost unrecognizable in their fury. Akeela covered her ears. The cries of men and the screeching of whiptails was something she'd never forget.

Suddenly, another sound caught her attention. She looked out of the opening. Hundreds of dwarf warriors burst out of the forest, their war cry ringing like the worship bells in the village. The dwarves charged into the whiptail army, roaring as they slew.

Riss'aird turned and blasted blue fire into the fray. He would've destroyed everything, but a whirlwind surrounded him, kicking up dirt and debris. Akeela could see the auras of the invisible air fairies, and she cried out in joy.

Over the clamor, a clear voice rose. "Keela! Keela!"

Akeela's heart dropped. No. It couldn't be.

Anon ran out of the forest toward the village.

Dear Celtar! He'd be killed! She left the protection of the sycamore and ran. "Anon! Here I am! Here!"

The faun saw her and started to run to her. Then, through the whirlwind, Riss'aird fired, striking him down.

"No!" Akeela screamed. She started to run to her beloved faun when something slammed into her. She hit the ground hard. "Akeela, no!" It was Hawk's voice.

She tried to push him away. "I have to get to Anon!"

"I'll get him," Ham said as he and Gilron ran up behind them.

"No!" she screamed, again. "Anon! I'm coming!"

Hawk grabbed her arms and held her. "Go!" he shouted at Ham.

Akeela struggled and screamed, but Hawk held her firm.

Just then, a waterspout slammed into Riss'aird. Water fairies whirled around and around him, singing. He roared and waved his hands, shooting blue fire at random.

Ham darted off.

Hawk and Gilron ran with Akeela back to the hollow tree. Akeela wrenched her arm from Hawk's hand.

Ham grabbed Anon and headed their way. Hawk and Gilron both restrained her now. Akeela pulled against them as she wept. *Celtar! Riss'aird is getting up!* "Ham!" she screamed. "Watch out!"

But it was too late. Riss'aird struck them down. Tar lunged at him, but Riss'aird threw him across the field as though he were a child. Air fairies whirled around him again, knocking him to the ground.

Ham picked up Anon and staggered toward the tree. Even from a distance, Akeela could see the faun's aura was out. Dead. Dead! No, it couldn't be!

She freed her arms and ran to her husband. They collapsed at the old oak. "Ham? Oh, Ham." *Please, Celtar. This is my fault. Oh, help me, this is my fault!*

He looked at her and smiled, touching her cheek. Hawk and Gilron ran up and stood guard over them.

Akeela began to weep. "I'm sorry. Lie still. We'll get you help. Krezma can heal you."

Ham's eyes locked on her own. "I love you, Akeela." His aura flickered and went out.

Akeela cried out once as Hawk pulled her up and forced her back to the tree. Gilron followed. When they reached the sycamore, Hawk shoved Akeela inside and followed her in.

Gilron said, "I'll try to draw Riss'aird's attention. Here, I thought you'd want this."

He tossed her Anon's bag of stones. She missed, and the bag hit the ground, spilling stones everywhere.

Anon was dead. The reality of that hit Akeela and crushed her chest. She dropped to her knees, gasping for breath. Poor little Anon! She picked up the empty bag and clutched it to her heart. How could Celtar let this happen? Of all the people she knew, Anon was the most worthy of life. Yet the battle raged on. A sob escaped her lips.

"I can't do it anymore," she cried out. "Oret is dead, and now Ham and Anon are gone. What am I supposed to do? I'm the chosen one, and I can't stop Riss'aird."

She hit the pile of stones and scattered it. A faint light caught her eye. One of the stones gave off a glowing, white shimmer. Akeela stared for a moment, then reached out and picked it up. It felt warm. Alive.

"Hawk—"

Images of Oret flashed through her mind. *Become the Fairy Guardian.*

The truth of it hit her. As the Fairy Guardian, she'd give her life as Oret had, wandering, always wandering, giving strength and encouragement to the fairies. And now, no marriage, no family, no home. Not now. Not ever.

Akeela reached into her tunic and brought out the small bag with the other three pieces of the Fairystone. She poured them on the ground and laid Anon's stone next to them. They glowed and pulsed with life. Akeela's heart pounded as she watched the outer shells disintegrate and reveal their true form. Four perfect jewels: red, clear, blue, green. They flashed and shimmered in the low light.

Hawk touched one. "Are they all here?"

Akeela nodded. She'd accomplished her quest. She had the four pieces of the Fairystone. But now she wasn't sure she could go through with it.

"Well?" Hawk said. "Aren't you going to put them in your birthmark?"

"I can't."

Hawk frowned. "You can't or you won't? Akeela, listen to what's happening outside. You have to do this."

"If I do this, that's it. No more Guardians."

Hawk grabbed her shoulders. "If you don't do this, there won't be a need for a Guardian!"

Akeela hesitated. She picked up the first stone, but before she could do anything, the sun went out. Akeela gasped. "The prophecy!" Still, she hesitated.

Hawk grabbed her hand. "I love you. I will always love you!"

He pulled off her archery glove. In the dim glow of the stones, he pushed the clear stone into her palm. It melted into the runes. Akeela felt a rush of power, almost painful, course through her, starting in her hand and rushing to her head.

"I will always be here for you."

He picked up the blue jewel and put it in her hand.

"Whenever you need anything, I will be there."

Small specks of light appeared inside the tree. Like stars, they twinkled and flashed. She gazed at her hand, the runes now glowing. Hawk picked up the green jewel. She held out her other hand. "I will do it."

She placed it into the runes. A song from far off began to ring in her head. She smiled as understanding flooded her mind. It all made sense. Her upbringing, her gift, her destiny. Celtar had chosen her from before time to fulfill this destiny. She felt honored. *I am happy to serve you,* she prayed to the One who'd made her for this task.

Hawk handed her the fourth stone—the red jewel. She took it.

Then she kissed him. "I love you. Don't be afraid."

He looked surprised and sad. "I'm not."

Akeela took a breath. She held the fourth stone over her hand. For a moment, regret filled her. How she would've loved to stay with Hawk for the rest of her life. She looked at him through her tears. "I love you," she said again.

"I love you," Hawk whispered. He put his hand under hers and nodded. Together, they pushed the stone into her hand. Akeela's head snapped back as her aura swelled and enveloped the tree hollow. She could only watch as Hawk was slammed against the side of the tree.

He slid down and did not move.

Akeela gazed at him. It was as though someone else controlled her body. The thought that he was dead flitted through her mind, but it didn't linger. She crawled out of the tree and faced Riss'aird.

The air fairies who'd been flying around him were gone. The fighting had ceased. Nothing moved as darkness covered the land. Riss'aird still didn't have an aura, yet Akeela could see him as though he stood in light. She walked to meet him in the field, unafraid.

"What's this? A mere girl? All this fighting to protect you?" Riss'aird sneered. "Foolish child. Now stand aside and see the power of the mighty Dark Lord, Riss'aird!"

He closed his eyes, raised his hands, and chanted a spell. The words were dark. Evil. Then he looked at her, his icy gaze penetrating her soul. She lifted her hands in a futile gesture to block his curse. He laughed and drew his hands back to strike.

The moons drifted away from the sun, and sunlight struck the Fairystone in Akeela's hand. Her body jerked and became taut. The far-off song she heard swelled and grew louder. Then the Fairystone came to life. All the auras Akeela could see grew as bright as the sun. She could hear every heartbeat of every fairy pounding in her ears. The song became recognizable. A song of praise to Celtar, ringing from the souls of every fairy and person who believed. A startling, fresh joy Akeela had never experienced before pulsed through her, and her soul joined in song with the others.

The song grew and became a wave. It emanated from Akeela and rushed toward Riss'aird. He shrieked and turned, but it crashed over him, enveloping him. Without warning, he disintegrated. His ashes floated for a moment before the air fairies whirled around them, sending them up and away.

The song faded, yet it remained just on the edge of Akeela's consciousness. She thought she heard a voice say, "Well done, chosen and loyal servant."

Then darkness surrounded her, and she slid to the ground.

Hawk groaned before he opened his eyes. The last thing he remembered was giving Akeela the fourth piece of the Fairystone. He looked around the tree hollow. Akeela was gone. He stood in a panic, banged his head, and sat back down. When everything stopped spinning, he crawled out of the tree. Anon's body lay near the opening, Ham's next to it.

Hawk stood. What had happened to the world? Everything looked sharper, brighter. The remnants of a song drifted away on a breeze.

Then he saw her, collapsed in the field. Without considering Riss'aird and his army, Hawk ran to her and lifted her in his arms while he wept.

Krezma came up beside him. "Cease your weeping. Akeela is not dead. Far from it. Give her some air."

Hawk looked at Akeela's pale face. She was breathing. Then he noticed a glowing around the edges of her body. He would've dismissed it as a Fairy Guardian thing, but he saw the same thing when he looked at Krezma and others in the field.

"What happened?" he asked.

Krezma shrugged. "She faced Riss'aird, brought forth the Fairysong, and destroyed him. It was as the prophecy said: 'Back to ashes, evil mourns. The Guardian will be reborn.'"

Hawk looked around the battlefield. The dwarves were caring for their wounded, as were the Acadians and the people of Broem. Iari ran from the village into Gilron's arms. An empty feeling passed through him.

"The wall," he said. "It's gone."

Krezma put a hand on Akeela's forehead. "Aye, it's gone. When the Fairysong destroyed Riss'aird, 'twas not needed anymore."

Tar ran to them, his face pale but relieved. "I see you made it through," he said to Hawk. "Thank, Celtar! I looked for you on the battlefield but didn't see you."

"I was with Akeela."

Tar studied him. Hawk faced his father's searching look without flinching.

"Is the Guardian going to be all right?" Tar finally asked.

Krezma nodded. "Aye, she will. But let's get her inside. We can take her to Queth's house."

Hawk carried Akeela. Vorrak'ira ran to them as they entered the village. "Cousin! I have to admit, I'm glad to see you. No broken branches, yeh?"

"No broken branches," Hawk said. *Just a broken heart.*

The villagers were busy with their own, some joyfully reunited and some weeping over their dead. They all stopped and stared as the group walked by. Hawk kept his eyes forward.

They came to the largest house, richly ornamented with carved window frames and flowering plants on either side of the bright-red front door.

A plump, round-faced woman answered their knock. "Why, bless me! Krezma, come in, dear. Come in."

"Thank you, Nirit," Krezma said. "We are weary, and Akeela needs a bed."

"To be sure, to be sure." Nirit wiped her hands on her apron. "The poor lass. Would you care for the same room as before?"

"Aye," Krezma answered.

Hawk followed Nirit into a small room with two beds. He laid Akeela on one as Krezma entered the room. "Nooph!" she cried.

Before Hawk could ask, a fat gray cat with black stripes looked up from the other bed. He stretched and meowed as if to say, *And who else did you expect?* Hawk smiled as Krezma lifted Nooph and held him tight. He never would've imagined cranky, sarcastic Krezma to show such love to anyone, let alone a cat. Celtar was full of surprises.

Nirit put her hands on her hips. "That cat has been eating me out of house and home. Now, how about a nice cuppa?"

"Aye, thank you." Krezma dropped the cat on the bed. "I will sit with Akeela. You go with Nirit." Hawk started to protest, but Krezma put up her hand. "Listen to me. You need a bath and something to eat. Akeela will still be here."

Hawk ate without tasting and hurried through a sponge bath. He'd refused the offer of a bathtub. Heating all that water would take too long. As he dressed, he heard voices and recognized his father's. He took the stairs two at a time and landed with a thump at the bottom.

His father stood at the fireplace. He waved Hawk over. Hawk clasped his hand, and Tar pulled him in for a hug. "Thank Celtar it's over. I'm proud of you, son. You are an honorable man."

Hawk worked his jaw, trying to swallow around the lump in his throat. "I didn't want to let her go, Father. It's going to hurt for a long time."

Tar nodded and flexed his claw hand. "I know the pain well."

"I'm sorry," Hawk said. "I know you do."

"Be not sorry for me," Tar said. "I will see your mother again in Celtar's kingdom. Until then, I do his will."

Krezma came to the doorway, a triumphant look on her face. "She's awake."

Chapter Forty-Six

Akeela was sitting up in bed, sipping a mug of tea. She dropped it as Hawk rushed into the room. "You're alive!" she cried.

Hawk hugged her as she thanked Celtar over and over. Krezma and Tar came in behind Hawk.

"Look at this. Tea all over the quilt," Krezma exclaimed.

Hawk let go of Akeela and jumped up. "Sorry!"

"I thought you were dead!" Akeela said. "I saw you inside the tree. After we put the stones into my hand."

"Well, he's not, so let's get this cleaned up," Krezma said.

Akeela didn't care how grouchy Krezma was. Hawk was alive!

"The Fairy Council is gathering," Krezma said. "They'll arrive soon. You will meet with them in Queth's garden."

Akeela nodded. Her heart ached, but she had to ask. "What happened to Ham? And Anon?"

"We took Ham's body to his parents," Tar said. "Anon is in the garden. We didn't want to bury him before you woke up."

Tears ran down Akeela's cheeks, and she took a deep breath. "Thank you. First, I must go to my husband's family. Then I'll meet with the Fairy Council."

Akeela, Mosset, and Kintcha held hands and wept. "I'm so sorry," Akeela said over and over.

Kintcha placed an arm around Akeela's shoulder. "'Twas the will of Celtar, not your fault, daughter."

They shared memories. They prayed. They wept some more. As Akeela was leaving, Ham's mother said, "Please do not wear mourning clothes. You and Ham had only one night. You are so young. Go on living." She kissed Akeela's cheek.

In her room at Queth's house, Akeela sat on the floor in front of the fireplace. She couldn't cry another drop.

Before the fire sparked, Akeela felt the arrival of a fire fairy. That was new. She'd have to get used to things being different now that she was Guardian.

"Greetings, Guardian!" The fairy bowed low, placing her hand over her heart. Another unfamiliar action.

Akeela nodded. "Greetings."

"I bring a request from the Ruling Fairy. She wishes Hawk, son of Tar, to also attend the meeting." The fairy bowed again.

What could the Council want with Hawk? This puzzled Akeela, although she was glad to have a little more time with Hawk. Akeela's heart ached at the thought of his leaving. She could only hope to see him from time to time as she traveled, doing her duty as Fairy Guardian.

"I will tell him."

Akeela, Hawk, Tar, and Krezma waited in the garden for the arrival of the Fairy Council. Poor Anon's body rested at the far end. Tar and Hawk would bury him after the meeting. Akeela struggled with the feelings that tore at her: grief, anticipation, love.

The Fairy Council arrived in a fluttering of wings, which again Akeela sensed before she heard. They settled on top of the long wooden table Tar had carried out. Krezma had told her about the

Council, but seeing them for the first time was overwhelming. Surreal. The auras almost blinded her, and the emotions! They filled her almost to the point of pain. They flew in and took their places as she recalled Krezma's words.

"The Fairy Council consists of representatives of each element. There is a Superior, Vice Superior, Historian, Translator. Also Subordinates from each of the four elements. That makes a council of twenty-four fairies, not counting the Ruling Fairy, also known as the Superior, who is always accompanied by three Warriors."

A brazier of fire rested to the left of a large block for the fire fairy representatives. Next to that, earth fairies sat on small wooden blocks. To the right of the larger block were water fairies and then air fairies, who, even though visible, still held an almost-transparent edge.

Next came three fairies Akeela had never seen before. They were dressed in robes instead of tunics. The one with parchment and a pen she guessed to be the Historian, and the one carrying a leather-bound book of the Holy Writings, the Translator. The last held a thick, folded piece of tapestry, which she opened and draped over the large block—the Vice Superior.

When they'd settled, the Ruling Fairy flew into the garden with her warriors: three large males dressed in leather armor and armed with bows and swords, one on either side and one behind the Ruling Fairy. The Council stood, and Akeela's heart swelled with pride and gratitude as the Superior landed in the middle of the Council with her arms outstretched. She stood like that for a moment, then gestured for everyone to sit.

A white light appeared. To Akeela's surprise, Queen Rowena Rayenath materialized, appearing just as she had in the Moon Dancer realm, and hovered to the right of the table. Her hair and dress floated around her, and two of her Moon Dancers rested on her shoulders. Rowena inclined her head, giving Akeela a small nod.

The Ruling Fairy spoke. "This special meeting of the Fairy Council is now assembled and come to order. Praise be to Celtar!"

"Praise be to Celtar," the fairies echoed joyfully.

She turned to Akeela. "Welcome, Guardian. It gladdens my heart to see you safe and complete."

Complete. Akeela liked the sound of that.

"This is my Vice Superior, Historian, and Translator." The Ruling Fairy indicated each as she named them. "You are acquainted with the Subordinates?"

Akeela nodded. She couldn't have said a thing if her life depended on it. Appropriate words weren't coming to mind, anyway.

"Krezma, welcome. You have done well," the Ruling Fairy said. "The Council is grateful for your help."

"It was my honor," Krezma said.

Ooh, Krezma sounded humble. How strange. Akeela hadn't ever heard her sound so contrite in her entire life.

The Ruling Fairy turned to Hawk. "I welcome you, friend and beloved of the Guardian. The Council is also grateful for your protection over her."

"You're welcome," Hawk said, looking pleased and puzzled. A stab of bittersweetness shot through Akeela's heart, but also pride. She thanked Celtar for sparing his life, even though it wouldn't be a part of hers.

"Guardian," the Ruling Fairy continued. She paused a moment, looking into Akeela's eyes. Akeela felt as though she was sending some kind of message, but she had no clue what that might be. "Since your grandfather was not able to train you in all our ways, I will see it done. You will come with us to learn and be strengthened. We are safe and at peace for the present, but we are not foolish enough to think it will always be this way. Still, we have time to prepare you."

Silence stretched on. Akeela realized everyone was waiting for her to say something and flushed. "Um. Thank you?"

The Ruling Fairy laughed. "Peace, Guardian. There is no need for embarrassment. No need for fear. We will help you with each step."

"When do I leave?" Akeela asked. She hoped it wouldn't be right away. She wanted to see Iari and Gilron one more time. She wondered where Krezma would go. She dreaded saying goodbye to Hawk. She couldn't. No words, however poetic and meaningful, could capture what her heart felt.

"As you know, the line of Guardians comes through your family," the Ruling Fairy said. "This must be preserved."

Pain knifed through Akeela's heart. "How? I'm the Guardian. I cannot have children now."

The Ruling Fairy stood. "Hawk, son of Tar, friend of Oret, step forward," she pronounced in a loud commanding voice.

What? Hawk? What was happening? Hope rose in Akeela's heart, unbidden. She mentally chided herself. Hope? A hopeless hope. How could she and Hawk possibly be together unless the Superior designated him to stay on as Akeela's protector?

No way would *that* work.

"When you helped the Guardian place the fourth piece of the stone into the runes, you were caught in the transformation," the Ruling Fairy went on. "Some of the fairy magic entered you. The Holy Writings say, when you sacrifice what you love, it will come back to you, bringing an extra measure with it."

Akeela glanced at Hawk. His eyes glowed with anticipation. Dreaded hope rose in her again, and she struggled to breathe.

The Ruling Fairy raised her hands. "You gave up she whom you loved in order to help others. For this sacrifice, I now declare you part Guardian. This enables you to marry and continue the line with Akeela."

Akeela gasped. *Celtar, oh, Celtar! Could it be true?*

Hawk caught her and spun her around. They faced each other, and Akeela put her hands on either side of his face. She was going to die, she knew it. Her heart couldn't hold one more emotion — until he kissed her and their auras exploded in a shower of silver sparks.

Everyone cheered.

After a time, Akeela had no idea how long, Krezma cleared her throat. She pulled away from Hawk, both of them laughing and crying. "Thank you, Superior!" Akeela said, not taking her eyes from her love.

Everyone cheered again.

"As soon as you marry, you both will come to the sacred tree of the Acadians," the Ruling Fairy said when the fairies quieted down. "I believe you know the place."

"We do," Akeela and Hawk said. Again, Akeela's heart overflowed, and she wiped tears from her cheeks.

The Ruling Fairy bowed her head. "One last thing. The little faun who was the bearer of the fourth piece of the Fairystone."

"Anon," Akeela whispered. How could she have forgotten him? She took a deep breath, and Hawk squeezed her hand.

"Yes," the Ruling Fairy said. "Queen Rowena?"

The queen of the Moon Dancers nodded. She turned to Akeela. "Guardian, thy friend is precious to thee. Take thy hand that holdeth the Fairystone and bring him forth."

"Bring him forth?"

What did that mean? Anon was dead. Dead! Akeela paused.

Krezma leaned over and whispered, "Go to him, child."

She let go of Hawk's hand. Each step to Anon's body felt impossibly heavy. His precious face was peaceful and relaxed, as though he were only napping. Only he wasn't. Akeela sucked in another shaky breath but kept going.

She knelt by Anon's body, and the power of the Fairystone sprang to life. She knew what to do. She passed her hand over Anon's heart, and a mist rose from his chest and hovered.

Queen Rowena called to him, "Anon, bearer of the Fairystone! I will take thee with me to the Moon Dancer realm. There you will live with us forever."

The mist grew and expanded. Akeela thought she could see Anon's face within, shimmery and full of life. "Anon!"

His image floated up and around her, filling her with his scent. His touch. She heard his voice. "Love you, Keela!"

Then he and the Queen were gone.

"Anon!" Akeela cried again. "Anon!"

Hawk came up behind her and rested his hands on her shoulders.

She put her hands on his. Tears of grief—and joy—ran down her cheeks. "I love you, too, sweet Anon."

Wings whirred once more. Akeela and Hawk turned as the Council rose from the table.

"We will say farewell for now," the Ruling Fairy said, "and await your arrival at the sacred tree."

Akeela and Hawk held hands as the Fairy Council rose and flew away in the opposite order in which they'd arrived.

Krezma grunted. "Well, that's a happy ending if ever I saw one. Come, you two. There are plans to be made."

Chapter Forty-Seven

A Month Later

Krezma adjusted the ring of bell flowers on Akeela's head. "Stand still and let me fix this so it doesn't fall off."

Akeela smiled. "I love you."

She grunted, then said the words Akeela had longed to hear from Krezma her whole life but hadn't. Until now. "As I love you, child."

"Are you sure you want to stay here in Broem?" Akeela asked. "Hawk and I truly wish you to come with us."

"Nay, I'm at peace here." Krezma touched Akeela's cheek. "Nooph and I will live out our days eating Nirit's food and listening to Queth's sermons. It's a good thing." Then she gave Akeela a happy grin. "And I have a labyrinth to plant."

Akeela sighed. "Celtar's plan is not what I would've chosen, but I can't imagine anything else now."

"Aye, the Holy Writings say Celtar takes all things and works them into a good plan," Krezma said. "Now, let's go get you married."

Akeela clutched Tar's arm. They walked slowly to the church where Hawk waited with Queth and Vorrak-ira. Tar, as usual, was quiet and a bit stoic.

"You're going to be my father-in-law." She nudged his arm.

Tar gave her a rare smile.

"And you were my grandfather's best friend."

"I was."

"Thank you for raising Hawk the way you did," she continued. "He's a good man, and he completes me."

Tar stopped. "Akeela, I had no idea when I met you how things would turn out. But it seems Celtar had a plan, and his plans always are accomplished."

They continued walking. Iari and Ves-rynia—her two sisters, as sure as if they were born to be—stood on the steps holding bouquets of bell flowers and Laureles leaves. Iari smiled as though it was *her* wedding day, and Ves-rynia wept with joy. Akeela's heart swelled and overflowed, as it seemed to do so often lately.

Iari handed her a bouquet and kissed her cheek. "You look beautiful. Radiant. Like I wanted you to be the first time. But today, it's even better. I look at you and see a woman healed."

Akeela clung to her, then Iari turned and walked into the church.

Ves-rynia placed a necklace of nacre seeds around her neck and hugged her. "My cousin. My sister. I love you."

"I love you too," Akeela whispered in her ear. Then Ves-rynia followed Iari into the church.

Akeela ran a hand down her borrowed gown. It'd been Iari's, of course. It wasn't the color Akeela would've chosen—gray silk— but the color went well with the yellow bell flowers, which were so plentiful around the village this time of year, and complemented the Laureles leaves Hawk had sent her this morning.

Tar paused at the door. "I am honored for you to become my daughter. Dar-dra would be also."

Akeela's heart swelled. "Thank you."

They walked through the doors, and everyone stood. Akeela was aware of people and fairies, but her eyes were only for Hawk. She saw the love in his face and felt it from his heart, and her heart answered without hesitation.

She handed her bouquet to Iari and joined her hands with Hawk's. They repeated their vows after Queth. "I promise to love you all through our lives. When there is sickness or good health. When there is enough or not. When Celtar seems close or far away. I promise to be faithful, never straying from my vows, providing what you need, for as long as we live."

Akeela felt Celtar's presense, and it filled her with joy, and yes, as the Ruling Fairy had said, completeness.

Thank you for placing me here. For choosing me for the task of Guardian, but not making me do it alone.

Hawk leaned in for their first kiss as husband and wife. Their auras blazed brightly, and her heart once again overflowed. But instead of crying, Akeela threw her head back and laughed. The crowd cheered and threw grains of wheat as they ran, hand in hand, out of the church.

Krezma was the first to greet them, and she placed her hands on their heads and blessed them. Everyone else filed out, and Akeela and Hawk were hugged and blessed until Akeela thought she'd suffocate. Then the people joined in singing a marriage hymn of praise.

Blessed are the people who love Celtar,
Who walk in his ways.
Blessings and prosperity will be yours!
Your wife will be like a fruitful vine,
Your sons will be strong in your house.
So is the man who loves Celtar!

Akeela looked at her husband talking to a group of young men, and for a moment, she felt a twinge of grief as she remembered another wedding. But as Hawk smiled at her, his love filled her heart, and she remembered Ham's father's words to her: be happy.

411

And she was.

Her joy was full—completely—and her heart couldn't hold any more happiness. She went without hesitation or guilt to the borrowed cottage that night.

Akeela and Hawk came out of the forest into the clearing where the sacred Laureles tree stood.

"Look," Hawk said. "There's the log where we first sat. I fell in love with you that night."

Two of the Ruling Fairy's warriors flew to them, their auras shining brightly. They bowed to Akeela and Hawk. "Are you ready for your training, Guardians?"

Akeela took Hawk's hand. "We're ready."

He kissed the back of her hand. "Together. Forever."

THE END

Don't miss the next book in the
Fairy Guardian Chronicles

Fairystone

Coming Soon from L2L2 Publishing.

Acknowledgments

I started writing *Fairyeater* twelve years before it was published. That's a long time to write, revise, submit, get rejected, and revise again. But it was worth it.

While an author does the bulk of their work alone, we can't keep going without the love and support of others. At least I know I can't, and God placed each one in my life at just the right time. So thankful for His love and creativity.

I'd like to thank The Crue: Nancy Rue, Joyce Magnin, Winnie Kutchukian, Candy Abbott, Dale McElhinney, Brenda Ulman, Floss Craig, Rosemarie DiCristo, Tim Shoemaker, and Dawn Moore. So blessed to have you all! Tim and Dale? Your fairywings are waiting.

Nancy Rue—I would have given up without you. Thank you for seeing the potential in my writing, encouraging me to keep going, and taking me from a picture book writer to a novelist. Loving you always.

My brother, Sam Still. Thanks for giving me Tar and Ode Janmar. And for always checking up on my writing. You're the best brother and friend. I love ya!

My daughter, Mary Halter. You never forget to ask me how my

writing is going. I appreciate your ideas and strange sense of humor, which you get honestly from me. Love you, babe!

Marlene Bagnull—thank you for helping me get started on this writing journey, oh so long ago. I won't mention when. That would give away our ages. Haha.

Storycrafters: Joy Kieffer, Rona Shirdan, Tammy Pfaff, and Floss Craig. We don't talk a lot at our monthly meetings, but boy do we write!

Becky and Scott Minor—thank you for starting Realm Makers. For giving me (and loads others) a tribe who understands the mind of the spec writer. It's great being weird together!

Joyce Magnin—you were the first to tell me I had found my voice in writing fantasy. If you hadn't done that, I probably wouldn't have gotten past the prologue. Thanks! You're my person.

Kim Sponaugle—thank you for Tzmet's window. It took my breath away the first time I saw it, and it still gives me a thrill today. Thanks for spending all those hours with me, drinking coffee, eating chocolate, brainstorming, and laughing until we cry. Love you, friend!

To all the people who helped send me to conferences and workshops in the beginning of this journey—thank you. Your money was not spent in vain.

Michele Israel Harper and the creative team at L2L2. Thank you for believing in me. Your expertise and encouragement have boosted my confidence. You were a joy to work with, and I'm delighted with what we've done together! I raise a cape of fairywings to you all.

My readers—thank you for spending time with Akeela and company. I hope I've entertained and blessed you in some small way.

To my husband, Daryl. While you're not a fiction reader, you never told me writing fantasy was weird. I'm so thankful for your love and support, which enables me to use the gift God gave me. I love you, with a full heart.

~Pam Halter

About the Author

Pam Halter is a fantasy and children's book author. The first book in her Willoughby and Friends series, *Willoughby and the Terribly Itchy Itch*, won the 2018 Realm Award in the children's category, and she also received a Reader's Choice Award in 2015 for her short story, "Tick Tock," in *Realmscapes*.

Pam lives in South Jersey, deep in farmland, where she enjoys gardening, cooking, canning, quilting, playing the piano for church, and walking on long country roads where she finds fairy homes, emerging dragons, and trees eating wood gnomes. Learn more about her at www.PamHalter.com.

ABOUT THE AUTHOR

Pam loves to hear from her readers! Follow her on social media, check out her website, or drop her a line to let her know what you thought of Fairyeater. *Happy reading!*

www.PamHalter.com
Facebook: @Pam.Halter.5
Twitter: @PamHalter
Goodreads: @Pam_Halter
Amazon Author: @PamHalter

Reviews

Did you know reviews can skyrocket a book's career? Instead of fizzling into nothing, a book will be suggested by Amazon, shared by Goodreads, or showcased by Barnes & Noble. Plus, authors treasure reviews! (And read them over and over and over . . .)

If you enjoyed this book, would you consider leaving a review on:

- Amazon
- Barnes & Noble
- Goodreads

. . . or perhaps even your personal blog? Thank you so much!
~The L2L2 Publishing Team

More from L2L2 Publishing

If you enjoyed this book, you may also enjoy:

Brenna James wants three things for her sixteenth birthday: to find her history notes before the test, to have her mother return from her business trip, and to stop creating fire with her bare hands. Yeah, that's so not happening. Unfortunately. When Brenna learns her mother is missing in an alternate reality called Linneah, she travels through a portal to find her. Against her will. Who knew portals even existed? But Brenna's arrival in Linneah begins the fulfillment of an ancient prophecy, including a royal murder and the theft of Linneah's most powerful relic: the Sacred Veil. Hold up. Can everything just slow down for a sec? Left with no other choice, Brenna and her new friend Baldwin pursue the thief into the dangerous woods of Silvastamen. When they spy an army marching toward Linneah, Brenna is horrified. Can she find the veil, save her mother, and warn Linneah in time?

More from L2L2 Publishing

If you enjoyed this book, you may also enjoy:

ENDING
FEAR
Deanna Fugett

Fourteen-year-old Fear learns she was a parachute baby, dumped over the edge of the Gliding Lands as an infant. Fascinated by the floating cities in the sky before, now she's desperate for answers. But a slave isn't likely to get those answers. When her abusive Downer family throws her from their hovel, Fear takes refuge with a family who shows her love for the first time. Surely they can't be trusted. Years of abuse and molestation has taught her that. Then her brother discovers where she's hiding and tries to kidnap her. Fear will never let him touch her again. Then Fear's new little sister, Happy, is kidnapped and taken to the Uppers' temple harem. Fear must go against her namesake and journey to the dreaded Gliding Lands before the little girl's innocence is ripped from her forever. Can she save Happy in time? And will she find answers to the burning question of why anyone would throw her away?

More from L2L2 Publishing

If you enjoyed this book, you may also enjoy:

Tales are often told of heroes who fulfill ancient prophecies.
Alara's Call is the tale of a woman who gives new ones.
A young clergywoman with a fiery passion for her Telshan
faith, Alara has been assigned to a mission abroad but longs
to lead a congregation in her homeland. Her father, the
prime minister, jeopardizes her dream and her safety when
he coerces her into what he calls a diplomatic mission. But
it's a ruse. The trip is meant to end with her marriage to the
crown prince of a foreign nation, where members of Alara's
faith are persecuted and women oppressed. All for a trade
agreement her father is desperate to enact. Her mentor
intervenes and takes Alara to Dorrel, the suitor she left
behind. They believe they are safe, but foreign soldiers
are under orders to bring Alara to the king's
palace . . . by any means necessary.

More from L2L2 Publishing

If you enjoyed this book, you may also enjoy:

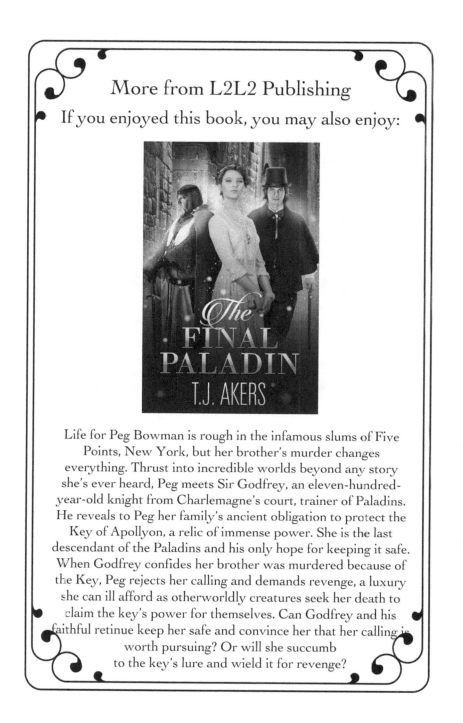

Life for Peg Bowman is rough in the infamous slums of Five
Points, New York, but her brother's murder changes
everything. Thrust into incredible worlds beyond any story
she's ever heard, Peg meets Sir Godfrey, an eleven-hundred-
year-old knight from Charlemagne's court, trainer of Paladins.
He reveals to Peg her family's ancient obligation to protect the
Key of Apollyon, a relic of immense power. She is the last
descendant of the Paladins and his only hope for keeping it safe.
When Godfrey confides her brother was murdered because of
the Key, Peg rejects her calling and demands revenge, a luxury
she can ill afford as otherworldly creatures seek her death to
claim the key's power for themselves. Can Godfrey and his
faithful retinue keep her safe and convince her that her calling is
worth pursuing? Or will she succumb
to the key's lure and wield it for revenge?

Where Will We Take You Next?

Discover *Spark,*
Relish *Ending Fear,*
Bask in *Alara's Call,*
Enjoy *The Final Paladin,*
and Savor *Kill the Beast.*

All at
www.love2readlove2writepublishing.com/bookstore
or your local or online retailer.

Happy Reading!
~The L2L2 Publishing Team

About L2L2 Publishing

Love2ReadLove2Write Publishing, LLC is a small traditional press, dedicated to clean or Christian speculative fiction.

Speculative genres include but are not limited to: Fantasy, Science Fiction, Fairy Tales, Magical Realism, Time Travel, Spiritual Warfare, Alternate History, Chillers (such as vampires, zombies, werewolves, or light horror), Superhero Fiction, Steampunk, Supernatural, Paranormal, etc., or a mixture of any of the previous or more.

We seek stunning tales masterfully told, and we strive to create an exquisite publishing experience for our authors and to produce high-quality fiction for our readers.

Fairyeater is at the heart of what we publish: a stirring tale with speculative elements that will delight our readers.

Visit www.L2L2Publishing.com to view our submissions guidelines, find our other titles, or learn more about us.

Happy Reading!

~The L2L2 Publishing Team

CPSIA information can be obtained
at www.ICGtesting.com
Printed in the USA
FFHW020041101118
49317665-53569FF